ESCAPE
FROM
BABYLON

Other books by Roger K. Young

As a Thief in the Night

Behold the Fig Tree

And there shall be Signs

When Ye shall see all these things

Zion, the Holy City of New Jerusalem

Dreams and Visions of the Last Days

To Your Tents O' Israel

They Must Needs be Chastened

ZIONS
REFUGE

ESCAPE

FROM

BABYLON

A Novel of the Events of the Last Days

By

Roger K. & Susan D. Young

Cover designed by Todd Duncan Asay
scottishmonkeygraphix.blogspot.com
scottishmonkie@yahoo.com

Published by AVOW: Another Voice of Warning.
Rigby, Idaho.

This book is a work of fiction. The characters, names, incidents, places,
and dialogue are products of the author's imagination and are not to be
construed as real.

Printed in the United States of America.
First Printing, July 2009

ISBN **13**:978-0-9821946-6-9

A NEW SERIES

This new series follows several fictional characters as they experience, first hand, the events of the last days, leading up to and including the gathering of the righteous, the miracles, wars and destruction of the last days, the places of refuge, the changes in the earth, the great false prophet, the building of Zion, the great Holy City of Light, the rapture, the 144,000, the Boys from the Mountains, the attack & defeat of the invading armies into America, the return of the Lost Ten Tribes, the return of the Savior in power and great glory, and the final destruction of the wicked which is the end of the world

In Book one

ACKNOWLEDGMENTS

First of all, to my sweet wife Susan who has put up with so much for over 32 years. Finally, after a year of begging her, she consented to help work on the project, to be a co-author on a book. (She actually has a degree in communications.) Her efforts have made a possibly good book become a much better book, even though she says I have been a slave driver. Also to my family, and especially to my daughter Rachel (who has a real talent for writing) who have been used mercilessly to bounce ideas and concepts off of.

Many thanks go to the many people on AVOW who have helped so much with so many different ideas and comments and even the naming of the book. Special thanks to AVOW'rs Suzanne Bullock, David Erickson, Barbara Parshley, Paul G, Pamela Bennett, Patty Gaither, Susan Edwards, Wade Smith, Cecil Champenois, Dianne Smith, Michelle Romney, and many more for proofreading and suggestions.

Also many thanks to Christopher Parrett, friend and publisher, who has worked with me and traveled a lot with me over the last year and has been involved in so many "what if" and "what would it be like" conversations as we have traveled all over the country, stuck in a vehicle for days on end.

INTRODUCTION

I have always wanted to try to do a fiction book because I thought it would be fun, but earlier attempts always ended in about three pages because I could not do dialogue. My wonderful wife Susan says I am a very good teacher, but not a very good conversationalist. (The answer came with the convincing of her to assist in the project primarily in fixing the dialogue and making the book so that it doesn't read like a lesson manual.)

Over a year ago I started in earnest on this project. Part of the motivating reason was that there were a few fictional novels on the last days that I felt were fun little books, but which trivialized, or missed most of the tremendous events that had long been prophesied. Others were essentially survival guides for gun and military enthusiasts.

Though I was intrigued with the idea of using this approach as a teaching tool, I also wanted to do something that made the events of the last days come alive, while at the same time have a good story line that engaged the reader. In other words make it fun and educational at the same time. Something like what the great author Gerald Lund has done for Church History with his past historical novels, but with these being potential "future" historical novels.

One of the problems has been that as I tried to imagine events happening in the near future, as in two, or three years, or more in the future, many of the events I outlined for happening in the future started occurring real time. This has forced me to try and forecast even more into the future. It has been an interesting exercise.

Overall, it has been a fun and a very different project and who knows, if I keep at it, perhaps one day I actually might become a good writer. Anyway it has been something that while I have been traveling a lot, has kept my mind occupied and me from falling asleep. And since lately I have been traveling even more, book two in the series is well under way already.

Please understand that the events portrayed in the book are my personal interpretations of some of these future events and their possible sequences/timing. Even though most of the events used in the story are based upon scriptural, prophetic, or dreams and visions of many people... this is still a fictional book. Characters are made up, though I have to admit they are based a lot on, or are a combination of different people I know. Also, some possible events and their potential timing have been adjusted a little to make the story line run a little better.

I hope you enjoy it.

Part 1

AWAKENING

"...they seeing see not; and hearing they hear not, neither do they understand."

Matt 13:13

PROLOGUE

The "New" Dollar, as it was called, had come about with the world wide devaluation of the old federal reserve note. Basically, one day, the rest of the world just wasn't buying it anymore. Hyperinflation started quickly, with prices dramatically increasing almost weekly. That was when the federal reserve, in conjunction with the administration, came up with the brilliant idea of using currency cards instead of actual cash and coins. In that way they could automatically change the value of the dollars that the card represented to keep up with the ever increasing official rate. It made everything easier and eliminated the need to print and issue new paper currency. There was a small, but very vocal opposing group that protested the cash cards vehemently, but they were appeased with the printing, issuance, and continued circulation of a trivial amount of the new currency.

The past winter had been a hard one, but finally it seemed to be over. Spring had come, though it was almost two months late because of a sudden arctic front that had arrived from Canada in the middle of May. It was unusual weather, but over the last five years everyone had come to expect "unusual" weather as the norm.

Regardless, it was a time of hope. The harsh and early winter, along with the nationalization of most of the agricultural system of the US, had thankfully put an end to the food riots. Food riots, brought on in most of the cities because of the tripling of basic commodity prices even after the introduction of the new currency, had prompted the administration to declare the food situation a national emergency and gave them the excuse they were looking for to take over distri, bution of food to the populace. The next step was an easy one. Wide spread crop failures spawned by the floods, droughts and disease allowed the government to take over food production as well.

The first step taken by the Federal government was to curtail all food shipments out of the country, a long overdue decision which, while desperately needed, fueled the already prevalent anti-American sentiment in the world .

After the takeover, FEMA started handing out free food that now, mysteriously appeared in abundance. Food rioting and anti-government protests drastically slowed until, across most of the country, they came to a dramatic end. Of course it didn't hurt that a very large, and very brutal mass of arctic air, unexpectedly came down and seemed to hover over most of the country for several weeks in late October. Freezing rain, snow and sub-zero temperatures have a way of dampening even the most enthusiastic protests.

The early, extreme and widespread Arctic cold blast had helped in another way as well, prompting the Feds to move most of the FEMA tent city inhabitants of the Northern states, to the much larger encampments in the warmer southern states. Ultimately over four million people were relocated to warmer climates, including Arizona, Texas, and Florida.

Volunteering to be relocated was simple if not painless. A person had only to turn their New Currency Card in for a tiny computer chip that was inserted just under the skin on the top of their right hand. It was essentially the same chip that had been in the card, but this new application just made it easier to keep track of everyone. An additional bonus was that it was almost impossible to steal...which had been a growing problem with the Currency Cards even with the biometric safeguards.

When the government offered added benefits with the "inserted" chip, including free food, relocation to a warmer climate with better tents and facilities, and finally a bonus of extra welfare monies, automatically deposited into the "chipped" persons account, people lined up by the millions. Many stores now also refused to handle the new cash, only selling to those who had been chipped, or who used the Currency Cards. Being "chipped" became the latest fad.

Now that the harsh winter and a severe flu epidemic that swept the country was finally past with the welcomed arrival of spring and the announcement that Martial law would be relaxed everywhere in the

US, there was hope in the air. Except of course, for those who were on the wrong side of Homeland Security...

CHAPTER 1

Northern Montana, near Glacier National Park

DATE: Current...
WEDNESDAY AUGUST 8

When it finally happened it shook him more than he had expected.

Luckily, Jared had prepared for this moment and had rehearsed his reaction many times in his mind. The thing that worried him was the call itself. He still didn't know who the voice belonged to... *"my guardian angel, if you believe in that sort of thing, or Tom,"* only it wasn't a voice that he recognized.

The male voice had simply said in a southern drawl, "They're coming, get out now"... and the line had gone dead.

He pondered over the questions in his mind, *"who had made this call? Who arranged it?"* He thought through the very short list of possibilities and came up with only one answer.

It had to be her.

A smile came to his lips for a minute at the thought that she had somehow arranged the warning in her mysterious way, and then a shiver went up the back of his neck.

"How did they find me?"

He reflected on the pain of having her cut the special chip out of his shoulder six weeks earlier and involuntarily flexed his shoulder and arm at the memory.

It was a foolish gesture, trying to feel an object that was no longer there and even when it had been there, as it had for so many years...he couldn't feel it. That was one of the features that made the chip so dangerous... you forgot it was even there.

The thought of it caused him to tense up. He was forty four and getting too old for this kind of adventure, but, then he thought, *"forty-four really isn't that old."* Then he remembered the old Indiana Jones line... *"its not the years, it's the mileage."*

"That's me," he thought with a slight laugh. *"Too many miles...I should be dead by now anyway."*

He had to take just a moment and calm himself and focus on the task at hand before he started moving. He had learned long ago that hasty action without focusing had the possibility of ending with any variety of bad results, including, but not limited to, a very violent death in his line of business.

He wished they would just leave him alone. That was the original goal when he had gone into hiding. Focusing, the mental checklist he had prepared for just this occasion appeared in his mind.

"Time to get going, " he said softly to no one.

He quickly extinguished all of the lights except for the one in the front room window of the small cabin and then placed his hat, with a small LED headlight attached, upon his head. He flipped the lamp over to its red light setting. It cast a dim light, barely enough to see by, but it would help his night vision when he went outside. The red light would also be almost undetectable from a distance unless the observer looked straight into the light.

He walked into the back bedroom, and grabbed his 45 from the small night stand next to his bed. It was a standard XD that he had put at least 1000 rounds through over the last couple of years, but had rarely shot recently. Ammunition for the gun had become too expensive for a while, and then after the government gun ban, it had become impossible to find.

He had come to like the XD a lot. It was almost as good as his H&K Tactical 45 he kept in his "D" bag below the foot of his bed. The H&K was bigger, and could be fitted with the silencer, which he had, which made it a little too long and just a little too heavy for the task at hand. Although a lot more expensive, and thought by most to be a better more accurate gun, Jared had come to prefer the shorter XD with its 4 inch barrel, for a personal defensive weapon.

The accuracy of the XD was just what he needed except for a possible long distance shot. It was always reliable and felt good in his hand. As he picked it up, he instinctively popped the magazine checking to see that it was still full of the 12 rounds while also making sure a round was chambered.

He slipped off the safety while reaching over to a nail stuck in the wall above where the gun had been and picked up his belt. Sliding the gun into the holster and feeling the quick release catch 'click' he buckled the webbed belt and gun on. He had gone through this process so many times that now he did it with the smooth and automatic motion of experience.

Reaching over to the small dresser and picking up his knife, he strapped it quickly to the inside of his left arm.   He fumbled for only a second as he tightened the knife sheath around his forearm in the dark. It was a flat, thin blade only about 5" long..., but exceedingly sharp and almost invisible under his long sleeve shirt. This was a part of his insurance.

Before the call, he had just about been ready to head for bed, sitting in his chair and reading as he had become accustomed to doing almost every night since arriving at the cabin, when the satellite phone had jumped to life. The sound of the unexpected ring had jarred him.

Cell phones were useless with the rugged terrain that surrounded the cabin. A satellite phone was really the only way to communicate with the outside world., but he hadn't even used it once since arriving here four weeks ago, though he kept it with a solar panel, just in case. He had grown accustomed to the peace and quiet with only the soft sound of the nearby stream and the rustling of the wind through the pines at this time of night.

He was glad he had not taken his boots off yet, as it saved him a good three to five minutes. Earlier however, he had taken off his ankle holster, which held a small 32 caliber Berretta Px4 subcompact. Another piece of insurance. He grabbed it quickly and strapped it on his left ankle, just below the calf.

Now, he was dressed.

Walking into the small cubicle that was the cabin's only bathroom, he opened the three tubes kept near the sink and smeared the greasepaint onto his face. Grabbing his camo jacket out of the closet, he slipped it on and the harness over it. The final touches were the thin shooters gloves which would camouflage his hands and also give them protection from the rocks and cold.

He wondered how much time he really had as he grabbed the modified Saiga SKS from the corner of the room and then went back into the bedroom. He liked the SKS because it was based on the famous AK-47 Kalashnikov system that was the best in the world. The Saiga was really a civilian version of the AK-47. Simple, rugged, easy to take apart, and very reliable, it didn't jam like the AR-15 often did and didn't require the constant maintenance. The SKS seemed to always fire wet, muddy, dirty as long as the inside of the barrel was clean.

Also, it fired a heavier slug than the American .223. Though you could carry more rounds for the same weight, the .223 (though the military referred to it as .556 mm) was just a little bit larger than a 22...and it wouldn't go through thick trees. Most everything stopped it, or deflected it. It was an excellent anti-personnel round, but it had its drawbacks. The heavier 7.62 x39 SKS round on the other hand, went through over a foot of wood, very handy when working in a heavy forest setting. The solid FMJ (full metal jacket) was essentially an armor piercing round and would go through most car metal, including doors, radiators, wtih ease, and often cause enough damage to engine blocks to make them seize up. He had alternated between full metal-jacketed rounds and the hollow points in all of this magazines to get the best of both worlds.

Though the American favored AR-15 was generally considered better at longer ranges, with the American made Saiga, he could consistently put a three inch grouping at 300 yards. And since he was in a heavy forest, he usually didn't see past 100 yards anyway...and so he had favored the SKS.

Reaching under the bed he pulled out the D bag and moved to the corner of the room. Moving the chest of drawers from the wall revealed a small trap door he had cut into the wall of the cabin about 3 weeks ago, for just such an occasion as this. He thought of the lesson he had often taught his men.... *"Always have a back door escape route. Always have a plan B and even a C and D if possible."* This "escape hatch" was his plan B.

He quietly shoved the D bag out first and then quickly and silently followed, pausing only to pull the chest back into position close to the wall, and then replace the door quietly.

Now he was in the covered wood shed behind the cabin and hoping that if they were watching they would think there was only one doorway in and out of the cabin and would be watching that. He hoped that the trick with the side trap door would confuse them for at least a little while, buying him more time as they searched the cabin.

He had debated with himself often over the last month in his preparations for the possibility of this kind of escape about whether, or not to leave any lights on in the cabin. In the end he had settled upon leaving at least one light still lit, giving him an edge that might prove invaluable. They would know within a few seconds of entering the cabin that it had recently been occupied and the light would draw their attention to the front room and the front door while also weakening their night vision as he slipped out the back and into the shadows that one light would help to create.

He could barely see out into the darkness past the stacked wood that surrounded him. The ground was only just visible under the dark shadows of the tall pines not more than 30 feet away because of the stars that were shining. With the Saiga dangling from the sling, he hefted the D bag and left the wood shed...observing as he went, that it was almost a perfect night with just a little chill settling in. He had always loved the mountains and especially this place. It held a lot of wonderful memories for him, but this was no time to reminisce as he brought himself back to task.

He quickly sprinted to the nearby forest, thick with lodge pole pine and underbrush, where the darkness deepened. Running past a couple trees, he stopped, crouching... listening. His carefully thought out planning had worked...so far. He had packed up and gotten away in under 7 minutes. *"I need to practice it a few more times so that it will be only 4 minutes the next time,"* he thought. He almost laughed at the possibility that might ever be a "next time."

Turning around he watched the cabin for a minute to see if he could make out anything, or anyone from this distance. Nothing was visible except for the faint outline of the cabin and the light shining from the front window. Behind the cabin over the ridge of dark mountains, he could see a slight silvery glow along the Western horizon. The moon would be up in about fifteen to thirty minutes. Until then he would still be able to take advantage of the darkness.

He reached down into the harness and pulled out his monocular night vision scope. It wasn't the best, but it was sufficient. Because of the urgency of his escape from his Arizona home, he had not had the time to get to his-top-of-the-line night vision, 'hands free' binoculars in his hidden storage room, but this one still worked quite well.

He looked around with it and found that he could see all the details he needed. His position was slightly above the cabin on the hillside, away from the road and the stream that flowed below the cabin. The clearing around the cabin appeared to be empty. He studied the tree line to spot any moving shapes among the trees and bushes. Nothing was visible to him from this position... so it was time to move.

Using the scope, he found the path easily that led him through the forest. This was part of the strategy that he had actually walked through a few times and had carefully planned out. This was still option A. Option B, if he had to choose it, would take him in a completely different direction.

Jared hiked about 200 yards on along the small trail, then, as he passed the large "elephant" shaped granite boulder, he turned off the trail and went down the hillside towards the stream.

He crossed the small stream carefully and traveled along its edge for a few minutes, back toward the cabin. There was a steep rock fall next, almost straight up the canyon wall. The moon had risen, and though only a third full, helped enough that Jared was able to put the night vision away and continued along merely by the light shining down on him from the moon.

Carefully, he took his time so as not to dislodge any rocks, or make noise as he started his climb. He knew that hidden behind and among the rocks he would be undetectable to any one near the cabin until he reached his destination near the summit.

At the top of the rock fall Jared stopped and took his position between two large boulders. From here he knew he would be able to see down into the cabin clearing, up the road a little and along the stream that flowed in front of the cabin.

He carefully laid his rifle down next to him, flat on the ground so as to be within easy reach, , but not in a position where it could be easily knocked over, creating a noise.   Just as he settled in and was reaching for his scope, he saw a couple of flashlights sweep past the front window from within the cabin. It was good news in a way... whoever was after him were amateurs.

Peering through the scope, he could barely see a green figure by the door and two lights moving around the interior of the cabin. *'That's three'*, he counted. After a short wait of only a minute, or two he spotted another figure among the trees down by the road, *'And that makes four.'*

"Still," he thought, *"It would be better not to underestimate them, whoever they are."* He wondered

if they were there to kill him, or just to take him back. Either way, it wasn't going to happen.

He watched a little longer just to see if there were others that he had missed earlier. He didn't see any. After a few minutes the two flashlights turned off and two figures exited out the front door. They apparently hadn't found the trap door into the wood shed.

As he watched, the figures in the distance split up and started searching around the clearing. Their lights were off, which probably meant they were also equipped with night vision, and probably a lot better version than the one he had, maybe even the same one that was still at his old home over 1000 miles away.

Watching them, Jared considered the idea that he should have left a booby trap to welcome them, and decided that he would prepare something if they found his trail and got too close. He meant them no harm..., but he would protect himself if he had to.

The moon was higher now, and things were actually quite bright through the scope, just varying shades of light-green and dark green. After several minutes, the person Jared had spotted near the road walked in and the four of them met by the cabin.

"Must be time for a pow wow," Jared said to himself in a quiet whisper. He continued the thought in his mind, *"Probably wondering what to do next...maybe even trying to radio for instructions, though that would be difficult unless the one running this operation was nearby, or they also had a satellite phone."* The area where they were was not too far from Glacier national park and the Canadian border. The area was heavily wooded mountains...extremely rugged and often very steep, terrain.   Jared was counting on the fact that he was familiar with this difficult landscape, and they were not ...which should be to his advantage.

He thought through his next step, considering the two "holes", or caches where he had buried supplies he had prepared. One nearby, only five miles away, and another nearly 35 miles away, and actually over the border into Canada. The second one was farther than he wanted to travel right now, but certainly doable under the circumstances.   Before he left however, he wanted to wait and see what this team of hunters did next. It might help him decide which hole he would go to.

As he was pondering these thoughts, he could see vehicle lights back along the road. He watched as a humvee slowly crawled over the rocky, rutted ground and stopped in front of the cabin.

Another person got out of the vehicle and joining the other four men, entered the cabin. Something in the way he walked made Jared think of Bennett. It had to be him! Somehow, he just knew it.

This turn of events was not good, not good at all. For Bennett to show up personally, something was wrong. Something terrible had happened. He felt that awareness settle in the pit of his stomach and turn into a burning. He had been out of touch for almost two months, the last month here at the cabin.

That thought brought her instantly back to his mind. He instinctively knew that she was in trouble. Somehow Bennett had gotten her to reveal where he was and Jared was now concerned about the methods that had used to obtain this information. He weighed his next thought carefully, *"Could he have tortured her? And if so... what had he done with her after she had given him the information he wanted? Had Bennett killed her?"*

Certainly, it was possible, but more than likely she was alive and had been tricked into revealing his whereabouts somehow. That was Bennett's way, at least at first. Bennett liked to tell himself and showoff to others, whenever possible, that he had the superior intelligence. The problem was that Bennett was extremely smart, but that also proved to be one of his greatest weaknesses. It often led to arrogance and sometimes sloppiness.

The other problem was that when his smarts didn't work he used whatever means he had to obtain what he wanted. He was an amoral and depraved, scoundrel, as Jared had been reminded over the last couple of months.

While in the military, Bennett had been kept in check. Now he worked for Blackbird, the private para-military group that supported Homeland Security, and they appeared to have given him free reign to accomplish whatever they wanted done. Ever since the beginning of the collapse and martial law, it seemed whenever and wherever trouble was, Bennett was right in the thick of it. At least that was what Jared's sources had told him. He had truly turned into a vicious and unfeeling animal.

Jared touched the SKS sitting next to him as he watched. If only he had a clear shot...he would be tempted to take it. If anyone deserved to meet his maker and receive judgment on an early time frame, Bennett was it.

He thought more about trying to shoot Bennett and then dismissed the thought. He wasn't even sure if it was him and it was dark. He could not risk the chance of making a mistake now. No, he would have to wait for another day. But, he decided, if Bennett had hurt her again...he would pay dearly.

A few minutes after watching the Humvee sit there in front of the cabin, Jared was deep in thought. He knew now that he couldn't go to the holes, either one of them for very long. He couldn't just hide away out of sight right now, not yet. Before all else he needed to get out of the forest and find out what had happened and what was happening now in the world.

He would first make a short stop at the nearest cache hole, pick up his supplies and make some plans. Along the way he would make a call and see what he could find out.

As Jared watched, the flashlights turned on, once again, inside the cabin and light shown out through the window and open door into the night. Bennett had to see for himself. A couple of minutes later the lights were carried out of the cabin, turned off and Jared observed that at least some of shadowy figures got into the Humvee.

He watched the dark military vehicle pull away. *"Did everyone get in it?"* He couldn't be sure. He hadn't been able to count them as they moved through the darkness. He scanned the area for a moment and didn't notice anyone left behind. It really didn't matter now, he wasn't going back to the cabin anyway.

Jared turned off his night scope and put it away. With the moon up higher, he wouldn't be needing it to see the trail.

He grabbed his SKS, backed down from his perch between the two boulders, and picked up his bag, slinging it over his shoulder. He reattached his SKS to his sling, and started off. The path here was very rocky, which was one of the reasons why he had chosen it. Here he would not leave a trail easily followed.

"It would take a bloodhound to follow me now" he thought, and if they did bring one, he would be long gone. Plus his scent was all over the place... helping to add to the confusion.

As he trudged along the moonlit trail, he thought again, *"I am too old for this kind of stuff anymore. It's time to settle down and take it easy. Raise a family."* After meeting her, he had been thinking of that possibility a lot. It was one of the reasons he had invited her to Show Low, to his home. But, then...his mind jumped back to the present, *"I have to find out what has happened to her."* As he started making his plans, he trudged along towards his first cache hide out.

CHAPTER 2

SOMEWHERE ALONG I-90
IN SOUTHWEST MONTANA

Friday Morning... August

Rachel Sinclair stared out the window of the Humvee as it sped along, for no other reason than to avoid the eyes of her captors. She simply didn't want to see their gloating eyes. Beside, the leaves were turning, and the contrast between the dark green of the pines and the yellows and golds of the aspen was truly spectacular. There was even a layer of snow on top of the mountains, something not uncommon for this time of the year in Montana.

"It looks like it is going to be an early winter, yet again," she thought. *"Just like the last few years across the entire country, since the weather had gone haywire."* The next thought came to her mind out of concern for others, *"It will be cold in the tents very soon."*

The Humvee hit a bump and she tried to shift her weight against the seat belts that held her tightly in place. She shifted her position and pulled on the handcuff chains, but all to no avail.

The handcuffs were constricting and had rubbed

her wrists raw where they came in contact with skin. *"At least they aren't behind my back like before,"* she thought. Instead, her hands were cuffed in front of her with the chain running through a ring attached to the metal frame of the front seat. The chain for these handcuffs was longer than the previous ones had been and allowed her to rest her hands on the edge of her knees, but nothing more.

They had caught her in Spokane, and were now taking her back to Ogden, Utah where Blackbird, the para-military, mercenary group employed by homeland security, had established their regional headquarters. Blackbird provided a lot of the 'muscle', or men for the Regional Intermountain Homeland Security offices for Utah, Idaho, Nevada, Wyoming, and Montana which were setup in Salt Lake City.

During the recent crises and the subsequent martial law, Blackbird "contractors" had been employed... along with the UN troops invited into the US to assist and provide manpower to the US Homeland Security since the majority of National Guard soldiers were still engaged in Iran & Afghanistan. Of course they were backed up by the Homeland Civil Defense Volunteers, the Federal presidential militia that had been organized two years earlier and were in the process of getting trained.

Although there were some UN troops in the Intermountain area, most of them, at least for now, were concentrated in heavy population centers like Los Angeles, Oakland, Chicago, Detroit, and D.C., where the food riots and unrest had been the worst.

Though things were much better of late, occasional there were still reports of running gun battles in Los Angeles and Detroit between Homeland Security forces and the gangs.

Rachel had been cautiously making her way to Montana hoping to catch up with Jared. She had been extremely anxious to see him ever since her nightmare, and it had taken her over 2 weeks to make her way from Arizona to Spokane. She had been surprised at how things had worked out for her along the way, especially allowing her to get past the road blocks without any federal ID.

Still, it was the constant fear of being caught and never seeing Jared again that had been the hardest part of the trip. And now it was all undone. *"Had they killed him? Had he escaped?"* She had sent him a message trying to warn him, but it was so vague. *"Had it even gotten through?"* So much had happened since she last saw him.

Rachel's thoughts turned to their parting moments when he had held her in his arms in the Arizona tent refuge, unexpectedly kissed her, and then turned and walked away.

He had simply said, "Think of me," and she had, more than she wanted to admit, and that was part of the problem. It seemed that she had done little else the last two weeks while traveling and the several weeks before that. Whenever she had a moment to pause, she thought of Jared and the tiny flame that he had kindled in her heart began to grow. Even she was surprised by the emotions that stirred within her. Then she remembered Granny's words... and then another bump in the road shook her out of her reverie.

She tried to adjust her body against the restraining seatbelts, but they wouldn't give. She crossed her feet the other way, closed her eyes again, and tried to relax. Her mind wandered, going back to the barbeque at her brother Todd's house. It seemed like it had been ages ago when it had all begun...

CHAPTER 3

August...two years earlier

It was a hot summer day in mid-August at Todd & Deedee Sinclair's backyard in Rexburg, Idaho, and they were all enjoying a friendly neighborhood barbeque, typical of this area and time of year.

There wasn't a cloud in the sky, and it was one of those rare occasions in Rexburg when the wind wasn't blowing. Rachel figured it was close to 100 degrees, made bearable only by the dryness of the air. She was glad she wasn't back home in Maryland, where the constantly high humidity at temperatures much lower than these made being outside in the summer time, insufferable. There the heat and sweat became almost suffocating during the summer. Rachel was glad she had made the decision to come out west and visit Todd and his family with their brother Bill and her niece Jill. It was a welcomed break.

Bill, the oldest brother of the Sinclair family, had come out the day before to drop off his oldest daughter Jill at BYU-Idaho. Rachel, who was Bill & Todd's little sister, the only girl and also the baby in their family, had come out 4 days earlier with Jill.

Rachel and Jill had become more than just aunt and niece, they had become good friends over the last several months. Even though Jill was almost 19, and Aunt Rachel was 34, their friendship was natural and genuine. The age difference didn't seem to bother either of them, Rachel was a young looking, youthful 34 and Jill acted and looked much older than she really was. Jill insisted that Rachel was her role model, and Rachel had to admit that there seemed to be not only a physical resemblance, as they were often mistaken for sisters, but also a similarity in their inclinations and enjoyments.

Beside the family trait of dark red hair and a few soft freckles, both women had a beauty about them that was rugged, clean and fresh, as much at home in the out of doors as the cover of any fashion magazine.

Jill had invited, or more accurately, insisted that "Aunt Rachel" come out to help send her off so they could hike the trails of the Grand Tetons that Rachel knew so well.

Even after a busy summer, Rachel had enough vacation days built up to enjoy this last outing of the season. In the past few years she had become a veritable workaholic and hadn't felt the need, or desire to use the paid time off she had accumulated, that is until time spent with Jill had become so enjoyable.

It all began when Aunt Rachel, making one of her every other month visits, had arrived at Bill's house that spring for dinner. Jill was preparing to graduate from High School and during the dinner conversation had been asked what she wanted to do this summer before heading off to college.

Jill's eager and surprising response was that she wanted Aunt Rachel to teach her all about hiking and rock climbing.

The stories Jill had heard about hiking trips and adventures from her Dad and Rachel, had prompted more than a few evenings filled by questioning Rachel about the other activities she had taken part in...once upon a time. Jill was especially intrigued with Rachel's summer activities as an Anasazi wilderness survival student and guide.

Enthralled by her stories, Jill insisted that Rachel take her out and teach her as much as she could during the remaining spring and summer. So the plans were made. It helped remind Rachel that there was more to life than work, genealogy and daily workouts at the gym.

And so, over the last couple months of summer, since Jill's high school graduation, they had spent a lot time together, with Rachel teaching Jill all of the finer points of hiking in the near by Appalachian Mountains.

Rachel kept telling Jill that they weren't really mountains, at least not by the standards of the western United States, but rather very large rolling hills. After hiking them, however, especially in the hot, humid weather, they may as well have been mountains to the girls.

On one of their first hikes together, Rachel had promised to take Jill, someday, to the Grand Tetons, which she claimed were some real mountains, and maybe do some rock climbing, or repelling. Jill had remembered the comment and suggested they could enjoy one last adventure near the end of the summer just before she went to BYU-I as a freshman.

Rachel had both good and bad memories of her time at BYU-I. She had grown up in Southern California and her father had been the Scoutmaster for what seemed her entire life. With five older brothers she naturally had been invited along on all of the scout hikes since she was 11 years old. By the time she graduated from High School, she had hiked 200 miles of the John Muir trail, hiked to the bottom of the Grand Canyon, and had climbed Mt. Whitney, twice.

While attending BYU-Idaho for two years, she added river rafting and rock climbing to her list of hobbies and hiked in the Grand Tetons, which were only about 2 hours from the campus.

As a freshman she turned down several offers of marriage, because as she said "I just can't see them taking me to the Celestial Kingdom". Rachel had pretty high expectations that most of the "men" at school just didn't meet. Then during her sophomore year she had found John Jackson, or, you could say, he had found her.

He seemed to be everything she had waited for, and their love blossomed quickly. They had discussed marriage openly and frankly, but just about the time she was sure John was planning to make it official, he got sick.

At first everyone thought it was the flu, and then maybe a bad case of bronchitis, or even pneumonia. When he had trouble breathing and became dizzy to the point of vertigo, his roommates forced him to go to the campus health center, which then sent him to the local hospital.

Shortly before the tests came back indicating that he had contracted the West Nile virus, John slipped into a coma and never woke up. Three days later, he was gone, taking all of Rachel's dreams for a "Happily-ever- after" future, with him.

John's death destroyed her and for months she seemed to wander around in a daze. Finally she pulled herself out by burying herself in school studies, church callings, and more time in the wilderness. She turned down all requests for dates in a polite, but firm manner which made it very clear to those asking that she just wasn't interested.

At the end of her sophomore year, just before her 21st birthday, Rachel applied to serve a mission and was called to Taiwan. After returning she decided to pursue a law degree motivated in part by her Mission President who had been a patent attorney before being called to serve in Taiwan.

She attended her last two years in Provo, graduating from BYU with a degree in physics. She applied to the J. Reuben Clark Law School, where she was accepted and did extremely well graduating

Magna Cum Laude, second in her class.

She landed a great first job, clerking in a prestigious patent law firm in New York for her old Mission President, where she proved herself to be a motivated, self starting, hard worker. She passed all of the bar exams and two years later Rachel had been hired by her current employer and put into a position where she had moved up quickly prior to the financial collapse.

On the occasion of Bill's, Rachel's and Jill's visit, Todd and Deedee had invited four other families to the barbeque, friends and neighbors who had been talking for a while about getting together one last time before summer was over and school was in full swing.

Bill's plans were to leave that evening, but Rachel was going to stay 2 more days and visit an old missionary friend before flying back, to Washington, D.C. on Monday.

Todd's barbeque specialty, Sanpete BBQ turkey, was a smash hit as always and the families, after eating, had divided into the usual two groups... with the men sitting in lawn chairs in the shade of the porch, talking football, baseball and sports in general while pretending to watch the kids play in the yard and in the little wading pool.

The women, on the other hand, were inside the cool of the house talking about husbands, children, and everything else. Jill and Rachel, not fitting well into either of the adult groups and their conversations, were actually playing with the little kids on the swings and in the wading pool.

The conversation had waned a little when Todd's next door neighbor Sam, a detective for the local police force and a good friend who also happened to be the ward preparedness specialist, asked if anyone had heard of an author named Robert Townsend, or read any of his books.

Charlie responded first, "No, who's he? I've never heard of him."

"My father in law has his books" Jeremy said, "keeps trying to get me to read them, but I just don't have the time."

Another neighbor, Gary, commented that he thought he had heard his name before, but knew nothing more.

Just then Denise, Jeremy's wife, and Roberta, Gary's wife, came out into the backyard where Roberta handed the baby to Gary. "Your turn" she said with a grin.

Deedee also came out and asked..."Does anyone want any more of this potato salad before I put it away?" and the consensus was that no one could fit another bite after that great meal.

Turning back to the conversation at hand, Charlie asked, "So who is this guy Townsend anyway?"

Sam, who had started it all, began to explain. "Well he's a guy who has written several books about the last days and the 2nd Coming of Christ. He goes around and lectures about what is coming. Julie and I just went to a lecture of his a couple of weeks ago down in Orem, Utah...along with about 700 other people."

Charlie's response was genuine surprise, "Really?" he asked.

Now others joined in with real interest. Jeremy asked, "What exactly did he have to say."

"Well... he said a lot more than I can tell you right now. It lasted for 2 days, there were a few other speakers, but he was the main one," Sam recalled. "It was all geared towards getting prepared for the last days and the main message was that we had better hurry."

Bill, ever the skeptic, always had his opinion and voiced it now. "Oh, one of those doomsday guys? There have been a lot of them over the years. They warn a lot, but nothing ever happens, just a lot of hot air. You know the 2nd Coming is still 100 years away, maybe more. Maybe my grandkids will see it, when they are old and have grandkids of their own."

"This guy is different," Sam tried to explain, "he's really good at what he says and very convincing. Julie and I have been reading his books over the last couple of months and have been pretty impressed. He really knows his stuff."

"So what does he say that's so different from

everyone else?" Jeremy asked with sincerity.

Sam answered, "He says that there are some pretty dreadful events that happen maybe thirty, or even fifty years before the actual coming of the Savior, including a 13 month war and a famine that happens in the United States. He says, that according to the scriptures... we are in the 7th seal and that these preliminary events are just around the corner."

Sally, having pulled up a chair next to her husband Charlie, joined into the conversation. "Really... Like what does he say is going to happen?"

By now, Deedee had stopped collecting plates from the picnic table and sat down on the bench next to her son Zack, to listen.

Sam went on, "He says that this recession is going to become a terrible depression and that we will have a complete financial collapse, food shortages, and then a terrible war here in the States. He says that the first Gulf War was the first great woe mentioned by John in Revelation and the second great woe will happen in a few years. He says that the second great woe is a terrible nuclear war that takes place here in the U.S. and the rest of the world."

Bill interjected with cynicism again, "The things people do to get attention always astounds me. All we are having is a market correction. It will last a year, or two, just like in the past, and then things will pick up again. This is no time to panic. Things are under control. You'll see."

"Is he one of the new Seventies just sustained at the last conference?" Charlie asked, "It's hard to keep track of them these days."

"Nope," Sam assured him, "he's not even a BYU professor. He's just a normal guy who writes books that contain a lot of quotes from Apostles and Prophets."

Bill was a retired U.S.A.F. major who took pride in identifying and placing everything and everybody into their respective categories otherwise known as pigeonholes. His attitude showed through clearly as he continued his argument, "Uh huh. It sounds pretty far fetched to me. He sounds like your average doomsday nut case with just a few different twists. What makes him think his interpretation of the scriptures is right? You just admitted he's not a General Authority."

Bill paused a little after his last comment and when no one said anything he continued. "He probably sells food storage and is just trying to scare everyone into buying his merchandise. We have some doom and gloomers in our ward and that's all they ever want to talk about. Famines, Ezra Taft Benson, and if we don't have a ten year supply of food we are all going to die." Bill emphasized the end of his comment by throwing both hands up into the air.

Just then, Sam's wife, Julie, came out of the house chasing their toddler, Buddy. As she caught up with the child and swooped him into her arms, Julie took the book he was carrying out of Sam's hands and gave him a look of exasperation before she sat down next to Deedee. She put Buddy down and he, sensing his freedom took the opportunity to escape, running over to the wading pool and jumping into the four inches of water.

Sensing a real conversation was taking place, Sally pulled up a chair next to her husband Charlie, while another Roberta wandered over to help supervise the wading pool.

Sam had become just a little defensive because of Bill's comments. "No, he doesn't sell food storage. As far as doomsday nuts, well... Julie and I sat next to a Stake President on Saturday who had traveled a day just to hear him speak. He had heard Townsend two years ago after having his books recommended to him by a retired General Authority. This Stake President believes he is absolutely right on. In fact, he predicted the recession that we are having right now over two years ago.

"Really?" Jeremy said, completely caught up in this conversation. There was a long pause where no one said anything as they considered all they were hearing.

Finally, Sam, turning to Todd, asked, "Do you have any food storage, like a years supply?"

"Sort of," Todd mumbled a little unsure of his response. "We have what is in our cupboards and in our pantry. Probably about a year's worth." He tried to sound convincing, but turned to Deedee for assurance. Deedee answered his unspoken question by shaking her head slowly back and forth. "Well, maybe not," he admitted.

Sam, turned to Charlie "What about you?" he asked.

"Yeah, we do." Charlie answered matter of factly. "My father-in-law is one of those preparedness nuts... and 2 years ago he gave us a year's supply of food for our whole family. It's still sitting in our garage, right where he delivered it."

As Sam turned to Jeremy, preparing to ask him the same question, Jeremy volunteered, "No," he said a little concerned. "We don't have anything except what's on the shelves."

"Well, I had some food storage." Bill interjected. "Had it for years and it was a total waste of time and energy. I dropped most of it off at the thrift store to be distributed to the poor after the Y2K fiasco of 2000."

Charlie, showing some interest now and trying to ignore Bill's comment added, "So what else did he say?"

"He also mentioned something that Brigham Young and others had talked about, a call out by Church leaders to tent cities." This mention of things never heard of, or considered by this group was more than a shock and Jeremy was the first to voice it.

"A what?" he asked. "You mean like the tent cities

I've heard about that they've set up in California because of the recession?"

Todd joined in, "Yeah, I've heard of those too."

"Well, he explained it this way." Sam went on "A lot of people are having dreams and visions. He says it's a part of the fulfillment of the prophecy in the book of Joel in the Old Testament that President Hinckley spoke about a few years back. In those dreams and visions many people are seeing the prophet inviting people to live in tent camps high up in the mountains. Going to these camps helps them to avoid the famine, plagues and fighting that occurs in the U.S. as part of the 13 month war."

Julie chimed in at this point anxious to be a part of the discussion, "In these dreams they also see the nuclear attack and invasion of the United States by Russia and China."

Bill exploded in a controlled rage. His face turned red and his eyes flashed the fiery anger that burned behind them, "That is the most absurd piece of apostate garbage I have ever heard." He railed, "It's simply ridiculous. And everyone knows that you can't trust people's personal dreams and visions and treat them like....like," Bill searched for words to express his disdain... "like reality. Who do they think they are?" Even knowing Bill and his attitude toward the topic of their discussion, Todd was taken aback by his outburst.

Bill paused with his question hanging in the air,

but no one said a word.

Seeing that no one was going to respond to his question and sensing that some of those present did not share his assessment, Bill continued. "And if you believe that kind of horse crap, you need to go see your Bishop and maybe have your recommend pulled."

Todd, hadn't seen his brother this angry in ages. The silence that hung in the air was a pall that had just overcome the group. After a long enough wait, and trying to smooth things over, Todd suggested, "Well, I guess everyone is entitled to their opinion."

Bill wasn't quite finished yet, but was calmer as he said, "I'm telling you, this is absolutely absurd and this guy Townsend is nuts. Certifiable. I don't know who this Robert Townsend is, or who he thinks he is..., but he sounds like an apostate trying to start his own cult. He probably has been excommunicated and you just don't know it."

Todd, in a further attempt at calming his brother, reflected, "Well, it is an interesting theory and makes for some lively discussion for sure." Then, looking at his watch continued, "Hey, look at the time, we need to leave in about fifteen minutes in order to get you to the airport on time for your flight."

With that official signal, everyone burst into motion, obviously relieved that someone had brought what had become an uncomfortable situation to an end. Grabbing kids, the last of the food, plates and decorations, clean up went quickly and within ten minutes Todd was on his way to the airport with his older brother.

In order to break the moody silence that had lingered from the party, Todd asked "So what projects are you working on now Bill, anything special?"

"No" Bill answered absent mindedly, but happy the silence had ended. "Just finishing up my doctorate in engineering and teaching some classes at the local community college, pretty boring stuff really. Linda is finally using her Masters Degree and teaching English Lit at the state college across town. She's always wanted to teach and now that Jill is off to college that leaves just Kathy and Mark at home and Mark will be gone to college next year."

Todd was relieved that his brother was voluntarily talking about the family and decided to keep the conversation going for as long as Bill would participate. "Where's Mark planning to go to school?"

"He hasn't said yet." Bill responded. ", but I wouldn't be surprised if he wanted to follow Jill here to BYU-Idaho."

"What do you hear from Bill Jr. in Germany?" Todd asked. The younger Elder William Sinclair had been serving in the Germany Frankfurt Mission for the church and would soon be reaching his half way mark.

"We don't hear much to tell you the truth." Bill

said with a slight disappointment in his voice. ", but he did mention in the last email that they are combining three more of the German missions into one, but that's happening a lot in Europe these days."

CHAPTER 4

A short time after Todd and Bill left for the airport and the clean up details from the barbeque had been taken care of, Rachel drove Jill back to her dorm on campus.

They had both listened in on the conversation about the last days, but neither had participated, content to let the others do the arguing.

In the car, on the short ride to the dorm, Jill asked Rachel, "So, what did you think about that discussion?"

Rachel, noticing the sarcastic emphasis on the word discussion answered her lightly, "Well your dad certainly has his opinion on the topic."

"Yea, Dad is like that. It's part of his military background. Anything new that tries to shake up his set paradigm will not be received well, especially if it comes from what he considers unauthorized, or through unofficial channels." Jill understood her father's opinion even if she didn't always agree with him.

Rachel asked, "What do you think?"

"I'm not sure. It sounds interesting, I just haven't

thought about it enough to really have an opinion I guess." Then, turning the tables back on Rachel, Jill asked, "What do *you* think about it?"

"I'm not sure either," Rachel answered trying to give her niece an honest answer. "One of the things that I have learned as a patent attorney is that you should never dismiss anything new as being impossible, no matter who is presenting it, or working on it. Inventors come in all sizes and shapes, from the sophisticated corporate researchers, to the crackpots living out in the middle of the desert doodling on post-it-notes in their basements. In fact, I could tell you a dozen stories that are legend in my firm...where a lot of respected scientists have said something couldn't be done, that it was, in fact, totally impossible, and then someone came along with some device that did exactly what they said couldn't be done."

Rachel paused just as they arrived at the dorm.

Jill sat expectantly, waiting for Rachel to finish her thought.

Finally, Rachel continued, "Let's just say that the topic intrigues me enough that I'm going to do some research on it. What we heard today is called hearsay from a second, or third hand source. What I need to do is get the original source material and review it for its salient points. Then, I can make a determination of its validity to one degree, or another."

"So, what you just said in legalese," Jill teased, "is that you are going to buy this guys book and read it to see if it makes any sense. Right?"

Rachel, with a grin on her face teased right back, "Didn't I just say that?"

Jill opened the car door and got out so her answer was given over her shoulder and with a small laugh, "Sort of," she said.

After hugs and goodbyes had been exchanged, Rachel got back into the car and drove off, reviewing the conversation at the barbeque in her mind and listing the points that had been made. She had a pretty good memory for such details, and by now this kind of analysis had become almost second nature.

CHAPTER 5

That night, after a late dinner of leftover snacks, Rachel busied herself downstairs in the guest room answering emails on her laptop over the internet while Todd, seated in the living room, read a newspaper. After a while, Deedee came in and sat down near him on the couch.

"Got a minute honey?" she asked.

Todd replied, "Sure D," as he quickly folded the newspaper and laid it down, out of the way. Twenty plus years of marriage had taught him that this was a signal for him to focus his attention entirely on his wife and what she had to say.

Her face seemed serious and Todd honestly didn't know what to expect as she began. "What did you think of the discussion at the party this afternoon?" she wondered.

"You mean about the last days and this Townsend guy?"

"Uh, huh, that's exactly what I mean"

"I don't know D., it sounds kind of interesting. I thought maybe I would drive over to the bookstore sometime next week, buy one of his books and read it to find out for myself what he has to say." Todd's words surprised her a little and made her eyes brighten up a bit.

"Well, I talked to Julie about it after most everyone else had left this afternoon, and Todd, I believe it." If Julie had been surprised by Todd's words, Todd was now flabbergasted by hers.

"Really?" Todd asked incredulously.

Deedee paused as if she were searching for just the right words to use. "Yes, really. When Julie and I were talking I asked her for more information about this tent city thing Sam had mentioned. She told me that Townsend mentioned it when he talked about the dreams and visions people have had. She said that a lot of people including men, women and children have all had dreams about the events of the last days. She also said that they were all seeing basically the same things over and over in their visions."

By now Todd was leaning forward. He didn't have to pretend interest, he was very much interested in what she was saying and wanted to hear more.

"I asked her, you know... about what they saw, and Julie said Townsend talked about three types of dreams. The first group was about natural disasters like earthquakes, floods, volcanoes, and diseases happening all over the country. The second group was about wars...especially about a war in the United States, with foreign troops and everything. Then, the third group was about what Townsend called the "callout," dreams about the people and church members living in the tops of the mountains in tent cities to escape all of the war and other disasters, and refugees coming to them with for help with just the clothes on their backs."

She paused again. Todd could tell that what ever was on her mind, it was very important to her and she was being cautious as she spoke to him about it. Now, instead of looking at Todd, Deedee was looking out the living room window into the darkness.

"I don't think I've ever told you Todd," she began. "I haven't told hardly anyone, but when I was 14 years old, I had a re-occurring dream for about a week. Every night I had the exact same dream of people walking, walking, and walking some more. They didn't have anything with them and I knew they were hungry and afraid. I didn't know where they were going, or where they came from. At the time it reminded me a lot of Lehi's dream where he is lost and walking in a large dark place and he is just walking. Anyway, in my dreams I would see lots of people just walking...only it wasn't dark and I knew they were going somewhere, but I didn't know where."

"That part of the dream would end and then I would see people living in tents high in the mountains, in the middle of a lot of trees with snow around them. There were a lot of people, they were very cold, and they had a lot of campfires. In fact it was like a big winter campground, but the thing that always impressed me was that they were happy, and they were safe. I don't know how I knew it, I just did."

Deedee's eyes had that unfocused stare of someone recalling something they did not need eyes to see. "I would watch them talking, laughing, and standing around fires to keep warm. I wanted to go and be with them they seemed so happy. As I looked at the campground sometimes I would see some kind of a special tent in the middle of the campground. It wasn't very big, but it seemed to glow and there were people dressed in white standing around it and they glowed too. I knew it was very special, but I didn't know what it was.

"Oh yes, something else that was very strange. I also saw what looked like really big Indians standing around the outside of the camp. They looked dressed up in some kind of armor with swords and shields, a lot like the pictures in the old copies of the Book of Mormon. Anyway, they were just standing there like they were on guard, or something all around the camp."

Todd's expression was complete and utter astonishment. "You have never mentioned this to me before."

"Well, to tell you the truth," Deedee tried to explain, "I wondered what the dream meant for a long time, but I never figured it out, so I pretty much forgot about it. I was only fourteen at the time and as a teenager there were so many other things going on in my mind that seemed more important. Anyway, this afternoon when I came out of the house and heard Sam talking about the last days, all of a sudden I stopped what I was doing and listened really intently because I just knew that it was important. Then, when he mentioned tent cities, the dream came back to me. I felt that I had just had received the answer to understanding my dream, what it all means.

"Talking to Julie later just confirmed it again. I don't know who Robert Townsend is, but the things that he is talking about, I have seen in my dreams a long, long time ago. I know it is true Todd and someday it is going to happen. I feel it is going to happen soon."

Todd paused, thinking over what his wife had just told him, and carefully forming the thoughts in his mind before he tried to put them into words. "Well honey, I think maybe we had better get a hold of some of these books as soon as possible and see what this guy has to say. Maybe he's right, and things are going to start happening soon."

Deedee was comforted by Todd's words, but still seemed somewhat anxious as she asked him, "When can we get the books Todd? I feel that this is urgent."

Todd assured her that he would speak with Sam the next day at church about obtaining copies of the books and while it wasn't as soon as she wanted them she knew it would have to do.

The next day at church after Todd had expressed their interest in Townsend's books, Sam gave him a website where he and Deedee could place an order and have them shipped in just a few days.

Later, Sam had dropped by their home and loaned them a DVD of a lecture that Townsend had given a couple of years earlier.

As Todd watched the lecture that night, he felt the spirit confirming to him several times, that this was indeed important as Deedee had said. He couldn't fault the logic, or the scriptures that Townsend used in his lectures and Todd noticed that he backed everything up with either a scripture or a quote from an Apostle, or Prophet.

As Todd and Deedee discussed what they had watched when the DVD had ended, it was as if someone, for the first time had finally explained to them the scriptures of the last days in a clear, concise and systematic way that made perfect sense and was easy to understand. Todd just shook his head. He considered himself an adept student of the scriptures and it was hard for him to believe that for so long he had missed so much important information.

Todd started watching it a second time, embarking on a serious investigation, pausing the DVD almost every couple of minutes to make notes and read in his scriptures. When he told Sam what he was doing, Sam told him not to bother, and advised that he just read the books. "It's all documented there," he stated as he handed over a copy of Townsend's book to read until their own arrived.

It took Todd five days to finish the book. What surprised him the most was that all Townsend had done was re-quote the Prophets and Apostles and the scriptures in a very simple way, and then relate them to current events. Todd had heard most of it before, but not presented in quite this way, or this clearly. It was like Townsend had started with the books by Gerald Lund and Cleon Skousen, two of Todd's favorite authors and had brought them up to the current time, linking them to the events happening in the world today.

After watching the DVD, Deedee didn't need anything more. She simply said, "I know what he is saying is true. This is what my dream was trying to tell me. We need to get ready, now." The next time Deedee saw Julie their discussion revolved around food storage and they started making lists.

Over the next couple of weeks, as they were starting to make their preparations, Todd and Deedee searched out the opinions of the families who had attended the barbeque and participated in the discussion about Townsend.

Jeremy and Denise were both intrigued. They were already reading a copy of a Townsend book that they had borrowed from Jeremy's father-in-law, who was delighted that they were finally showing some interest.
Todd, with Sam's permission, gave them the DVD that he had watched. Jeremy was getting ready to move, as his company was consolidating and relocating them to a big construction project in Vernal, Utah.

Charlie and Sally were sort of interested and thought maybe, there was a chance that it might be true. But, Charlie basically had said that they didn't have time for it. Todd got the impression that it really wasn't a priority for them. Charlie and Sally spent a lot of time out camping and playing. They rarely missed Church, but right after Sacrament...they were gone to the hills, or to the lake.

The last couple, Gary and Roberta were not interested at all and agreed with Bill that it was a bunch of wild talk, and sure that anything important would come from their Bishop, or Stake President.

CHAPTER 6

On the plane flight home, Bill couldn't keep his mind off of the discussion with Sam. The more he thought about it, the more infuriated he became. Even he was surprised how angry just the memory of that confrontation made him.

The next day, at home, when his wife Linda asked how the visit had gone, Bill replied that it had been fine, except for a crazy neighbor of Todd's who had talked about the end of the world and fairly ruined the barbeque. "This guy even believed some stupid idea by an apostate that the church is going to go live in tents up in the mountains," Bill complained. Linda made a comment about what a strange idea that was and promptly put it out of her mind.

It was on Bill's mind however for the next two weeks. Every time he thought about it, his neck got hot and his temper flared. It bothered him that his brother, or anyone else would be duped by some crazy guy spouting apostate doctrine. He had even considered writing a letter to Church headquarters to complain about Townsend being an apostate, trying to start his own cult, and leading innocent people like his brother Todd astray, but he never got around to it. After a couple of weeks and the regular business of everyday life, the memories started to fade until finally the conversation and all the negative feelings associated with it had left Bill's mind as well.

About three months later, Linda arrived home one evening, deep in thought and asked Bill, shortly after she walked through the door, "Didn't you tell me a while back about somebody named Townsend who was writing apostate stuff concerning the last days?"

Bill was caught off guard at first. He hadn't thought about that encounter for months, but just as quickly it all came back to him. "Yeah" he remembered, "It was while I was at Todd's house. It was a neighbor of his who talked about it. Why do you bring it up now?"

"Well today, Liz and I were having lunch together, and she mentioned him." Elizabeth, or Liz as she was known to most of her co-workers, was a department head at the college and one of the few Mormons on the campus. Linda and she had become fast friends and often ate lunch together. Linda's respect for her friend was tremendous and Liz's opinions carried a lot of weight with her. Her husband had been a Stake and a Mission President and was currently serving as first counselor in the local mission presidency. Liz was one of the few people Linda could talk to, and enjoy stimulating conversation without worrying about being misunderstood. She could just be herself with this friend.

Linda began to unfold the events of the day to her husband. While having their usual lunch together, Linda had noticed the book Liz had laying on the table next to her meal. She casually glanced at the name of the author and it seemed to strike a familiar chord. So she had asked Liz who he was.

"Townsend?   Why he's one of my favorite authors." Liz had responded. Azeal and I have been reading his books the last couple of years. This one is his latest."

Because of Linda's respect for Liz and her husband, she couldn't help, but ask, "What's it about?

"That's a long story." Liz said as her mood visibly became serious. She then fixed Linda with a solemn look, paused a moment and then asked, "Do you believe in the last days?"

"What do you mean? Linda asked

Liz continued to search Linda's face and asked, "Do you believe that we are in the last days, perhaps in the very last days and that the events mentioned in the scriptures, leading up to the Savior's coming are starting to happen around us now?"

The look on Linda's face was surprise, but not so much as someone might have guessed. These two often discussed ideas that caused them to debate, but always with a trust born out of admiration and respect. No topic was out of bounds for them, so Linda's answer was an honest one. "I guess so," she said thoughtfully, considering the answer even as she gave it and not sure that she fully understood the ramifications of the question.

Linda's thoughts quickly reviewed the topics that she mentally linked to the "Last Days;" the Jews returning to Israel, the growth of the Church throughout the world, the Lamanites blossoming as a rose, which had been discussed in Church just last Sunday and her answer became more confidant. "Yes, I do believe that."

Liz looked at her again and said, "Okay then. Let me ask you a couple more questions. Do you *really* believe it, or are you just saying that because you think that's what is expected of you? " Liz reached over and laid her hand gently on the arm of her friend, "And one more thing, do you believe in the gift of dreams and visions?"

This was something she had truthfully never considered. "I don't know," Linda responded. She was startled by the intensity of Liz's expression and tone of voice. Also, the second question threw her for a loop. It was as if someone were questioning if she really believed the gospel was true. She took just a moment to settle down and engaged her analytical mind.

"In answer to the first part of the question... I am not sure what you mean. Yes, I believe that we are in the last days. The signs that say so are all around us and the Prophets and Apostles have confirmed that fact.
"As far as the second question," she paused a moment and then continued, "Our whole Church is based upon the reality of visions and prayer."

", but Linda, do you believe that individual members of the church can have dreams and visions that are intended to personally guide and direct them?"

"Well, sure Liz. Dreams and visions of Prophets and Apostles are for the whole Church, so it follows that members could also have dreams and visions to inspire them and their families."

"If Azeal, or I had a dream, or vision for our family," Liz went on, "and in that dream we were told to prepare for an earthquake that would shake our house next Wednesday at noon, would you be interested in knowing about it?"

Linda pondered that for a few seconds before responding. The answer seemed rather obvious to her. "Absolutely, I would be very interested in hearing about it...mostly because I respect you and Azeal, but I would want to find out for myself if it were true, or not."

"Would it also interest you if many other families had dreams and visions about the same earthquake?"

Linda replied quickly this time, "Even more so."

Liz breathed a little sign of relief for Linda's answers. "Exactly," Liz said. Pausing a little longer, she looked at her watch, recognizing there time together would soon have to come to an end. "Briefly, Robert Townsend writes that the signs and events prophesied in the scriptures are happening at an accelerated rate all around us. The world, and most of us who are members of the Church, don't recognize these events for what they are, or their significance because they are a part of our everyday lives.

"Townsend is no one special, just a regular member of the Church, without any credentials of any kind. His writing may not be refined, but if you can get past the poor grammar and sentence structure he actually makes some excellent points."

Liz took a breath and continued, "The main point of his writing is that the events outlined in the scriptures are speeding up and some catastrophic events are about to take place."

"Life as we know it very soon is about to change, possibly in the next few years, and he believes we had better get ready for it. This book," Liz said holding up the copy of Townsend's book that had been the catalyst for this discussion, "is a collection of dreams and visions he has put together from Prophets, Apostles and members, all talking in some detail about what is about to take place in the near future."

Linda responded with a question of her own. "If that is the case, then why haven't the Prophets and Apostles been telling us this stuff in General Conference?"

"They have, almost every general conference for over sixty years, probably longer," Liz replied almost as a teacher with a favorite student. "You're not old enough to remember this, but in essence all Townsend has done is to gather material on the last days from the old Relief Society, Priesthood and Sunday School manuals from the fifties, sixties and seventies and put it together in chronological order.

It's there and it has been taught for a long time to the members. The problem is, too many members of the Church nowadays act the same as the ancient Jews, hearing, they hear not," seeing they see not. It's being taught all the time, but it seems to go over most members' heads."

"And that," said Liz as she looked at her watch again, "is all the time we have. I have to go Linda. I'm already running late."

Liz stood up. "Let's continue this conversation next week. I'll be in town." And she had rushed away to her next class.

That was the end of the conversation and Linda's explanation of it for Bill. Linda waited for a moment before she asked her husband, "What do you really know about this Robert Townsend person?"

Bill shook his head and said, "Nothing, except he sounds like a kook."

"What if he's right honey?" The concern in Linda's voice was evident.

"What are you talking about?" Bill asked with disbelief.

"What if he is really on to something?" she continued.

"If he were on to something" Bill said, feeling the redness crawl up the back of his neck, "why wouldn't we hear about it from the pulpit, or at General Conference? I am telling you this guy is a kook and he is just trying to scare people to sell canned food and his books."

Linda paused. She could see that this conversation with Bill was going nowhere, so she decided to drop it. Bill was not ready to discuss this with an open mind.

"Well, thanks honey, you're probably right," Linda said, as she rose from her seat and gave Bill a kiss on the cheek. "I just wanted to get your opinion."

As far as Bill was concerned, the discussion was over and he had convinced Linda that her thoughts about Townsend and his ideas were pure foolishness. He never considered for a moment that Linda felt otherwise and would have been more than a little irritated if he had known that the very next day, she called her friend Liz and asked where she could order her own copy of the book.

CHAPTER 7

After returning from Idaho, and once more becoming deeply immersed in her work, Rachel promptly forgot all about the conversation at the barbeque. Four months later however, she was at Bill and Linda's for dinner one Sunday evening.

As Rachel was helping in the kitchen with the final preparations, it was Linda who broached the subject by asking, "Rachel, you were there at Todd's barbeque last summer, weren't you?"

After Rachel's answer to the affirmative, Linda went on.

"Did you hear any of the conversation that took place about the last days?"

Again, Rachel's answer was a simple "Yes,", but now she couldn't help, but wonder where Linda was going to take all of these questions.

"Tell me, what did you think of it?" Linda asked.

"What do you mean?" was Rachel's reply.

"To tell you the truth," Linda started to explain, "I

am a little confused. Bill came back and was all concerned that Todd and Deedee were being persuaded to leave the church, join a cult and go live up in the mountains in a tent someplace. Is that what you heard?"

Rachel almost started to laugh at the image Linda's comment had painted in her mind, but then stopped and composed herself as she tried to recall details from the infamous conversation.

"No Linda, that's not what I heard." Rachel assured her sister-in-law. "A friend of Todd's, named Sam, talked about the need to get food storage because, in his opinion, things are going to get bad very soon. Really, it was nothing more than that."

"So what do *you* think about it?" Linda was determined to get Rachel's feelings on the matter.

"To tell you the truth, I haven't thought about it much. I've just been too busy."

Linda seemed to be just a little exasperated that she was having to work so hard to get the answer she was looking for from Rachel. "What was your impression of what you heard at Todd's?" she continued.

Realizing that she was going to have to make some kind of definitive statement regarding her feelings before Linda would give up this interrogation, Rachel finally spoke, "I didn't see anything wrong with what was said. The whole conversation was about someone named Townsend who wrote a controversial book, stating his opinion that we need to get prepared because events of the last days are happening now and things are going to get worse very soon. Really Linda, when you think about it, it's the same thing that we've been told for over a hundred years."

While Rachel's answer had helped it obviously did not satisfy Linda's desire to know more. "Do you think that maybe things really are going to get bad soon?" Linda asked solemnly.

"Well, things are not terrific right now." Rachel conceded. She could see that Linda was very serious about the questions she was asking. This was not just idle conversation to her, so she continued. "There are some who believe that we are already in a major recession and that it will turn into a real depression next year. Of course, here in the beltway, everyone is saying that after the elections things will improve, if we can get a change in the scenery." Rachel smiled with her last comment. "You know, hope and change."

"I know that's what others are saying around town, but really Rachel, what do you think? Is that what our future looks like?" Linda stood in the middle of the kitchen now ignoring anything that had to do with meal preparation and just waiting for Rachel's response.

It had always been Rachel's policy to avoid the subject of politics with family members, but now she felt she couldn't sidestep her sister-in-law on the matter. "Well, I certainly think that we need a change." She began. "I'm not really political, but things aren't working and so, perhaps it is time for a change."

Linda paused, as if deciding what to say next. "What if this person is right, and things are starting to happen, and it is going to get really bad, very quickly?" Linda had more to add to that question, but just then Bill walked into the kitchen and asked, "How long before dinner?"

Linda, a little disappointed at the interruption, recovered quickly and replied pleasantly, "Just putting it on the table now. Tell Kathy and Mark to come in and sit down."

When Bill had walked out of the kitchen, Linda turned to Rachel and made what she knew would have to be her final comment for awhile. "I am starting to believe strongly that Townsend is right and things are going to get bad really soon. I really do think we better get ready before it's too late." With that, Linda carried the last of the dishes into the dining room, leaving Rachel behind contemplating the future.

Throughout dinner, Linda's words kept echoing in Rachel's mind. Though the topic was not brought up during dinner, as Rachel was leaving, Linda gave her a knowing look that said; "Think about what I told you." It was a look of shared secrets and something special between women that had existed since the dawn of time.

On the drive home, Rachel thought about Linda's

words even more than she had during dinner. Arriving home, she attempted to put the subject out of her mind, but had no success. Finally, she drifted off to sleep.

Nevertheless, in the morning, it was the first thing she thought of, and that disturbed her. She could not shake the feeling that her sister-in-law's opinions were correct. Finally, Rachel determined that she had to know if Robert Townsend was right, or not. With an action that made it official, she wrote the memo in her daily agenda to call Todd and get the phone number for his friend Sam.

That afternoon, during a break in her regular, Monday meetings, Rachel called her brother Todd. When Deedee answered the phone, Rachel was direct, asking for Sam's number without an explanation. However, with the closeness of her family, Rachel expected she would have to give a reason and had decided beforehand that she would be honest about her intentions. When Deedee pressed for a reason, Rachel openly told her that she wanted to call Sam and learn more concerning the books he had spoken about last summer. Rachel, matter of factly, said that she needed to know if what Sam had said was true.

That led to nearly an hour of discussion, ending with Deedee sharing her dream and feelings. Finally she told Rachel she *knew* it was true and that time to prepare was running out.

Before the conversation ended, Deedee had mentioned a website where Rachel could order the books she wanted to purchase and a preparedness expo that was going to be held in Mesa, Arizona, where Robert Townsend would be speaking in a few months. Deedee and Todd were thinking about attending the Expo and suggested that Rachel might like to hear it, "straight from the horse's mouth."

What Deedee said intrigued Rachel. The more she talked, the more Rachel wanted to hear. It was like a light that had just been turned on and was gradually growing brighter.

By the end of the day, Rachel had ordered all of the books Townsend had written as well as a few others along the same topic by various authors. She had re-arranged her work schedule to attend the two day preparedness expo, and wished that it wasn't still three months away. There would be several speakers on various preparedness topics including Townsend, and Rachel estimated that by then, she would have done her homework and would be ready.

CHAPTER 8

PHOENIX

As Rachel's plane traveled the four hours to Phoenix, she ignored the in-flight movie and read an article in USA Today describing how well the cleanup from the 6.0 earthquake in Salt Lake City was coming. She also skimmed over articles on the new FEMA tent encampments in Texas, and the continued plunge of the stock market. Rachel folded the paper neatly and shoved it into the back seat pocket before leaning back to mentally review what had occurred over the last several months.

After the books arrived, she had immediately setup a reading schedule, which had been promptly thrown out the window after reading just the first book. She read through the entire first night and then every minute she could spare thereafter. Finishing all of the books in just under a month, she began re-reading them all. They were already marked up with copious side notes in the margins and each book was beginning to resemble one of her professional working legal briefs.

Rachel went online and ordered a year's supply of freeze dried food after the first week of reading. For her, money for the purchase was not a problem. In fact, in Rachel's mind, the only problem was the three months it took for the food to arrive.

Regular weekly conversations with Deedee about the things she was reading became something she looked forward to. Deedee and Todd were doing the same thing Rachel was, preparing like crazy. Their problem was that they were preparing for six people instead of just one and their budget was tight. Todd had already been informed that he would probably be laid off the following month.

Rachel had mentioned these conversations to Linda and invited her to join in, to which invitation Linda had politely expressed her thanks and said nothing more. Last days and food storage were still pretty much taboo subjects at her house, she had briefly explained. One day, though, Linda had announced to Bill that after listening to a Relief Society lesson and message from the First Presidency on preparedness she had decided to rotate and update their food storage because that was what they had been asked to do. Actually, Linda had begun to restock and substantially add to their food supply. And, at least for now, money was not an issue for them. Linda confided to Rachel that she had purchased a lot more than the basics and was adding substantially to it almost weekly. So far, Bill had not complained about it, or even seemed to notice.

So much had already happened, involving her family and herself and yet, deep down, Rachel had a feeling that this was just the beginning.

The first half day of the Expo was very enlightening. Rachel learned the "hands on" and "how to" of preparedness—from sprouting seeds, which made everything sprouted four times more nutritious, to the many applications of solar power. Vendors lined the halls of the building and she stopped to chat with many of them between speakers. It was surprising and wonderful to find so many people who believed as she now did. She didn't feel so alone any longer and was surprised at how much she appreciated hearing their stories and experiences.

It wasn't until the next day, on Saturday morning, that things got interesting for her personally.

As Rachel entered the hotel dining room looking for breakfast, she recognized many of the vendors she had only met the day before, some already deep in conversation over breakfast. Passing a table where one large group was seated, she heard someone call out her name.

"Rachel! Rachel from D.C.," a man called to her, waving his arm and already shuffling chairs to make room for her. "Come and join us!"

Rachel recognized the man calling to her as Dave, the vendor with all of the solar equipment, who had also been one of the featured speakers the day before.

"Oh, Hi," Rachel called back as she headed toward the table. "Are you sure you don't mind?"

"Not at all," several said, nearly in unison. "You're just in time, we're just starting to order." By now, most of the faces had moved their focus from their menus and had turned towards her. "Everyone," Dave spoke louder so that everyone could hear, "this is Rachel Sinclair from Washington, D.C. She flew out from the East Coast for the expo..., but be careful, she's a lawyer." The last remark had brought a little bit of laughter from the group as they waved her on to come join them.

Rachel took a seat between two women, one of whom she recognized as the wife of a vendor she had talked to briefly the day before who sold sprouting seeds. The other woman was a Master Herbalist who had lectured on locating and identifying herbs in the wild.

Rachel gave her order to the waitress and then just sat enjoying the excitement of the conversations around her. Most of these people obviously knew each other and appeared to be old friends. It had occurred to Rachel on more than one occasion since arriving at the Expo that they almost seemed like one big family.

After sitting at the table for just a few minutes, Rachel chose to get into a conversation with the herbalist. She had been fascinated with what she had heard in the lecture the day before and wanted to learn everything she could. The whole subject of herbs was one of those things she had always wanted to know more about, but had never taken the time to research.

About an hour later, when almost everyone had eaten and started to drift away from the dining room, Rachel found herself still listening to the herbalist, soaking in as much information as her mind could contain, until finally the woman's cell phone rang. She excused herself from the table, stood and walked away to take her call. There were only three people left at the table now, including Rachel. Two men sat finishing the last of their breakfasts, one she had not yet met, at the far end of the table, and the other, seated directly in front of her.

Rachel had noticed the man sitting across from her when she had arrived and sat down at the table, recognizing him from the nuclear preparedness booth from yesterday. During the breakfast conversation she learned that his name was Jared Davis, but some of the people had called him J.D.

Rachel had also caught him looking at her more than once during the meal and she smiled slightly to herself. Even though it was not unusual for her to receive that kind of attention, she had never really become accustomed to it, and so she made an effort to continue the conversation with her new herbalist friend, ignoring the looks.

Jared Davis was a distinguished looking man with his short cut, dark hair. She guessed he was probably 38, or 40, and in excellent shape. If she had to guess from his bearing, she would have supposed him in the military, possibly retired. Occasionally, as part of her job, she worked with military people and he had that look about him.

As she watched him, out of the corner of her eye during the meal, Rachel noticed that he didn't quite seem to fit in with everyone else. It was as if the others were family and he was a guest, or a friend, like she was. She also noticed a couple of other things about him, one was that he didn't say much, except to answer some questions that someone had asked. The other thing was the absence of jewelry on his left hand. He wasn't wearing a wedding ring.

After her new found friend had left to take her call and just as she took her last bite of toast, Rachel caught him staring at her again, this time intently. His boldness was unnerving and caused her to forget herself for the moment. "Is something the matter?" she mumbled through her bite of toast, immediately regretting speaking with her mouth full. Rachel knew the importance of a first impression and this was completely out of character for her.

Jared grinned, which in a way, was even more flustering, and continued to stare at her. "I just noticed that you have beautiful eyes," he said. ", but one of them is blue," he said leaning forward in his chair. "And if I'm not mistaken, the other one is green."

Though she had been reminded of this difference all of her life, the remark still caught her completely by surprise and she flushed a deep red. "Yes, I am a little abnormal," she replied, "My brothers used to tease me mercilessly."

"Ms. Sinclair," Jared said, still grinning, "on you, abnormal looks good."

His unexpected comment flustered her again. Looking away, Rachel could not bring herself to meet his gaze as he continued to stare in her direction. *"He's flirting with me,"* she thought with a smile, while instinctively looking down, first at the table and then over, at his hand, confirming once more that he wore no ring.

Her thoughts were racing while she reverted to her analytical self. *"Just because he doesn't wear a ring...,"* Her thought trailed off as she warned herself. *"Lots of married men don't wear wedding bands."* She had met more than one man without a ring whose intentions were not to mention the wife at home, but there was something different about this man and Rachel found herself hoping this time, the absence of a wedding band really did mean he wasn't married.

It took her another moment to regain her composure and respond to his complement. Looking him straight in the eye, Rachel said with a smile, "Why, thank you Mr. Davis." She could see, in his blue-gray eyes, that he was enjoying her discomfort just a little too much for her liking.

Just then the herbalist returned to the table and communicated to Jared in no uncertain terms that they needed to get to their booths before the crowds gathered and the onslaught began. Jared agreed and reluctantly stood to leave. He casually threw his napkin on the table, gave Rachel a parting smile and said, "See you later," as he walked away.

Rachel watched him as he left, guessing his height

at six feet two, maybe three. She was slow to get up and leave the table, not quite ready for the end of whatever had just transpired between them. Since she wasn't a distributor and the expo doors didn't open to the public for another 45 minutes, she lazily signed for her tab and went back to her room. In the room she picked up and searched the day's schedule to see when Jared was speaking. His name didn't appear on the list and that made her curious.

Later on in the day, Rachel discovered that Jared was a substitute for a scheduled presenter and he would be speaking at three o'clock that afternoon. Seated in the audience near the back she listened attentively as he thoroughly covered the topic of nuclear preparedness. He explained that Greg Hanson, the planned presenter, had asked him to fill in as he tended to a family emergency. Jared lived not too far away, within the state, making it easy for him to stand in at the last minute.

The lecture was extremely informative and he certainly knew what he was talking about. Rachel learned that, contrary to what she had been taught, nuclear winter was not a true reality of modern nuclear war. Yes, the devastation of a nuclear bomb was tremendous within a two to twelve mile radius, depending upon the size of the blast. However, excluding ground zero, the actual bombing site, most radiation was greatly dissipated after only a few weeks.

Also, she learned that with the more accurate weapons available presently, an enemy would only need to hit a few specific targets to completely disable a country, and did not need to blanket everyone and everything, as was the concept of nuclear war in the late sixties and seventies.

Rachel also learned that the most devastating part of a limited nuclear attack was the EMP, or Electro Magnetic Pulse. The EMP was a product of a nuclear blast and would set off a massive radio wave pulse that would effectively shut down the entire power grid in the U.S. It would completely melt most, if not all, of the computer chips that control the communication and transportation systems.

Instantly, it would transport the entire continent back to the horse and buggy days. Such a drastic and sudden change would be catastrophic, with numerous deaths due merely to a lack of water, since almost all cities depend on well water that is pumped electrically. There would also be immediate food shortages and a large scale famine because there would be no machinery to plant, harvest, or transport the food. Without food, or water, tens of millions would die within the first six months.

The information on the subject was probably the most startling she had heard. It was difficult to acknowledge the truth of Jared's words, but Rachel knew that to be prepared she had to be informed. Admitting the harsh reality and possibility of a nuclear attack was part of that preparation.

During the question and answer period at the end of his presentation Rachel also learned that Jared

Davis was, indeed, ex-military, single and she was pretty sure, not LDS.

CHAPTER 9

Later that evening after the expo, Rachel had just sat down to a quiet dinner alone in the hotel restaurant when Jared walked by the entrance. Seeing her, he changed his direction and entered the dining room, walking over to her table.

Rachel steeled herself to appear as professional and nonchalant as she possibly could.

"Good evening." Jared greeted her. "Dining alone tonight?"

"Good evening Mr. Davis," Rachel responded in an effort to keep this encounter a little more formal than the last one. "Everyone else has left and I frankly didn't expect to see you again. I thought you would have gone home too since you live so close."

"I'll leave in the morning. It's a four hour drive to my house and I just don't feel like making that trip tonight."

"So you don't live here in Phoenix?" Rachel asked, glad for an opportunity to learn a little more about him.

"Oh, no," Jared declared, "It's way too hot down

here in the valley. I live up on the Mogollon Rim, in the White Mountains."

"What's the Mogollon Rim?" Rachel wanted to know. "I've never heard of that. And just what do you mean by the valley?"

With a little smirk on his face Jared teased, "Obviously, you haven't been here before."

"No, this is my first time in Arizona, if you don't count layovers at the airport, waiting for a connecting flight." Rachel found she was relaxing a little and allowed herself just the slightest hint of humor.

"I tell you what," Jared offered, "join me for dinner at a much better place than this and I will tell you all about Arizona. Have you ordered yet?"

"No, I was just starting to look at the menu." Rachel answered casually, not wanting to appear too anxious at his invitation.

"Great!" Jared responded "Will you join me then?

Rachel wondered if he could hear her heart pounding as loudly as she could, but decided to answer him anyway, "Okay," she said as she laid the menu on the table. "Sounds good to me."

"Ok, well then allow me." Jared walked behind her, carefully pulled out her chair and offered his arm as they walked out of the restaurant and through the hotel lobby towards the entrance.

As she took his arm, Rachel was on high alert, reminding herself that people were not always who they seemed to be. There was a quick, passing thought about the mace and whistle in her purse that caused a smile to come to her face, feeling confident that she would not be using them tonight. Searching her inner feelings, she said a silent prayer. If this was wrong she wanted to know, but all she felt was peace.

Exiting through the hotels doors they were blasted by the late night heat, even though it was dark outside. Rachel had spent all of her time in the hotel for the past two days and nearly wilted under the unexpected inferno.

Jared, noticing her reaction, commented, "Still pretty hot isn't it."

"Yes, it really is." Rachel agreed.

"My guess is that it is still probably ninety five degrees, or so." Jared spent a lot of time in the valley and prided himself on his ability to accurately determine the temperature at any given time. "It's actually hotter than normal for this time of year. In a couple of months it should get another ten to twenty degrees warmer. He laughed as he explained, "It get's so hot that radio stations actually have contests to see who can cook eggs on the sidewalk the fastest." He continued, "It's interesting that most of the rest of the country is experiencing abnormal cold, but we have abnormal heat and drought."

Rachel searched for words to express her thoughts

adequately. "It feels like a blast furnace, and it's so different than when it's hot at home, on the coast. When it gets hot there, it's like a steam bath. This is like a hundred blow dryers set on high. I've never felt anything like this before."

They stopped at a brown Jeep Grand Cherokee and Jared warned her, "Stand here for a minute while I turn it on and cool things off. It's probably a hundred and twenty inside the car right now and I would hate to have you get burned on the hot metal."

Jared got in, started the car and rolled down the windows. He said, "Actually it's not too bad. It's probably only a hundred and ten. Give it a few minutes and it'll cool down." He climbed back out of the car and stood for a minute with Rachel next to the driver's side.

"How do people survive here?" Rachel asked with sincerity.

"Oh, they get used to it, or so they say." Jared sounded like he wasn't one of the people who really believed that. ", but it's really the air conditioning that makes living here tolerable. It's too hot for me. That's why I live up in the mountains in the cool pine forests."

Now Rachel thought Jared was teasing her again, "Arizona has cool pine forests?" she asked with doubt in her voice.

"Oh yes," he responded quickly, "and lots of them,

up in the north and northeast corner of the state." Looking at his watch he said, "I think it's cooled down enough for you to get in now." Jared walked around to the passenger side of the car and opened the door for her.

As they pulled away from the curb, he asked, "What kind of food do you like?"

"Almost everything." Rachel replied happily.

"Mexican, Chinese, Japanese, what's your pleasure? What are you in the mood for?" Jared asked, not realizing how that last question might be interpreted.

"It's your town." Rachel conceded. "Go ahead and choose. I promise not to complain."

Jared thought for a minute and then made an abrupt right turn at the next intersection. "I think you will like this place. It is one of the best kept secrets in this town. People here tend to think that the only kind of food in Arizona is Mexican."

In a minute they arrived at "La Paris," a restaurant with a sign out front that boasted "Gourmet French Cuisine."

"Alright," Jared said as they walked into the restaurant, continuing the discussion started at the hotel, "all of the metropolitan area including Phoenix, Mesa, Scottsdale, and all of this city down here among the cactus and painted green cement grass, is called the valley. To the north and east it rises up to a high plateau and mountains, including a couple of ski resorts."

"Its called the Mogollon Rim because it rims the valley. The valley is approximately 1500 ft. above sea level and the Mogollon rim is around 5000 ft and higher. The rim also is heavily forested; in fact, the largest white pine forest in the world is located along the Mogollon Rim."

"Really?" Rachel hadn't spent much time in the southwestern United States and so she hadn't thought through the geography of this state. "I just imagined that Arizona was all desert and cactus," she clarified.

"Just the southern and western half of the state." Jared continued.

"So where do you live?" Rachel asked anxious to know more.

"I live up in the mountains just above a little town called Show Low." Jared was sure that Rachel had never heard of this town, but mentioned it anyway.

"I've heard of Show Low." Rachel exclaimed, rather excited that she could add something to the conversation. "Isn't it near a town called Snowflake?"

Now it was Jared's turn to be surprised and just a little impressed. "Very good," he said, showing his approval at her knowledge. "Yes, Snowflake is about 20 miles north of Show Low. Just out of curiosity, how do you know about Snowflake?"

"I met someone on my mission from Snowflake," Rachel explained casually.

By this time they had arrived at the front desk and the maître d was seating them.

"La Paris" was a small restaurant in a part of town not known for restaurants. Jared had described it as "The Valley's best kept secret." And for the most part, that was the case. The clientele of 'La Paris' tended to be those of the upper class who had actually been to France and enjoyed the authentic cuisine. Menus were written in French with the prices omitted, in keeping with the adage, "If you have to ask the price, you probably can't afford it." Jared apparently didn't have to ask.

Xavier, the maitre d, seated them at a small table in a dimly lit corner, seemingly familiar with Mr. Davis and his usual requests for discretion and obscure dining. Jared liked to keep things private and was happiest when no one knew anything about him. Quiet dining in a bistro with excellent food that was close to empty was just to his liking.

Taking the proffered menu, Jared began to order in a way that made it clear he was intimately familiar with this restaurant and its food. He may not have been speaking French at this moment, but from his pronunciation as he ordered, Rachel was fairly sure he could have.

Jared turned to Rachel and stated, more than

asked, "You don't drink do you?"

"No, I don't," Rachel responded.

"Good, that makes it easier."

Rachel gave him a puzzled look and asked, "Makes what easier?"

Jared smiled, "The choice of wine, of course."

With the slightest of bows the man doubling as maître d and waiter disappeared. When he was gone, Jared turned to Rachel and asked, "So you were a missionary for your church?"

"Yes, I was." Rachel said between sips of water.

"I thought only Mormon boys went on missions."

Rachel found it interesting that Jared knew anything at all about the church. "A few young women serve missions as well, also a lot of older couples."

"And where did you go on this mission and what did you do?"

This was really not the kind of conversation she would have expected in a place like this and with a man like him, but he had asked the question and she was glad to respond."I went to Taiwan," Rachel said, "and taught people about Jesus Christ and our church."

Jared was completely charmed by this beautiful woman and continually surprised the more he learned about her.

"Taiwan, really? How long were you there?"

"About eighteen months."

"So, do you speak Chinese?" He asked.

"As a matter of fact, I do." Rachel said proudly. "I speak Mandarin Chinese. You'd probably be surprised at how often that has helped me at work. Do you speak any foreign languages?"

"Yes," Jared said with a little smile, truly enjoying his company this evening. "I speak Russian fairly well, a little Spanish and Portuguese, and I was starting to learn Farsi when I retired."

"Retired from the military?" Rachel asked.

"Yes." Jared's response, and their conversation, was momentarily interrupted by the arrival of their salads.

It was then that Rachel realized how hungry she was, and also, that it was four hours later on the east coast. Two days was not enough time to grow accustomed to the time difference and it was catching up to her. At least it had caught up with her appetite.

Rachel would not make the mistake of talking with her mouth full again, but picked up her fork ready to take a bite while Jared was speaking. She asked, "So, did I hear correctly that in the military you were a nuclear bomb specialist?"

Jared answered with a nod as he had already taken his first bite of salad.

Eating slowed the conversation down a little, but with small bites and patience it went on. "So, what does that mean you really did?" Rachel asked.

Jared put down his fork for a moment and answered with his usual reply to the question he had been asked what seemed a million times, "My job was to prevent things from going boom and killing a lot of people."

Now it was Rachel's turn to put her fork down and give the conversation more of her attention. "Do you mean that you *really* disarmed nuclear bombs?"

"Uh huh," Jared said swallowing, "and biological weapons."

Rachel had underestimated this man and his experience. "So why did you retire?" she asked him quietly.

"In the second Gulf War, I was injured," Jared paused, "and almost died. I figured it was a good time to retire. Besides, the army didn't give me much of a choice in the matter."

"You almost died?" Rachel asked, almost in a

whisper.

He grinned, "almost, as you can see, it didn't take."

Jared was trying to lighten the mood that had suddenly turned morose at the mention of death, but Rachel could not contain her curiosity, so she asked, "What happened?"

In a brief flashback, Jared went back to that day before responding to Rachel's question. "After we entered Bagdad, we were finding munitions dumps all over the place. My team's job was to search them for nuclear and biological weapons. And we found some- no nuclear, but quite a lot of biological weapons."

Rachel was a little confused with her memories, "I thought there weren't any biological materials found."

"That's what the news reported back here, though I can tell you that we found several hundred biological warheads and other materials. Even with that, the vast majority of it had been shipped out several weeks before we got there, at least that's what the people we interrogated said."

"Shipped where?" Rachel asked, now completely ignoring the remnant of her salad.

"Some of it was buried in secret locations in the desert, but most of it went over the border into Syria," Jared explained.

"Why wasn't that ever reported in the news?"

Rachel wanted to know.

"Well, it was in some newscasts," he went on. ", but you have to remember that it became a political hot potato, and so, the real story never got told by the main news agencies. The truth often gets buried in politics."

"Are you sure?" Rachel wanted to believe what Jared was saying, but was finding it difficult to accept that there was some kind of censorship keeping the truth out of the news.

"I was there." Jared said with just a hint of defensiveness. "In fact, a few months later some of the stuff that had been shipped to Syria ended up in an attempted attack on Israel. Luckily, Israel stopped the truck that was full of biological material before it had reached its designated target and prevented it from being set off."

"Why would this happen and who would not let the truth be told?" Rachel was certainly no Pollyanna, but this was new territory in her education about the world.

"Politics," Jared answered simply. "Politics over the years has become more about grabbing the brass ring of power and money and less about doing what's right for the country. If the truth gets in the way of the power and money, then it gets thrown to the side and stepped on."

After taking another bite of salad and chewing it

thoughtfully, Rachel asked a little cynically, "So what are you, Republican, or Democrat?"

"Neither. I guess that you could say I am an independent, conservative, constitutionalist, if such a thing exists. I believe that both of the major parties have become corrupted by power hungry opportunists., but forgive me," Jared stopped and raised his hands as if to halt not only their words, but their thoughts as well. "That's enough about me and I've forgotten my manners. Discussing politics at dinner usually leads to indigestion. Let's change the subject back to you. So you were a missionary in Taiwan, and as a missionary, what did you teach the people in Taiwan?"

The conversation's change in direction was so abrupt and truthfully, Rachel's head was reeling with doubts and questions that would keep her busy with research for some time, however, dropping the topic of politics was a welcome change, so she began to explain a little more about her mission to Jared. "We taught them about Joseph Smith and the Book of Mormon."

In a teasing tone, and with a big smile, Jared said. "Ah, the infamous Joseph Smith and the Book of Mormon"

Rachel thought his teasing was innocent enough, but couldn't be sure. "What do you know about Joseph Smith, or the Book of Mormon, for that matter?" She was challenging him now and wondered how he would handle it.

"Actually, I don't know very much at all." He answered. "Only that Joseph Smith reportedly found some gold plates and supposedly translated the Book of Mormon from them. He founded the Mormon Church and was killed by a mob because of it."

Rachel didn't take long to debate in her mind whether posing the next question was wise, or not. She asked, "Have you ever read the Book of Mormon?"

"No, I never have, though a couple of your people have tried to give me one. I just never have had the inclination, or the time." While Jared's answer was not exactly what Rachel was hoping to hear, neither of them seemed offended, or put off by this discussion.

A little of the old missionary zeal came to the surface as Rachel pushed a little farther and said, "If you ever get the chance, or the inclination, just remember as you read it, that Joseph Smith only had a third grade education, and completed the translation of a book of over four hundred pages of very small print, in just less than 90 days. Furthermore, he translated the whole record to a scribe during that time as he read from the plates, never repeating a sentence and never losing his place. Just some things for you to keep in mind." Rachel smiled.

"Huh...," Jared replied, somewhat impressed by the recitation. "Maybe I will someday."

"Have you ever known any Mormons before?"

Rachel continued, not wanting to change the subject.

"I have known a few Mormons," Jared admitted. "None of them very well. Probably the Mormon I know the best was the one who saved my leg, and possibly my life."

"That sounds like a story waiting to be told." Rachel quipped, encouraging Jared.

"Well, when I was injured they tried putting me back together, but there must have been some parts missing and it didn't work very well."

"By the way," Rachel interjected, "you never told me how you were injured."

"Well, there really isn't much to tell." Jared didn't share this story very often, but he found it difficult to keep anything about himself from this lovely woman, so he continued. "There were three of us working together that day. As we finished checking out a warehouse munitions dump, somebody touched a wire, or something, and it set off a hidden booby trap. My two team mates were killed instantly, but they saved my life. They were on my right as we walked out of the room. The blast killed them and their bodies blocked a ton of debris and shrapnel headed straight for me.

"As it was, my arm was broken in three places, the right side of my chest was caved in, and my leg got smashed up pretty badly. It was just lucky for me that the whole warehouse didn't go up.

"I woke up ten days later in the Landstuhl Army Hospital in Germany. They basically said I should have been dead, but somehow, I survived. I'd lost a lot of blood, and the broken ribs had punctured a lung. I was in pretty bad shape.

"Anyway, they pieced me back together and put a metal rod in my arm along the bone. My leg was so smashed up that they tacked the pieces of bone to another piece of metal, hoping they would grow back together. A week, or so after that, I was shipped back to the States to heal, with both my leg and arm in casts." Jared paused and took a drink of water.

"Three months later, the arm had healed somewhat, but the leg hadn't. By this time, I had come back to Show Low and was visiting the V.A. hospital in Phoenix every other week. For some reason, the leg just wasn't mending. The doctors started talking about amputating it because an infection was starting and not responding very well to the antibiotics.

"Every time the doctors brought up amputation, I refused to even consider it. After a while, they said it was either my leg, or my life and I needed to make a decision quickly. Well, right after that, someone in Show Low told me that I needed to contact an old woman named Granny. They said that she could fix it with herbs." Jared smiled to himself and shook his head as he remembered the skepticism he had when he first searched out the old herbalist, only because of utter hopelessness.

"I was desperate enough by then to talk to anyone who had even a sliver of a chance of helping me. She lived in a little bitty town called Shumway and was at least 80 years old then. She was, and still is a Master Herbalist. One look at my leg, and the x-rays and she told me to start taking a handful of capsules every hour; and, she put an old fashioned poultice on my arm. I actually helped her cut off the cast on my leg. At the time, I didn't know what else to do. She was my last hope.

"Several times each day I soaked my leg in some herbal concoction made mostly of Comfrey that was slimy and green. Within three days, the infection had completely cleared up. Six weeks later, when they did another x-ray on my leg, the doctors said that the bones had moved back into position and were starting to grow together. After three months, they operated and took out the metal because I didn't need it any longer and it was in the way."

Rachel was amazed by his story and couldn't help, but ask him, "So how are your arm and your leg now?"

Jared put down his fork, unbuttoned the cuff of his shirt and rolled up the sleeve. A huge, ugly scar covered most of the inside of his forearm from elbow to wrist with numerous, smaller scars crisscrossing the remaining skin.

Looking down at the arm as if it belonged to someone else, he said, "It's actually looking pretty good compared to what it used to look like. The concoction Granny taught me how to apply got rid of a lot of the scarring. I got the same results with my leg, but I don't think I'll show that to you right here." Jared glanced around the restaurant with a smile.

Rachel was just about ready to come up with another question to ask when he stopped her, and with a shake of his head said, "Uh, uh, now it's your turn. I've done enough talking for one evening."

By now the salad plates had been removed and entrees that looked as good as they tasted were brought to the table. This was truly an elegant restaurant with the candle light and soft music in the background. Now that her stomach was getting filled and the hour was growing later, Rachel was relaxing and decided to share with Jared as he had shared with her.

"Okay," Rachel said with a smile as she pushed her plate away. "What do you want to know?"

"Tell me what you did after your mission." Jared replied

"Well my life is nothing in comparison to yours, I'm afraid. After my mission I went to Brigham Young University-Idaho, graduated and then I went to the BYU- J. Reuben Clark law school in Provo, Utah. Pretty dull by your standards" Rachel said with a sigh.

"You've never married?" Jared asked in astonishment.

"No, I never have." There was a little sadness in her voice, but just a little, and Rachel hoped that Jared had not detected it.

"Hmm, I thought Mormons were all about families, settling down and having kids." He thought he had understood that much about the Church.

"Well," Rachel felt a little awkward having to explain this to him. "They are. I just haven't met the right person yet." Rachel thought about how tired that old saying sounded, but figured it was alright because Jared probably hadn't heard it before. She went on, "I thought I had found him once, or that he had found me, and we were planning to get married, but he died suddenly." The look on Jared's face was asking the question, so Rachel hurriedly explained, "He contracted the West Nile virus."

Even though this had been a devastating part of her life, most of the pain from the memories was gone, or at least had become manageable and now Rachel was able to discuss this loss without depressing herself and everyone around her.

The rest of the evening was delightful as they chatted back and forth about many things, but nothing of great consequence. At the end of the evening, they went back to the hotel where he escorted her to her room, bid her a goodnight's sleep and left.

Rachel couldn't help herself and admitted that she really liked him. It was one of the most enjoyable evenings she had experienced in a very long time. Jared was fun, witty, and full of surprises, a little mysterious and very good looking. He had been a perfect gentleman, and then some, the entire evening. "Too bad he's not LDS," she said to herself as she finished her prayers, climbed into bed and went to sleep.

The next morning, there was a huge news story being reported. The President of Pakistan had been assassinatcd. The huge bomb blast had also killed thirty eight others and completely demolished four vehicles, including a truck full of soldiers. A top army general and several cabinet ministers were also among the casualties.

Immediately, Pakistan's Vice President, with the support of the army, declared martial law throughout the country while an investigation was put into motion to determine who was responsible. The next day, the army was put on full alert and began mobilization. Two days later, intelligence reports blamed India for the attack.

When Pakistan mobilized, India, feeling threatened, did likewise, rushing troops to the border. The United Nations hurried to send negotiators into Pakistan while China volunteered to assist Pakistan in peacefully resolving their dispute with India.

Quickly, the U.N. and Chinese negotiators helped work out an agreement between the major political parties to hold an emergency election within the week, with the U.N. and Chinese acting as observers.

Despite the presence of three thousand United Nation and Chinese peace keeping forces to oversee the elections, along with an aging Jimmy Carter, bombings and riots were widespread.

When the election was over, the Pakistan Peoples Party had been defeated and a coalition of pro-Islamic parties had been officially declared the victors, with the radical Asim Hussain Sharif declared the new President. His platform had been decidedly anti-U.S., anti-India and pro-Iran. It was especially noteworthy, but evidently not newsworthy, that Sharif was supported by the Taliban in both the north and west.

Thirty days after he was sworn in as President with a newly organized government, Sharif announced that all of Pakistan would have the choice of living under Pakistani law, or Sharia law. Immediately, pro-Taliban, pro-Sharia rallies and marches were organized throughout the country. Their cry was for hope and change from the politics and policies of Western influence that had corrupted the country and driven it into economic chaos. Within sixty days, the entire country of Pakistan had chosen to join their neighbor Iran and live under Sharia law, though the vote was called into serious question.

During this time, troops had been marshaled into the Kashmiri region and started exchanging artillery fire with Indian troops. Though tensions ran high, no major conflicts occurred as the whole world waited with baited breath to see what would happen next.

As the drumbeats of war with India continued to emerge from the new administration, an interesting development occurred. A troubling report surfaced in the Western Intelligence papers concerning a group of Pakistani military officers. Fearing the worst if Pakistan's nuclear weapons came under Taliban control they pulled the cores from the nuclear weapons and while the cores were being smuggled out of the country, blew up the several depots where the weapons had been stored.

The Pakistani government vehemently denied the loss of their nuclear weapons and declared they had more than enough munitions to take care of their arch enemy, if necessary.

However, within days of the incident, in order to prevent an escalation of the war and, supposedly, to help keep the peace, China, at the invitation of the new Pakistani government, rushed 80,000 troops into Kashmiri.

The official statement was that they were there to support the new fragile, democratically elected government of Pakistan from any encroachments by their aggressive and war mongering neighbor to the south.

CHAPTER 10

Two months later, right after the US government had declared a state of emergency due to anti-government protests and food riots all over the country, Jared's services were requested to observe and advise on a covert operation involving an anonymous 'desert country.' At least that was the official word at his quick briefing. Still recognized by his peers as one of the best in his area of expertise, and certainly with more experience than anyone else, Jared was never told the exact location of the operation, but to him it was obvious the country in question was Iran. He just wasn't sure where in Iran.

His assignment was to observe via satellite video link as four members of his former team completed their part of the operation on the ground. They, and the 24 Rangers who led the assault under the leadership of a Major Ramsen, had been covertly inserted under cover of night.

After the area had been secured and the link established, Jared was invited into the observation room to watch. It was a dimly lit room with theater style seating for ten people. Four technicians sat at computer consoles on the left of the room. On the front wall was a large screen, covering almost the entire wall, which displayed the main image, and along the right side were several smaller screens with various camera perspectives, maps, and radar images.

As Jared entered the room he was handed a com head set and informed that Captain Keith Bailey was on the other end. Jared had trained Keith some time ago, forming a friendship that had endured over the years.

"Hey snot nose, this is JD, what do you know?"

"Hey Captain, glad to have your eyes with us on this one. We're not sure what we're going to find. The plan is to see what it is, defuse it and get out. We have an hour before we need to leave. Response time is estimated to be an hour and a half from now. Anything we can do to shave off some of those minutes helps."

"Affirmative that." Jared responded. "I don't think you'll need me on this ride, but it's nice to be invited to tag along."

"Yeah, it's almost like old times." Keith's voice and words expressed the respect and confidence he had in Jared that time did not permit. "I'll just keep a running monologue of what's going on."

"Affirmative that."

"This area had heavy defense, but it has been eliminated. It's a warehouse complex out in the middle of nowhere. Intel said it might be hiding some nuclear materials and we have had some tentative satellite confirmation. The building has already been swept for any booby traps. It appears to be clean. "

The video, green and a little grainy, was streaming from the camera attached to Keith's helmet and jumped with his movements as he walked over uneven ground. So far the only thing that could be seen was one distant wall of the building Captain Bailey and his team were approaching. As they continued their cautious advance, a door came into view, surrounded by three soldiers of the Rangers team, all of whom were heavily armed and with night vision binoculars flipped down on their helmets. The three were facing away from the door looking out into the night and the door was open.

As Bailey went through the door he was met by another soldier who, giving a quick nod, invited him, "this way." The screen now showed the back of the soldier as he led the way across what appeared to be a light machine shop.

They continued through another door into a large room into the main part of the warehouse.

"What do we have here?" Keith said to no one in particular as he stopped and panned the area, making sure that the 'observers' were seeing everything that he saw. As he did so, what looked like forty, or more Coke and Pepsi machines appeared on the screen. Some were lined up as if they were ready to be shipped. Others were in various stages of assembly. One thing they all noticed, the writing on them was in English.

The green video display centered on one of Bailey's team holding a Geiger counter who was pointing it around the room. "There is a reading of 23 rads, above normal, but not dangerous" the soldier offered.

Another soldiers voice said, "Sir, there are no windows. We could risk light without detection."

"Do it. Have the outside perimeter watch for any light leakage from the building."

"Yes sir."

In about 15 seconds the video went bright white and then, as the camera adjusted to the illumination, everything quickly came into focus again in bright colors.

Keith asked someone, "Any light leakage?"

"No sir," was the quick response.

Then, for the benefit of those who were observing and the soldiers around him, he voiced his thoughts out loud, "So what's up with all of the pop machines? Iran doesn't allow these machines in the country. Something isn't right here."

Some of the soldiers in the room moved closer to the machines and the crates that already had been prepared for shipment. "Sir, these machines over here that are all boxed up have shipping labels with U.S. addresses on them. This one here says, C Avenue, New York, New York and this one here is labeled,

Portland, Oregon. Across the room another soldier added, "This one says Kansas City and the one next to it someplace in Dallas, Texas."

At this point Jared and Captain Bailey were putting two and two together and coming up with the same results that had them both concerned and instantly on guard. Baily spoke first, "Why would anyone buy a coke machine from Iran and ship it to the US?" The unsaid answer to that question left a sinking feeling in everyone's stomachs.

As another soldier crossed the room an additional discovery was made.

"Sir, these machines over here look like they've just arrived, and they've all been shipped from the United States."

"Okay," Bailey said studying the scene. "Someone here in Iran is buying soda machines from the U.S., modifying them somehow, and then sending them back to the United States. I think it's time to have a look inside. Do you agree Captain?" The last question was posed to Jared back in observation.

"Absolutely," Jared answered. The mood in the observation room had become tense and cautious with the discovery of the machines. "Something is definitely rotten in Denmark and it isn't fish. Take it slow and easy."

Bailey set down his rifle and the tool box he was carrying, and after pulling out a socket wrench carefully began to open the pop machine closest to him. He began his inspection all the while speaking so as to keep the observers up to speed on his findings.

"This machine already has cans of pop in it. Why would anyone put product in a machine BEFORE it is shipped? That does not make sense." Poking around a little more, Bailey got down on his knees and looked at the machinery mounted in the bottom of the machine. He pulled out a small, but powerful flashlight and shined it on the wires and fan assembly to get a better look.

"Wait a minute. Yeah. The inside of this machine has an interesting cooling unit in it. I'm pretty sure this isn't normal. It's like it has two cooling units, but one isn't hooked up to the rest of the machine." Keith paused and then spoke quickly to a soldier nearby. "Johnson, bring me that Geiger counter and the meter."

Keith was mumbling to himself as he began a closer inspection of the cooling unit, flipping on the sensor and then panned around at the other machines.

"Okay," he called out to everyone within sound of his voice. "I just found out why we are here." This was sure to be one of those "Good news, bad news" situations. "The second cooling unit is a little hot. And it looks like they might have some tamper proof devices on them.

"Alright, everybody come over here and watch what

I'm going to do. Then we'll each grab a machine and I'm going to talk you through what's going to happen." Momentarily turning his attention to the ever present, but unseen observers he asked, "Can you see this JD?"

"Sure can." Jared replied. "Watch that blue wire. I think you'll find it's the hot one."

"Affirmative, Cap."

"Check it with a voltmeter, but I believe that if you'll run a bypass with a 6 volt battery on that wire you should be able to clip the wire and pull that 2nd cooling unit out."

"I agree." Bailey did the procedure, and after 20 minutes of dismantling several screws and bolts, and withdrawing the first cooling unit, the second cooling unit finally slid out of the pop machine and was placed on a nearby workbench. It was very heavy and took two men to lift it.

Bailey spoke to his team. "I think it's time to put on some suits. The rest of you better clear out of this room, just in case." The four rangers in the room left while the bomb squad put on their radiation and biological protection suits.

After they were prepped, Bailey stepped back up to the second cooling unit and opened it up.

"What the....?" Captain Bailey didn't have to finish the sentence. His ashen complexion made everyone watching keenly aware that something was wrong. "J.D., can you see what I'm seeing?"

"Yes, I can Keith," Jared did recognize the armament, but wished he hadn't. "It looks like it's a heavily modified SDAM 17." An SDAM was a small Russian nuclear weapon, commonly called a suitcase nuke. It had been a while since Jared had seen one, but he was sure he was not mistaken. In his career he had personally disarmed six of them.

"Look here," Bailey said, pointing to the red digital read out. "The old timing circuit has been replaced with this new timer." He cocked his head slightly to get a better look. "It appears that this core is already armed and set for about seventy five days from now, if I'm reading this right. What's going on in about two and a half months?"

With Bailey's helmet mounted camera within inches of the read out, Jared could see it clearly. "My guess is that if you were to put them on a boat and make it look like normal cargo it would take just about that long for transport and set up. If the machines already have product no one is going to mess with them for at least five, or six days after they are put in place. That gives you more than enough time to make it look like a normal machine replacement and not arouse suspicion."

Bailey responded, "That's not good."

Jared said, "We better see if they are all the same, or if we have different setups."

Bailey quickly opened three more at random and found that they were all exactly the same on the inside.

On inspecting the third one, Bailey commented, "Well, that makes it a heck of a lot easier, and a heck of a lot harder." He gave instructions that all thirty seven of the machines and crates be opened and inspected.

A full bird Colonel standing in the observation room with Jared turned to him, and with his hand over his headset mike asked, "What does Bailey mean by that?"

Jared replied, "Sir, the team probably only came prepared with containers to secure three, or four weapons. Now, it appears there are many more. The problem is, we need to determine how many weapons are actually here, then defuse them, extract the cores of the weapons, and figure out how to transport those cores out of there without killing everyone in the process with radiation."

The colonel nodded in understanding.

J.D. asked over the com, "Captain, how many containment systems did you bring with you."

"Five." Bailey said with a little sigh. Then attempting to lighten up the situation added with a chuckle, "I think we might be a little short. I'll take a look around in a little bit and see if there is something

-116-

we can use here to make up the difference."

"Good idea." Jared concurred. "The SDAMS in the cooling units must have come in something."

Bailey paused a minute, and then finally spoke to the team around him, and a little to himself, "Okay people, get a grip. We have a job to do and we don't have enough time to get it all done. Everyone gather around and watch closely."

J.D. and Captain Bailey, working together, went through the steps of disarming the first weapon. In turn, Captain Bailey walked the rest of his team through the procedure for the second device. With the disarmament of two weapons behind them, Bailey instructed the three other men in his team to each choose a machine, at which time he repeated the instructions for each cautious move. The work went slowly, too slowly for all they had left to accomplish. In the observation room, they were prepared for "bad news" at any moment.

To J.D. and the others watching the slow, methodic neutralization of each weapon, the tension was tangible. Each man stood in a suspended animation, silent and waiting. They'd found that each of the eight machines already in shipping containers had hot and active cores. Of the twenty nine remaining machines, only six had active weapons, but it took valuable time to open and inspect each one.

After the first five cores were put into their lead lined containers, Captain Bailey went looking to see what else he could find. After searching around, he came across a stack of lead lined boxes against a wall, in the other room. These were obviously what the weapons had arrived in.

"J.D., I have some bad news. I count twenty seven lead lined boxes and so far, I've only found fourteen weapons. That means we are missing thirteen more SDAMS."

There was something else Bailey had noticed and proceeded to explain to Jared, "Also, there are a total of forty five pop machines here in all, every one of them outfitted with a second cooling device. So, we are missing thirteen weapons that have already arrived and it looks like they were expecting to have another eighteen weapons arriving soon. The Majors' team is looking for documentation right now to help us figure out this setup."

"That's an affirmative." Jared responded. "We have at least 13 missing Russian suitcase nukes, and probably more on the way." After hearing Jared repeat the words, the colonel gave Jared a forbidding look and slowly, shook his head.

Two and a half hours later, the disarmament process had just begun on the last machine. With all, but the last of the cores removed and placed into containment boxes, one of the techs in the observation room who was monitoring the radar feed from a circling AWACS plane over two hundred miles from the action, reported, "Colonel, we have multiple bogeys approaching at a range of about 200 clicks, and closing in at 500 knots."

The Colonel quickly walked over to the tech, watching the radar screen and asked for clarification, "Alright what do we have?"

"Sir, it looks like four high speed planes, probably jets, approaching the target zone. At current speed their E.T.A is 15 minutes. Also, I am picking up other slower moving bogeys with speeds at 125 knots, probably helicopters following behind."

The colonel immediately spoke into his headset to the commander in charge of the Rangers. "Major Ramsen. You have visitors approaching at high speed. I repeat, you have visitors approaching at high speed at 27 degrees. It looks like four jets, followed by helicopters. E.T.A for the jets is 15 minutes. Jim, get your teams out of there now and blow the place. You're out of time. They're late, but they are finally on their way."

A voice crackled over the speakers. "Affirmative, Colonel. We are ready to go as soon as this last machine has the core removed. Demolition charges are set."

The Colonel then turned to J.D. and asked, "How much longer for your team to finish, Captain?"

"I estimate about 10 more minutes, Colonel. It's one of those things we just can't rush." Jared realized the Colonel was aware of the time constraints, and wished he could hurry the process along. "We only expected one, or two devices, not forty five machines with eleven nukes."

"I understand Captain. Just tell your men to hurry if at all possible."

"Bailey, you are about to have visitors." Jared explained, "You need to get your rear in gear and out of there A.S.A.P."

"Affirmative. I heard that. We've just about got it- just another five minutes."

"Keith, I don't mean to rush you, but you don't have five minutes." Jared's words were a vast understatement of the situation at hand.

"Affirmative that," Bailey replied.

J.D. knew the real danger was not in having the jets attack the team on the ground, but rather, in having them down the three extraction Black Hawk helicopters with the team and nuclear cores on board. Once they'd lifted off and headed for safety, wherever that was, they would be sitting ducks. Jared could see the Colonel talking in hushed tones on his headset.

The colonel flipped a switch and spoke again, addressing the Ranger team leader, "Major, we have no available assets to assist you in time. There is one Predator in the area, but it does not have air-to-air, only air to ground."

One of the techs spoke up, "Sir, the jets are coming in real low. If we fly the Predator high above them, we might be able to lock on to them, fire the two Mavericks, and guide them by wire. We probably won't be able to hit anything, but it might buy us some time."

The Colonel, grateful for an option, replied, "Do it," then continued,

"Major, on second thought, we have an idea that just might buy you some time. An extra eight minutes puts the Black Hawks in the mountains, where hopefully, they can lose our "friends" in the ravines. Intel reports these are probably either old F4's, or Mig 21's. They don't have infrared and they do not have any 'look down' radar. They may have some Russian AA-2, or AA-5 air to air missiles and maybe some ground ordinance, but once you get into the mountains, you should be able to lose them. Worst case scenario, you can put down and shut down."

"Affirmative Colonel, birds are spooling and we are loading the last of the boxes onto the Black Hawks now."
The Major was running through the warehouse as he spoke. "Charges are set to go in five minutes."

"Sir," the radar tech interjected, "Bogeys are at 100 clicks and closing. ETA is four minutes."

The tech who was in direct contact with the Predator control and command base in Nevada said, "Sir, Predator is at 4500 feet and we have targeted the first and second lead bogeys, which look to be at about 3000 feet. They are now within range of the Predator's Mavericks. Permission to fire?"

The Colonel was prepared for this event, "Permission granted." He spoke quickly, "Fire. Fire. Fire."

"Missile one away; missile two away, Sir." This was quickly followed by, "Missiles tracking on targets, Sir"

"Son," the Colonel directed to the Predator tech, "have them fly the Predator directly at that lead bogey. Let's see if we can scare the hell out of him."

"Affirmative sir." The Predator tech then started speaking into his headset.

The third tech, monitoring the satellite thermal imaging as well as being in direct communication with the pilots of the Black Hawk helicopters, announced, "Colonel, the extraction team has lifted off."

"Tell them to be ready for defensive maneuvers. This is going to be close." The Colonel knew these men were always prepared to be on the defense.

"Affirmative, Sir" the tech acknowledged.

"Sir," the Predator tech announced, "the lead bogey is jinking to his right to avoid the Maverick. I am having control direct the Maverick to follow the target, but it is having difficulty maneuvering with the jet."

"Do the best you can," the Colonel encouraged.

"Sir," the radar tech reported, "the lead bogey is turning left to avoid the second missile. The plan appears to be working."

"Follow the bogeys as best you can with the Mavericks," the Colonel continued, "try to make them think that they have a couple of sidewinders chasing their ass."

"Yes, sir," the young tech added with enthusiasm.

With an afterthought the Colonel added, "Have the Predator follow them as well. Make them think it's still armed and hunting them."

"Affirmative, Colonel."

Suddenly, on one of the small screens there was a flash of light. The satellite tech said, "Sir, the target complex has been destroyed."

"OK, let's get our guys home." The Colonel directed. "What's their ETA to the mountains?"

"About three more minutes, Sir."

The Colonel was thinking about the next command. "Once they hit the mountains, have them split up and follow their assigned B routes home."

"Yes, Sir"

"Sir," the radar tech was speaking now, "bogey jets have failed to return to target, it appears they are going home. The Mavericks have detonated on the ground."

"Excellent," replied the Colonel. "Have the Predator return to base."

After the last command, Colonel Hill turned toward J.D. and gave him a look.

It was a look of concern Jared recognized on the Colonels' face. Jared's words voiced the concern showing in the Colonel's expression, "Now all we have to do is figure out where the rest of those machines went?"

Colonel Hill didn't say a word, but nodded his head.

"Well, at least there'll be hell to pay when they find several billion dollars worth of their nuclear weapons are gone." Jared attempted to point out the successful objective of the mission, now completed.

The Colonel smiled and looked back towards the screen and the three techs that had monitored the entire operation. He clicked his com switch and spoke to the Major and his Special Forces Ranger team, "Good work gentlemen. Now get your, butts back home, A.S.A.P."

As an exhausted J.D. left the building and started on the journey home, he couldn't help, but wonder if the missing machines were, already in the United States. If they were and if they were set the same as the ones in the warehouse, he surmised two and a half months from now would mean sometime around September 11th. He decided he better get ready, just in case.

CHAPTER 11

ONE WEEK LATER

Bennett saw the man in uniform first, and then noticed the sign with his name "BENNETT" neatly printed on it, at the airport. He was wearing the new Blackbird uniform, similar to that worn by the U.S. military, except the patches were different, and the pattern was a classic camo instead of a digital ACU print. For most people, this man would look like he belonged to some military unit, but anyone with military experience would spot in a minute the differences, and the unique HOMELAND SECURITY patch above the right breast pocket, not to mention the Blackbird insignia on the shoulder.

Walking up to the mercenary he stated, "I'm Bennett."

"Yes sir." His response was what one would expect from a soldier, minus the salute. "A car is waiting for you at the curb. Do you have any bags?"

"Yes, Just one," Bennett answered.

As they walked to the baggage claim he thought how unexpected this greeting was. It was reserved more for a high ranking officer than for the equivalent of a captain in this organization. Two days earlier, he had been south of the border, sitting in a dingy

Columbian hotel, when he had received a message from Blackbird headquarters to return immediately to the U.S. for reassignment.

It was just as well, he had completed his mission in that god-forsaken place; having extracted the information his superiors had requested, and eliminated the targets.

As he identified his bag to the corporal, he wondered what was next in store for him. Part of the mystery was that he had been ordered to report here, in North Carolina, and not at Blackbird headquarters outside of Houston, Texas.

As the door was opened for him, he saw someone else sitting in the back seat of the dark blue Continental. Getting into the back seat, he recognized the Special Ops commander, who was the third highest ranking person in Blackbird. It was usually from this man that his special orders came. He was in civilian clothes right now, but the driver was in uniform.

"Evening sir," Bennett extended the greeting with respect.

"John, did you have a nice trip?"

"Yes, sir." The relationship between these two was not one of peers, so Bennett's responses were fraught with military decorum.

"Oh, we don't need to be so formal right now." He

paused. "You have done well." The commander's words seemed to have some hidden agenda behind the compliment. It had always been military formal prior to this moment.

The car pulled away from the curb and entered airport traffic leaving the Corporal who had helped with the bags nowhere to be seen.

"Thank you." Bennett was wary now and a little anxious as to what was going to be asked of him next.

The commander pulled an envelope from his pocket and handed it to him. "This is just a little token of our appreciation for a job well done. Your work has not gone unnoticed."

Taking the envelope, Bennett said, "Thank you." It was very thick and without looking at the contents, he stuffed it into his inside coat pocket.

The commander continued, "In fact, I would like you to meet with someone tonight. They have an offer for you that I strongly suggest you not refuse."

"Yes sir. Thank you, sir."

The agenda was beginning to unfold, and John Bennett was more curious than ever.

The rest of the 45 minute trip was driven in silence. Bennett itched to reach inside his pocket, pull out the envelope, and count the bonus money. The last time he had gotten an envelope it was stuffed full to the tune of $50,000. This one seemed fatter than that one had. Together with his monthly salary of $10,000, plus expenses, that would make at least $60,000 for this month, possibly more. As soon as he could, he would convert most of it into gold, silver, diamonds, a few other commodities, and then he would go have a good time. He hadn't been to Bangkok, in a long time and he was due.

He wondered what this offer that he shouldn't refuse would turn out to be. He had never refused any of the offers presented to him, no matter how mean, or nasty they had been. Usually, these requests for his service came from the Commander sitting next to him.

After driving in the darkness through the jungle-like forests of North Carolina, they finally arrived at a series of large buildings. It appeared to be a typical out-in-the-woods business park. There were no other cars in the three parking lots that he could see as they drove to the side of the closest building, and down a ramp to a small underground garage, *"Probably reserved for the company big shots,"* he thought. In the garage he saw four other cars, two black Mercedes SL 500s, and a Lincoln that was a twin of the one he was riding in. Bennett noticed that all the vehicles had North Carolina license plates.

They walked quickly through the door and into the elevator, which opened into a simply furnished waiting room on the top floor. "Wait here," the Commander directed, and Bennett took a seat, watching as the man pushed through a large wooden double door.

Within two minutes, one of the doors opened with the Commander motioning to him, "John, come in."

It was a large office with most of the lights either turned off, or dimmed making it fairly dark inside except for two lights shining on a single chair in the middle of the room. In the corner, behind a desk that was shrouded in complete darkness, a large, shadowy figure sat in an executive chair. A light shining through the window next to his head aided in the illusion of mystery.

There were two other men, in the room, one sitting on each side of the big desk and somewhat illuminated although John didn't recognize either of them. Both were in dark suits and reminded Bennett of the movie *Men In Black*. John looked at the single chair in the middle of the room, facing the mysterious man behind the desk thinking that this was all a little over-the-top, melodramatic.

"John, have a seat" the Commander said as he motioned to the chair, obviously meant for him. As John sat down the commander continued, but now to the others in the room he said, "Gentleman, may I present John Bennett."

The man on the left was the first to speak, "Welcome Mr. Bennett, I hope you had a pleasant flight?"

"It was uneventful." Bennett was not one for chitchat.

"Good," the man replied. "Let's get right to the point. We have been following your career for some time now with great interest, ever since your time with the Legion. You have done extremely well and have earned the trust of your superiors, even with the most difficult of assignments."

"I try to do my best." Bennett affirmed.

"Indeed. That is why you have been invited here." The man continued, "We would like you to come to work for us, but let me explain exactly what that means. You will continue to work for Blackbird. In fact, you will be given a promotion along with a new assignment, where you will be placed in a position of great importance and authority within the Blackbird organization. However, from time to time you will receive instructions from us, for special assignments. These assignments should not conflict with any assignment Blackbird gives you. However, if they do, our assignments will take priority. Is that understood?"

Bennett answered with a thoughtful nod as the explanation continued.

"Also, your compensation for working with us and completing our assignments will be extremely generous. This will be in addition to the increased pay and prestige we will arrange for you through Blackbird." There was a pause, as if to give Bennett some time to consider what he was being offered, and then he went on.

"Are you interested in working for us?" This question, and Bennett's answer to the affirmative, were completely unnecessary and merely a formality. If there had been any chance that the answer would be no, the offer would never have been made.

"Yes."

"Do you have any questions concerning your position, or responsibilities?"

"Just one," Bennett replied. "When do we start?"
The speaker smiled slightly at Bennett's question, then turned his gaze to the man seated in the shadows. There was a perceptible nod, presumably of approval. He then looked to the man sitting on the other side of the desk and the commander, both of whom also nodded. The voting, it appeared, was unanimous.

"Excellent. It is agreed then." The man reached over and lifted a large manila envelope off the desk, stood and handed it to Bennett, saying. "Please open it now."
While Bennett was opening the package, the man continued to speak, "The small white envelope is your acceptance bonus, let us say, to seal the agreement between us. The cell phone is your way of communicating with us and us with you. It is a perfectly normal cell phone in all respects, except one. If you hit star, the pound sign, numbers nine and five, and then star again, the phone automatically switches to a new line in a secure mode. While in the secure mode the number is completely untraceable and all

communications, including texting, will be automatically encoded and scrambled in either direction. If you hit zero while in the secure mode, the phone will automatically dial a number that is monitored live 24/7.

"If we initiate the call, your screen will turn red with the words 'Call Home' on it. You will then enter the security code and connect to us to receive any message we have sent, or to talk to someone live by hitting zero. Do you understand?"

"Yes," Bennett repeated the code, "Star, pound, 9, 5, star. I understand."

"Good." The man looked around at the others as if to detect any concerns they might have, but no one moved.
"Thank you Mr. Bennett. We look forward to your complete loyalty and efforts on our behalf." The whole meeting had been rather short and now it was apparently over.

With that, the other man on the right side of the desk and the Commander rose from their seats, leaving only the man in the shadows seated. The spokesman for the entire meeting now extended his hand toward Bennett. He shook it firmly and then turned to the Commander, who was now holding the door, signaling that it was time to leave. The man in the shadows, behind the desk didn't stand up, or even move, as far as John Bennett could detect.

In the car as they left the underground garage, the

Commander spoke to Bennett for the first time since the meeting began. "You will find, John, that you have made a wise decision. I'm sure that you understand never to play games with these people and to do everything they ask of you. They are not to be trifled with and also not to be discussed with anyone. Not even with me, after tonight. Do you understand what I am saying?"

"Yes, sir." Bennett answered.

"But, also remember," the Commander continued; "these people have enormous connections and resources that can assist you in whatever it is you need to get the job done, and they reward success handsomely."

The Commander paused for a few minutes and stared out the window at the passing lights. He began to speak without turning toward Bennett. "You will receive your new Blackbird assignment in a couple of days. All I can tell you now, is that you are being promoted to Major and will be posted in Utah as part of the Homeland Security support detail. There are some special reasons why they choose you for this assignment and you will find out more when the time comes."

CHAPTER 12

AUGUST, TWO MONTHS LATER

The CIA and FBI, working in conjunction with the military, had done a great job during the last two months since the successful disarmament mission. They had tracked down and intercepted the two missing shipments of pop machines. One shipment was caught just as it was arriving in the port of New York, and the other one, a week out of Long Beach, California. A total of thirteen nuclear devices had been recovered.

Unbeknownst to them, however, a third shipment was already sitting in the Chinese port located in Vancouver, Canada. It was actually the first of the three nuclear weapons shipments and had arrived three months earlier. It became the test shipment, not in disguised pop machines, but rather, in containers labeled as "tractor parts."

Only after that 'test' shipment had successfully arrived in Canada was the idea conceived to smuggle the additional weapons, rather suddenly acquired by the Iranians, into the country using pop machines. After the apprehension of the two previous weapon shipments by the combined U.S. forces, decisions were made at the highest level to delay things, proceeding carefully and with great caution. The

Iranian agents in Canada were instructed to pick up the Vancouver shipment and hide the weapons in three separate locations. The attack these weapons were intended for would have to be delayed for several months, maybe even a year. After all, they were very patient. It was hoped, by that time, that additional weapons might be acquired and positioned for one large coordinated devastating attack. However, the lesson had been learned and they would never again put all of their eggs into a single basket, or location, at a given time.

The plan would remain the same, to set off multiple weapons, in numerous cities, throughout the United States. In one fell blow, the great Devil would be reduced to a land of quivering infidels at the mercy of the growing legions of Jihadists scattered throughout North America, ready and waiting for the great day of Allah's victory.

ONE WEEK LATER

Rachel arrived at the motel in Salt Lake City later than she expected. She was amazed at the number of checkpoints she had gone through since leaving her apartment in Virginia earlier in the day, in order to get to the motel. The armed soldiers with sandbag barricades at the airports stood as a stark reminder that things were not going well and had definitely not gotten back to normal in the country.

Because of the food riots in Los Angeles, Oakland,

Detroit, Philadelphia and other large cities, martial law had been declared throughout the nation, and, in fact, most of the world. The world economy was in poor shape, with riots and civil unrest widespread.

Most of the banks had already been nationalized by their respective countries throughout the world, to one degree, or another, along with many major corporations. Now, there was talk of a global currency being readied that would solve the problems. Rumors abounded everywhere about what would replace the US dollar and the possibility of national, or even global banking holidays. The inflation rate was at an official 100% annual rate in the US, though many believed it was much higher in the things that counted, like food and energy. Food prices had already doubled in the last few months, with some items even tripling, adding to the government's woes.

Because of the unrest due to economic conditions, the governments of many countries had been overthrown, or replaced and it was becoming increasingly difficult to keep track of them. Most seemed to be under siege to one degree, or another, with much of the civil tension resulting from the high cost of food and oil and the tremendous unemployment that was rampant around the world.

Additionally, in Great Britain, France, Germany, and other Western European countries, there were almost daily riots and protests by Islamic dissidents, especially affected by the economic downturns. In France particularly, the country seemed on the verge of civil war.

In the U.S., unemployment had surged to an official 19%, though most analysts judged it to be much higher. In some cities it had actually reached a shocking 35%. The stock market had dropped almost a thousand points during the last two months and was still headed down despite the massive changes and federalization programs the new administration had made, or initiated. The oft repeated lies and promises no longer had the effect of providing even a false sense of hope.

In order to board the plane Rachel had to display a 'new' chip implanted, Federal I.D. card, or passport. Some of the most recently issued state drivers licenses also qualified as federally approved identification, since many of them also had the chips and were tied into the new federal system. Most states had already begun the process of issuing the new cards.

However, several states, including Idaho, Texas, Oklahoma, Montana, Arizona, and Wyoming, refused to do so. These states were part of the secession movement that had sprung up throughout the country and was now being fought in the courts. Utah, to the surprise of many, had been one of the first to become part of the new Federal I.D. system.

Violence was rampant, in addition to the food riots and anti-government protests. Spilling up from Mexico, the turbulence reached even into the Northern states and Canada. Crime had skyrocketed everywhere, especially violent crime. There were so many home invasion robberies that many homes now resembled fortresses complete with iron bars at doors and windows as people attempted to protect them selves from the onslaught. Home security companies offering alarm systems were one of the very few businesses experiencing growth and sales.

Texas and Arizona had both declared a state of emergency and had National Guard troops situated along the borders to reinforce border and state security. However, it was too late to prevent some of the most dangerous and deadly of infiltrations. The Mexican Drug cartels now had spinoff drug gangs already operating openly throughout the U.S. in almost every major city, and among the tent cities that had been created in the warmer, southern states. The carnage perpetrated by these gangs was widespread and valid reason to fear for your life. Many big city streets were generally unsafe by day, with only the bravest, or the most foolish going out unarmed after dark.

Though started by local communities and state organizations, almost all of the urban tent cities had been taken over by FEMA, under the direction of Homeland Security, in an effort to increase and guarantee safety. Observation towers had been erected and tall fences, topped with barbed wire, built surrounding the camps. During the summer months the camps had simply exploded across the country. It was hard to get a handle on the exact population in the camps since it changed almost on a daily basis, but most estimates put it at over eleven million.

Drug violence had become such a huge problem

that a powerful movement was under way to make many common street drugs legal and cheap, in the hope of making a painful dent in the huge income and power of the cartels. The administration promised, in their usual vague and confusing language, to pass a new "Anti-Drug Legalization" law the next month. The wording was so complicated that few of the voters would truly understand what they were asking for.

Rachel had flown into Utah, to attend another lecture on preparation. Her brother Todd and sister-in-law DeeDee had invited her to come out with the hope that after the meeting she would drive back to Rexburg with them and visit for a couple days before leaving for home. On Monday, she was supposed to spend time with Jill, hiking in Yellowstone. In addition to being able to visit with family, another fact that helped make her decision easier was that Jared was listed this time as an official presenter.

At the seminar on Friday, almost immediately Jared spotted Rachel and approached her to ask if she had dinner plans for after the seminar. Admitting that she was free for the evening, after just a minute of conversation, she agreed to a dinner date.

Later that night during dinner everything was going very well until Jared asked her what she thought of the problems in the economy and the new administration's efforts in that regard.

Rachel's reply was not what Jared had expected. "Well, I think we just haven't given them enough of a chance yet. After all, they inherited quite a mess and it's bound to take a couple of years, or more, before everything is straightened out and the economy starts to bounce back."

"I take it then that you voted for the new administration, for hope and change." Jared's words were tinged with just the slightest bit of sarcasm.

"Yes, as a matter of fact I did." Rachel confessed.

"You are an intelligent person." Jared said leaning forward across the table, intent on understanding what she was thinking. "Why would you do that? I thought Mormons were conservative."

"Well, the system was broken. It needed to be changed."

Jared had heard these same words often enough from misguided, but well meaning people. "Did you know what kind of change they were going to implement, or have implemented? It's called radical socialism."

"What's so bad about socialism, really?" Rachel asked a completely bewildered and frustrated Jared. "I would rather live under socialism than fascism. Wouldn't you?"

Jared paused for a minute, took a bite and chewed on his food for a minute to calm down before answering. "Rachel, what if the changes they are making don't fix anything, and in fact they actually make things ten times, or a hundred times worse?

What if I said that I can show you that what they're doing will destroy this country completely in five years, maybe less?"

"Then all of the experts would be wrong and we have been lied to."

Jared started to smile and shake his head from side to side. "You don't get it. Do you?" Before giving her a chance to answer he continued, "Have you ever heard the joke, How do you know if a politician is lying?"

"No, I haven't", Rachel said, a little defensive now.

"It's simple actually." Jared went on to finish the joke. "The way to tell if a politician is lying is if his lips are moving."

Rachel just sat there with a blank stare and Jared could see by the quizzical look on her face that the full import of the joke hadn't struck home.

"Do you spend a lot of time trying to understand politics and government?" Jared wondered.

"Not really." Rachel admitted.

"Have you ever lived in, or traveled to a socialist, communist, or fascist country?" Jared's question was serious and to the point.

Rachel thought for a moment and replied, "I don't think so, no."

"OK, then," Jared continued. "Let's go back to your comment about socialism and fascism. You've probably heard someone talk about socialism being on one end of the spectrum and fascism on the other end of the spectrum. Correct?"

"Yes." Rachel nodded.

"Ok, then. That comparison is actually incorrect, because a fascist government and a socialist government are, in fact, the same type of government. They are exactly the same, except for one thing. In one, there is a small group of people running the government, and in the second, there is a dictator running the government."

Jared could see her furrow her eyebrows with a puzzled look on her face. "One thing?" Rachel asked.

"Ok, just follow me on this one." Jared continued the lesson in politics. "There are eight major types of governments. There may be different versions and combinations of them, but still, just eight actual individual types." Jared grabbed a napkin and started drawing on it.

"The idea of fascism on one end of the spectrum and socialism on the other end is incorrect, or actually very misleading. And it shouldn't be left, or right...it should actually be turned this way, with the scale going up and down." Jared turned the napkin accordingly.

"On one end of the scale, at the top, is total freedom. There is no government. This is where the people just govern themselves. Each person owns what they own, does what they want to, and no one can tell anyone else what to do.

"On the opposite end at the bottom, is total slavery of the people. It is a kingship, or a dictatorship which is completely totalitarian. The king, or dictator, owns and controls everything. He owns the people, the land, the crops, the production, everything."

"Feudalism." Rachel commented, showing that she understood his explanation so far.

"Exactly." Jared kept going, "The king rides down the street and says off with his head...and the head comes off. The king is the law and owns everything and everyone. The people have no rights and are serfs, or slaves to the king."

"Now, in this totalitarian type of government, the king IS the government. And so, in essence, the government owns and controls everything. Are you with me so far?"

Rachel nodded once more.

"Good. Now, fascism is just another name for a dictatorship, or kingship type of government. The phrase was coined by Mussolini in the 1930's. Hitler was a fascist. Stalin was a fascist. Pol Pot was a fascist. The government owns everything and the people are essentially slaves to the government."

"Now one level up from fascism is socialism, or communism. It is almost exactly the same, with one small variation. The government still owns and controls everything and the people are still essentially slaves. The difference is that instead of having just one person completely in charge, there is a small group of people running the government. They are the elite royalty, or ruling class. In a way, it means that there is no one dominant person, such as a strong king, ruling the country...instead it is a coalition of a few powerful people that control everything. They are the elites and everyone else is the working class."

Rachel had been listening intently and now had a question. "I thought that in socialism, the people owned all of the property and ran the government?"

Jared was pleased that he was making things clear enough for Rachel to have questions and happy also for the opportunity to answer them.

"That is the most common misconception that people have. And it is perpetuated entirely on purpose primarily to confuse people. On the one hand, those who push communism and socialism tell everyone that the people will own everything... but, in reality, it is impossible because by definition socialism and communism is where the government controls everything and the people have no power and own nothing. In socialism and communism there is no private ownership. Everything is owned by the government and everyone lives to serve the government.

"Historically, what has always happened, without exception, is those who promote communism and socialism say it is for the people; that their intention is to help put the people into power...however, when they overthrow the existing government, instead of putting the people into power, they put themselves into power. They then change it into a totalitarian government, often with a dictator at the head, or an elite ruling class.

"In other words, socialism, or communism, whichever you call it, because they are essentially different names for the same thing, is the system most often used throughout history to overthrow existing governments and replace them with dictators and their friends."

Jared paused for a minute and then asked, "Have you ever read a little book called *Animal Farm*?"

"No, I never have." Rachel answered. "I've heard of it though."

"Well, you need to read it." Jared suggested. "As I mentioned, throughout history communism and socialism have always been used by elite groups of people to take over governments and put themselves into power. ALWAYS, it has been used for this purpose, without exception. It has always been about power.

"Another problem that arises when they stage the takeover is the destruction of the country's economy. Economically, socialism just doesn't work very well, and again, always destroys the economy, because the elites take most of the money from the people and use if it for themselves and their friends.

"In other words," Jared said, now with a smile, "what I am trying to say, with this rather long explanation, is that this new administration has followed the same path that took Germany from a completely free republic to a complete dictatorship under Hitler as their fascist socialist leader in less than eight years. The full name of the NAZI party was the National Socialist party.

"The Fascist Party of Mussolini was also a Socialist Party. The NAZI party of Hitler, was started and funded by the Russian Communist Party, another Socialist party, under the direction of Stalin.

"What I have found to be uncanny and actually very scary, is this new administration has followed the same process as Hitler's NAZI Party of the 1930's. It has been line by line, step by step, and the topics of many of the speeches are even the same, or at the very least, extremely similar. Like I said, it is very scary..."

At this point, Jared suddenly stopped talking in mid sentence and looked at Rachel. His demeanor changed immediately.

"You'll have to excuse me." He stuttered for just a moment. "I apologize; it's just that this subject is very dear to me. I know people who have died for this country, and now I see a very convincing group of power hungry liars trying to take it and set themselves up as a ruling class. So far, everything they're doing is putting money into their pockets and those of their corrupt and crooked friends to secure their power and destroy the freedoms I have fought for and my friends have died for."

There was silence for a while. Jared's passion regarding this subject was clearly evident. As they both turned to finishing their dinner, Rachel understood that she still had much to learn about politics. After a few minutes Jared broke the silence.

"Ok...let's change the subject. Enough of my lecturing. That isn't what we came here for tonight." He paused again, "Tell me about your work as a patent attorney. Who do you work for?"

Rachel responded, "I work for Richardson, Lowery, Vacuvic, and Johnson, Limited, out of D.C."

"I have heard of them, pretty good firm, as I recall. Well respected."

With a little surprise on her face, Rachel asked, "How do you know that?"

"I have patented a couple of inventions, so I know a little about this area, just enough to get me into trouble, or, try to keep me out of trouble." He smiled.

Now the subject was in her area of expertise and Rachel was curious. "What kinds of things have you invented?"

"First off, don't act so surprised," Jared feigned offense at the implications in Rachel's question. Then, breaking the act with a smile, he went on. "I can't tell you much because they have top secret classification, but, let's just say that my toys help dissipate heat buildup in a unique and efficient way."

"OK." Rachel said a little intrigued.

There was a pause in the conversation as both took a few more bites of the epicurean fare before them. After a few minutes Rachel asked timidly, "May I ask you a question?

"Shoot away," Jared answered.

Rachel queried, "You say you have retired from the military, so how long did you serve?"

"I was in the military for exactly twenty one years and three months. I joined the ROTC as a freshman in college and retired a little over five years ago. And for your information, I am 44 years old, and yes, I was married once, a very long time ago."

Rachel was surprised and a little embarrassed. First, Jared didn't look his age at first glance. She had guessed 38 maybe 40. Second, Jared had apparently anticipated her line of questioning and left her feeling just a little more transparent than she had hoped to be. After that, the conversation was almost non-existent as they finished their meal.

THE NEXT DAY

At the beginning of the seminar on Saturday morning, it was announced by the promoters that this would be their last preparedness expo, and all future expos already scheduled were being canceled. With martial law and the civil unrest, there were just too many complications to allow future events.

During Saturday, everyone was talking about the recent Supreme Court decisions on two cases involving the hate crime legislation that had been passed several months earlier. They both had been fast-tracked through the system. The first case involved declaring the Boy Scouts as a hate group, making them an illegal organization, unless they changed and accepted homosexual leaders.

The second case was very similar and was decided the same way. The decision declared a small religious group in Massachusetts also a hate organization, and the Supreme Court upheld the lower court ruling that took away their status as a non-taxable religious organization. Therefore, they were liable for paying taxes on all of their income since they had been organized in the early 1960's. Essentially, it meant that the Church was declared bankrupt and the government took over overseeing the liquidation of the property that belonged to the Church. In addition, the leaders of the Church were mandated to serve ten year jail sentences for their hate crimes.

At the conclusion of the seminar, Rachel drove

home with Todd and DeeDee to Rexburg. Things had not been going well for them. Four months earlier, after working several months with his hours, and consequently his salary, cut almost in half, Todd had finally lost his job. Searching in vain for work, along with thousands of other unemployed people, he had only been able to find part-time work. Luckily, Todd had the attitude of willingness to take any job that he could find, so, he had managed to bring in enough money to barely scrape by.

DeeDee, who had been a stay at home mom ever since they were married, also got a part time job working at a friend's restaurant as a waitress. Somehow, they had managed to keep the house and pay the monthly bills.

The biggest reason they were able to make it work was their lack of debt. That, and they owned more than a years supply of food storage. Another thing that had also helped immensely was the ward garden. About the time things started to get rough economically, their stake had purchased a little over twenty acres and divided the land between wards and members who wanted to have a garden, but did not have land of their own. Working hard in their section of the ward garden, they and the children had received many benefits, including most of the fresh vegetables on their table.

Unfortunately, several of their neighbors who had invested a lot of time and money into boats and snowmobiles had lost their homes and were now living in one of the many government camps. Other neighbors were on the verge of losing everything. As part of a stimulus program some of them had been allowed to stay in their houses for an additional six months before being evicted. When the government aid ran out, and they still had no income besides the handouts, they were moved out of state and assigned to work in the Civilian Work Corps program.

Todd was in the Bishopric and was able to share some ward statistics with Rachel. It seemed that fully one third of the ward was unable to find full time work. With so many members unemployed, the big problem facing the Bishopric was that the Church could not possibly help all of the people who needed it. There just wasn't enough Fast Offering money to go around.

Todd told them that the Church had implemented some new rules tightening the requirements for assistance. Any help was temporary and would only last three months. If the father of the family didn't work, or was too proud to work when presented with a job opportunity, then there was no assistance provided by the Church. Also, the Bishop's Storehouses and canneries had closed to all outside canning and purchases. They were only open now to Bishops helping the needy in their wards.

Todd told them stories about some of the backlash coming from affected church members, always careful to omit the names of those involved. A lot of people were very angry when the Church would not help them with their house payments for longer than three months, or if the Bishop suggested they move into a smaller house to lower their monthly payments. The attitude of many was, they had paid their tithing for years and helped others, and now when they needed help, the Church was failing them.

There had been anti-Church protests concerning the new policy, even in Idaho. Todd had observed that many of the people he knew who were protesting were, or had been, living in huge houses, with no gardens, and no food storage. Many of them were in the process of losing their homes, or had already lost them. He also noticed, to his shock and sorrow, that some of them had joined the anti-LDS, pro-homosexual protests that had grown throughout the U.S., swelling their ranks substantially.

When Todd brought up the anti-LDS, homosexual movement, the conversation abruptly changed. They began discussing two U.S. Supreme Court cases concerning the homosexual/gay rights issue in process. A U.S. Federal District court in the northeast declared the Catholic Church was in violation of the new hate law when a Priest refused to marry a homosexual couple. The Catholic Church lost the case and the Priest had been ordered to perform the marriage by the District Judge. He refused and went to jail rather than violate his principles.

As an additional punishment, the judge had ordered the confiscation of the Catholic Church property used to promote the so called hate crimes, in order to prevent "further abuses," which, in this instance, included the cathedral, school, and rectory.

The case was on appeal to the Supreme Court and it looked like it was going to be sustained as everything else had been. Todd told them that a friend of his, "in the know," said that the LDS Church had filed a brief as friend of both the small Massachusetts Church and the Catholic Church, but, the outcome still didn't look good. The LDS Church expected to be attacked by the government very soon as a result of these two cases.

Todd indicated that his friend, who worked for the LDS church had said three lawsuits already existed at various stages in the court system, trying to force the LDS Church to perform gay marriages, since gay marriage was now legal in many states and had been recognized as the law of the land. He said, if the Catholic Church lost its court case the LDS Church was planning changes in policy that would no longer allow any church leader to perform a marriage in the United States and only sealings to be performed in the temples within the U.S. borders.

However, the Church, expecting the opposition to continue, realized that the temple sealings would be challenged as well and were in the beginning stages of making plans to close all of the U.S. temples rather than be forced by federal courts to perform ordinances of any type involving homosexuals.

Part 2

WHEAT & TARES

"Therefore, let the wheat and the tares grow together until the harvest is fully ripe; then ye shall first gather out the wheat from among the tares, and after the gathering of the wheat, behold and lo, the tares are bound in bundles, and the field remaineth to be burned."

D&C 86:7

CHAPTER 13

NINE MONTHS LATER IN MAY

Rachel had just finished greeting Janet, the receptionist, as she walked through the office this morning. Most of the desks were empty, reflecting the cutbacks of over two thirds of the staff. Where once they had fifty three people working at her firm, they now had only seventeen.

As she stopped and looked around to see if there were any more empty desks after the weekend, she mused how times had changed. She reminded herself again for the umpteenth time that she was lucky to have a job at all in this economy, even though she and the others that remained had all taken substantial pay cuts.

Still, she had survived the job cuts up to now, primarily because much of her work involved large companies with government contracts. These companies had managed to survive the wave of bankruptcies over the last couple of years and their executives liked working with Rachel. They also had several large Chinese contracts, which Rachel, with her ability to speak Chinese, was key to.

She reminded herself that even with the pay cuts,

she still was paid relatively good money, though everything these days was relative. Still, she missed the hubbub of a really busy office, with lots of people rushing around in a purposeful way.

As she entered her office and sat down at the desk, she saw the two large stacks of folders, placed there by her one remaining assistant. Where she previously had five, now there was only Jimmy.

Ultimately, she was forced to make the decision over the last several months who was to go and who was to stay, finally settling on Jimmy as the best and brightest, not to mention the hardest working one of the group. It had not been a pleasant exercise and she shuddered at the prospect of having to let Jimmy go one day. He had a young wife and two little children. She knew how badly he needed this job. She hoped that it wouldn't come to that.

Lately, she thought hopefully, things had been looking up in the economy. The numbers had shown a positive creep upward for the third month in a row, at least that was what the newspapers reported.

Of course, experts and government officials had all been proclaiming that the bottom of the depression had been reached every other month for the last two years. But, recently a good friend of hers had told her that now, it appeared there was finally something to it. Maybe now it wasn't just the usual expert economists lying through their teeth.

Her   friend   had   said   that   the   new

United/Canada/Mexico dollar, more commonly referred to as the UCM, had gained traction, that it was being more readily accepted by China and other countries, and people were actually talking about some parts of the economy, at least, returning to normal. The UCM dollar had stabilized somewhat against the International Monetary Unit which was the standard currency now in use throughout most of the world. It was supposedly backed by gold...as was the UCM. The UCM was currently holding steady at about one thousand UCM dollars per ounce. Rachel did a quick calculation and figured that would equal about ten thousand dollars of the old Federal Reserve Notes.

Additionally, her friend had said that unemployment really had dropped another tenth of a point to an official 21.6%, the third such increase in jobs over the same number of months. It was also encouraging to see that there hadn't been a new major bank foreclosure, or nationalization in the last sixty days.

The new welfare programs were feeding a lot of people, and the government job programs seemed to be helping. Even martial law in many of the large cities had been relaxed a little when the daily occurrence of food riots had all, but come to an end.

Just as she was about to reach for the first folder on her desk, the phone buzzed. "Call for you on line six, a Mr. Jared Davis," Janet said over the speaker.

Immediately, Rachel brightened, while at the same

time becoming slightly confused. Her mind flashed back to the dinner conversation she'd had with Jared about nine months ago.

"Thanks Janet, I'll take it."

She picked up the receiver, "Jared, this is a pleasant surprise. To what do I owe the pleasure of this phone call?"

Jared quickly replied, "Well, I want to hire you."

"You want to what?" Rachel asked incredulously.

"I want to hire you for a couple of days, maybe a week."

Rachel started to stutter a little, completely taken aback at the offer. "Uh, I'm sorry...but, but, I don't understand."

"You are still a patent attorney aren't you?"

"Yes," Rachel answered.

"Well, I have another patent that I am working on and I would like to hire you to work on it for me." Jared paused for a moment and then added, ", but, before I hire you, maybe I should ask you another question. Are you a GOOD patent attorney?"

Jared's phone call and first question had caught her a little off guard, but now she was on firm ground. She knew that she was good. "Yes," she said a little coyly, I'm very good." Flipping into attorney mode, she went on. "OK then, tell me about your patent."

"Exactly. What I would like to do is have you fly out here to Arizona for a few days so I can go over it with you and discuss the specific approach to the patent and the whole works." Jared continued to explain himself. "There are a lot of angles on this particular idea and I would very much prefer not to do it over the phone."

Rachel replied, "That would be nice, but it would be highly irregular and I am not sure if I can work it out. Besides, I don't think you can afford me for a whole week," she added.

Jared countered, "Don't you fly out and visit large companies to work out details concerning their patent issues?"

"Occasionally," she acknowledged, not sure where he was headed.

"Well, just think of me as one of your big, stuffy corporations, and come out to our corporate headquarters."

Rachel thought she could hear the smile in his voice as she considered this for a moment and then said, "Ok, I guess it's possible, but it'll take some time to get approval from my boss and make arrangements."

"Actually, I have already talked to your boss, a Mr.

Richardson, I believe; a very nice man by the way, and he has agreed to it. This saves me the time and trouble of flying out there to the east coast, which I detest. I can easily afford to hire you and pay for all of your expenses to fly out here and meet with me since I have already made arrangements for the wire of a sizeable retainer for your services."

When Jared finished, Rachel stammered a little more. This man never ceased to amaze her. "Well, I, uh, uh, I am totally flabbergasted and at almost a total loss of words. I'm not sure what to say."

"Don't say anything, just do. Check your schedule and let me know when you can fly out here so I can make the arrangements on this end."

"OK," Rachel gave in, "I'll call you sometime later today."

Rachel was a little flustered, something that bothered her a lot. She was someone who was not easily surprised, or caught off guard and she very much liked to be in control... as she was most of the time. It disturbed her that Jared could get to her the way he did and keep her so off balance. She made a mental note not to let that happen again, though in the back of her mind she remembered that he has done it to her just about every time they had been together, which made her more determined not to let it happen again.

Rachel stood up from her desk, walked out the door and down the hall, past a couple of secretaries and knocked on the slightly opened door of Bill Richardson's office. "Got a minute?" she asked, as she leaned in through the opening.

Richardson looked up when he heard her voice, "Oh, hi Rachel. Have you talked to Mr. Davis yet?"

"Yes, I have." The feeling of being off balance started to return.

Bill noticed the momentary look of confusion on her face. He broke into one of his big grins, and with an understanding nod said, "Good, very good. He and I had a nice chat yesterday afternoon and he asked me to wait until he cleared it with you this morning before you and I discussed it. Tell me, how did you luck out in finding such a big new client? He even said he was single." There seemed to be a little mischievous twinkle in her boss's eyes as he said that.

She had always liked Mr. Richardson. Of the four senior partners in the firm, he was like the big papa bear, almost always jovial and good natured, besides being incredibly intelligent. Long on customer service, when they needed someone to schmooze a potential client and close the deal, it was usually Bill Richardson who was brought in. As an attorney, and especially in this business, his approach was completely unique.

He maintained that most everything in life that was important was meant to be person to person, friend to friend, especially when working with crackpot inventors and that it was best to approach it like that.

He always preached to them about befriending their clients. "Love them as a dear friend," he would say. "only then can real trust be developed." At any rate, his approach worked. Though times were hard, and a lot of their competitors had fallen, Richardson, Lowery, Vacuvic, and Johnson, still had their clients.

Rachel enjoyed working for him, and had become friends with his wife Suzanne, even accepting the occasional dinner invitation to their home in Virginia. She remembered, after the first dinner, as she was getting her coat to leave, overhearing Suzanne say to her husband, "Such a nice girl and very pretty. She should be married and have a house full of kids." Then lowering her voice, she had asked, "What's the problem, is she gay?" Rachel had heard Bill reassure his wife that he was pretty sure she wasn't because she was a Mormon. Suzanne had replied, "A Mormon, they are such nice people. It's a shame what the government is doing to them and their church."

Since that time they had almost treated her like a long lost daughter...even taking the opportunity of lining up a couple of blind dates for her. She started to laugh as she remembered what a disaster the last one had been.

As Rachel started to laugh, Richardson said, "Oh, this could be interesting."

She awoke from her trance, shook her head and waved her hand as she said, "Too long a story for now...but, tell me, what is your impression of this guy? Do you think he is on the up and up?"

Bill Richardson was known for his ability to quickly and most often correctly size people up and categorize them. His first impressions were most often right on.

He seemed slightly disappointed when Rachel refused to go into details about this new client, but since she had asked the question, he replied thoughtfully, "He seems to be. His money is good and I verified that he has done some patent work before, but it appears to be classified military, so there are no details in the file. Besides that, he was pleasant and straightforward to talk to. So far, I like him. I think we will be able to do business with him."

She paused for a moment, trying to slow things down in order to get her mind wrapped around everything before she said. "Well, I guess with your permission then, I better make arrangements to fly out to Arizona for a couple days."

"Do you have any idea what his invention is about?" Bill asked.

"Not really," Rachel responded. "We met at a convention about two years ago and have run into each other a few times since then. We've even had dinner a couple of times."

At this revelation the mischievous twinkle was back in Richardson's eyes, along with the big smile.

Catching the look, Rachel shook her finger at him and chided, "No, it is nothing like that." She continued, "All that he has said is his hobby has something to do with gathering and manipulating energy. I got the impression that it might be something like a new kind of circuit, or something like that. Something to better handle heat and energy transfer off of computer chips."

"Hmmm, that could be interesting and fruitful." Bill thought for a minute and then asked, "Is there anything hot on your plate right now?"

"Nothing really," Rachel said after mentally scanning her schedule. "At least nothing that can't be put off for a few days. I can have Jim finish cleaning up the new Tascom 3 patent descriptions. It's mostly done anyway and I can review it when I return."

Richardson nodded his approval, "Ok, let me know if there's anything you need and have a good trip, relax a little. You could use the break."

About an hour later, Rachel called Jared to let him know that she could leave as early as the next morning. He told her to go ahead and book her flight and send him an email with the details of her itinerary. They exchanged email addresses and cell phone numbers and Jared asked her to call him when she landed in Phoenix.

CHAPTER 14

THE NEXT DAY...

Rachel had a late morning flight and used some of her flyer miles to upgrade to first class. The flight was almost full and the movie was terrible, but she watched some of it anyway on the screen of the person sitting next to her after she went through the usual flight magazines. Unfortunately, she had learned long ago to read lips. Usually, that was to her benefit, but with the unsavory dialogue of this movie, it was a distinct disadvantage for the parts of the movie she did see. Next time, she promised herself to bring a good, thick book.

The time was 12:30 pm when she landed at Phoenix Sky Harbor International Airport. With the time change she had gained 4 hours. Though it was May, and still a little on the chilly side in Maryland, the thermometer had already risen to ninety-eight degrees here in Phoenix, with most of the day and hotter temperatures yet ahead. "How do these people do it," she wondered.

Jared had requested she call him as soon as she touched down and so she did. In their short conversation, he explained that some things had come up, and he would be unable to pick her up at the airport, however, he had reserved a rental car for her, and requested that she drive up to Show Low on her own, if she didn't mind too much. He suggested she take her time and enjoy the drive. There would be a map in the car with directions clearly outlined. She smiled as the agent at the desk described the classy four wheel drive vehicle, which would be waiting for her, parked just out side.

The drive was more than pleasant; it was invigorating. Along the way she also discovered the secret to survival in this sweltering valley was, very simply, air conditioning. The car had been started and cooled down with the cooling system softly purring by the time she got in. The agent behind the desk had a map on the counter already marked with directions on how to reach her destination, along with an unexpected ski map and brochure. As she started the climb up into the mountains, the temperature cooled off enough that she was actually able to turn off the air conditioning and roll down the windows. Rather abruptly the dry rocky desert had given way to the mountains with miles and miles of lush pine tree forests.

As the climb continued along the tree lined roads, Rachel finally understood what Jared meant when he called Phoenix the valley and the area where he lived, the rim. The contrast was like night and day. The desert with its heat, rocks, and cactus was just as it was depicted in the movies and photos she'd seen; dry and hot, but picturesque in its own unique way. As she drove along, the landscape invoked images of the old west. In her one and only previous visit to Phoenix she had not escaped the city limits and so hadn't seen any scenery except at a distance.

This state, and it's varied landscapes never ceased

to surprise her, and she loved every moment. The road was twisting and curvy, but not overly so. It was a relaxing drive with few other cars on the road. Rachel was tempted to close her eyes for just a moment as she breathed in the wonderful pine aroma.

As Rachel drove along, she recalled in detail her previous encounters with Jared, especially the last one in Salt Lake City. She had thought a lot about the things he had said to her concerning socialism and freedom. It had disturbed her quite a bit at the time, but when Todd had described what was happening to him personally and to the Church, she couldn't help, but reflect on the words Jared had said and his opinions that this new administration was destroying the country.

Because of that conversation, she had decided to take an active interest in government and try to find out what was really happening in politics. She really started to listen to both sides of the arguments and did not automatically accept as fact everything that was reported on the nightly news. It had taken her only about three weeks of concentrated study and research to realize that Jared was absolutely right. The facts supported him again, and again. She was looking forward to apologizing to Jared and telling him she had become a convert to the cause of liberty and freedom.

When she arrived in Show Low, Rachel pulled off the road just to survey her surroundings. It was now 5 pm and what she could see was absolutely gorgeous. There was a slight, warm breeze, barely rustling the limbs of the tall evergreen trees. She loved the mountains and the forests and spent as much time as she could afford in them, but had no idea such beauty existed in Arizona. Rachel felt as if she were coming home. Of course, she felt this way every time she left the city for some time out in the wilderness. She stepped out of the car for a stretch and mused to herself, looking around, *"One of these days I need to think about retiring, abandon the city completely and just live high in the mountains among the trees."* The thought immediately brought a sense of peace and contentment that she rarely felt these days.

After a few moments of enjoying the scenery, Rachel pulled the cell phone out of her pocket and called Jared per his instructions, to get the last of the directions to their meeting place.

Jared answered the phone simply, "J.D."

"I am in Show Low," Rachel stated. "Where would you like us to meet?"

"Are you hungry?" Jared asked thoughtfully.

"Well, yes, I am as a matter of fact. I haven't had anything to eat since the flight, and I am famished." His question had awakened her recognition of the hunger pains coming from her stomach.

"I tell you what," Jared went on, "why don't you just come up to my place and I'll rustle up something edible. We can eat dinner and discuss my project all at the same time."

Following the directions he'd given her, Rachel found herself ascending higher into the mountains. She found the cross road, and then watched the odometer, going exactly the 4.6 miles Jared had directed before turning off onto the graveled dirt road with its twists and turns. After another six miles, and a small bridge, she found a smaller dirt road that revealed infrequent use by the grass growing between the two rolling ruts in the caked mud. The entrance to this road was marked only by a large dark green rural mailbox and a sign which read "PRIVATE PROPERTY-NO TRESSPASSING."

Rachel drove the next three miles, or so, through heavy pine trees that towered above the small road, sometimes seeming to over take it. She crossed a quaint bridge over a small stream, then shortly turned and then broke through the trees into a large clearing. In the middle of the clearing, she guessed perhaps four, or five acres in all, was a sprawling, ranch style house.

The initial view was so breathtaking, she stopped the car. It wasn't the house so much as it was the sudden effect of going from the shady darkness of the forest, with its various hues of browns and greens, out into the bright sunlight with the bright colors now presented before her. The dissimilarity made it all at once different and peaceful.

The first thing that caught her attention was the color. The opening was awash in vibrant shades of white, pink, bright green, red, and blue. She realized with a smile that she felt a little like Dorothy in the movie version of "The Wizard of OZ," opening the door of the farmhouse from black and white Kansas to the bright, multi-colored land of the Munchkins.

There were four horses in the fresh green pasture on the left side of the clearing, near a red barn with a dark shingled roof. All along the opposite side of the rustic looking barn was a modern solar green house with curved, clear, Plexiglas ceiling and walls leaning against the barn. The windows were open, exposing the bounty of plants growing inside. Just past, and a little bit behind the greenhouse, was a small garden area with a very tall chain link fence around it. There were rows of what, from some distant memory, reminded her of peas and still other rows of plants that she could not identify.

Rachel became aware of a swishing sound on her right and turning that way, saw a large circular sprinkler lazily watering the lawn near a small grove of fruit trees.

Of all she saw, however, the most striking were the trees in front of the house which was right in front of her. Along the outer edge of the large front lawn were mature trees with thousands of white and light pink blossoms. Behind those, in a double row, closer to the house, were trees with blossoms of a richer, darker pink hue, almost red. There was an opening between them with a walkway that led from the large circular driveway to the front of the house. To the right of the stone path was a small rock water fall and pond, with what appeared to be weeping willow trees baring white blossoms hanging down into the water.

Rachel had never seen such a variety of foliage as what lay before her except in a Japanese garden she had seen once, and it was a pleasure to behold. There were white flowers floating in the pond, lightly stirred and moved by the gentle breeze. The scene had her almost mesmerized.

The house was a cheery, bright yellow with a clean, white trim, and rock accents surrounding the entryway and under the windows. The lawn looked well cared for with many colorful flowers and bushes arranged in borders surrounding the house and trees.

Instantly, Rachel was jealous and envious of this veritable Eden. She quickly made a silent vow to get out of the city, soon. *"This is the way people were meant to live,"* she thought.

Just then, Jared came out of the house and onto the front porch, waving her in. She got back into the car and drove up the long circular driveway, stopping at the walkway entrance.

As she stepped from the car, the aroma in the air almost overpowered her. "What is that I smell?" She asked him, incredulous, as he stepped off the porch and came toward her.

"That, my dear city girl," he said, with a smile on his face and a slight wave of his arm as if to introduce her to the country, "is a combination of cherry blossoms, pine trees, honeysuckle, and lilac."

"Beautiful." Rachel's reaction may have seemed a bit trite, but it was truthfully all she could come up with at the moment, as she turned in a full circle, attempting to take the panorama all in at once.

"Welcome to my little oasis." He paused, allowing her time to enjoy the view. He had grown accustomed to this type of reaction from first time visitors to his home, but having it come from Rachel especially pleased him.

After it appeared she had overcome the initial shock of her surroundings, Jared spoke up. "Are you still hungry?" he asked. "Or, in other words, do you want the tour before, or after dinner."

Remembering how long it had been since her last real meal, Rachel answered reluctantly, "Actually, I am rather hungry, "adding quickly", but I will definitely take you up on the offer of a tour after dinner."

"Good, then come on in. You can leave your things in the car. I've made reservations for you at a comfortable motel in town." And, with that, Jared turned and started back towards the front door.

Rachel was experiencing a strange mixture of emotions, feeling relieved and sad, all at the same time. On the one hand, she had been a little worried that Jared would suggest that she stay at the ranch, but when he had mentioned the motel in town, she had experienced a confusing combination of deliverance and hesitancy. She did not want to leave this beautiful place and go into town; she wanted to stay here, in Shangri-la. She had to mentally remind herself of the task at hand and the reason she was even having this experience. *"Get a hold of yourself girl, this is just business, nothing more."*, but in the back of her mind, she wasn't so sure, and she had half a hope that it wasn't.

As she entered the house, it became immediately obvious that this was a man's home, devoid of any feminine touch. She passed the huge grandfather clock and wood bench in the tiled entryway past the double French doors crafted of white pine and bubbled glass. Behind the double doors, was a western living room furnished with dark brown leather couches and decorated with cowboy sculptures, Indian artifacts, rope, and lots of wood, something that she found surprising. She hadn't taken him for a cowboy.

Rachel absorbed it all in a glance as she followed him past a long hallway, around a corner, and into the kitchen/family room. As Jared walked around to the working side of the counter, she stopped, scrutinizing the living space. It was open and spacious, thoroughly a modern Southwestern design. Without a doubt, this was where he spent most of his time. This was the heart of Jared's home.

The kitchen where Jared was standing was on her right and had a large gray granite counter that dominated the area, with a large stainless stove top towards one end. Across from it, against the wall, was a side-by-side stainless, built in refrigerator, and more open counter space with a large built in microwave above, and a double built in oven. The cabinets and trim were a wood, light in color. This was a state of the art kitchen as functional as it was beautiful. Just past the kitchen was a formal dining room complete with an eight foot long table.

To her immediate left was a heavy mantle above a large rock fireplace with a black metal insert. In front of and on each side of the fireplace was a protruding rock shelf which had a large multicolored round throw rug in front. Rachel decided not to fight the impulse and started grinning

"Care to let others in on the joke?" Jared teased casually.

"No joke," Rachel assured him. "it just came to me that all you need is a dog lying by the fireplace to complete this homey picture."

Jared gave a little laugh. "No dog, I'm afraid. I don't have any animals. I travel too often now, with the Community Emergency Response Training."

"What about the horses in the field?" Rachel asked remembering the image of them running as she came out of the forest.

"Actually, the horses are not mine," Jared explained. "They belong to my neighbor. I take care of them when he is gone and I happen to be in town. For that, I get to ride pretty much whenever I want to. In fact, one of the reasons that I couldn't come down to meet you this morning was because he called and asked if he could bring them over this afternoon. He had something come up suddenly and needs to be out of town for the week."

Rachel continued her relaxed inspection of the room. Turning the corner, on the far wall past the fireplace, was a large, mostly blank area, maybe ten feet wide, with narrow ceiling to floor cabinets on each side. She wondered why there were no paintings hanging in the space, until she noticed the small LCD projector hanging from the ceiling aimed directly at the blank wall and the wrap around leather sectional facing it. It had all been carefully arranged for a theater seating area. Farther down the wall there was a large sliding glass door to the backyard.

Through the glass of the back door, Rachel could see the back porch with its informal patio furniture, past to the green field, and the forest beyond. On the right side of the porch was a pool that seemed to come right up to the house.

As she walked a little further into the room, she saw that the barstools were attached to the bar and didn't have any feet on them. They just swung out. There were four of them facing the granite counter. Then, she walked a little further, and noticed that not only did the pool come up to the side of the house...it actually came into the house about six feet. She stopped for a minute and said, "You have a swimming pool in your house."

Rachel felt stupid and quite childish the minute it

came out of her mouth. She was a grown woman from the east who had been many places and seen many things. She wanted to appear more sophisticated and not be so impressed by the things she was seeing here, but it slipped out because, frankly, she was impressed. She stood nearly hypnotized, staring at the clear, blue, tranquil water of the pool.

Jared, by this time, had stepped further into the kitchen and stood with his hands on the counter, just watching her as she visually explored her new surroundings. He started to laugh when she discovered the secret of the pool, but thought better of it, knowing that she would be feeling foolish after that comment. There was something special about this woman and he did not want to offend her in any way.

"When I got injured, the doctors recommended that swimming was the perfect way to rehabilitate." He explained. "However, we are at an elevation of about seven thousand feet. The snow can really pile up here in the winter and things have a tendency to freeze." His attitude was friendly now and comfortable to help put her at ease and diminish the importance of the issue. "So, I had them bring one end of it into the house. I can cover the outside portion of it during the winter and still swim. I don't use it that much anymore, but occasionally, it is kind of fun."

He motioned toward the couch and invited, "Go ahead and make yourself comfortable." Then, as he turned and opened the refrigerator he asked, "How do you like your steak-medium, rare, or well done?"

Rather than go over to the couch Rachel sat down on one of the barstools at the counter, where she could watch the preparation of the food. She swiveled for a minute. "I like my steak medium rare," she replied.

"Medium rare it is then." He responded.

Jared pulled a plate out of the refrigerator, stepped to the stove, and turned on the grill. It appeared that he had forgotten something and went back to the fridge, rummaging around for a minute before he asked over his shoulder, "What kind of dressing would you like on your salad?" Then, with a mock serious tone he added, "I have a really nice selection of Paul Newman's very own dressings, including his famous raspberry vinaigrette."

Rachel started to laugh at his silliness and admitted happily, "Raspberry sounds good to me."

"Raspberry it is then for the lady, and my old standby ranch dressing, for me." His arms were full with a large salad bowl and a couple bottles of dressing as he nudged the refrigerator door closed with his side.

"Would you like to eat at the counter, or at the table?" Jared asked.

"It doesn't matter to me." Rachel felt strangely at home here and was, once again, confused by her emotions.

"Well, I have my papers and diagrams spread out on the table already, so let's eat there."

With the mention of the invention, Rachel was brought back a little to the reality of why she was here. It was almost like a rebuke. *"Yes...business,"* she thought.

In a few minutes the steaks were cooked, the table was set and they had started to eat the salad.

"You built all of this by yourself?" Rachel managed between bites.

"Yes. It was good therapy." Jared acknowledged. "When I came home, I wasn't expected to live, and then I wasn't expected to walk. This gave me a purpose and a focus. I did actually hire a lot of it out when I had to, but I acted as the architect and general contractor on everything. As I got to the point where I could do more, I did. For example, I made all of the cabinets and did most of the trim throughout the house. The barn isn't really for housing livestock. Most of it is actually a woodworking shop for me to putter around in. I've even made some of the furniture in the house." He looked with some satisfaction at the furnishings around them. "In fact, I made this table and the chairs that we are sitting in."

"You're very good." Rachel was truly impressed by his craftsmanship. "How long did it take you to complete everything?"

"About five years, though I am still working on

details here and there." Jared confessed. "For example, the greenhouse and garden are my latest projects. Lately, I've been working hard to make this place completely self sufficient. My goal is to even grow all of my own food, especially since the economic collapse and the price of everything going through the roof. I have come to find out that gardening is much harder than I thought and I have developed a new respect for farmers."

"You know," Rachel allowed, "when you mentioned that you had kind of retired to this little place up in the mountains, in my mind I pictured a small cabin. This is quite different than anything I could have imagined."

"Funny, you should mention a cabin," Jared's thoughts came back to the conversation. "Originally, all that was here was a small cabin which still stands behind the barn. You can't see it from here." He, paused a minute, collecting his thoughts, while still staring out into the darkness.

"Yeah, well, after my forced retirement from the military I had to have a place to heal and I needed the peace and quiet this place affords. I've seen a lot of ugly in this world and I wanted something different." Jared's words seemed personal and Rachel was happy that he was willing to share these feelings with her.

"The property had been bought a long time before my injury, but nothing had really been done with it. I'd made a lot of plans though." He smiled with the memories. "In fact, in the first war in Iraq we had infiltrated the outskirts of Baghdad and were hold up in a house spying on what was going on at a military complex. Our job was to watch and possibly identify any biological munitions they were deploying out of there. There were six of us, and we were only supposed to be there for about a week, although luckily we had enough food for two weeks."

"Things happened that we hadn't anticipated and we sat in that house for almost six weeks. I had a lot of time on my hands during that 'field trip,' and I spent most of it building everything you now see here in my mind. It helped keep my thoughts off of starving to death. When I got hurt, I came here and started working on making those plans come to life."

Jared paused as he looked off, through the window and out to the trees. By now, it had gotten quite dark; night seems to fall quickly in the mountains, so the view out of the window left nothing to see, but the blackness of the forest and a darkening sky, with the disappearance of the last rays of the sunset.

"In the military, you are always traveling, and when you are in battle, you tend to talk about when it is all over, and if you survive, about settling down, putting down some roots, and raising a family. In combat, coming home is the thought that makes it all worthwhile and keeps you going, even when you don't have anyone, or a home to come home to." Jared's voice trailed off as memories seem to swirl inside his head.

Rachel couldn't think of anything to say. She

realized that she had gotten a glimpse into a world she never had imagined let alone even thought about. Jared had opened a hole in his armor, had lifted his warrior's shield and let her look into his heart for a moment... and it was so terribly lonely. She wanted to reach out across the table and hold him, offering some of the comfort and peace he said he needed and tell him thank you.

Instead, she just sat there; watching him and his exposed emotion while he continued to stare out the window. The silence was starting to become uncomfortable when suddenly, Jared said, "Well, enough of that. Let's get down to business." Immediately, she felt the armor, back in place and the shield moved into position for protection.

He reached over to a stack of folders lying on the table near his arm while saying, "Let me show you what I have been working on. By the way, don't you have some legal documents that I am supposed to sign before we talk about this stuff?" Although Jared had no worries about the honesty of this woman, he had experienced enough business deals gone bad to be cautious even under the best of circumstances. When money was involved, people often changed into something almost unrecognizable.

"Oh, yes." Rachel remembered. "They're still out in the car." She arose from her seat to go get them. Turning towards the door, she instantly saw a man, standing there, all in black with what looked like a black ski mask over his head. Her first reaction was disbelief. It was just so unexpected. At first she looked at the eyes peeking out from the mask, and then her gaze went to the gun in his hand. It too was all black...and it seemed huge.

"Going some where?" the man in black questioned. "Never mind, I'll get them." Jared turned to face the intruder. There was a puzzled, angry look on Jared's face as he took in the scene.

Now the figure spoke directly to him. "Don't you remember me, Jared? That's too bad" he said in a mocking tone. "I remember you." The look on Jared's face became even more puzzled as if he was searching his memory, trying to place this man's eyes and his voice.

Just then, another intruder dressed in black stepped through the double doorway, also holding a gun.

"Perhaps this will help," said the first man in black as he reached up with his free hand and quickly pulled off the ski mask. Short blond hair was revealed, and Jared immediately scowled. "Bennett!" he spat out. "I thought I was rid of you for good." The disgust on Jared's face expressed clearly his feelings about this man.

"Yeah, well, maybe you were able to forget about me, but I've never forgotten you." The words were almost growls dripping with contempt. "And so, along comes this opportunity to run into you again. Too bad the people I work for want you in one piece and in good condition, or this would be a very short, but memorable reunion. As it is, put your hands on your head and come on out to meet the family, and," Bennett paused for effect, "don't try to be clever, or your girlfriend here will reap the consequences."

The man named Bennett motioned with his gun as he and his accomplice stepped back into kitchen/family room. He spoke again to his captives. "The girl comes first and then you follow."

Rachel entered the other room and saw two additional men. They were holding different types of guns that she failed to recognize in the brief moment she saw them. As Jared stepped into the room after her, this second group walked behind them leaving Bennett and friend, training their guns on them from the front.

"Nice place you have here." Bennett said with a sneer. "And, I heard that you were walking again. My, and without even a limp." He stepped over to right in front of Rachel, eying her up and down with an obvious leer on his face. His look sent chills up and down Rachel's spine. "Very, very nice. I'm sure it would have been a lovely evening JD...sorry to spoil your fun."

Jared spoke with fire in his eyes and steel in his voice. "Let's get to the point Bennett and get this over with. What do you want, and who are you working for?" Jared's anger was rising and Rachel was seeing a side of him he hadn't shown before.

Bennett didn't take his eyes off of Rachel as he

answered. "Well, everyone knows about the fame of Jared Davis, including my bosses. You still hold the record for the most experience with live nuclear weapons, and you are still alive, which makes you a very rare, and valuable commodity. When I learned that my people wanted you and your unique expertise, I jumped at the chance to help find you and bring you in." It was all a lie. The truth was that Bennett had been specifically contacted via his "company" cell phone to find Jared, pick him up, and hold him unharmed.

"They could have just called and I probably would have come. I've done a few assignments since my retirement. All this," Jared said gesturing toward the guns, "isn't really necessary."

Bennett replied, finally taking his eyes off of Rachel and glancing at Jared. "Yes I know, but it is a lot of fun. Too bad I can't bring you in like I would like to, but, as they say, 'first things first'

With that, he suddenly reached out, back handing Rachel across the face with the gun in his hand. It caught everyone by surprise, especially Rachel. She didn't even see it coming because her attention has been fixed on Jared.

The blow hit her hard, half lifting her off her feet and she fell backward onto the carpet, landing on her side. Jared, seeing her fall, took a big step forward and then suddenly screamed out in pain as the man behind him fired a high powered stun gun into his back. The barbs went through the thin fabric of his shirt and pierced Jared's flesh, sending 10,000 volts of electricity screaming through every muscle in his body.

Jared staggered, went down to one knee, and froze there, concentrating all of his will power on not to fall over. With muscles cramping and shaking in pain as the electricity coursed through his body, drops of sweat immediately formed on his forehead, as he struggled against the attack.

Bennett nodded slightly, and the pain subsided as the man in back released the trigger.

Rachel was sitting on the floor, dazed, and holding her hand to her bleeding cheek and bruised eye. She had never experienced this type of excruciating pain.

"Cooperate, and she lives." Bennett warned. "I was told to bring you in unharmed, but I don't have to play nice with anyone else, understand?"

Jared nodded his head as he looked down at Rachel.
"Cuff him," Bennett directed, "hands behind the back and... slowly."

Jared slowly stood up and placed his hands behind his back. The man, who a moment ago had stunned him, now put the handcuffs around his wrists. Jared grimaced slightly as the cuffs were tightened so that they bit into his skin.

"That's good." Bennett said, directing his words to

the one who had just cuffed Jared. He then continued, "Pick her up and put her to sleep." Then, looking directly into Jared's eyes to be sure the threat was understood, he repeated, "Just to sleep."

The accomplice reached down under Rachel's arms and bodily picked her up, slipping one of his arms quickly around her neck and applying a choke hold as he tilted her backwards and lifted her off the ground. Rachel involuntarily struggled against the constraint, but within just a few seconds she was limp in his arms.

"Good, let her go and let's get our friend here to the car." Bennett was anxious to deliver his package and be done with it. He knew the longer a job took, the more chances there were for something to go wrong.

The man now holding Rachel's limp body pushed her forward and let her drop to the floor, where she fell face down onto the carpet. Her dark red hair was now disheveled and lay spread out around her face, held back only by a single bobby pin above her ear. The blood slowly began to drip from the gash on her cheek.

Jared watched Rachel fall and then took a large step towards her. Instantly, he was struck by another two barbs, but this time he was ready for it, and didn't go down. No sound came from him as he stood there trembling for a moment, but keeping his eyes still focused on Rachel lying motionless on the floor.

Bennett calmly watched Jared's futile struggle

against the pulsing electrical charge and ordered angrily, "Juice it some more."

Another wave of electricity hit Jared as the power was increased. He staggered one more step forward, then teetered and fell face first on top of Rachel, his face smashing into the side of her head. Once the flow of electricity had been cut off, Jared relaxed, and quickly moved his lips as if to kiss her ear.

Bennett watched this apparent show of affection and said sarcastically, "Oh, how sweet," then barked abruptly, "Okay, let's get out of here. We have a schedule to meet." Motioning toward Jared with a nod he ordered, "Pick him up and take him to the car. We'll meet you at the airport in a few minutes after we clean up here."

As two of the men reached down to grab Jared's arms, Bennett squatted beside him and hissed into his ear, "Remember, be good, or she'll hurt like she never thought she could." Jared nodded slightly, indicating that he understood what was expected of him.

Bennett stood up and shouted, "Okay, take him out, but be careful."

The men, one on each side of Jared, half dragged him, staggering out of the house and to the car waiting for them with a driver behind the wheel. They pushed him into the back seat and then, got into the car themselves-one of the men in the front to ride shotgun and the other in the back with Jared.

When they had gone, Bennett spoke to his lone remaining helper. "Drag her over here." Bennett led the way out of the room, paused for a moment, then approached the front hall closet and opened the door. Looking into it he saw a couple of jackets, hats, and rain boots inside, nothing dangerous, and no weapons. "This will do...put her in here," he said. The man followed him dragging the unconscious Rachel. Then he unceremoniously shoved her head first into the closet, picked up her legs and thrust them in as well. Bennett quickly closed the closet door.

"Go find me something combustible. It's time to make a fire." Bennett pointed to a door down the hall and suggested sternly, "Check the garage." The man obediently strode down the hall and opened the door to the garage.

Bennett returned to the front hall, looked at the closet door and then around the entry way until his eyes settled on the large grandfather clock. Walking to the side of the clock he wedged it away from the wall until he was able to position himself behind it completely. He then moved it away from the wall a couple of feet and then he pushed it over, watching it smash against the closet door with a deafening boom and the tinkling sound of broken glass. The gong sounded a deep, resonating noise within the wooden cabinet that reverberated throughout the house.

"Time's up," he muttered to himself. He then went to the stove and the oven in the kitchen and quickly blew out the pilot lights, turning everything on full.

He was just finishing this process as his man returned with a red, plastic gas can.

"It's about three quarters full." He told Bennett, raising it in his hands.

"That'll do it." Bennett said as he grabbed the can, took off the cap and started dousing everything with gasoline. There was a grin on his face as he splashed the kitchen and family room and their furnishings with the gasoline. He then poured some down the hallway, and the entryway. He kicked open the French doors to the front living room, sending glass shards everywhere, and continued to douse the furniture. Noticing that he had about a gallon left, he carefully poured a puddle from the living room, through the entry, out the door, and down the steps. He saturated the steps again, and then poured a line carefully down the paving stones leading from the front steps, and out to the edge of the circular driveway.

"Get the car," he shouted impatiently to the man who had been watching him throughout the operation, but who now ran off to his appointed task.

Bennett walked to the edge of the porch and threw the now empty gas can through the front door and back into the house. He then walked to the end of the gas trail just as the man drove up in a dark blue sedan. Bennett pulled out a couple of long matches he had picked up from the fireplace, and struck one against one of the paving stones. As the flame appeared he said, "This is for ruining my life Davis."

Then he reached over and threw the match quickly onto the still wet stones. Instantly, a flame appeared and started back along the line he had poured. Satisfied that his revenge was just about to be completed, he got into the car, watching as the flame now moved rapidly towards the house. He then closed the car door and said, "Let's go, quickly." The wheels of the sedan sprayed gravel as the arsonists and kidnappers took off down the lane, without looking back.

CHAPTER 15

Jared knew that Bennett's promise to not hurt Rachel had been a meaningless lie. Jared had seen the lie in Bennet's eyes and knew instantly that Bennet meant to kill her, eventually. Jared had kept tabs on Bennett for a short while after running him out of his Special Forces team and subsequently out of the service. Bennett had become a scheming, vindictive, son of a B who used morals only when it suited his mood and goals.

After he got Bennett cashiered from the service, Jared had found out that Bennett had joined the French Foreign Legion and then a couple of shady groups operating below the radar. Word on the street said it was CIA black ops down in South America, doing things that no one else had the stomach to do.

Part of the trouble with Bennett, besides his arrogance, was that he thought he was smart and while he was, to a degree, he was also careless. He didn't give a damn about anyone around him, which was against everything that Jared stood for. The first rule was duty to country. The second was taking care of each other, especially those under your command.

Bennett's personal self interest and carelessness had resulted in the deaths of two men on Jared's team. They had been good men, good soldiers and good friends who Jared had worked with for a long time. Jared had trained them personally and knew their families. 'It should have been Bennett that died instead of them...' he thought, for the millionth time.

All of those thoughts and memories came streaming back into Jared's mind when Bennett had removed his ski mask. He immediately had a gut feeling that whatever Bennett was up to, it wouldn't end well for Rachel, and, for that matter, probably not well for him either. He immediately started to think of ways to get out of this jam, without getting Rachel hurt, or killed.

When Bennett hit Rachel, Jared's blood had reached a boil. If he'd had a chance he would have torn Bennett limb from limb. When he was shot from behind with the taser, he knew that Bennett was purposely goading him, using Rachel to get to him and any effort he made to resist would only give Bennett an excuse to hurt Rachel more.

As Rachel passed out and hit the floor, Jared saw his chance. It took all of his willpower to withstand the 10,000 volt kick of electricity, but, he had mentally prepared for it the second time and knew it was coming. Even when they jacked up the juice, he willed his paralyzed muscles to obey; falling on top of Rachel had not been mere accident, and he hadn't kissed her ear when the pain had stopped. Desperately searching for something to help them out of this position, Jared had spied the bobby pin holding Rachel's hair behind her ear. It was a small chance, but the only one he could see at the moment and so, he had taken it. With his mouth close to her ear, he had clenched the bobby pin with his teeth and maneuvered it quickly so that it was hidden in his mouth.

As he was thrown into the car and the door shut, Jared assessed the situation. There was the driver sitting in front of him and another of the men standing by his door as a third man went around and opened both doors on the other side of the car. Jared coughed a couple of times and spit the bobby pin out onto the seat; he turned and picked up the pin with his hand.

He knew he had only a short time before Bennett did something to Rachel, and he needed to hurry. This might be his only chance and he had to make it good. He adjusted and squirmed in the seat as if he were trying to get comfortable while he positioned the bobby pin properly behind him. He turned his body, facing the man sliding into the car beside him while he frantically worked with the handcuffs and bobby pin. First, he had to bend it into the form of a small h, then insert it into the cuff's lock, just above the center pin.

He had practiced this move many times in the distant past, but it had never been a matter of life and death before. On the third try it worked and he had a wave of relief come over him as he felt the pressure from the handcuff on one wrist give way. The front door slammed shut and the guy sitting shotgun directed the driver, "To the airport," while the man sitting next to him pulled out a taser and pointed it in his direction.

It had been easy to see that these guys were not professionals, though they tried act like it. Their actions were careless and overconfident. Come to think of it, they were a lot like Bennett himself. *"Leave it to Bennett to surround himself with incompetence,"* he thought, but now, their sloppy work would be to his benefit, as he noticed the driver had neglected to activate the electronic door locks.

The car started and drove off down the dark road. Knowing the road, Jared waited until he timed his move perfectly. As the car slowed down for the right turn, just before crossing the larger bridge, there was a bump in the road, one that Jared had hit a hundred times. When the car hit it now, everyone jumped in their seats for a split second and Jared was ready when they did. While they were distracted by the jostling, he made two moves simultaneously. He quickly swung his right leg up and kicked the hand holding the taser, catching the guard completely by surprise when he did. The taser went off and the two barbs shot into the padded ceiling of the car. At the same time, Jared opened the car door with his free hand. The force of his kick against the taser combined with the force of the turning car, propelled him like a cannon out of the car and onto the dark, gravel road.

He rolled a couple of times and was up on his feet before the brake lights turned bright red and the car skidded on the gravel, to a stop. Four long strides and he was in a gully off the side of the road. Even though it was late spring, it was still a dry bed, which suited his situation perfectly now. As he ran down the ravine, he heard the shouts and curses coming from behind him.

Bennett had mentioned more than once, that whoever wanted him, wanted him alive, so Jared was counting on them not to shoot. Taking into consideration, however, the aptitude of these guys, he knew that they might forget that order and shoot anyway. Luckily, the sound of gunfire and bullets whizzing by him never came. Instead, he heard the car doors slam shut and one of the men cursing him. "Where did he go?" he yelled, while one of the others cautioned, "Remember, we need him alive."

It was pitch black among the trees now, so after running for just a few minutes along the streambed, when it made a sharp bend Jared climbed up the bank and into the forest. He moved silently through the trees, listening, but never heard any footsteps in pursuit. The stars were out, but the moon wasn't and he tried to recall what phase the moon would be in when it finally did come up, but he couldn't remember. He stopped and leaned against a tree while he worked on the other handcuff before it finally gave way, then, with a thought, placed the cuffs into his back pocket. Just then in the distance far behind him he saw the glow of three flashlights. *"Amateurs"* he thought with a thankful grin.

Jared knew exactly where he was as he had traveled this area many times on horseback. He circled around his pursuers and went back to the road. Some of his associates had said he was born with an internal compass, and tonight, it served him once again. Crossing the road, he walked along the edge of the trees until he came to where the car had been left. Though it was dark in the forest among the trees and the foliage, here in the open road, there was enough starlight for him to see clearly.

He approached the car from the side, cautiously, just in case one of the men had stayed behind. Once he was satisfied the car was empty, he popped his head up and checked to see if the keys had been left in the ignition. It was too dark inside the car for him to see and he thought to himself, *"No, even they aren't that stupid."* He resisted the impulse to open the door and be sure, because he knew that if he did so, the lights inside the car would probably turn on and reveal his location.

Debating for a few seconds on what to do, Jared decided that even if the keys were in the car, and he headed back to the house, he would probably run into Bennett again, and he didn't want that. With that thought, he fished the bobby pin out of his pocket, silently moved to the front of the car and let the air out of the tire. Watching the woods and listening intently he moved quietly to the back tire and did the same. When he had made sure Bennett's associates would have to travel on foot from here on out, he went back along the road walking briskly. He could barely see by the starlight here, but, it was enough. When he found the trail he was looking for, he turned off the road and disappeared into the black forest.

He knew he had to hurry and traveled as fast as he dared in the dim light. He could barely see the lighter shade of gray defining the edges of the trail, but it was enough and he started to jog. This trail, he knew, led straight to the side of his property, coming out of the woods near the barn.

He had been jogging for about three minutes when he heard a tremendous explosion that startled him. It was a deep explosion, like a bomb instead of a howitzer, dynamite, or mortar shell. "Oh hell," he swore under his breath, and began running faster.

CHAPTER 16

The explosion shook the house, blowing out all of the windows, displacing part of the roof and sending a huge fireball through the now vacant hole where the glass doors had been. The fumes from the gasoline and propane had filled the house, making it, in effect, a huge bomb, which was the effect that Bennett had wanted. After the explosion, flames immediately engulfed the entire inside of the home.

Bennett smiled as he heard the blast and looked back in time to see the fireball rise above the tops of the trees. He was pleased with the effect, *"Loose ends taken care of,"* he thought to himself.

The explosion woke Rachel up from a drowsy, pain filled sleep. Her head was pounding, she couldn't open her right eye, and her cheek hurt badly when she brought her hands to her face. It took her a minute, or two to awaken completely, but when she smelled the smoke and heard the crackling of the fire she roused herself. *"Where am I?"* she thought, confused by her close surroundings. *"What's going on? Why can't I see?"*

Rachel felt around as she moved her hands to the floor and turned over to kneel. She could feel the shoes and boots around her, and looking through the crack at the bottom of the door, she could see the red glow of flames on the other side. She started to stand up, but hit the clothes and heard the clatter of hangers. *"I'm in a closet,"* she suddenly realized.

Locating the metal door knob, she grasped it, but it was now hot from the fire in the entry and it caused her to jerk her hand away. She laid her hand carefully against the wood of the door, feeling the heat radiating through it. In an attempt to evaluate her situation, she thought, *"I'm in a closet, the house is on fire, and I can't get out."* By now, the smoke was starting to come in through the cracks around the door, causing her to cough. *"Okay, keep calm,"* she thought. *"I need to keep the smoke out."*

Rachel, reaching up, found what she thought was a light jacket and tore it down off its hanger stuffing it along the bottom of the door. Then, she felt along the floor to see if she could find something else of use. *"Shoe, boots, hangers, what's this?"* she thought to herself as she touched the contents of the closet strewn about her, on the floor. It took just a couple of seconds to identify the item she was holding as an old fashioned umbrella, not the collapsible kind she was used to. An idea sprang into her mind.

Standing up carefully now, Rachel pushed all of the clothes hanging on the rod down to one end of the closet to give herself some room. She grabbed the umbrella and started jabbing the metal tip of it into the wall at the back of the closet, near the floor, with all of her strength.

As a teenager she had helped her dad and brothers build the family house. She remembered her father yelling at her once for accidently sticking her foot through the drywall they were hanging. "Hey be careful," he had said. "It's not as thick as you think. This stuff is fragile and can easily be damaged."

As she jabbed harder and harder she felt the wall start to give way and then the hole in the wall getting bigger. Rachel jabbed harder yet through the middle of the hole and broke through the dry wall on the other side of the studs. By this time, her one good eye was stinging badly and the tears were streaming down her cheeks. Being locked in the closet was good, for one thing, in that it kept most of the smoke and heat outside longer, but she knew it would not last forever. Rachel needed to make her way out of this closet soon, before the smoke overtook her. She worker harder and with the exertion came even more coughing. She was beginning to see a trickle of light from the hole her work had produced and felt a slight rush of clean air coming into the closet, but it was what she didn't see that excited her the most. She didn't see any flames.

Rachel put the umbrella down and started pulling the sheetrock away with her bare hands finding the space between the studs. It would be tight, but she could make it. Sitting down on the floor of the closet and scooting as close to the wall as she could, she kicked with her feet at the other side of the wall, sending pieces of drywall flying. The low heels she was wearing for beauty suddenly had become functional as well, as they dug into the sheet rock.

Each kick broke another piece away, and with that, brought more light. Rachel could see that the room was bathed in an orange glow, but she didn't feel any heat yet and that brought her hope.

After a minute, she turned around and placed her face up next to the hole. It was a bedroom and it wasn't on fire. However, now she could see black smoke had already started filling the top half of the room. Rachel determined the smoke was still about two feet above the floor. *"Good enough,"* she thought, and she started the process of wiggling through the opening. She placed her arms above her head and pushed them through first to take advantage of the cleaner air in the bedroom. When she was about half way through, her pants caught on something for a minute, and she almost panicked not being able to progress forward, or backwards. Finally the fabric of her pants tore slightly and she was able to pull herself out completely into the bedroom. She lay on the floor panting for a moment.

Now, she could see the fire down the hall and realized in a few more minutes it would be in this bedroom as well. She crawled towards the doorway of the room, remembering to keep low. As she reached the opening she felt the heat of the flames on her face and hands and hastily grabbed the door and swung it shut. Instantly, the heat she had felt subsided. *"That should give me a few more minutes,"* She thought, just as the coughing started again. Rachel lay on the carpeted floor, face down, trying to control her hacking and wiping the tears away from her face so she could see. Her injured eye was swollen completely shut and throbbed steadily while her other eye had a constant stream of tears, reacting from the smoke.

Closing the door might have given her more time, but it had taken away her one source of light. As she lay on the floor in the darkened room, trying to control her breathing, she thought to herself *"What now?"* In answer to her own question she spoke out loud, perhaps in an attempt to summon strength for the next step. "I've got to get out of here, out of the house." Trying to remember the layout of the room she had seen before she had closed the door Rachel once again spoke to herself, "Where is the window?"

With that she turned around on her hands and knees and started crawling back in the direction of the bed. She tried to picture in her mind the probable layout of the room, and hoped that the bed was directly underneath the window. *"There is only one way to find out,"* She thought. As she reached the place where the bed was pushed up against the wall, she took a big breath, reached up, and grasped the blanket to help pull herself onto the bed. By the time her head rose to the top of the bed she was in the smoke so she closed her eyes. She couldn't see anything anyway, the smoke was thick and black.

Rachel crawled forward on the bed, and then, suddenly unable to hold her breath any longer, exhaled sharply. She couldn't stop the instinct to breathe in and inhaled a lung full of the smoke filled air. Immediately she started coughing hard, her body trying desperately to ride itself of the poison in her lungs. With that, she started to panic, and the coughing became even more violent. She was about to the point of retching when, in the middle of a spasm, she felt a brief gust of fresh air. Her spirit immediately lifted; she had guessed right. The window was here, and it was open, she was going to escape.

Rachel forced herself to calm down and think clearly. She put her face into the pillow at the head of the bed and breathed in, filtering the air as she did so. That seemed to help and the coughing abated. Rachel took as deep a breath as possible and pulled herself to a kneeling position on the pillows, feeling up, along the wall for the window sill. When she found it and pulled herself up, she held her face close to the sill. The fresh air flow was stronger now and she allowed herself a deep breath of almost completely clean air.

Rachel reached up to push out the screen, still with closed eyes, but it wasn't there. As she groped around to find the edge of the window, she suddenly felt a sharp pain and jerked her hand back away from the window. Not knowing what had hurt her hand, she opened her eyes. As she did so, she looked out the window, the light from the fire lit up the sky and she could see that the window was gone, except a ridge of sharp broken pieces still clinging to the frame. Without hesitation, Rachel lifted her knee, pulled the bedcovers back and grabbed the pillow out from under her. She draped it over the window sill laden with shards of broken glass.

Suddenly, she felt dizzy, and paused for a moment to try and clear her head. *"I can do this"*...she thought with determination. Rachel reached over, grabbed the other pillow and placed it on top of the first. Now she stood where the pillows had been, and reaching down, grabbed as many of the covers as she could, pulling them up, and pushing them out of the broken window. Using the blankets to shield her hands, she then pulled herself up, leaned her body forward, and with a deep breath for courage, gave a push that propelled her out of the window, head first, covered in blankets. She was out of the house.

Lying on her back, where she had landed, Rachel opened her one good eye and saw a black sky and the stars above her. She tried to move her right hand, but it was trapped in the blanket beneath her. Her left hand stung badly from the cut and her eye teared up again. But this time, she closed it and began to cry, not even attempting to hold back. These were tears of joy and gratitude; she was alive and breathing fresh air.

Her reprieve lasted for only a moment, before she was startled by a small explosion, then another, and another. Suddenly, Rachel became aware of the loud roar and crackling of the fire. It was a deafening noise that was making it difficult for her to reason.

An instinctual desire for self preservation took over and the thought came to her mind, *"I've got to get away from here, away from the house."* Every inch of her body hurt and the exhaustion was almost overpowering, she so badly wanted to just lay there and rest. Once again, something else took over, clearing her mind and the thought came again, *"This is still a dangerous place to be, I have to get away from here.*" She slowly rolled to her side until she was up on her knees freeing her right arm. Then, she slowly stood, up resting her head against the wall of the house. She turned around and leaned her back against the wall, looking around. Rachel was standing on the side of the house closest to the barn. She could see the red of the barn and the greenhouse walls that were reflecting the flames coming from the house. She pushed herself away from the wall, and staggering slightly, made her way to the barn, gaining strength with each step.

As she got to the edge of the structure, she turned around to look at the house. It was totally engulfed, with flames and smoke shooting up into the night sky, lighting up the forest around the clearing. Even from this distance, Rachel could feel the heat of the flames. As she gazed in horror at the scene, she was suddenly struck by a thought too frightening to ignore. *"What if they're out here somewhere, watching the fire too? They might see me and come back to finish their job."* The thought panicked her. Suddenly, she turned and ran past the barn and greenhouse, in the direction of the back of the property, towards the forest. As she rounded the barn, she saw the small cabin Jared had told her about, but she couldn't stop. She began to run, in earnest now, towards the edge of the forest, towards the darkness, to safety.

Rachel reached the edge of the woods in just a few minutes, but didn't stop running until she had run another ten feet, or so. Finally, she did stop and hid, cowering behind a tall pine. She peered around it, looking, not at the house, but past it, into the darkness, searching for something she couldn't see. Just then, near the trees by the side of the barn where she had been, she saw the figure of a man walk out into the clearing. The fear rose up in her throat as she watched, trembling. But, he wasn't looking at the fire, he was looking, could it be... he was looking straight at her. She was sure of it. Then, without warning, the man ran to the barn and disappeared into the shadows. He reappeared almost as quickly as he had vanished carrying something in his hands. From this distance Rachel could see it was a large ax. He started running, heading for the trees close to the barn, but now angling towards her. Just before he entered the darkness of the forest, he glanced once more in her direction and then disappeared into the shadows. The fear grew within her and she held her breath...she knew he was coming to kill her.

CHAPTER 17

The fear that gripped her was unlike anything she had ever experienced before. Rachel had an uncontrollable urge to scream at the top of her lungs, but she resisted.

"Run! Run and hide!" The thought screamed in her head. Rachel turned around, looking away from the flaming house and into the dark forest. For a moment, she couldn't see in the darkness and the panic resurfaced. *"He's coming,"* she thought. Gradually, her eyes began to adjust to the dim light; she could make out the trunks of the trees now and with the increased vision started walking quickly, deep into the woods. As she walked, a branch she hadn't seen scraped at her face, close to her good eye, catching some strands of her hair and pulling it as she passed. Instinctively, she raised her arm and brushed it away. The farther she went into the woods, the darker it became and now she could hardly see anything. She walked with one arm stretched out in front of her, the other shielding her head and face. She noticed with every step she took, there was a rustling of leaves and an occasional snapping of twigs. The sounds were audible now that the roar of the fire had been put behind her.

Rachel stopped and paused for a minute, leaning back against a large tree. She tried to collect her thoughts, and realized that she was breathing hard and loudly, so she tried immediately to quiet her breathing, but failed. It was so dark she really couldn't see, but, she thought, *"he can't see either...unless he has a flashlight and I could see that."* Rachel crouched down, and peeked around the trunk of the tree with her one good eye. She was looking for any lights now, and saw nothing. By this, and at this distance, there was just the slightest glow of the fire through the trees.

Just then, she heard a twig snap. Instantly, she froze, holding her breath. She couldn't tell how far away it was, but thought she could tell the direction it came from. *"He's coming and maybe he can see,"* She thought. *"I need to find a place to hide. Some place dark. But, if I move, he'll hear me."* Her thoughts were only partially frantic and she couldn't make up her mind what to do. She huddled, next to the tree, drawing her knees in close to her chest and resting her head between them. She tried to make herself as small as possible, invisible in the darkness.

Rachel was brought alert by a loud sound, over to her right which startled her and caused her to half jump up, making her own noise. The noise was close and she had just given her position away. Standing up, Rachel started to walk as quietly as she could away from the direction of the sound she had heard, arms outstretched, in front of her face.

Then, close by to the left she heard another noise. *"Maybe there are two of them,"* she thought. Without taking time to think through her actions, Rachel started to run off to her right, head down, trying to see the darker shadow of the trees with her good eye, arms out in front. She heard the footsteps behind her; they were loud now and getting closer. She brushed a tree and went through some branches. She was making plenty of noise now, but all she could think about was getting away. The footsteps were coming faster...and they were right behind her. She started to pray as she ran... *"Heavenly Father, please don't let me die, please, please, please."* She hit a tree hard and bounced off of it, which almost knocked her down. Stumbling now, she tried to start running again and just as she did so, she stepped into a hole and went down. The pain in her ankle was sharp and she let out an involuntary yelp as she fell with her foot still stuck in the hole. Rachel tried to dislodge her foot, but, tremendous pain shot up from her ankle through her leg. She couldn't move, and just lay there, as fear overtook her with a vise like grip.

She heard a noisy snap of a branch and footsteps running towards her. Again, she began to plead in silent prayer, *"Please, Heavenly Father, don't let me die like this. Please..."* Gathering her courage to endure the pain, she pulled again and her foot came out of the hole. Slowly she stood up on one leg, determined to hop away if she had to. As she took one step, testing her hurt ankle, the pain shot up her leg again, but, this time she didn't cry out. Just then, Rachel was distracted by a noise behind her. Turning toward the sound, she felt a huge form run into her that knocked her off her feet. As she and the man fell, he landed on top of her, knocking the air out of her lungs in one great exhale of breath. Her head hit the hard ground, and she saw stars. Trying to keep consciousness, she felt the man on top of her, pinning her body with his weight, his hands holding her hands in a vise like grip spread eagled out, and felt his breath on her face. It was then she heard a whisper, "Rachel, is that you?"

JARED

When Jared heard the explosion, he increased his speed to something like that of a deer. He knew the trail pretty well and though it was very dark, he could see just enough of the path to keep on track and not run into a tree. After only a few minutes, he could see the slight glow of the distant fire through the trees. *"Oh, NO!"* he thought, *"they're burning the house down! Where's Rachel?"* It took another ten minutes, or so, before he came to the clearing.

As he approached the edge of his property coming out of the trees near the barn, it was as he feared. The house was totally engulfed by the fire. Huge flames shot out from the back and the front of the house, lighting up the entire clearing. Black smoke tinged with red, billowed upwards into the night with sparks, first shooting into the sky, and then drifting back down to the earth. The roar and crackling of the fire was tremendous.

As he watched, the flames started shooting out of the bedroom window facing him. *"I'm too late,"* he thought with sadness.

Jared looked for a possible way into the house, not ready to accept his fears as fact, but it was totally over run with the fire. Despair shook him. He could think of only one thing. *"Rachel, what have I done to you?"* He knew that Bennett meant to kill her. It had been a gut feeling and his gut feelings were never wrong.

That was why he was still alive.

Then, his blood began to boil with anger in a way he had never experienced before. The emotion swept over him with his next thought, *"Bennett has killed her. Bennett, and whoever he worked for, has killed her."* Then one word entered his mind and refused to be moved, *"**Revenge**."* He would track down and kill whoever had hurt her. They would pay. Bennett would pay the price for his crimes. He would administer justice. He didn't care how long it took; Bennett, and the others involved, would pay with their very lives. A guilty life, for an innocent life.

At that moment, out of the corner of his eye, Jared saw a movement near the edge of the forest. He saw a dark figure moving among the trees and turned just in time to see it disappear into the shadows. *'They must have left someone to watch,'* he thought. It wouldn't be Bennett; it was one of the others. That was alright, he would be the first to pay for Rachel. Ultimately, they all would pay the same price, but this one was here now. He had helped in the misdeeds of this night and he would pay the price. This was a war now, and he had killed in war before.

Jared needed a weapon, but, didn't have time to get anything. *"Except, yes,"* he thought, as he quickly ran over to the back of the barn near the cabin, and grabbed the ax he used to cut fire wood. *"This will do,"* he thought, hefting the heavy ax in his hands. He glanced again quickly to the spot where he had seen the shadowy figure, consumed with the thought of revenge for Rachel's death. He was in full combat mode now, a hunter seeking his enemy to destroy him.

He ran to the edge of the forest closest to him, looked again, making a mental note of the distance to the spot where the person had stood, and entered the forest. Near this edge of the clearing was a horse trail that he often used. He started jogging along it, solidifying his plans and making mental notes as he went along.

"They have guns so I need to be cautious. I can easily stalk them, I know these woods, and they don't. I definitely have the advantage. And they probably don't have any night vision with them." He hadn't seen any on them at the house and the three who chased him from the car used flashlights. He thought, with some satisfaction, *"They are amateurs...and probably have never been in real combat."* Jared had played this game of life and death, of hunting and being hunted, in thick jungles in Central America, and in the back streets of desert cites. He knew this game well and he would win because he knew all of the tricks.

As he arrived at the spot where he figured the person had been, he slowed down, stopped and listened. Then, he silently slipped off his shoes, leaving his socks on. In this forest and darkness, this would be a game of sound. His feet would probably get bloody and sore, the socks would help a little, but hard shoes made too much noise. He reached down and by the light of his burning home, picked up two rocks and a large stick. This would do.

Jared started moving deeper into the forest, slowly at first, and listening. He stopped and closed his eyes. That was when he heard the sounds he was listening for...footsteps. *"Good,"* Jared thought, *"I'm heading in the right direction."* He opened his eyes and started walking quickly in the direction of the footsteps, feeling with his feet...in what his grandfather used to call Indian, or hunter fashion. Using his peripheral vision, he scanned the area as he walked. He had learned long ago that in the dark you could see better using the periphery of your eyesight rather than looking directly at something. He had always had good night vision and was pleased to see it still worked.

Jared started moving faster, every once in a while hearing a sound and adjusting his direction. This person was definitely an amateur, moving in generally the same direction, with no change of direction, or circling around. His left hand gripped the handle of the ax tighter in anticipation of the confrontation he soon would have.

Another sound, like branches brushing clothing, caught his attention. It wasn't too far ahead. He quickened his pace just a little. Just then, he stepped onto a small branch and it broke, breaking the silence he was trying to maintain. *'Damn.'* He froze and then quickly and quietly stepped two paces to the left and crouched down. He expected to hear a gun go off, but nothing happened. All was quiet once again. *'Let's see what this does,'* he thought, as he stood up and threw the large branch he had been carrying over to the right. It landed with a thud that he knew would be easily heard by his quarry.

Almost immediately, he heard movements and then footsteps again, walking quickly. *"Works every time..."* he thought. He started towards the sound of the footsteps, judging it to be only twenty to thirty yards ahead. He picked up his pace in anticipation, angling to his left, away from the noise, hopefully cutting off the person ahead, who was now, running away from the noise of the branch. In his hurry, Jared brushed by an overhanging branch and made another unwelcome sound.

Immediately, the footsteps were running and they were very close. Jared picked up his pace and started the chase. His quarry had been flushed from cover and the stalking was over. He had wanted to get ahead of them and try to set up an ambush, but now the race was on. The person ahead of him was now making enough noise that he instinctively matched the timing of his steps...hoping to hide the sound of his own footfall. The sounds of swishes and someone going through branches helped determine his direction as he ran. They weren't even trying to hide their sounds now.

The footsteps went faster and so did he. He gripped the ax with both hands now in expectation of the encounter. Suddenly, there was a loud noise and cry. Obviously his prey had tripped and fallen, just up ahead. But, now his mind, made cloudy by the flood of emotions since coming upon the fire, was registering that something was wrong, but in the heat of his emotions and the chase, he did not register what it was. He slowed his steps now, listening and looking hard out of the corner of his eye for a flash of skin, a shadow, or anything.

He gripped the ax tightly, drawing closer. It was then that he heard the sound and saw the shadow rise up, right in front of him. He quickly dropped the ax, took a step, and lunged at the shadow person, tackling him and driving him to the ground. As they fell, Jared's hands searched for his enemy's hands to gain control of the gun that he was sure to be holding. However, when they landed on the ground, with Jared on top, the sound coming from the person under him was not that of a man. Jared was slightly disoriented, "*Could one of them be a woman?*" he asked himself. The possibility made him pause, preventing the transition into full combat mode.

He lay there for a second on top of...whoever it was. The person underneath him did not try to struggle. Their faces were close, and as he breathed, he smelled her perfume. But, this was not just any woman's perfume, this scent was familiar and brought with it a string of emotions that culminated with a sense of profound relief that enveloped him at just the thought, the possibility. He had to know... "Rachel" he asked, "is that you?"

CHAPTER 18

"Jared?" came the whispered, confused, questioning response from the, now obvious, woman he was pinning to the ground. It was Rachel's voice, uttered between gulps of air.

Hearing her voice was answer enough, and Jared raised himself up, and then rolled off of Rachel to lie beside her on the ground.

"I thought they had killed you." He said still recovering from the wonderful shock. "I thought you were dead."

"They tried, but I got out," Rachel began to explain. "I thought you were one of them and so, I ran." She was nearly in tears now with the abrupt ending of the chase, the flow of adrenalin, and the pain of her wounds.

"I thought you were one of them, and I was going to kill you..." Jared paused, and grinned, realizing that what he was going to say to finish his sentence, became rather comical, but, he finished it anyway. "...For killing you." However, the humor was a luxury that could not last. While the immediate danger had passed for both of them, there still a lurking danger that had to be faced, and dealt with.

Rachel, missed the humor. "Ohhh," she moaned. Just then, everything seemed to hurt at once. "Can I go home now?" she asked, sounding a little like a tired child after a long day of play. Jared remembered Bennett hitting Rachel with his gun, her being choked unconscious, and then being dropped face first on the floor.

"I wish it were that easy," Jared responded, coming back to a full sense of their situation. "But probably not. We need to get out of here and go someplace safe. They're probably looking for me right now, and if they find us, it will not go well." He paused for a moment, and then continued. "I think I know of a place where we can go, and I think I can even get us there. We need to be quiet though. Let's go." Jared stood up and grabbed her hand to pull her up.

Rachel jerked her hand away. "Not that hand," she said. "I have a bad cut there. And I don't think I can stand up anyway, I'm pretty sure my ankle is broken."

Jared reached down and gently felt her ankle. She cried out softly at the pain of his touch. "No bones sticking out," He said quietly. "I can carry you; it's not far from here. Can you stand on your good foot and climb on onto my back, or do you want me to carry you over the shoulder?"

Resigned to the fact that, either way, she would not be able to travel on her own volition, Rachel answered, "Let's try piggy back." Jared knelt down as she got to her knees, then climbed onto his back. He straightened up, paused a minute to get his bearings, and said "I think we go this way"... and started off into the darkness.

As they moved through the forest, they approached several strings of barbed wire Jared could just barely make out in the darkness. Jared spoke softly, "If you had kept going, you would have run right into this barbed wire fence. It would have been nasty." Rachel could just make it out as Jared turned and walked along it. All of a sudden, the sound of sirens pierced the night and they knew that someone had finally reported the fire.

Jared, with Rachel on his back, walked in the darkness for another fifteen minutes, finally reaching a house in a clearing. Jared explained, "This is the house of my friend who owns the horses." Rachel remembered Jared's earlier account of his generous neighbor. That conversation seemed like it had been days ago instead of just a few hours.

Jared, with Rachel still on his back, went to the back door. He reached up and retrieved a key from one of the cross beams in the porch roof. Unlocking the door, they entered the kitchen. Jared walked over to the refrigerator and turned on the small light near the ice dispenser, then backed up to the table, and gently deposited Rachel on top of it. Jared was worried that any more light might attract attention that they were definitely trying to avoid.

Jared started opening kitchen drawers. On the third try, he found a small paring knife and tested its sharpness on his left arm. It was extremely sharp and easily shaved off a small patch of hair. He pulled some paper towels from a dispenser under the cabinet and, after searching through a couple more drawers, found a small roll of duct tape. "This will have to do," he said.

Turning to Rachel, Jared asked solemnly, "Before we go any further, I have to ask you to do something very important. I need you to cut something out of my back. Are you up to it?"

"What?" Rachel asked him, not understanding his request.

Jared knew that his explanation might startle her, but he had no other recourse; this needed to be done now. "I carry a special military tracking device in my shoulder. These men who nearly killed us could make a couple of phone calls, and know exactly where we are. I figure they will probably figure that out and get a fix on me in about half an hour. You need to cut this chip out of my shoulder so they can't track me. It should be easy. It is just under the skin near my shoulder blade."

Now Rachel understood why he had searched for a knife so quickly. The experiences of this evening continued to take her down unexpected and perilous paths, but she was a willing participant now, not seeing any other options. "Okay," she answered with resignation. "But, I'll need more light. I can't see well enough to perform surgery." She tried to make that last comment sound a little like a joke and realized it was the truth.

Ignoring her attempt at humor, Jared suggested,

"Let's move to the bathroom then. It's an inside bathroom without any windows. Climb back on." Jared turned his back towards her, scooting in closely so she could resume her position.

Rachel refused, and said, "Just let me lean on you. I think I can make it with your help."

"Alright." Jared said and helped her down from the table so that she was standing on her one good foot. He draped her arm around his neck, placed his arm firmly around her waist, and helped her into the bathroom, pretty much carrying her anyway.

Within ten minutes the surgery had been performed and the chip was out. Rachel had used a piece of the paper towel as a bandage and duct taped it to the shallow wound. While he put his shirt back on, he asked, "I need to ask you Rachel, have you been chipped?"

She knew he was referring to the fact that almost all of the U.S. population had been implanted with the Federal I.D. chip. Very few people used cash anymore, and the chip had made payments and purchases so convenient that most people gladly accepted the device.

"No," Rachel replied adamantly, "I'm not chipped. I could never bring myself to have that thing inserted into me, especially not after all I've been learning lately."

"Good," Jared said with relief. "We can go then."

The bathroom light was turned off, and Jared helped Rachel out the back door, and to the side of the house, stopping only long enough to pick up a key hanging by the door.

After helping Rachel into the passenger side, Jared got in and started the ten year old Ford F-150 pickup truck, driving off without turning on any of the lights. Jared said, "There's a back road here that he uses to reach the county road to get fire wood. This is a pretty round about way to get us where we are going, but, we can get there without having to go on any of the main highways."

They bounced along a rutted, dirt road not much more than a worn path among the trees for a few minutes, eventually coming out onto a smooth dirt road. Every bounce and jiggle made her ankle hurt, shooting pain up her leg. Rachel just grimaced and bore it in silence. Jared kept the lights off the whole time.

In about ten minutes they reached a smooth, paved road where Jared turned on the head lights, opened the window, and tossed the chip out into the brush.

When he rolled up the window, he turned to Rachel and said, "We should be there in about twenty minutes. Hang on Rachel, we'll get you taken care of."

She didn't say anything, but gratefully, leaned up against him, laid her head on his shoulder and closed her eyes. In a few minutes she was sound asleep. The adrenaline produced by all of the excitement had finally worn off and the exhaustion had taken over. When they passed a street light Jared took his first really good look at her since their sudden encounter in the forest. Her dark red hair was almost black with soot and hung in a messy tangle with leaves and twigs still attached. Her face was caked with a combination of black soot, blood, and smeared tears. Her right eye was swollen shut, but the cut on her cheek had stopped bleeding some time ago, and now had crusted blood on and around the wound. The tears she had cried had caused the blood and mud to streak down her face, and her clothes were in the same pitiful condition, torn and smudged with soot, dirt, and spots of blood. He remembered how beautiful she had been upon her arrival this afternoon and that her blouse had been a lovely lime green.

He looked at her now and realized that she was still beautiful. Quietly, he whispered to himself, "Oh Rachel, what have I done to you."

CHAPTER 19

Bennett was chuckling to himself with satisfaction, until he came around the bend and saw the car. He had his door open and was stepping out before the car he was riding in came to a complete stop. He marched up to the abandoned car and looked in, trying to open the drivers' side door. It was locked. Looking around, Bennett used the light from his car's headlights to inspect the ground around the vehicle. He saw footsteps in the dirt all heading off in the direction of the woods to the left. He balled up his fist and hit the top of the car with a burst of fury. "Those *%@#% idiots," he shouted.

Bennett saw a distant light in the forest off in the direction the footsteps had traveled. He called the names of his associates loudly into the night, and shortly, they emerged from the woods. After their story of the escape, Bennett thought for just a moment before he directed with confidence, "I know where he is headed...back to the house, fast." They all jumped into their vehicles and Bennett's car had already started it's turn when the driver in the other car discovered the problem with the tires. With all four of their car doors opening at the same time, Bennett's driver turned to him and said softly, "Sir, there appears to be a problem."

After assessing the damage, Bennett changed his mind, instructing them to drive the car in it's present condition, and follow him with it's two tires flapping as they limped along. After about ten minutes, Bennett spied another side road and on a hunch, directed his driver to turn off.

Parking so as to take advantage of the lights from Bennett's car, they secured the spare tires from both vehicles and in about ten minutes were ready to go. While the tires were being changed, Bennett made a phone call starting the process to trace Jared's chip. Just as they were replacing the tools, they heard the approaching sirens. Realizing that they were too late to search as he wanted, Bennett advised his men to turn off the cars headlights, remove their black stealth clothes and apparatus, and to look as normal as possible. Through the trees, they watched as one police car passed them, then another, followed finally by a volunteer fire truck. Slowly, they pulled out, turned on their lights, and tagged slowly along behind the procession, with an apparent casual interest in the raging fire.

As Bennett and his men pulled up, the pumper truck was unrolling its hose. In the distance they heard another siren approaching. *"Probably another fire truck,"* Bennett thought.

Bennett walked straight up to the Sheriff's deputy, watching the firemen unload their truck. He identified himself and his men as federal agents that just happened to be in the area, and having heard the explosion and seen the smoke came to offer their assistance.

The deputy responded gratefully that things seemed to be under control, but, he appreciated the offer. When asked whose house it was, the deputy said that he didn't know yet, but would shortly. "It's probably some rich guy's house; there are lots of them up around here." He then went on, "We found a rental car sitting in the driveway with some women's luggage in it. We called to see who rented it and we're just waiting to hear the report. The house is pretty much destroyed," he said matter-of-factly. "And the guys will just try to contain it and keep it from spreading to the other buildings and the forest."

Bennett asked if the deputy thought the fire was suspicious in nature, or just an accident. The deputy responded, saying, that the cause had not yet been determined and that an arson investigation team would be dispatched in the morning to check it out, just as soon as it was possible. There had been problems lately with vandalism in the area, so this fire would be investigated thoroughly.

While Bennett was talking to the deputy, his men had scattered about the area doing their own reconnaissance. Just as he and the deputy finished talking, his cell phone rang. They had the number of Jared's chip and could now track it real time. Currently it was about five miles from their location and it wasn't moving.

Bennett finished the phone call and had the

coordinates transferred to his cell phone as he was joined by his five henchmen. He gave them a one word question, "Well?" to which they all shook their heads. "OK, let's go then," he commanded quickly. "We have a lock on his coordinates." About forty five minutes later, after searching in the heavy brush, and finally discovering the discarded chip, the string of profanity had begun and continued all the way back to the Show Low airport.

On the drive back Bennett's anger escalated with each minute, and mile that passed, with the tiniest addition of an emotion he rarely felt... fear. However, by the time they arrived back in Ogden, Bennett had his cover story ready for the report on the failure of his mission. The excuse would be that someone must have tipped Jared off. He had disappeared and set a booby trap for them at his house. As part of the fabricated story, he planned to say that it appeared Jared still had friends everywhere, with Intel about their plans, and he would encourage his higher ups to start looking for the informant, as he would surely do in his own office.

CHAPTER 20

The next thing Rachel knew, upon awakening, was that she was in Jared's arms in front of a wooden door, and it was still night. She mumbled drowsily, "Where are we?"

Jared replied softly, "at Granny's...everything is going to be alright." He added as he adjusted her body in his arms. "Just hang in there. I think you're in a little bit of shock."

The small yellow porch light came on and there was a thin voice on the other side of the door asking, "Who is it?"

Jared answered in a whisper, "Granny, it's me, Jared. Open up. I need your help. I have someone with me who's hurt."

The door slowly opened and a small face peeked out of the door, still held by a chain. "Oh, it's you," she said in surprise. Then, seeing the girl in Jared's arms she asked, "What happened?" Without waiting for a response, the door closed, and the voice added, "Give me a minute." Jared could hear the chain lock being undone, then the door was opened up fully and the screen door pushed aside.

Granny was about five feet two inches tall, and

thin as a rail. He didn't know for sure, but he guessed her age to be about eighty-five, though you would never know it from looking at her. She had the appearance and behavior of a spry sixty year old. The only clues as to her true age were some of the dated photos on her mantel that Jared had seen before.

Granny immediately took control of the situation. "You bring her right in here out of the night air and just put her down on the couch there," the little woman directed him, with authority that he knew well, and respected. "Let me go get my bag," She said as she disappeared into another room. Moving quickly, she returned just a minute later.

"Alright dear," directing her question now to Rachel, "what happened?" Then, after a second thought, correcting herself, and stopping whatever answer Rachel might have been considering, she said "Never mind; that can wait. Where do you hurt besides your face?" She asked soothingly. She was already daubing at Rachel's face with a damp cloth, wiping away some of the soot, and very carefully cleaning the cut on her cheek.

By this time Rachel was more alert, but finding it difficult to put into words all that had happened to them; she didn't know where to start.

Jared decided to help by answering the old woman's question for Rachel. "Nothing life threatening Granny, but, I think her ankle may be broken and there is a cut on her hand."

"That's nice Jared," Granny spoke in a condescending tone, "but I wasn't talking to you. I was asking her." Looking now into Rachel's eyes, she asked her directly, "Dear, where do you hurt the most?"

Rachel responded softly, "my ankle."

Granny lifted Rachel's pant leg and looked at her ankle. "Can you wiggle your toes? Can you move your foot?"

"Yes" Rachel answered wincing as she did so, ", but it is extremely painful."

"Well, it is pretty swollen. How long ago did this happen?" Now Granny's look invited Jared to share the information she needed.

"About an hour ago." Jared answered.

Granny removed Rachel's scuffed up shoe and dropped it to the floor as she gently felt the swollen ankle. She reached over and grabbed a throw pillow from the corner of the couch, lifted Rachel's leg, and put it under the foot. Rachel thought to herself that Granny was stronger than she had first appeared. While the old woman did this she spoke, once again with gentle, but firm, direction and confidence. "Jared, go in the kitchen and get me some ice from the refrigerator, will you? Put the ice in a bowl and bring it to me. That's a good boy."

With that Jared left the room.

Granny then reached down into what looked like an old time doctor's satchel, but larger, and pulled out a plastic bag, and a small jar of ointment. She laid them on the floor next to where she was kneeling. As she worked on Rachel she explained calmly, "I'm going to check a few other places to make sure that nothing else is broken dear, please tell me if it hurts."

She began pressing on Rachel's left leg, starting just above the ankle and continuing up to her waist, then switched to the other leg, and repeated the process. Finding no additional injuries on her legs, she continued the examination by poking gently around her ribs.

"Ouch, that hurts a little," she said as Granny touched a spot on her side.

"Hmmm, you might have a bruised rib, but I'm pretty sure it isn't broken." Granny checked both arms and her neck, and finally looked at the palm of Rachel's left hand. She dabbed at it a little with her damp cloth, carefully cleaning around the wound with the touch of experience. It started to bleed a little. "That might need a couple of stitches, but we will see." Granny's tone, when speaking to her, was much different than when she spoke to Jared. To her it was soothing and kind. A wonderful change from the previous encounters she'd had tonight.

By this time, Jared had returned with the bowl of ice and stood there watching. Granny turned, handed him the plastic bag she had pulled out, and instructed, "Put some of that ice into this bag and put it on that ankle." Then, she added a reminder, "and be gentle."

Turning to Rachel, she warned, "This is going to hurt a little, but, it should help the swelling and lessen the damage. I don't think it's broken, but, it is at the least, a very nasty sprain." She watched Jared gently put the bag on the ankle. Rachel clenched her fists a little and made a face, but, said nothing.

Granny went into the kitchen and brought back a chair to sit on. As she sat it down, she commented with a smile, "I'm not as spry as I used to be and kneeling too long begins to be a little uncomfortable. Ok, let's look a little more at that eye, shall we?" she said as she tenderly pushed Rachel's matted hair away from her face, and washed a little more of the soot and dirt away. "Doesn't look like anything else was damaged, can you see with your eye honey?"

Rachel forced her swollen eye open just a crack and replied hesitantly, "Yes."

Granny's attention left the eye, and she started washing more of Rachel's face. While she was doing this, she spoke to Jared. "Would you like to tell me now, how this pretty girl got all beat up?"

"Well, the short version," Jared began, "Is that we were having dinner at my house..." At this, Granny paused a moment, lifting her hand away from Rachel's face for just a split second. With the slightest hint of a grin on her wrinkled face, she resumed her task of washing the soot off of Rachel's face. Rachel caught the look of surprise in Granny's face with her one good eye, and realized there was a story to be told that unfortunately would have to wait.

Jared continued, "Some men broke into the house, basically to kidnap me. It was Rachel's bad luck to be a witness to the plan, so they tried to kill her and burn down the house. Rachel managed to escape from them, but, not without sustaining some injuries along the way."

"Is this true?" Granny asked Rachel with genuine concern in her voice.

Rachel whispered, "Yes." As tears welled up in her eyes and she began to cry silently, burying her head in the back of the couch, away from Granny and Jared.

Granny kindly soothed Rachel, stroking her tangled hair and hushing her softly, "There, there, it's going to be all right. You're safe here; no one is going to harm you now." The woman went on with determination. "Granny will take good care of you. You just relax and leave everything to JD and me. We'll have you up and around in no time."

Granny opened the little jar beside her, and started to spread the ointment on Rachel's face, cautiously placing some on the laceration. She added some more of the salve to a small piece of gauze, and placed it lightly, over the wound.

"This will help heal it quickly, and reduce the swelling a little." She cut some surgical tape and deftly secured the gauze to Rachel's face. After finishing the procedure, she went on to the injury on Rachel's hand, and spoke once again to her willing assistant.

"JD, in the freezer is a small bag of frozen peas; would you go get that for me?" It was a rhetorical question with no need of response.

Jared returned quickly, handing Granny the bag of peas. Granny hit the bag to the floor once to break up the frozen contents, and make it a little more pliable, then placed it carefully over Rachel's swollen eye.

"Ok." Granny announced with some satisfaction at completing her task. "That is as good as we can do for now. The best thing for you now is to get some sleep, honey. Then in the morning we can get you really cleaned up." She turned to Jared now, "JD, do you think you could pick her up, along with this pillow, and carry her upstairs into the spare bedroom?"

Rachel watched with her one good eye, that wasn't covered with the bag of frozen peas, and looked at Jared as he dutifully reached down and picked her up while Granny observed.

Granny said to Rachel, "Can you hold this bag in place while he carries you up?" Rachel reached up with her good hand and dutifully put it over the bag of peas.

Jared quickly carried her up the stairs, following

Granny, down the hall and into a small room with an old fashioned four poster bed. Granny leaned over and turned down the covers.

Granny guided Jared, "Just set her here on the bed."

Jared did as he was told, gently placing Rachel on the springy mattress.

"If you like honey," Granny offered, "I can send JD out and help you get undressed. I have an old nightgown that you can use."

"Yes, please," Rachel responded thankfully. "I am so filthy; it would feel good to get out of these clothes."

As Jared left the room he could hear granny say, "The bathroom is right through that door there. Here let me help you up, just lean on me..." then, closing the door he went down the stairs. He had a lot to think about.

Twenty minutes later, Granny came down the stairs and found him sitting on the couch. She sat down in an old wooden rocker, and started rocking briskly, as she always did when something was on her mind. She gave the report she knew he was waiting for, "She is already asleep, poor dear."

She sighed, and then asked. "Why would anyone want to hurt you? Why would anyone want to hurt that pretty girl, and burn your house down?" Then unexpectedly, she asked, "Could it be because she is a

Mormon and you were with her? It has been happening a lot lately, I hear."

Jared shook his head slowly. "No, they were after me. She just happened to be in the wrong place at the wrong time. But, how did you know that she was a Mormon? I never mentioned that, did she?"

Granny gave him a knowing little wink and reassured him, "I have my ways, JD." She rocked for another couple minutes, and then asked with sincerity, "Why would anyone want to hurt you?"

"I don't know," Jared responded, "but, I'm going to find out. The guy who came after me has an old score to settle, and a grudge he has been carrying for a long time. He was once a member of my team, but was responsible for the deaths of two of our team members, because of his sloppiness. I had him thrown out of the service for it. However, he contended tonight that he was under orders from someone else, someone who needed my services, and was told to come and get me.

"Anyway, they took me away in handcuffs, knocked Rachel out, and then set fire to the house with Rachel in it. She managed to get out. When I got away from them, I immediately ran back to help her, but they had already gone. I found Rachel in the woods a little worse for the wear, but, at least she was alive. I thought they had killed her." The tone in his voice did not go unnoticed by the perceptive old woman. "I had no place else to go. I thought about you, and knew that you could fix her up."

Granny nodded. "You did the right thing, JD. That's me, that's what I do, fix people up, just like I did for you." She continued her steady rocking, in silence, for a few minutes. "What are you going to do next?" she asked.

"I'm not sure," he answered honestly, "but, I know that they'll be looking for me. I don't know if they know yet that she got away, but they will figure that out in a day, or two. Then they will be looking for her too...to try and finish the job they failed tonight. I'm not so worried about me...but, I am worried about her."

There was silence in the house now, except for the creaking of Granny's wooden rocker as both of them were lost in their thoughts.

Granny spoke up after some contemplation, "If you need a place to stay, then you are welcome to stay here until you figure out what to do next." Then, with a little chuckle to punctuate her confidence, "They will never find you here. Most of the world doesn't even know Shumway exists, which is just fine with us. Both you and she will be safe here."

"Thank you." Jared said earnestly. "Again, I'm not so worried about myself, but, she's far from her home on the East Coast. She was only out here to discuss some business between me and her company."

Granny arched an eyebrow and asked slowly, "Is that so?" as if figuring something out. Then, thoughtfully she continued, "Well, it's going to be a busy day tomorrow.   Why don't you sleep on the couch tonight and we can make plans in the morning." She rose from her rocker, and walking out of the room for a minute, she returned with some blankets and a pillow. Granny then added, "Things always seem a little clearer after a good night's sleep."

CHAPTER 21

The next morning, Jared awoke early and walked out into the small field behind Granny's farm house. He perched himself atop the split rail fence and surveyed the ground before him. He guessed it was about ten acres, and it looked like it had been either freshly plowed, or planted. He was curious what she had planted, as he was trying to learn how to grow a garden of his own, with the assistance of his green house, and so, such things now interested him.

After a long while, the back screen door creaked as it opened, and Granny called out, louder than necessary, "JD, breakfast... come and get it." With that, he jumped down off of the fence, strode back to the house, and into the kitchen. It had the wonderful smell of home cooking that he loved so much, bacon and eggs, gravy, and biscuits.

"Jared, why don't you grab that tray there, and bring it up to Rachel?" Granny had placed a plate full of hot, delicious food on the tray. She held a glass of orange juice in one hand, and a glass of milk in the other.

As they entered the room, Jared saw Rachel sitting up in bed with a bunch of pillows behind her. She had obviously had time to bathe, and her red hair seemed to glow in the morning light that was streaming in through the window. Her eye was not as swollen as it had been last night, but, it had turned a deep purple. She still had the bandage on her cheek and her left hand was still tightly wrapped in gauze. She was wearing an old fashioned flannel night gown, sprinkled with a print of pink and blue flowers.

As they entered the room, Granny greeted Rachel, "Hungry darlin'?" She noticed the way that Rachel brightened, and watched Jared as he entered the room with the tray of food...and also, that her attention was not entirely on the food. Rachel managed a timid half smile, and said, "Good morning." There appeared a slight blush in her cheeks, behind all of the scratches and scrapes on her face, that also, did not escape Granny's notice.

Jared asked her, "How do you feel? You look a lot better." He smiled as he said it, and anyone listening could tell from his voice that he meant it. Jared set the tray down in front of her and backed away.

"I feel much better." Rachel spoke with a smile in her voice indicating that the night's sleep had been restful for both her mind and body. "Granny is just wonderful." She looked at Granny and then at the tray of food Jared had just presented to her. "Wow! You are really trying to make me fat. How can you afford all of this food? This must cost you a fortune."

"Well, we grow most everything you see here within our little community," Granny explained. "And we trade among ourselves a lot. We even raise our own pigs," she said with a little laugh. "Though not like we used to. This is mostly farming and cattle land, and we do alright. A lot of us here are related between Shumway, Taylor, and Snowflake, and almost all of us are members whose ancestors moved here in the 1800's by direction of the prophet. Most everyone else has left, and moved down to the valley to be part of the government work force...and receive the government rations. Those of us that are left, are pretty much off of the map and ignored."

"Well, I'll gladly pay you for my stay here and for the food as soon as I can." Rachel was trying to be considerate, thinking of the times they were living in and the scarceness of commodities, but she really didn't comprehend the situation in this community.

"Oh hush now. Are you trying to insult my hospitality?" She quickly looked at Jared, and saw the concern on his face that was evidence of his deep thoughts and unspoken words. "But, I think you and JD need to talk a little in private. Excuse me, I'll just go downstairs. You can call me if you need anything else, or just help yourself."

Jared turned and watched as Granny left the room. When he had turned back, Rachel had her head bowed and her arms folded. She was silent for about a minute as Jared watched and patiently waited. When she opened her eyes and looked up, she broke open her biscuit and asked, "What do we need to talk about?"

Jared pulled a chair from an old fashioned writing

-242-

desk against the wall, turned it around and sat down. "We need to talk about last night." He said with a serious tone.

"Oh, yes." Rachel acknowledged. "You know... it almost seems like a dream, a nightmare to be more exact. I can't seem to believe that it really happened." She paused, putting her fork down for a second as she recalled the horror of last night. "It did happen though, didn't it?" She raised her hand to her eye and touched the swelling.

"Yes," Jared replied solemnly, "it did. There were people last night who tried to kill you, and kidnap me."

"Why?" Rachel asked. "Who were they?"

"I'm not sure why they want me," Jared answered, "but, I will find out. The 'who' part of it is simple. When I was in Iraq, I was assigned a new member of our team, a Lieutenant Bennett"

"Wasn't that the name of the person who hit me?" Rachel remembered.

"Yes." Jared stated. "To say we didn't get along was an understatement. I had a really great team, all handpicked except for him. The rest of the team had been working together for a long time. Well, we trained together for a few days, and it soon became obvious that he didn't fit in, but before I could replace him we were suddenly deployed on an important mission.

"In the field things got worse between us, actually, between him and everyone else. He was careless, and arrogant, and didn't care about anyone else except himself. That's an attitude that in our line of work gets people killed quickly."

Rachel was remembering more of their conversations, before the horrific events of the previous day. "Didn't your team defuse nuclear bombs?" She asked.

"Nuclear and biological," Jared clarified. "Well, we were behind enemy lines looking for some weapons. We found them, and we got into a firefight. Long story short, his carelessness cost me two of my best men. So, when we got back I recommended that he be demoted and cashed out of our unit. Soon after that, he left the military. I heard a rumor that he joined the Foreign Legion, and another one that he was doing free lance work for the highest bidder. I really don't know who he is working for now...but, from the conversation, and a couple of things I saw when they had me in the car, I believe it's the Blackbird outfit the government is using, along with the U.N. troops, to help enforce martial law in the cities."

"What's Blackbird?" Rachel asked.

"Blackbird is basically a private security force, one of the larger ones." Jared explained. "A lot of ex-military guys join these private armies because the pay is great. Most of them are decent outfits, but, I have heard some stories about Blackbird guys before, that they are more on the shady side of things. They were used in Afghanistan when things started to turn ugly and some other places." He paused, thought a moment, and then continued, "If I remember right, when the food riots started, and Homeland Security declared martial law, Blackbird was one of the groups that got a contract to assist Homeland in the Intermountain region, primarily up in Utah. There weren't too many problems there like there were in Los Angeles, and Oakland, and other big cities. In those places they were using Federalized National Guard troops, and some U.N. troops, since most of our soldiers were still over seas."

"So what does this Blackbird want with you," Rachel wondered. "And why would they want to burn down your house with me in it?"

Jared thought for a minute before replying. "I don't know if it is Blackbird. It may not be. The Blackbird identification might just be a cover. Bennett hates me, and apparently wants revenge for my getting him kicked out of the military. To tell you the truth, until last night, I had no idea he hated me that much."

Jared paused again. "According to what he said, whoever it is that wants me, wants me unhurt. Bennett just used you as leverage to get me to cooperate. And since he couldn't hurt me, he hurt you instead. Also, you were a witness, so, after he had me, you were just a loose end to get rid of. When I knew Bennett, he wasn't a cold blooded killer of innocent women, but, apparently he is now, and he got a real thrill out of hitting you, which is even worse.

"When he hit you, I saw the look on his face, and I knew I couldn't trust him, no matter what he said. I have seen that look before; it's the look of a sadistic power hungry man who likes to hurt people. It's hard to explain, but I've seen it in the face of people who enjoy torturing, and killing others. To them, killing is an experience to enjoy, not just a matter of business, or an assignment to get information. When I saw that look on Bennett last night, I knew what he might do to you, and I knew I had to get away quickly and take him out. I was almost too late; actually, I was too late.

"They set the fire just to cover their tracks, with possibly a little revenge thrown in as well." He looked up at her. "I'm so very, very sorry, Rachel. I am so sorry that you are now a part of this mess. You just happened to be in the wrong place, at the wrong time, and it is entirely my fault. I should never have brought you here. I should have flown to see you in D.C."

Jared's remorse was as sincere as he had ever felt as he added, "If I had thought for a second that this kind of danger was possible, I never would have asked you to come."

For several seconds they looked into each others eyes in silence, each of them lost in their own individual thoughts.

Finally Rachel broke the silence, "So, what do we do now?" she asked.

"There is no doubt in my mind that they are putting all of their energy into finding me. I am pretty sure they don't yet know that you are alive and so they won't be looking for you, yet. The problem is... you. I have places I can go. Where, I can essentially get lost, even for a very long time. I have resources to call upon and people I can trust. But, you," He paused again. "I'm not sure what to do about you. This makes things very complicated. I just don't know what to do yet.

"I need to gather more information and find out what is going on. Meanwhile, as soon as you are better, we need to get you to a safe place. You can't go home for a while." He said this last with an unspoken, but clearly evident, apology in his voice. "You can't even travel very far because you don't have any I.D. with you. Do you?" He asked.

Rachel shook her head, acknowledging what he already knew. "No. It was all in the house and the car." She was starting to feel overwhelmed as the reality of the situation was finally sinking in.

"You can't use your credit cards, or get any cash from your account, because they will be watching, and can trace the transactions, at least in a lot of places, especially the bigger cities. But, the cash scanners aren't out in a lot of rural areas like this, so there might still be a way. I'll have to think on it for a while." Jared hated having to put Rachel in lockdown, but right now his only concern was for her and he would do whatever it took to secure her safety.

"In any case," Jared went on. "I have some unregistered cash stashed away that we can use. I'll have to go and get it tonight, or tomorrow. In the meantime, Granny has invited us to stay here until we can make other arrangements, then we will leave. The biggest challenge we have before us right now is figuring out where we should go. Let me ask you a couple of questions."

"Ok," Rachel responded. Her head was starting to spin with all of the details and problems Jared was discussing, but deep inside of her, there was a feeling of peace. Somehow, in the midst of all this confusion, she trusted this man who stood before her.

"Do you think you could travel tomorrow for most of the day, if I do the driving?" Jared questioned.

"Yes, absolutely," Rachel responded with enthusiasm.

"Also, do you by any chance happen to bank, or have a credit card, with Wells Fargo Bank?"

This time, Rachel again responded affirmatively, but with a questioning confused tone, "Yes...but, why does that matter?"

"Wells Fargo is one of the few big banks that still allows the use of plastic credit cards. I have an idea that I think we can use that to your advantage." Jared continued, "Let me think out a plan, and a back up plan just in case, and we will leave early tomorrow morning, probably before it is light, and then return later in the day, maybe at night."

That night, Jared traveled back to what was left of his house. After approaching from the forest, he observed a couple of guards watching the area, one from the barn and another from the greenhouse. This development prevented him from accessing his main supplies which were stashed in the hidden basement of the barn. Jared had been expecting some kind of lookout, but had hoped otherwise. Instead of recovering the stash in the barn he went into the forest and dug up a heavy green, water proof, canvas bag. It was his Deployment bag, or 'D' bag, as he called it, that he had buried months ago, for just such an emergency as this. Everything inside it was also double wrapped, and sealed in plastic.

The following day, Jared and Rachel drove east to New Mexico along several dirt back roads. At a carefully selected, small Wells Fargo Bank branch, Rachel went in to replace one of her credit cards. She explained that she had been in a car accident and that her ID and credit cards had been destroyed. After answering their security questions concerning her account, along with her thumbprint, they replaced her ATM-Debit card on the spot. While there, Rachel withdrew five hundred dollars cash from the ATM, the maximum she was allowed on her new card. Jared made sure that neither they, nor the vehicle they were driving in, had been observed, and only Rachel had been photographed by the bank, or ATM cameras. He then destroyed her new ATM card so she could not be tracked by the RFID chip in it. Together, they then drove southward where Jared withdrew money from his account through another ATM. After doing so, he went to a gas station where he put his card in a southward heading, eighteen wheeler semi-truck, with Mexican license plates. The goal of all this subterfuge was to give the impression that they had split up and were headed in different directions, she to the east, and he, south to Mexico.

On the car radio they listened to the news reporting that the civil war in Egypt was going badly for the government forces and that a coup appeared to be in process in Saudi Arabia. The information was sketchy, but, according to the correspondent, the majority of the royal family was believed to be safe, having fled the country, leaving it now in the hands of the Islamic insurgents the government troops had been fighting for the last four months.

Also reported, was the Pakistan-India war, which had heated up recently with several border clashes in Kashmir between the Indian and Chinese-Pakistani forces. Also, Chinese forces had crossed the border into the Pradesh area of Assam, the North-East region of India opposite Pakistan, in order to assist rebels in their fight for "liberation" from India. One news commentator had reported that with that move, China now controlled the productive Digboi oil fields and refineries that were in the area, and one of the main sources of oil and gas for India.

At the same time, a little further east, Chinese troops had crossed the border into Myanmar (Burma) to help in humanitarian efforts, in order to assist the government against another group of rebels, and to protect substantial Chinese investments in the Myanmar oil and gas fields.

Syria was in the process of consolidating its takeover of Lebanon, and though pledging to keep it a separate and independent country under Sharia law.

In South America, US Embassy officials and staff had been asked to leave Brazil, and Columbia, and vacate all embassy offices.

The top headlines, being reported in the U.S. domestic news, was the government announcement concerning the relocation of an additional 1.2 million refugees from the colder, northern FEMA camps to the warmer, southern states camps. This would expand the Civilian Work Force, and the Civilian Defense Force, with the necessary people to keep the peace for the coming summer, build new camps, assist with other FEMA construction projects, as well as working on the farms that had been nationalized the year before.

Listening to the news on the radio as they drove, Jared and Rachel couldn't help, but wonder, how much longer the world unrest could go on before everything imploded, or exploded. It also gave them a slightly different perspective on their own dilemma.

CHAPTER 22

When Bennett returned to the Blackbird regional headquarters in Ogden, Utah, he immediately began to set things in motion. After calling several of the staff together, he told them, "Get me everything you can on Jared Davis. I want to know everything he has done, what his favorite restaurants are, any friends, family, old army buddies, everything. We need him, and we need him now." Most of what Bennett said, he shouted just to make sure everyone got the point. "If he uses his credit card, I want to know three seconds later. Put out a BOLO (Be On the Look Out) on him, complete with photographs. Say that he's wanted for questioning on a federal investigation for multiple weapons violations. He could be armed, and therefore, should be considered dangerous.

Later, the grilling he received over the phone was not as bad as he had feared. When he offered his idea that Jared had been tipped off, and the need to search for the tipster, the voice on the other end of the phone responded that they would look into it. Regardless, Bennett's orders were to concentrate on finding and bringing in Jared Davis. They re-emphasized, unharmed and to do it quickly. Bennett was told they were running out of time without any further explanation.

Three days later, Bennett was informed that the

police had reported that no bodies had been found in the burned out remains of the Davis residence near the outskirts of Show Low, though they had determined it was definitely a case of arson. They also reported that they were looking for one Rachel Sinclair of Virginia, who was a person of interest, and currently missing. They had not yet been able to locate the owner of the property, a Mr. Jared Davis. The local police believed that he might be in Mexico because of information they had received, indicating he had been headed in that direction.

Bennett already knew about Jared and his use of the ATM in Socorro, New Mexico, and wondered if Jared had gone underground in Mexico. His credit card was tracked going into Mexico, but then the signal died, and there had been no official record of him entering into Mexico. Though Mexico had become pretty much a no-man's land of anarchy and violence, it was possible that Jared had gone there. However, in his mind, Bennett didn't think Jared had gone to Mexico, and he had his people looking for any sign of him across the U.S.

However, when the news that Rachel was still probably alive reached him, Bennett went through the roof. An hour later, as they searched for anything concerning Rachel Sinclair, they found her at the Bank, and then the ATM in Santa Rosa, New Mexico withdrawing cash. Bennett wasn't fooled for a minute. He knew they were traveling together, and somehow Jared had gotten her out of the house that night, though for the life of him, he couldn't figure out how.

Bennett contacted Homeland Security in Texas and asked for their help in searching for the two of them there, just in case, though he didn't think they actually went in that direction. Bennett figured, from the information they had gathered, that Jared wanted him to think they had gone south, and east, and had separated. That left just two other directions, and so, Bennett concentrated his efforts searching to the north, and west of Show Low, Arizona.

Bennett also wondered if Jared had developed any contacts on the Indian reservations of Northern Arizona. If he had, they would be very difficult to track, since all Native American reservations were now officially recognized as sovereign countries, and Homeland Security had no official presence there. He also wondered if his real bosses had resources on the reservations.

"Find out who she is and what she does. Put out a BOLO, 'Wanted for questioning in a murder and arson investigation.' If you find her, I want her brought here. She might know something about where Davis has disappeared to. I need him, and I need him now. Time is running out."

One of the newer members of his staff asked, "What if she doesn't know where he is?"

Bennett replied with a sneer, "If she doesn't know where he is, then maybe we can use her to smoke him out. Bait for a trap."

The naïve staff member had not yet learned to keep his mouth shut when Bennett was talking, and dared to ask another question. "You think he would fall for that?"

"Yea, he would." Bennett said, and then added with a touch of disgust, "He is soft like that." Bennett thought back to the night at Jared's house, remembering him falling on her and kissing her hair. "*Yeah,*" he thought, *"Davis would come for her. Hell, she is pretty enough that I would come for her."*

Recovering from the moment of thought, Bennett yelled at the staff with finality. "FIND HER NOW! IF WE FIND HER...WE CAN GET HIM."

CHAPTER 23

SATURDAY MORNING

Granny and Rachel were sitting on the back porch of the farmhouse, in old wood and cane chairs, stained a faded red, as they watched Jared split firewood by the shed.

They were sipping warm peppermint tea, made from mint grown on this very farm, according to Granny.

Rachel's foot was propped up on a short stool and Granny had just finished packing it with a poultice of comfrey and plantain. She covered this with a plastic bag and then wrapped an elastic bandage gently around her foot and ankle to hold it all in place. For a little extra protection and padding, she covered everything with a big white sock.

Granny said, nodding toward Rachel's foot. "It looks like it's coming along nicely; the swelling is pretty well down, though there is still a lot of discoloration. How does it feel honey?" she asked.

"Much better," was the reply from Rachel. "It doesn't hurt much at all anymore, except when I stand up, or you are bandaging it." Rachel was truly grateful for Granny's constant care and only wished they had met under different circumstances.

"Well, let's not push it too fast. In about a week, or two, or three, if you behave yourself, you should be able to put those crutches away and get around on your own." Granny had found an old pair of crutches in her basement that she had kept, "just in case of an emergency."

"The best thing right now is to keep you off of that foot, and keep it elevated so that your body can use the herbs to repair the damage."

Granny checked her handiwork over for a minute. "Let's wait a while before I put your protector back on."

The amazing Granny had also come up with a plastic blowup cast that she put around Rachel's foot and ankle to immobilize it. "This will help protect and cushion it, in addition to preventing it from bending." she explained.

Rachel had finished her first cup of tea, so Granny poured her another one and freshened her own cup before returning to the chair next to her.

It was an absolutely beautiful morning. The sun was shining and there were only a few distant clouds in the sky. The back porch faced the east so the morning sun hit them and warmed them considerably, along with the peppermint tea.

Rachel closed her eyes and sat absorbing the warmth of the sun as she felt it caress her body. It was heavenly and she couldn't remember feeling this peaceful in a very long time.

For a while she just sat there with her eyes closed, not thinking about all of her troubles, not even her black and blue face. She listened to the birds singing in the nearby trees and wondered what they were called, they sang so sweetly. Everything was perfect. *"This is wonderful,"* she thought.

As she felt the sun on her face, she thought with a smile, *"If I'm not careful I'm going to get a tan."* Then as an afterthought, *"I am going to get a tan on my face and have a white patch right on my cheek where the bandage is."* Instinctively, she opened her eyes and touched the small bandage on her cheek and laughed at her silly thoughts. With her eyes open now, she focused on the scene in front of her.

From the porch she could see the field that had indeed been recently plowed. Granny said the ten acres behind the house had been planted in corn just the week before. There was another forty acres to the side of the house that had also been planted in wheat.

Rachel heard another crack and looked over at Jared splitting another piece of wood. Jared had asked Granny if there was anything he could do for her to which she had replied, "I can always use more firewood split." Rachel watched as Jared picked up a piece of wood, set it on the stump, and swung the big combination ax and sledgehammer over his head, splitting it with a single stroke and sending the two pieces flying off the stump in opposite directions. He then picked up another piece, put it on the stump and started all over again. He had been working in this fashion for the better part of half an hour and by now there was a large pile of split wood surrounding the stump.

Rachel thought about the conversation she and Granny had the day before. Taking a chance with a private subject she had asked about Jared's wife and what had happened. Granny was open enough about it and told her that Janet and Jared had married after he had been in the military for three years. She had been a Show Low rodeo queen and somehow they had met at the University in Tempe. Six years later she died in a car wreck caused by a drunk driver, while Jared was overseas.

The way Granny understood it, they had just purchased the mountain property above Show Low with some inheritance money Janet had received, and they planned to build their home there and raise a family. Jared had also planned to quit the military and do something with electronics, but with Janet's death, he decided to discard his plans and just stay in the military. He had never remarried.

When Jared was injured in Iraq, he came back and after Granny had helped him to heal, had built the house on the property as a sort of therapy. Granny said that it was very special and very unusual for him to have invited her to his house. As far as she knew, Rachel was the only other woman to be invited to the house, beside herself.

As Rachel pondered the meaning of that comment, Granny interrupted her thoughts and brought up a memory. With a sad smile she looked out at the scene before them. "You know, I used to come out here in the morning and watch Robert work the fields. It was such a beautiful site."

Granny paused and Rachel saw her eyes sparkle with her memories, "He loved this farm and he loved to work."

"Who works it now?" Rachel asked.

"My nephew Jimmy, down the road, does it now." Granny answered, reluctantly coming back to the present. "When Robert died eight years ago, I sold Jimmy the back one hundred acres, near his house. For the last fifteen years he had worked it for us anyway, and Robert always said, when he passed away, I should sell it to Jimmy."

There was another long pause, though not uncomfortable in this relaxed setting.

Rachel could tell that Granny was in a reflective mood, but also felt she wanted to talk. "What did he die of?" Rachel asked politely.

"Oh, old age, I guess," came the reply. "He was 81 when he passed away.

"We had just come home after another mission, this time as family history missionaries at the library in Salt Lake. When we got home, they made him the acting Stake Patriarch again, since the person who had taken his place was ill and needed some help. He did that for about six months before he had a small stroke. His left side was paralyzed and he couldn't walk.

"After about a week, Robert announced that his father had come to visit him during the night and told him to prepare to come home in three days."

Rachel was listening attentively as Granny shared these precious memories.

"Robert instructed me on what to do and asked Jimmy if he would watch over the farm and me when he was gone. The family all came and we had a wonderful time with them. Three days later he went to sleep and never woke up. Well I guess that's not exactly accurate," She said. "He just woke up on the other side."

As she watched Granny's face, Rachel detected a small glistening in her eyes. "Do you miss him much?" Rachel asked, already knowing the answer.

"Oh, honey," Granny said, "after fifty nine years of putting up with him," she stopped talking, and just shook her head slowly. A half smile came to her face with a little twinkle in her eye.

Wistfully, she said, "Yes, Rachel, I miss him. It's like a part of me is missing. I've gotten used to it a little, over time, but I sure don't like it.

"The thing that seems to help the most is to keep myself busy, so I take care of people like you and Jared., but on days like today, it brings back memories."

Granny paused again before she added, while looking off in the distance. "You know, I can still see him like it was yesterday and we were newlyweds. It's the body that gets old and doesn't work very well. In my mind, I'm still 19 and he has just come off of his mission." She paused, then continued. "My, he was a good looking man."

It was at that moment that Granny turned to Rachel, noticing that she was watching Jared chopping the fire wood and said, "He loves you, you know."

"What?" Rachel exclaimed, embarrassed at the mere suggestion and sure she hadn't heard Granny's words correctly.

"Honey," Granny addressed Rachel. "I've been around men a long time. I raised five boys and three girls. I have thirty three grandchildren and some fifty great grandchildren. Trust me when I say he loves you. I know the look."

Deep emotions flooded Rachel from head to foot. It almost felt like she couldn't breath, and she knew that any parts of her face not purple with bruises were now a bright red. She had thought about Jared as a good looking man, and he was fun and interesting to be around. All of the thoughts and daydreams she had thought of came rushing into her mind, including the one reason why it could never be.

Rachel hadn't intended to blurt it out, but that is exactly what happened as she quickly told Granny, ", but, he, he's not LDS Granny. He can't take me to the temple." Rachel knew that the sadness and frustration of that thought was showing on her face and in her voice, but she could not hide that from this sweet woman.

Granny looked back at Rachel again with tenderness, and with a bit of insight she stated more than asked, "You have never married because you could never find the right man who could take you to the temple?"

There was a long pause, followed by a deep sigh from Rachel, as she considered her life.

"Yes." Rachel said finally. "When I was in college I had a couple of proposals, but they weren't the kind of men I wanted, not the kind that would help me get to the Celestial Kingdom.

"When there was no one in my life, I served a mission to Taiwan and when I came back, it was the same. None of those that asked me were of the caliber that I wanted to spend my life with, let alone all of eternity. I concentrated on my degree, and then my career, hoping one day to find someone, or actually hoping that someone would find me, but he never came." Rachel's story was so sad, but Granny just sat and listened while she went on.

"After a while I just gave up and decided that I was going to be an *unclaimed treasure*." There was another pause.

"I met Jared about two years ago." She looked over at him chopping the wood, and oblivious to the fact that he was being talked about. "He is very nice, and very different, unlike anyone I've ever met really., but I put him out of my mind as marriage material because he isn't a member. I have my standards and ...." her voice trailed off.

Granny looked at her for a few moments and then at Jared before replying after a long pause.

"Rachel, Jared is just a dry Mormon. He just doesn't know it yet. When he came to me five years ago to heal him, I helped him because I could sense he was a good man. As I got to know him, I found him to be honest and kind. Yes, he's got a lot of rough edges, but a good woman can take care of that in a man. That's part of our job." The twinkle was in her eyes again. Then she added, "It's nice to see that you love him too."

Rachel nearly choked on her herbal tea at that comment. After sputtering for a minute she turned to Granny and asked, bewildered, "What did you say?"

"Dear, you listen to granny for just a minute," the kind old woman told her. "There is something in the future for you and this man. I can feel it. He's not LDS, yet." She added, punctuating the last word. ", but you give it some time. There are going to be a lot of changes in the near future. The whole world is going to go completely upside down, not just sideways like it has been the last few years. You hold on to those standards of yours. You're on the right track." And then with a touch of tenderness she added, "Heavenly Father has not forgotten you."

At these last words, Rachel's eyes teared up and drops turned into streams that slowly coursed down her cheeks. The ache she had buried deep inside her, and tried to cover up so many times, rose to the surface. She had wanted to be married for such a long time. She had longed to be loved, to be held in strong arms, protected and safe, to be one with someone special. She had dreamed of kneeling in white at an altar in the temple. But, in all these years, there was never anyone kneeling across from her in those dreams. She wanted to be loved and she wanted to love someone with all of her heart, to make him happy, to give him children, and raise a family. Someone to grow old with.

Rachel closed her eyes, wiped away her tears, and didn't say a word. Granny reached over and patted her arm softly and said, "Just a little more patience, honey, and a little more faith and you will have it all, just like you have imagined. And it will have been worth the wait, I promise."

CHAPTER 24

The next day, though Rachel wanted to go to church with Granny, Jared thought it was a bad idea and convinced her to remain at home. "First of all," Jared had pointed out, "your face is still badly bruised and that would draw attention to you even more than normal. Secondly, 'Our Friends,' are undoubtedly out looking for you and by now they probably know you are LDS, so they might be looking for you among church members and congregations." In the end Rachel admitted that Jared was right, so Granny went to church that Sunday, alone.

Rachel contented herself at the house by sitting on the back porch, reading her scriptures. The sun was bright and warm and it was almost as nice a day as it had been the day before. After a while, Jared came out and sat in the chair next to her and watched her read.

"Reading that Book of Mormon of yours, are you?" he asked, breaking the silence of the morning and her concentration.

"As a matter of fact, yes, I am," Rachel replied with a happy smile on her face. "You ought to try it. You might find it interesting. I'm sure that Granny has another copy around here somewhere you could use." Rachel lifted her head and looked around as if trying to spot another copy of the book for him.

Jared had a smile on his face as he answered Rachel calmly, "actually, I have my own copy already. Granny gave it to me." Then with a sudden realization, he added, "Though now, I guess it has gone up in smoke with the rest of my things in the house."

The missionary zeal grew within her, and Rachel chose to ignore his comment about the burned house, not wanting to let a potential missionary moment go by, especially in light of what Granny had said yesterday. "Have you ever picked it up and read it?" Rachel asked pointedly.

"No, never have." Jared responded. "I just haven't found time yet I guess." In his mind Jared reflected that he had picked it up a couple of times, soon after Granny had given it to him, and was going to read it, but something always seemed to happen that drew his attention elsewhere and made him put it down. "Maybe, one of these days when things calm down a bit and we get this mess straightened out I can get another copy and make some time."

Before she had time to reply, Jared continued, "Rachel, we need to talk about what's going on and what we need to do. We need to make some plans for the immediate future."

"Alright," Rachel answered, "what do you think we should do?"

Jared had been thinking about this late last

night and again early this morning, so he had some plans already formulated in his head. "We can't stay here for much longer. Maybe a week, or two at the most, but as soon as you can travel we need to go. I can't make any phone calls from here, or anyplace in this area since they arc sure to be monitoring all of our communication and they would be here in a flash. So, I haven't been able to check with any of my contacts to find out what's going on. The good news is that we have plenty of cash that's not registered to us. On the other hand, we need to be careful not to frequent too many places with video cameras tied into the national face recognition program.

"They will, a without doubt, be using everything at their disposal to locate us. That means we have to avoid big cities, airports, bus lines, essentially any public places where crowds would need to be observed via camera. It's probable that they have the police and other agencies looking for us also. Hopefully, they ate the breadcrumbs we left them and think we headed to Mexico, or back east, so we want to lay low and not give them any reason to think otherwise.

"Bottom line, Rachel," Jared said looking at her with raised eyebrows, "The real problem is you. I have a place to go, where I can hole up for months if I need to, but you can't go. It's up in Montana near the Canadian border, high in the mountains, and in the middle of nowhere. And, well," Jared was trying to find the correct words, finally settling on simple ones so she would get his meaning. "It just wouldn't be right. Anyway," he went on, "it's a place of last resort that I have prepared just in case."

Jared continued, "You can't go home, at least not until we get this straightened out, and I don't know how long that will take. These are strange times with new rules. What we need to do is find another place where you can go, somewhere safe, while I work on finding out what exactly is going on."

"Do you have any place you might go?" Jared asked with hope. "Any place nearby by chance?"

"I have my brother Todd up in Idaho I could go and stay with." Rachel considered out loud.

"No good... that would be one of the first places they would look." Jared knew operations like this and spoke with certainty. "It can't be family. It has to be a trusted friend that you haven't seen in a long time. Someone they would not be able to associate with you."

"I have an old missionary companion in Cedar City, Utah." Rachel remembered. "I know I could probably go and stay with her, for a while. She has a small house on the edge of town and I've stayed there before. They wouldn't have any records of her as being associated with me."

"That's a possibility." Jared replied. Before he could say another word in the conversation, they heard a car coming down the road. Jared immediately got up and went to the side of the house, and peered through a large lilac bush that was just starting to bloom. He had pretty much done this every time he heard a vehicle come near the house. Luckily, the road was fairly deserted, so it didn't happen very often.

"It's Granny." Jared called back to Rachel, "But, something is wrong.   She shouldn't be back this soon." He walked back to her and started helping her out of the chair as he finished. "I think you better come into the house; let's find out what's going on."

Granny pulled into the driveway and calmly walked up onto the porch. Her calmness eased the tension, considerably in Jared.   He pushed open the screen door for her and asked, "Back so soon, I thought your church lasted for three hours?"

Granny answered his question as she walked through the door. "That was before they changed it. Now it only lasts two hours instead of three. In fact, in California they don't even have any meetings at the church houses at all anymore, just home meetings."

The information Granny was sharing was nice, but the suspense was killing both Jared and Rachel as they suspected she had something more important to tell them by the look on her face. They all sat down with Granny in her wooden rocker and she continued to talk, as she began rocking. "However, today, after we had sacrament, they ended the meeting early and sent everyone home except for a few of us." At this, Rachel leaned forward in her chair, very much focusing her attention on the little old woman.

Granny went on, "After sacrament, the Bishop got up and read a letter from the First Presidency. It asked all those who had obeyed the commandment to have a year's supply of food storage for themselves and their family to meet in the Relief Society room for a short meeting with the Bishop. In our ward, just about half stayed."

"In the relief society room," Granny continued, "the Bishop read another letter, which invited all those present to a special meeting at the stake center this afternoon at four o'clock for a televised broadcast from the First Presidency, who have an important message for us."

"I take it that this is unusual?" Jared said, noticing the shock on Rachel's face.

Granny, ignored Jared's question for the moment as she watched Rachel's expression. Rachel's eyes opened wide in amazement. Then Granny asked, looking directly at Rachel, "Honey, what do you know about the last days and the second coming of Jesus Christ?" Before Rachel could reply, Granny revised her question. "Better yet, let me ask you, back at your home in Virginia, do you have a year's supply of food stored away?"

"Yes Ma'am," Rachel responded proudly.

Then Granny surprised her with her next question. "Why?" she asked.

This question had caught Rachel off guard, but she took a moment to clear her thoughts and finally answered. "Well, because the prophet said to, but," she continued slowly, "also, because I have come to believe that a day would arrive when the prophet would call the members of the Church out to places of refuge and it will be necessary to have it there."

A large grin spread across Granny's face. "Wonderful." She said as she stood looking into Rachel's eyes. Jared interrupted with a question. "You think that is what this special meeting is about, this call out that you told me about years ago? Is that what you are talking about?"

Granny nodded her head in answer to Jared's question, and then added, "My Robert told me that this day would come and that we would probably be alive to see it come to pass."

Jared, a little confused, asked Granny, "What does this mean, exactly?"

"We will find out the answer to that question," Granny said, looking at the clock on the wall, "in about four hours."

The rest of the time, before the meeting, was spent discussing preparations while Granny showed them what she had stored away. Granny informed Jared and Rachel that if the meeting went as she expected it to, she would need to get things ready to be moved. The basement of the old house was full of food and other preparedness items all neatly stacked in buckets and boxes from floor to ceiling.

She had Jared get the old truck out of the barn to

make sure that it started. She showed him where she kept a large horse trailer. "We bought this several years back just for this kind of thing," Granny explained, when Jared wanted to know why she owned the trailer, but no horses. Not knowing for sure what the afternoon would bring, she wanted to be ready, just in case.

Before she left for the meeting at the stake center, Granny turned to Rachel. "Jared tells me that you can't go home for a while because of all that's happened. If I am right, and this afternoon turns out the way I think it will, would you consider coming with me and helping me up at the camp?"

Rachel had actually considered this possibility and was very happy that Granny was bringing it up now. "Besides," Granny persisted, "you can't go home right now to get your food supply and go anywhere with your stake."

"If you're sure that would be alright with you," Rachel answered, her words confirming the look on her face. "I would be delighted, though with this ankle I don't know how much help I'll actually be."

"Well, we will just have to see about that, won't we?" Granny said, smiling from ear to ear. "Robert used to say that he didn't believe in coincidences, and so maybe your coming here, just at this time was supposed to happen, at least as a help for me."

Then turning to Jared, Granny asked with a sly grin on her face. "Would you be willing to help an old lady and an invalid setup camp, somewhere?"

"It would be my great pleasure to help in any way I can." Jared answered with a little bow., but the joking ended as he got serious and continued, "I owe you both so much, anything I can do to help would be only partial payment for what you have done for me, or to make up for the pain I have caused you. But, are you sure they would invite a non-member to come?" Now Jared was seriously questioning whether, or not it would even be possible for them to continue together.

"I'll just have to ask, won't I," Granny said with a laugh. As she stepped out of the door she added, "Now don't you two go away. I shouldn't be too long, at least I don't think so."

After Granny drove away, Rachel watched as Jared backed up the truck and hooked up the trailer.

When Granny returned, both Jared and Rachel had been watching for her out of the front window. The anticipation was about to kill Rachel, but Jared, for some reason, was taking everything in stride as if it were just preparation for a Sunday picnic.

As she came through the front door, Rachel asked Granny, anxiously, "Well?"

"Well," Granny said, back to Rachel. "They will be by sometime Monday evening to pick up our food storage. We need to be at the stake center Tuesday morning at six am ready to leave."

Rachel stood there, not really believing that this event, long hoped for, planned for and talked about, was actually happening. It was almost too much to take in all at once. As Granny had explained earlier, many people had looked forward to this day for so long that countless people had given up hope that it would ever really come. For those who had not given up, however, it had finally arrived.

Granny turned her attention now to Jared. "I asked about you son, and you are definitely invited to go. Is there any way to have them pick up the food storage and supplies from under your shop?"

"Probably not, but let me think about it." Jared answered. "There might be a way."

"Well, I have some paperwork here to fill out." Granny sat at the kitchen table and pulled out a folder filled with papers. "I am going to deed this farm to the Church, since I own it free and clear. There were several present at this afternoon's meeting who asked about what to do with their houses and properties that were owned outright. The Church anticipated this possibility and has setup a trust account wherein you can donate everything to the Church or, you can have the Church just hold it for you and be caretakers until you revoke their limited power of attorney. Most everyone it seems, is just giving property to the Church with no thought of ever getting it back."

"May I see those," Rachel asked, pointing to the

papers. "I am an attorney and I would be interested in seeing how they have set things up. Besides, I think I would like to donate what I have back in Virginia to the Church."

As Rachel reviewed the papers, Granny started telling them more details at the afternoon's gathering.

"I was a little disappointed," she said, "in how many showed up for the meeting. The chapel was filled, and the overflow, but that was it. I hope the Snowflake and Show Low stakes had a better showing than the Taylor stake."

"Please tell us what happened at the meeting." Rachel asked, having finished looking over the forms.

"Well, we all came in and the Stake Presidency was up on the stand along with a Member of the Seventy, Elder Pinetree. It was just like any other stake meeting. There was a prayer and then at four fifteen exactly, the First Presidency came on the screen just like at General Conference. Only, it wasn't the Conference Center." Granny seemed a little puzzled by that difference, but went on. "The First Counselor spoke and said, after much prayer and fasting the First Presidency and the Quorum of the Twelve were united in inviting all of those present to participate in a special wilderness camping experience in places of safety that had been prepared over the last several years.

"He said that they didn't know how long we would be in these wilderness places, but we should be prepared for a long stay, if necessary even over the coming winter. For those interested in participating, each stake would pass out packets explaining what we should take and how we should proceed.

"They emphasized that this will be temporary and different from the existing camps the Church is already operating for those who have lost their homes.

Granny paused just long enough to take a sip of water, then she went on with the description of what had taken place.

"They specifically asked us not to talk about today's meeting with anyone who had not been invited to attend. And, we were further told, if asked about the meeting, or what it concerned, by anyone that had not been present, we were to reply that we had been asked not do discuss it. Those instructions were given to everyone, even those who decided not to go to the camps.

"We were told to direct any specific questions to those presiding at our individual meetings. I don't think the video lasted for more than half an hour.

"After the video, Elder Pinetree got up and asked for a raise of hands of those that were interested in participating in this wilderness camping experience, then excused those who did not want to participate. I didn't see anyone leave though I know there were some who didn't raise their hands.

"Then, they started handing out information

packets that we had to sign for. While that was going on, Elder Pinetree answered questions. Someone asked, 'what about those people with jobs, what should they do?' He was told that it was entirely up to each person to decide what to do about their jobs. Honestly," Granny couldn't help a little commentary at this point, "people should just use their common sense and then listen to the Spirit. Some people want to have the whole journey laid out for them before they are willing to take the first step."

"After the meeting," Granny went on, having vented enough for the moment, "I talked to my cousin's son, who is the First Counselor in the Stake presidency, about you Jared. He didn't know what to say, so we talked to Elder Pinetree. He made it very clear that anyone could come and participate in this second group who had their year's supply and were willing to keep the rules of the camp. I told him that would be no problem."

"What did he mean second group?" Jared asked.

"I'm not quite sure and I didn't think to ask." Granny admitted. "Anyway, I turned in your names as those who were coming with me and I made a list of what we would bring."

Seeing the look on Jared's face at the mention of their names, she raised her hand as if to calm his fears and added, "Don't you worry about that Jared, I gave your name as Jeremy and Rachel as Rhonda and you are both now honorary, distantly related Shumway's. I also wrote down that we had a truck and trailer, but no livestock since Jimmy has all of that now." Addressing Rachel, Granny explained, "For special skills, I put down that you and I are herbalists and that Jeremy here, is ex-military."

", but, I don't know anything about herbs!" Rachel exclaimed.

"Don't worry about that dear." Granny assured her. "You might not now, but after I get through with you, you will. For now you will be my assistant. You've already started having lessons," she added, pointing to Rachel's foot."

"What will the church pickup and transport and what do we have to fit into the truck and trailer?" Jared asked already thinking about getting the supplies loaded as soon as possible.

"Here is the list of things they will transport," she said as she handed Jared another page. "Everything else we will have to bring, if we want it with us."

Jared looking over the list, said, "Okay, it looks like they'll pick up most everything that is in a bucket, or a sealed box not bigger than an apple box. Also, they will transport some furniture, including one small table, and one kitchen type chair for each person going, also one small bookshelf not more than five feet tall. Any hand tools such as axes, hatchets, shovels, rakes, saws, hammers and the like, they'll also pick up and deliver to the camps. Special arrangements can be made to transport farm animals such as chickens, horses, cows, sheep, and goats. Everything else we will have to bring."

"And for that list of things," Jared paused as he turned the page over, "we are encouraged to bring our genealogy and family history records, summer, and especially winter clothing, including hats, jackets, gloves, and winter boots, temple recommends, whatever that is, and extra garments, any musical instruments and sheet music for them, one set of scriptures per person, a small selection of good reading materials, and school books, or materials for any children."

"We are also encouraged to bring laptops and communication devices, such as two way radios, any guns we may own and ammunition for them, preferably in lockable cases. We are to make sure that we bring any life sustaining medicines and first aid supplies. Blankets, or sleeping bags, pillows, a small selection of cooking utensils, plates, pots and pans, cups and silverware. Tents, or camping trailers are welcome, along with bicycles. If we are bringing pets, then we need to bring food for them and they must be on leashes. We are cautioned to remember all legal documents including birth certificates."

"Then there is a warning against bringing motorized four wheelers, motorcycles, or snowmobiles, unless specifically authorized. Also, one vehicle per family, unless specific permission is granted and all vehicles that come, must be completely paid for. Proof of ownership must accompany all vehicles, or they will be turned away."

"If you do not have a vehicle that you can bring, then a bus, or other form of transportation will be provided by the church to the camp."

"Don't be late," Jared continued reading. "The group will leave at 6:00 a.m. sharp. It is suggested that you arrive early and check everything twice. Do not plan on going back to get anything. Please fill gas tanks and bring any cash you might have."

Jared had finished reading the list and looking up at the women he said, "Guess we better get busy."

They proceeded to put things into two piles—Those items that would be transported by the Church, and those they would be responsible for. It helped tremendously that Granny already had things labeled and ready to go.

Later that night, Jared went to the store and returned with several bottles of hair color. He had Rachel change from her natural red to almost black, the darkest color he could find. He said it was just a precaution.

With their excitement about the adventure that lay ahead of them, Granny had chosen not to tell Jared and Rachel about the grumbling and complaining she had heard in the parking lot of the church, after the meeting. It was amazing to her that the same people who qualified for an invitation to the camps would be among those objecting to the First Presidency's decision and direction.

CHAPTER 25

The next morning at the Show Low Stake center the crowd had arrived early. There were about 50 cars and trucks, two buses, and a large moving van in the parking lot by five thirty. Shortly before six there were also three large fifth wheel trailers, five travel trailers and one, very large motor home.

The Stake President casually walked through the parking lot listening to the various conversations and assessing the emotions.

Next to a 4-door pickup truck, packed to the top of the homemade side rails, was a heart wrenching scene involving a pleading mother and father, arguing with their oldest married daughter and son-in-law. The three small children of the young couple were still at home as their parents had come to persuade Grandma and Grandpa not to take part in this "mistake." The older father had given up talking to his grown children, but the mother, unwilling to give up, was begging them to come. The man stood by the side of the truck with his arms folded, looking off into the pine trees, as his crying wife begged her children one last time.

Their daughter's husband spoke in a loud voice that the Stake President could not help, but overhear from a distance. "Absolutely not," he insisted, "I have a good job. I'm taking care of my family, things are looking up. I'm not retired like you and Dad. I still have my job and I have responsibilities as the bank manager. Why didn't the Church do this when we needed it, a year ago? Now things are improving. We'll see you back here in a month, or two."

The frustrated daughter chimed in, "Mom, don't go on this crazy move. Please don't do this. It's not safe, both you and Dad have health problems. It's just not safe for you to be out in the woods away from the conveniences you've worked so hard to get. Do you really want to be away from your grandchildren? They will miss you so much."

The Stake President walked a little further and was just about to call out an announcement for everyone to meet inside the church for prayer and instructions, when several cars arrived all at once. At first thought, the President was hopeful they were travelers that had gotten a late start, but, as the people started to get out of their cars, he realized that none of them had been present at Sunday afternoon's meeting.

As more cars arrived and unloaded he recognized several people who had met with him in the last several months. These were people who disagreed vehemently with the Church's stand on the issue of homosexuality. A few he recognized as former members who had been excommunicated over this very matter of contention. It was clear these people were not here to see the travelers off, or to accompany them. The more that showed up, the more arguments erupted with those about to leave. At one vehicle, the instigators had started pounding on the windows of a small car, yelling at the frightened family inside.

Immediately, the Stake President decided to forego the prayer meeting and just get on the road as fast as possible before things turned really ugly. He quickly walked back to the group of leadership standing by the entrance of the Stake Center, watching the arriving cars and said in a rather stern voice, "We are leaving. Now! Get everyone in their cars and head out." The men sensed the urgency for quick obedience and started to leave, but before they had taken more than just a couple steps he called after them. "Wait," the President said. Then, turning to his first counselor who was to be the driver of the lead car in the caravan, he gave the instructions. "Go ahead and pull out, but go slowly, so we don't lose anyone. If they follow us..." and he glanced in the direction of the agitators across the parking lot. "We will turn and head towards Snowflake. If they don't, then we will follow the map and go straight east. I'll bring up the rear and we will be in constant radio contact. I'll let you know what's going on from the back of the line."

Earlier that morning, all those with portable short wave radios had checked to make sure they were in good working condition and on the same frequency. The President was grateful that those details had been taken care of and not saved for the last minute.

"If they don't follow us, then stop at the gas station as we planned. If they do follow us," he let out a sigh and paused, "then I will let you know what to do.

Understand?"

"Yes," with a nod, was the quick response.

Addressing the small group again, he added, "Alright let's keep our cool and be calm. Remember, no confrontations. Go ahead and tell everyone to avoid contention, to get into their vehicles quietly and to follow the cars in the caravan. We are leaving now. Let's go."

With that, the group broke up and quickly made their way around the parking lot, letting people know that it was time to leave. There were about thirty people who had gathered to protest the departure. As the caravanning cars left the parking lot, the unruly crowd gathered on each side of the exit, yelling at the occupants of the cars as they drove away. Occasionally, they pounded on the car windows and even tried to rock the motor home as it left, but thankfully, they didn't follow them.

Later on, after they arrived at their destination, the Stake President heard what had happened to prompt this disruption. After the meeting on Sunday, a couple who had been invited to the Stake Center and heard the broadcast because they had their food storage, decided they didn't want to have anything to do with the callout. They had gone home and immediately called some of their friends to talk about the meeting and the plans discussed.

One of the men they called felt it was his duty to tell everyone what was going on. He believed it was a false and feeble prophet who had persuaded or, more than likely, was forcing everyone to go along with him so he could fleece the members and steal their property. For him and his crowd, this was the last straw. He had been one of the most vocal of those in the area who disagreed strongly with the Church's stand concerning the homosexuality issue. It had then become a bitterly personal argument when the Church was not willing to help him and his family as they lost their 5,200 sq ft house after he was laid off from work.

He and his friends had protested against the Church before, and recently had disrupted a meeting during the sustaining of Church leadership when they voiced their opposition by yelling their disagreements. The Stake President had met with them a couple of times after that to try and work things out, but, he admitted it was not going very well. Since the President had received word, two weeks ago, about the callout, he had been too busy to meet with them again and hold a disciplinary council.

LATER THAT DAY...MONDAY EVENING

Jared had spent all day Monday packing everything Granny pointed out to him, into the truck and horse trailer. He was especially excited about the old fashioned wood working tools that he loaded out of the shed and hoped to have an opportunity to use them soon. By dinner time, everything was about as ready as it could be.

Granny called Jimmy to ask what he was doing and what his plans were. He replied that he had been asked to accept a calling to stay on the farm as part of a group that would stay behind working and helping each other. He understood there were additional groups with other specific assignments as well. One group he knew of had been assigned to watch over the temple and other Church buildings in the area even though the temple had been closed for over a year and the other Church buildings would be empty and closed.

The church truck had come around midnight Monday evening, along with two cars, full of men. They pulled in front of the house and one of the men got out with a clipboard. Granny and Jared were waiting for them and went out to talk. He confirmed that Granny, "Jeremy" and "Rhonda" were still planning to leave with the group and said they were prepared to pick up the food storage and other items, if they were ready.

Granny signed a form that authorized them to pickup and transport the food. He then asked where the food storage was and the easiest way to get to it. Thanks to Jared, most of it was now stacked throughout the house, with a lot of it in the living room. The brother with the clipboard then spoke with the driver of the truck, which hadn't been turned off, and he backed right up and put the ramp down on the front porch. The eight men from the cars formed a line and started loading the boxes into the truck. Just before each container was picked up, the driver peeled off a sticker and stuck it on the box, or bucket in order to number and identify it. Each stake had a different color label, with the Taylor Stake's being purple. These labels showed that these containers belonged to Margaret Shumway, of the Taylor Stake. For official business she used her "official" name even though there were a few people in the Stake who would not have recognized her by anything other than Granny. As the stickers were put on each box the brother counted out loud.

As the last of the supplies were loaded and the truck pulled away, the men stood around. It had only taken about forty minutes to load everything on the truck, even though Granny had stored enough food and other provisions to last ten people for one year. Jared was pleasantly surprised at how fast the loading had gone, since it took him almost a full day to gather it all together.

When the truck and helpers didn't leave immediately Jared asked what was going on and the brother with the clipboard had said they were waiting for the furniture truck that would pick up the table, chairs and bookcase. He and his team were actually ahead of schedule because it appeared that not many families had decided to go. He guessed about seven, or eight families per ward were going when they had originally anticipated about fifteen families.

Jared talked to him a little more and learned that the man had been called two weeks earlier and that his family was already up at the camp. He reported that there were others like him who had been up at the camp for six months getting things ready, even during the previous winter. The other seven men in his team had volunteered on Sunday to help load everyone else up because they were all ready to go. These men had loaded their supplies into the trucks on Sunday afternoon, right after the satellite broadcast, and had then taken their families to the camp that same day. Jared had no way of knowing before that conversation, but the camp was apparently only about an hour and a half away from town.

The driver of the truck was a Church missionary who was assigned to drive. The brother with the clipboard explained that the truck driver had been moving people for over two months to many different places. This team was just one of three truck teams in the area picking up the food storage from the various families. When their truck was full, they took it over to the stake center and loaded it onto a semi-truck that had been parked there. Then the process would start over and they would go out to get some more. They figured that they would be completely done in about two more hours since the Taylor Stake was the last one in the area to leave. While the men were talking another truck pulled up and backed into the driveway. Granny signed more papers and pointed out the kitchen table, chairs and bookcase that she wanted to take. Loading the furniture only took about ten minutes and then everyone left.

The last thing they did before they left was to inform Granny that the departure time had been changed because of safety concerns to 4:00 a.m. instead of 6:00 a.m.

The whole gathering and loading process for the stake took only about eighteen hours.

CHAPTER 26

At the Taylor Stake Center very early Tuesday morning, there were more than five hundred people gathered with scores of vehicles of every kind. There were also two large yellow school buses. Groups of men in florescent vests and carrying flashlights, directed traffic and walked around checking titles of ownership on vehicles and trailers against the lists of people who were going with them. It was all organized down to the last detail. Only one family neglected to bring their car title and they quickly ran back home to get it. Within thirty minutes they were all accounted for. Everyone entered the stake center where they were told how the caravanning to their place of refuge would happen. It was not very far, and they would make only one stop before arriving at the camp in order for everyone to fill up their gas tanks one last time.

The instructions were to not lag behind and if a serious problem arose, drivers were to simply flash their headlights, signaling, and the whole caravan would stop and pull over to assist them. The leaders encouraged everyone, especially the children, to go to the bathroom, one last time, as there would not be another bathroom available until the refuge. With that, the Stake President offered a prayer for safety and peace on their journey and they walked out into the darkness, got into their vehicles and drove away in a long orderly caravan of vehicles and lights.

They drove for about an hour, and just as the morning sun was cresting the mountains to the east they turned off the main highway, taking a dirt road for another forty-five minutes. They were high in the mountains now, Jared guessed at about eight thousand feet. Snow still clung to the rocks in shadowy places among the trees and as they came over a small hill they saw the camp for the first time nestled in a small valley. The camp seemed to surround one end of a small mountain lake and was interspersed among the trees. Many people and tents were already present and Jared guessed the number to be around two thousand plus, already there milling about. *"Apparently,"* Jared thought to himself, *"We are in the second, or third wave to arrive."* It appeared to him that the camp was not filled to capacity yet because of the land still available on the other side of the lake. He estimated they could hold another thousand people, at least.

Later that day, the Round Valley stake arrived at the camp, en masse. Where the Snowflake, Taylor, Show Low, and Winslow Stakes had brought a total of about 1800 people, the Round Valley group alone, brought with them 1600 people, almost half of the stake.

As each vehicle arrived they were met by a person with a clipboard who directed them where to park and supplied them with a map showing the location of their family tent site. People were organized and grouped by wards and stakes, with each family site clearly marked on the ground with chalk dust and a number. The distance between where they parked the horse trailer and their campsite was about one hundred yards, and luckily for them, someone loaned them a homemade handcart to help move their things.

After they unloaded their trailer and truck, Jared unhooked the battery cables as they had been instructed. Later on, someone from the Church went through and put a little bit of a liquid they called PRI-G into each vehicle's gas tank, which would keep the gas fresh and usable for a longer period of time.

The camp was organized a lot like many military field camps that Jared had been a part of. He later learned, that a half an hour after the Sunday afternoon broadcast meeting, each stake had telephoned in how many families were coming from their individual units. They also faxed lists with the names and numbers of people in each family. It was originally estimated that most stakes would have between one hundred fifty and two hundred families. However, Granny had heard that most stakes ended up with only about one hundred families coming, roughly less than seven percent from each ward. There were a few exceptions, of course, from stakes that had many more, such as Round Valley, but they were exceptions and not the rule. Organizers had been up at the camps for several weeks prior to the actual call out, and especially the last few days, busy re-arranging the stake areas and placing family names tentatively on the camp sites as information came in.

It was a busy and exciting time getting things

setup at the camp over the next few days. About one in ten of those who came owned their own tents; the others were given a tent of one kind, or another by the Church. After Jared, with some help from their new "neighbors," set up the outfitters tent for Granny and Rachel, he found a nearby "bachelors" tent that had room for him where he could spend his nights.

It quickly became obvious to Jared that someone with military field experience was involved in setting up the camp. It was well organized and well laid out. Having helped set up a couple of military field camps in the past, he expected that over the next several days, and even weeks, things would be organized chaos as people who had never been involved in such a camp before were trained and came to understand the daily workings of the camp. However, he was pleasantly surprised at how different things were in this camp and how rapidly things had become organized and orderly. The transformation was almost overnight. Jared asked Granny why that was so and she explained that it had a lot to do with the experience and training received by church members with either the Boy Scouts, or something called Young Women.

On the third day after their arrival, units were organized with groups of ten, fifty and one hundred families. Each group had a temporary leader who oversaw the welfare of the people in his assignment. Finally, there was the overall camp leader which was Elder Pinetree. Since each ward had between seven and ten families, they usually chose the highest ward leader present, for the 'ten family' leader. Often, this was the Bishop, but sometimes it ended up being the Elders Quorum president. In one ward it was the Sunday School President. Later on, over the next month, the camp would be re-organized and formal callings extended.

On the fourth day, a camp meeting was called for each of the groups of fifty families, since that was all that could fit into the three large rooms of the log buildings. A larger, open air pavilion was planned for construction later in the summer that would alleviate the problem of too little space for larger meetings. At the meeting the overall camp leadership was introduced. For their camp it was the Seventy, Elder Pinetree, with two other men who would serve as his counselors. Rules of the camp were presented and it was made clear that they would be strictly enforced for everyone, without exception. Common sense was the basis of the rules and could be summarized in three simple main statements or laws:

1. Honor and serve God.
2. Honor and serve others.
3. Duty to the Camp and its inhabitants.

The idea was discussed concerning the importance for every camper to voluntarily learn to place the needs of others ahead of their own as an outgrowth of the second law. This included the concepts of service and sacrifice. However, at the same time it was emphasized that personal property remained their own, and would be respected as such. No one had a right to anything belonging to another and the only real communal property were the camp buildings and various tools that were specifically designated as camp property.

If people could not keep the rules, they would be asked to leave and forced to leave if necessary. Once someone left the camp either voluntarily, or otherwise, they would not be allowed to return.

Problems that came up would be handled by the camp leadership, starting with a family, or group head, then working their way, as necessary, up through the groups to leaders of ten, leaders of fifty, and so on. Only when more serious problems arose would a group of leaders be called together, modeled after church councils with half to support the accused, to prevent injustice and half assigned to speak for the accuser. The most serious offences would find the accused turned over to the local law enforcement authorities for investigation and punishment under the jurisdiction in which the camp operated.

While the camp regulations were founded on the "Basic Three" as they were called, there were in fact five detailed rules, clearly written and posted in an attempt to prevent misunderstandings and complications.

Rule 1. Camp rules apply to everyone.

Rule 2. All men are required to work to the best of their ability on their camp assignments.

Rule 3. God will be honored and no conduct will be

tolerated that will cause the spirit of God to leave. (Including, but not limited to: contention, lying, stealing, vulgar language, and sexual misconduct).

Rule 4. If a person does something that hurts, or affects someone else, that person would be expected to make complete restitution. If the offence was intentional, or through misconduct, a penalty will be issued by camp leadership.

Rule 5. Any activity, or conduct that is determined as detrimental to the security, or well being of the camp will not be tolerated.

It was explained that during the next few weeks the whole camp would be reorganized into new Stakes and Wards. Three Presidents would be called and assigned to Stakes consisting of two hundred families each and Bishops would be called to serve each ward of fifty families. This would put about two hundred fifty people in each ward. As the camp expanded, new wards and stakes would be organized as needed.

While the normal stake and ward organizations would be setup, home and visiting teaching would be handled a little differently. Everyone would have a home teacher and the Elders Quorum, or High Priest Group Leader working with the Bishop would then choose a home teaching supervisor responsible for ten families.

Everyone should expect to have specific work assignments given them while at the camp which would need to be carried out everyday except

Sundays. Women were invited to take care of their families first, and then to volunteer to help in the general camp, when available. Each Ward and Stake would take the lead to make sure the needs of their members were taken care of as everyone prepared for winter. There was a lot to accomplish before cold weather set in and there were preparations necessary for the large influx of people expected over the next several months and particularly, this time next year.

Jared volunteered to work in the security group for the camp and was quickly put in charge of it. He sought out those who had military, or law enforcement experience, then quickly set up twenty four hour perimeter security, with checkpoints, and guard patrols. Because of the increased martial law in the country over the past two years, armed security did not seem out of place; in fact, it seemed to provide a sense of calm for everyone. Jared also setup a schedule of weapons training classes for the entire camp, since almost everyone had brought their own firearms.

Mornings, in the newly defined daily schedules, were reserved for breakfasts, family chores, scripture reading, and simple assigned tasks up until 8:30 am. Exercise was also strongly encouraged during this time. At 8:30 group devotionals were held which included the Pledge of Allegiance, a hymn, group prayer and finally, announcements and assignment changes.

In the late afternoon and evenings there were classes on just about everything from using and cooking food storage to blacksmithing. During the day many of the men were assigned to go out and collect firewood and building materials. Other groups were assigned to work on building more camp structures and fences. Garden plots were created and cared for and still others took care of the cattle and sheep, and prepared winter shelters for the livestock.

Granny and Rachel volunteered and were assigned to the First Aid/Infirmary group. The camp was blessed to have three doctors, one dentist, three EMT's and several nurses. There were also four experienced midwives, which thrilled both the doctors and Granny. The doctors were all from the same small town clinic, one of which had married a Shumway great niece and so was well known to Granny. The doctors were there because of a dream that one of them had had about tent cities and famine when he was growing up. The impact that one dream had on the clinic was tremendous and they were all well prepared for the callout.

A facility was arranged as well and as quickly as they could, which included two birthing rooms, since there were several women expecting in the next few days and weeks. One of the nicest trailers in the camp was generously donated to serve as this hospital.

One of the doctors was always assigned to go out with each logging crew, along with an EMT and a nurse, just in case. There were also two other first aid stations setup at other locations in the camp, staffed by nurses and the EMT's. Fortunately, they spent most of their time giving first aid classes and tending to minor injuries. A goal was made, to have everyone in the camp above the age of twelve, learn enough to essentially satisfy the requirements for the First Aid Merit Badge. They also wanted every family to have an adequate first aid kit. One final goal of the medical group was to have one, more fully trained lay medical assistant and a midwife for each group of ten and fifty families.

Granny was well received and respected by all of the medical people because of her reputation. The doctors actually drew straws to see who got to sit in on her first herbal classes. They had the attitude and understanding that in the wilderness, far away from modern medical facilities and medicines, though they had brought as much as they could with them, ultimately she was the best trained and qualified for what they faced. They had decided to reserve their medical materials as much as they could for the larger and more severe emergencies, relying upon herbal remedies to take care of most problems.

Rachel was learning a lot as Granny treated her as her assistant, explaining everything she did. After a week, Granny asked her to perform some of the treatments for the patients who filtered in from time to time. Rachel was learning that the heart of herbal medicine was to cleanse and nourish. That after poisons and toxins were cleansed from the body, and the body provided proper nourishment, then the body could perform almost miraculous feats of self repair.

Breakfast and lunch were often a "family" affair for

Granny, Jared, and Rachel, eaten together since they had the necessary supplies and preparation to cook for themselves. Often, they invited others to join them since most families were forced to group together according to their needs, cooking skills and preparations. Dinner was often a group of either ten, or fifty families with a potluck, or something where everyone contributed.

Rachel was amazed at how long it took to cook and prepare food from scratch and then to clean it all up afterwards, even though Granny was a master at it. Rachel really missed her food processor, refrigerator, and dishwasher, especially her pre-packaged foods, though she had to admit the meals Granny cooked from scratch were delicious and the bread was divine. Part of Granny's preparedness was a large wood burning cook stove with attached oven, she called it a modified sheep herders stove. Granny was now starting to teach Rachel to cook from scratch, considering such basic knowledge the other half of her basic education.

Since Granny seemed to know everyone, she was a constant source of information, which she often shared at meal time. One day she heard that even though the main callout, or 'invitation' was extended to the members of the Church in many places simultaneously, 'invitations' actually had been extended over a three week period.

She also learned that not everyone was invited to the long term camps up in the mountains like they had been. There were a few locations in remote areas where people were asked to stay behind and host others in their yards and homes for a period of time. These were temporary gathering places. With the arrival of more people, they would be moved as a group to the long term camps.

Also, there were those who were asked to remain in their homes, like Granny's nephew Jimmy, to work the farms and ranches for a period of time with the intent of harvesting the crops, and moving all of the animals quickly up to the camps as soon as possible. Those were the additional people that the camp was preparing for and expected to arrive later in the summer and fall.

They also expected a much larger group of refugees with nothing, but the clothes on their back, to start arriving the following spring. It was expected that the camp would more than double, possibly even triple in size by that time.

During the first couple of weeks, Elder Pinetree asked anyone who had brought cash, to consider donating it to the camp treasury. Many did, including several who gave large amounts of silver and gold coins that they had brought with them.

As part of this, camp needs would be assessed from time to time and when there were critical items needed that had to be acquired from the outside, a determination would be made if it was safe to travel and purchase the necessary items. One of the things that Jared insisted on was some barbed wire, not just for the cattle pens, but for security as well. He had also requested some heavy electrical wire, very large lights, and some batteries with solar panels to charge them.

Granny also heard about the main stream news reports about the callout. It was simply presented that the LDS Church had increased its tent encampments and invited its membership at large to gather to them. For the most part, the news went unnoticed in the world, at least for now. It appeared there were just too many other, more critical events, taking place that occupied the news and the interest of the people.

The Associated Press did release a story, reporting that the 'Homophobic Hate Organization known as the Mormon Church,' was expanding its tent encampments. The story included interviews with neighbors of the people leaving for the camps who were happy that such 'hate mongers' were finally gone from their area. As far as those who had been interviewed for the story were concerned, such hate groups could not only leave the city, but were also free to leave the country as well. "American freedom has no place for such bigoted, homophobic and racist people..." was one of the quotes from the article. The largest of the apostate organizations called 'Mormons For Equality & Freedom,' made their usual plea for those still confused members of the LDS church to become enlightened, to show forth true love and compassion for all of God's children, to become free of the tyranny of the Church, and to join them in their struggle against oppression.

Most of the news agencies relegated the AP article to an unnoticed spot on the second, or third page of their web sites since the day before the announcement from the Church, the rhetoric between mainland China and Taiwan heated up again, and the Egyptian government had capitulated completely to the Islamic Brotherhood forces, and were in the process of negotiating a cease fire with the Iranian backed group so that they would leave the country.

Other top news stories occupying the front pages included one stating that the Afghanistan war was going badly. It reported a further setback in a battle with the Iranian and Pakistani backed Afghani Freedom Fighters. The U.S. President was considering sending more troops into the region and at this time, he was asking for volunteers from the Federal Civilian Defense Force to become full time military. There was some heavy debate taking place concerning the possibility of mandating up to 20% of the CDF, some two million men and women between the ages of eighteen and twenty eight who had received CDF training, into the full time military and sending many of them to Afghanistan.

These stories of the world in commotion, plus the fact that over four hundred so called 'tent cities' which were already functioning across the country, many of them run by various denominations, but, most by state and federal government, for the nation's homeless...made the gathering of church members appear fairly mundane.

The LDS Church had previously constructed 13 of

these tent encampments, in various locations across the nation a year earlier as part of its welfare program to provide its members an alternative to the government camps. One of the major differences between the LDS Church camps and almost every government run camp was that those living in the LDS camps did not receive welfare, or assistance from the government, and therefore were not required to have the Federal ID chip implanted in their hands.

The homeless had become a new and growing part of the U.S. population. Most were on government welfare programs, and many were involved in the Civilian Defense Force or the Federal Jobs program. The newscasts had been flooded with stories about the constant construction of new tent cities and the increase in the homeless over the past year. People in general were tired of such stories, and now that the economy was starting to improve, everyone was looking for good news.

For many of the people watching the news, hearing that the LDS Church had expanded its camps, was just another demonstration of its antiquated views, when so many were already talking about tent city cutbacks in the future. In fact, just a few weeks earlier, the big news had been when one of the largest camps in the country, run by the State of Georgia, just outside of Atlanta, announced that they were beginning the process to dismantle it and expected that within the next two years all families in the camp would be moved into homes.

On the day after the Church wide callout to the

camps, an LDS Church spokesperson simply announced that the Church had decided to set up additional temporary facilities for those of its membership who needed a place of refuge in these troublesome times.

Granny also told Rachel and Jared what she had heard regarding the situations at several wards and stakes after the callout. Most of the local church buildings had been closed because of the security issues with vandalism and the lack of leadership. The week following the main callout, hundreds of buildings were set on fire and/or vandalized. Arguments and even several fist fights broke out in chapels where remaining members tried to hold meetings anyway.

Several of the apostate groups were claiming that Church leaders had finally shown their true colors and pronounced them as fallen. Great recruiting drives were made by these organizations claiming that it was time for them to step out from the shadows and take the true lead over church membership. One of the scriptures they used quite effectively was Matthew 24:26 *"Wherefore if they shall say unto you, Behold, he is in the desert; go not forth: behold, he is in the secret chambers; believe it not."* The apostates said that anyone who counseled people to leave their homes and go into the wilderness was obviously a false Prophet, or Apostle trying to deceive the elect. Granny said it reminded her of what had happened in Kirtland and Nauvoo after the main body of the Saints had left. When Jared said he didn't understand, it took Granny over an hour to explain it to him in great detail.

CHAPTER 28

It was evening, eight days after their arrival in camp, when things were finally organized and life had started to settle into a routine. It was hard for Granny to keep Rachel down and off her foot, but in spite of her frequent use of it, it was still healing quite well. In another two weeks Granny felt that she wouldn't need the crutches. However, after each day filled with so much activity, especially using the crutches, Rachel climbed into her sleeping bag and almost immediately fell asleep. Occasionally, if she wasn't quite so tired, she would practice unlocking the handcuffs with the hairpin, as Jared had taught her, all the while hoping to never again have the need for the technique.

As Granny sat in a chair near one of the large group fires that had become a gathering place at the end of the day, Jared sat down next to her.

Without much of an introduction Jared jumped into what he needed to say. "I need to leave in the next couple of days and find out what's going on and work on getting our names cleared." By now, Jared had grown a stubby beard, peppered with gray.

"I knew this day would come." Granny acknowledged. "Do you know what you're going to do exactly?"

"No," Jared admitted, ", but my staying here would

put everyone in jeopardy, especially you and Rachel. Eventually, they will come here and find out our true identities, I expect sooner rather than later. In fact, I'm surprised they haven't shown up yet.

"I understand." Granny said, and then paused, a little sad at the inevitable turn of events. "When you get things cleared up, do you think you might return? You know you are welcome here and there will always be a place for you at my table."

"I've considered that, and I think that I might. There are some good reasons to want to come back." Jared's eyes twinkled slightly as he allowed himself to say those words, knowing that Granny would understand his meaning.

"Have you told her yet?" Granny asked with the knowledge that they shared a secret without any words having been spoken.

"Not yet," Jared confessed. "I have a couple of things to do with the security team yet and then I can leave. The day after tomorrow I know of a car that is leaving to go south on some camp business. I have made arrangements to hitch a ride with them."

Jared placed two pieces of folded paper into Granny's hand. "Just in case I don't return and you need it, here are the instructions on how to get to my storage under the barn. I've also included a power of attorney to my property. If I haven't returned in a year, you can do whatever you want with it. It'll be yours. You might consider giving it to the Church if you want to, or to Rachel. It's up to you."

With that, Jared got up and walked off into the darkness.

The following night, after the evening activities and just before Rachel headed off for bed, Jared asked her if she would take a short walk so they could talk a little. She said, "Of course," and, on her crutches, walked with Jared side by side a little ways past the tents, out among the tall pine trees. There was enough light that they could still see each other's faces clearly here. Where she had been exhausted just a few minutes before, she was now very much alert.

Jared stopped her by touching her shoulder softly and then turned to face her. Rachel looked up into his face, lit by the glow of a distant lantern. It was framed by his almost black beard touched with the slightest bit of gray here and there. Jared looked into her eyes silently for a moment then reached up to stroke the side of her face. His gentle touch was so soothing and yet electrifying, all at the same time. "Rachel," he began with a whisper, and then hesitated. He looked at her for a moment longer before continuing.

"You, more than anyone understand that I have to leave. I have to find out why they want me and I have to clear our names." He paused, as if searching for words that would make this less painful for both of them. "These people are killers and unless I take care of things, eventually they will find you and me and finish what they started."

Tears started to well up in Rachel's eyes as she listened to him and continued to look into his face. Jared was finding this much harder than he had imagined. *"She is so beautiful,"* he thought.

"I've explained everything to Elder Pinetree and President Garland, and they agree. By the way, they now know who you and I really are, but will keep it to themselves for our safety. They're good people and I am very impressed with them."

Jared had the opportunity as head of security to work closely with both of these men. He had learned that Elder Pinetree was a retired Lieutenant Colonel in the Air Force and they had gotten along famously. It was under Elder Pinetree's direction that Jared had been put in charge of camp security.

"As soon as I discover who's behind all of this and clear it up I will return. I have permission from Elder Pinetree to return to the camp at any time after I take care of this situation."

Rachel continued to stare into his eyes, hesitant to ask the question that she already knew the answer to. But, she asked it anyway, in almost a whisper, "When are you leaving?"

"Early in the morning," Jared said with a sigh. "There is a car leaving on some camp business and I've arranged to hitch a ride with them."

He continued reluctantly. "There is a chance that I might not be able to return as soon as I would like. I have people I trust, but they're up north. If you need to get a message to me," he pulled a small piece of paper from his pocket and held it out in his hand for Rachel to take. "This is where they are located. They'll know how to contact me. I'm sorry, I don't have his telephone number, but this is his address up in Spokane. He's an old army buddy that I trust with my life. I'll leave information on how to get hold of me with him. If I have to, I have an old cabin of my grandfathers up in Montana on the edge of Glacier National Park, near the Canadian border where I can stay for a time."

Rachel looked down at the paper in his hand. She let go of her crutch with one hand to take the note, and the crutch fell with a slow motion thud to the ground. She carefully removed the note, from him then spontaneously let go of the other crutch and threw her arms around his neck, leaning her head on his chest. She closed her eyes and held him not wanting to let him go, but knowing she must. There were so many things she wanted to tell him. She wanted to say "I'll miss you,' and 'hurry back," but in the end she didn't say anything because she wasn't sure what would come out of her mouth.

Her move surprised Jared at first, but happily he returned the embrace, holding her close to him. They stood that way for a few minutes, not saying anything, with Jared nuzzling her hair as she listened to the beating of his heart.

After a while, she pulled away just far enough to look up at him. With both his hands, Jared softly caressed her face, and then used one hand to brush her hair out and away from her eyes. She wanted to kiss him and as he leaned over towards her she closed her eyes in anticipation. At that moment, they heard a voice behind them say, "Please excuse me folks. I'm very sorry to intrude here, but there's a little problem and Elder Pinetree sent me to find you."

Unwilling to lose this moment, Jared replied without looking away, "Okay, I'll be right there. Thanks." The messenger departed quickly, anxious to report that his assignment was complete. Not knowing what to expect now, after the interruption, Rachel felt his hands gently tilting her head down, just a little and then felt his lips on her forehead as he softly kissed her there. He held her close once again with her head against his chest and his face in her hair. He tightened his embrace for a split second and said, "Think about me while I'm gone." He let her go, reached down to pick up her crutches, handed them to her, then turned and walked away.

CHAPTER 29

JARED, THREE WEEKS LATER

Jared had finally made his way up to Spokane. First, he had gone to the outskirts of Tucson, where he had obtained a throwaway cell phone, and had then started making inquiries. What he heard wasn't good. Bennett was head of the Blackbird unit that was providing support for the Intermountain Homeland Security region, a position of power and authority, and more importantly, one with a great deal of resources. No one knew why, or who wanted Jared originally, but now there was a warrant out for his arrest as a material witness on a sealed federal charge. Rachel was also wanted as a witness to a murder and arson investigation.

Jared decided that he needed to go to Bennett's "back yard" so to speak, to Ogden, Utah and see what he could find out there. It took him longer than he expected ...a full two weeks...to make the trip, but after three days in Ogden he had learned nothing new about his situation, and had nearly been caught twice at surprise checkpoints. After the second time, he had decided that the best thing he could do was to hunker down for a few months, or so, at least until after winter and see if time would take care of things. He then headed to Spokane to visit with Tom on the way to the cabin.

He had not been able to get any messages to the

camp in Arizona.   He soon discovered that while people knew about the camps, they were generally glad that the Mormons were gone.   He also found out that there was basically no communications into, or out of the camps. That, for all intents and purposes, they had cut themselves off from the world.

Jared arrived at his grandfather's old mining cabin in the Kootenai National Forest, riding on a silenced Honda 400 motorcycle.   He had made good time, even driving the back roads at night, after getting the motorcycle with the help of his friend in Spokane and fixing it up, "special ops" style.   By this time, Jared had a full beard, and had picked up a false ID. It was still amazing what one could do with a little cash. The black-market in Spokane was alive and doing very well. The ID was actually a backup, just in case he could not avoid the officials and got stopped.

Everything at the cabin was as he had left it two years before, the last time he had come and spent three weeks at the cabin.   He started getting ready for a long, cold winter.

RACHEL

Seven weeks after Jared left, Rachel was walking and running around on her ankle without crutches, or even a limp. Life in camp had become routine and she soon found herself as the second counselor in the Young Women's Presidency for her ward.   She actually enjoyed working with the youth and was having a wonderful time with the enthusiastic girls.   For most of the girls it was like a super long girl's camp. Every week seemed to bring a new adventure with it.

Between keeping up with the girls, learning from Granny about herbs, cooking from scratch and all of the other things that just came up, Rachel kept herself very busy. So busy, that she only thought about Jared a couple of times a day, wondering what he was doing and if he was safe. In the whole time since he left, they had not heard a word of any kind from Jared.

During the seven weeks, eleven families had chosen to leave the camp for various reasons, mostly because it was too much work and they missed their television, play stations, and X-boxes. However, fourteen new families had come to take their places.

Saturdays at the camp had come to be a wonderful time, full of activities, and games. A softball tournament had been organized with a co-ed team from each ward. Rachel had been told that she played a great first base and she was learning how to place her hits better. Though hard and different, life was wonderful and for the most part, everyone was happy. Romances were blossoming everywhere and Rachel had been asked a couple of times to attend the dances that were held almost every Friday night, but each time, she had declined.

One night, Rachel had a dream. It was a wonderful and familiar dream. She was in the temple, dressed in a long, white, flowing gown. The room was filled with many people. As always, she couldn't see their faces, but she knew that they were all very happy for her. She was again kneeling at the all too familiar altar, but this time, when she looked up from her hands, clasped with someone else's, she looked into Jared's face. Even in her dream, she caught her breath with surprise. Jared was dressed all in white. There seemed to be a glow around him. His eyes were not gray anymore, but a deep blue and he was clean shaven. As she gazed upon him, he broke into a wide happy grin. And that was when she woke up.

The next day she couldn't stop thinking about that dream. She felt it was more than just a regular dream, that it was something special, but she was afraid to think about what it could mean. Finally, she broke down and talked to Granny about it. Granny told her that dreams are sometimes hard to interpret and sometimes it takes a long time to understand their real meaning. She told Rachel that the same thing often happens with spiritual impressions.

Granny said that her husband Robert had repeatedly told her that too often when people receive a message from the Lord, they are in such a hurry and get so excited, that they don't wait for the message to be completed, but they try to finish the Lords revelation for Him...sometimes missing the full nature and meaning of what the Lord was trying to say. This is because we are impatient and our personal desires cloud, or warp, our view of things.

Granny counseled Rachel to learn patience and let the Lord finish his message for her, and teach her Himself what it meant in His time frame. She also counseled Rachel to remember that along with messages; sometimes we have tests, to see what we will do with the information.

Rachel had the exact same dream the next two nights.

BENNETT

Bennett was beside himself. Pressure was mounting to find Jared. The last message over the secure cell phone had been very cryptic and insistent. They were definitely not happy.

He believed that Jared and the girl were hiding in one of the Mormon camps. There was no other place for them to go, and so, he was going through the list he had just received, line by line. Bennett sat at his desk, scanning the names of all the people who were at the camps, specifically, the Mormon camp east of Show Low. The federal government had requested from the Church the list of those who were in the camps, supposedly to see if wanted felons were hiding among them. It had taken a while, but the lists finally came.

Also, because of the rigid new bankruptcy laws, they were looking for anyone who was trying to skip out on their debts. The government had nationalized just about every company, including the credit card companies, which meant that the government owned most of the credit card debt in the nation. The new laws allowed the government to collect on delinquent debt by having the debtors work it off in either the civilian labor force, or the defense force, with the government taking a portion of their government "pay." The labor force now employed over sixteen million people in one way, or another. The defense force had close to five million involved.

By this time, the government had informants in several of the camps. They had also sent teams, who took pictures of everyone using telephoto lenses and now they were in the process of identifying the people in each camp, matching names to photos. Bennett had received a tip from the informant at the Show Low area camp about someone who might possibly fit the description of the girl, someone named Shumway. He was waiting now for the picture to be sent to him.

About ten minutes later he was handed the fax. The angle wasn't good; the hair was the wrong color, but he thought as he scrutinized the photo, "*It could be her.*" It was close enough that Bennett decided to fly down and see for himself. He would be in the camp by tomorrow afternoon where he would meet her face to face. If it was her, he knew that the camp would not harbor wanted felons. They had already picked up a couple of people from other camps wanted on various charges, and he knew there would be more as soon as the identification program was complete.

Bennett picked up the phone and started the process rolling for him to fly to Arizona for the investigation.

RACHEL

Rachel was pondering her dreams and Granny's advice when she finally went to sleep. Before crawling into bed she had spent twenty minutes on her knees, asking for guidance and direction. Her prayers were becoming longer and more focused. She had been persistent in asking that Heavenly Father's will be done rather than hers. She had dreamed of Jared for three nights in a row, and it hadn't varied at all..., but didn't want to jump to conclusions that might not be correct. She was still not sure what the dream meant.

This night instead of the wonderful familiar temple dream, Rachel had a terrible nightmare. She saw Jared chopping down a tree in a pine forest. The tree fell and it landed on him. She didn't see exactly how it injured him, but the next thing she saw was him lying on a bed in a cabin. There were wolves surrounding the cabin, pacing and trying to get in. Jared was trapped, he couldn't get out. There was a bear coming toward the cabin that was big and very powerful. The bear ripped the door off of its hinges and the bear and the wolves rushed into the cabin. At the moment just before they killed Jared, he looked at her and said, "Help me. Save me. I need you. I need you NOW."

As the animals started to tear into Jared, Rachel started to scream. Then the dream ended.

Rachel woke with a start and realized that it was just a dream. It was pitch black in the tent and her breath was coming in gasps as her body was shaking from head to toe. She sat up on her cot, swinging the bottom of her sleeping bag to the ground. Trying to calm herself, she slowed her breath and tears, and thought about her dream. It seemed so real, as if she was there. Jared's words echoed in her mind. "Help me. Save me. I need you. I need you NOW." The feeling was so strong and the need so immediate.

Not knowing what else to do, she turned around and knelt by her cot to pray. She asked her Heavenly Father what the dream meant and if it was important for her to understand it's meaning, to be given the interpretation. After several minutes her mind was completely calm. She suddenly felt sleepy and decided the best thing for her to do, was to go back to sleep and forget about the dream. She crawled back onto her cot and very quickly fell asleep.

The dream began again, exactly as it had before and she woke up, again just as the bear and the wolves were rushing into the cabin. Jared again seemed to look up at her and said the same thing as in the first dream. "Help me. Save me. I need you. I need you NOW." Only this time, he added the words "Come help me in Montana," at the end.

When Rachel woke up this time, at the end of the dream, she didn't scream, but quickly sat up again, pondering the dream in her mind. It was almost like she had been watching a movie, knowing what was going to happen, before it did. She wasn't panicked like she had been before, but she did feel an urgency that she had something to do, but again, she wasn't sure what. Once more, she knelt down and prayed for guidance and understanding. Again, at the end of her fervent prayer, she felt drowsy and crawled back onto her cot, and once again, she fell quickly to sleep.

For the third time, she had the dream. There was another difference this time, as the wolves and bear rushed into the cabin to kill Jared, they transformed into men wearing black clothes. She didn't see them carrying any guns, and it seemed as if they were going to rip him apart with their hands and teeth, just as if they were animals. Again, just before they reached him, he looked directly at her and said "Help me. Save me. I need you. I need you NOW. Come help me in Montana." Then he added the words, "Rachel, only you can save me." His look seemed to burn into her soul and she noticed that his eyes were not gray, but the same brilliant blue, as they had been in her temple dream.

This time after her prayer, she was wide awake. Using a very small key light, Rachel got dressed and went outside. It was a beautiful evening. The stars were brilliant and they filled the sky. Though she had spent a lot of time out in the woods before coming to this camp, and had seen many beautiful nights, she couldn't remember a time when the night had been so black with the stars so visible and bright. They seemed close enough to reach out and touch.

Rachel sat down in one of the chairs at the front of the tent and pondered the nightmare she had just experienced. The first time, it was truly a nightmare and she had been terrified, but with the next two repetitions, it wasn't overwhelming panic she had felt. It was concern and urgency. She sat pondering, and tried to figure out what the two dreams meant. As she pondered them, wondering if they were related, she remembered Jared's eyes. In both dreams they were the same color. They were blue. As she thought about it she seemed to feel that the dreams were connected, though how, she was not entirely sure.

The more she thought about the nightmare, the more she pondered the words Jared spoke to her. "Come to Montana," he had said. "Come now." The more she thought about the words, the more she felt she needed to go to Montana, though she didn't understand what she could do to help. She thought about the tree falling on Jared and wondered if he had been injured. With the training that she had been receiving from Granny, she felt that she could help him.

As she sat thinking, Rachel heard a rustling and turned to see Granny emerge from the tent, her small figure dark against the pale, star lit canvas. Granny took the chair next to her and looked up into the sky and after a minute spoke, "Beautiful aren't they?"

"Yes, they certainly are." Rachel agreed, also staring up into the night sky.

"Robert used to call them the lights shining through the windows of God's home...our old home." Rachel and Granny just looked at the stars for a few minutes, not speaking.

"I've had another dream." Rachel confessed. "Actually, another three dreams, all in one night."

Granny looked at Rachel with curiosity. "Would you like to talk about them?" she asked.

"Yes." Rachel was actually anxious to discuss what she had seen with Granny. She paused, collecting her thoughts and then began. "They were very different from the temple dreams, though I think they are related." Rachel then went on to describe her dream in detail.

As Rachel finished relating her dreams and her feelings about them, there was a slight glow beginning to show in the eastern sky.

"I think you're right." Granny finally said. "These dreams are important and I also think that they're related." She paused for several minutes while they both watched the light in the east grow brighter and chase the darkness away.

"I also think you are right about leaving and going to Montana. I'm not sure why, but I think you need to leave quickly."

Rachel was surprised to hear Granny's suggestion and she became confused. "How would I get there?" She asked. "I am not even sure exactly where his cabin is. He gave me the address of a friend of his in Spokane who would know how to contact him, but there is no phone number."

"Well, I am not sure," Granny went on, ", but I think we should go and talk to President Garland.

Let's see what he thinks. In fact, I happen to know that he is a very early riser and we should be able to talk to him if we go right now, before breakfast gets underway."

With that, they both got up and walked to President Garland's tent. When they approached, he was sitting in a chair, out in front of his tent with his scriptures and a little battery powered reading light in his lap.

President Garland listened quietly as Granny and Rachel related the dreams and impressions, and the feeling that Rachel needed to leave and travel north to see Jared.

After listening to everything they had to say, President Garland turned to Granny and asked seriously, "Sister Shumway, do you really feel that Rachel should leave the safety of this camp, leave friends and family, and head north to a place that she has never been, to help someone who hasn't asked for her help, when she is not even sure of where he is, or if he really needs her help, all without a means of transportation to get there?" President Garland paused and waited for her response to his sincere question.

Granny thought about what the President had just asked her, realizing the dangers that would surely be involved and then answering with a firmness that surprised even her, said, "Yes, President. Yes, I do."

President Garland looked into Granny's eyes for a moment and then into Rachel's. Rachel felt as if he were searching her soul and that he could see everything, even those things she might try, in vain, to hide.

President Garland then spoke. "I think you sisters may be right. It just so happens that this morning, in about half an hour, there is a car leaving for Salt Lake City. I do not think that your coming here to see me this early morning is just a coincidence. I feel God's hand in this." Turning to Rachel he said, "I will talk to Elder Pinetree and make the arrangements. Can you be at the main flag pole in about twenty minutes, ready to go?"

"Yes sir." Rachel answered.

"Good." President Garland responded as he stood up and shook their hands. "I will see you in about twenty minutes then." he said, as he turned and started walking towards Elder Pinetree's tent.

BENNETT

Later that same afternoon, Bennett was a passenger in a tan Humvee riding over a dusty Arizona road to the Mormon Camp. He was wearing his official Homeland Security uniform, with the Blackbird patch on the shoulder. Another Humvee carried four additional uniformed Blackbird soldiers, all armed. He had arrived at the Show Low airport two hours earlier and the anticipation was growing and eating at him as he impatiently endured the two hour drive.

When they arrived at the camp gate, they presented their credentials and were immediately ushered into the camp.

To Bennett, it looked like just another of the tent encampments that he had seen all over the country. This one did seem more orderly, however and quite a bit cleaner, plus, it had much nicer surroundings being among the pine trees and by the small lake.
In his mind, Bennett had immediately begun making plans on how to attack the camp, if necessary, overcoming the meager security detail and hauling everyone off to one of Homeland Security's large *secure* camps.

Bennett had heard that such plans had already been discussed. Homeland Security had considered, when the time came, that they would just take over the Mormon camps, and put a double fifteen foot chain link fence topped with barbed wire around them, transforming them into 'secure' government camps. It would save them the cost of transportation, not to mention that these camps were already isolated and full of the dissidents that they were most concerned about.

Standing in front of the three leaders of the camp, Bennett proceeded. "We are looking for two people, wanted for questioning in conjunction with a federal investigation into a homicide and arson case. We have reason to believe that they might be here. I would like to talk with a Rhonda Shumway to see if she knows anything about them."

The three leaders looked at each other and then the white haired man who had been introduced as Elder Pinetree spoke for all of them. "We would be glad to cooperate with Homeland Security, but the person known as Rhonda Shumway left camp just this morning. She is not here."

Bennett response to this revelation started out as a low growl. "What do you mean she is not here?" he said

"Early this morning, she decided that she needed to leave." Elder Pinetree explained. "And so she left about 6:30 this morning. As you are probably aware, everyone here is free to leave whenever they choose."

Bennett's mind was seething and he had to consciously make an effort to control his anger and not yell at these three men. "Can you describe her?" Bennett asked, regaining a semblance of control. "Who did she spend time with here at the camp? Who did she leave with this morning? How did she leave and where might she be headed? Also, I would like to question anyone here who she spent time with. In fact," turning around and grabbing the folder from the soldier standing directly behind him, "here is a picture of the person we are looking for."

As Bennett was opening the folder, Elder Pinetree said, "Certainly, President Garland here can answer most of those questions." Turning to another man standing to the side, he asked, "Mark, would you be so kind as to get Granny and tell her that we would like see her? She is probably over at the clinic." The man immediately turned and left without saying a word.

Bennett pulled the color picture out of the folder and handed it to President Garland. "Is this her?"

President Garland studied it for a minute before replying. "Yes, that is Rhonda. Though the hair is a different color, it is definitely her." He then handed the picture to President Pinetree.

Bennett's excitement was difficult to conceal. He had her; his instincts had been right. She had been here just this morning. She had not gone to the east as the clues had suggested, she hadn't gone anywhere. "What color is her hair now?" he asked.

"It is a very dark brown." President Garland answered directly. "She arrived in June when the majority of the people came to the camps. She was with Granny Shumway, I mean Margaret Shumway and a man who went by the name of Jeremy Shumway."

Bennett almost jumped at the mention of the man. "Who and where is this Jeremy?" He reached back and got another folder from his aide. Opening the folder, he pulled another picture out, "Is this the man?"

President Garland took the picture and after just a

second nodded, "Yes," he said, "That's Jeremy. He left almost two months ago. He got a ride and was dropped off in Tucson, I believe. We haven't heard from him since." President Garland returned the photo.

Bennett went on with his explanation. "These are the two people we are after. His real name is Jared Davis and her real name is Rachel Sinclair. They are both fugitives from the law."

By this time, Elder Pinetree's assistant, Mark, had returned with Granny.

"Major Bennett," President Garland began the introduction with his arm stretched out in Granny's direction, "this is Margaret Shumway." Granny nodded her head in greeting to Bennett, but stood back, eyeing him suspiciously.

"Do you have any idea where this person is, or might be headed?" Bennett asked as he handed her the photograph of Rachel.

Granny looked at the photograph and then at Elder Garland, who nodded. "I believe that when she left this morning she was headed for Salt Lake City," she answered.

Bennett handed her the second photograph, and asked, "What about this man? Do you know where he was headed when he left?"

Granny held the photo of Jared in her hand and

shook her head. "No. He never said where he was going. He just said he had to take care of some business about clearing up his name." Granny used her words to let out some of the concealed frustration she felt toward this man who had tried to hurt people she loved.

Bennett controlled his instinct for a violent confrontation with this old woman and asked, "When she left this morning did she give any indication where she was ultimately headed? Some place besides Salt Lake City?"

"She really didn't know where she was headed," Granny said truthfully. "It was all kind of sudden. She had thought about it all night long and just said that she had a very strong feeling that she needed to head north, towards Spokane. A car was leaving for Salt Lake, and so she got a ride."

Bennett was in a hurry now, "Can you describe the car she was riding in, and who she was riding with? I need names and a license plate number if you have it."

Within five minutes Bennett was back in the Humvee, talking on the radio heading towards the Show Low airport.

"When we find the car do you want us to stop it and arrest everyone?" the voice coming from the radio asked.

"No, something better," Bennett directed. "Find the

car and track it. I want to know where it is and who's inside at every minute. Don't stop it. Don't let anything stop it. She might be headed for Spokane after Salt Lake. She doesn't' have any relatives, or close friends in Spokane. We know because we've monitored all of her relatives for the past three weeks. The closest one she has was in Rexburg, but he's now up in one of these stupid Mormon camps in southeastern Idaho. My guess is that she is going to see Jared. If we follow her, she'll lead us right to him." Bennett thought to himself, with satisfaction and cunning, *"Better yet... she is coming into my territory...where I am king."*

As Bennett's plane was nearing Ogden, he received a call and was told that they had located the vehicle and were tracking it. It had crossed the border into Utah, had just left Kanab, and was now heading north on I-89. There were four people in the vehicle, two men and two women. At their current rate of travel, they were expected to arrive, or pass through Salt Lake by late evening. The photograph of the occupants taken at the Page, Arizona border crossing was already sitting on his desk at the office.

When he got to his office, he picked up the folder and opened it to see the first picture, blown up to reveal Rachel sitting in the back seat of a tan Buick. Even in grainy black and white, he could identify her. "Well, well... I guess I'm not finished with you yet." he mumbled to himself.

About the same time that the car Rachel was riding in passed through the checkpoint at the Arizona-Utah border, the nuclear bomb went off in Los Angeles. It wasn't very big by bomb standards, though it did destroy three city blocks of the financial district and the power grid immediately went down throughout most of California. Luckily for neighboring states, the safety system stopped the cascade from going outside of California and southern Nevada. With the electrical power off and a small mushroom cloud rising above L.A., panic and rioting set in almost immediately. Within ten minutes, every nearby store of any kind was a complete mob scene and stripped of anything that wasn't nailed down. Food went first, but then televisions, appliances, and anything that could be carried, went through the broken doors and windows. Even though the damage from the blast was kept within a two mile radius, fires seemed to erupt simultaneously all over California. The usually crowded freeways and over passes became instant parking lots as millions more vehicles tried to squeeze onto them, in an attempt to escape.

Within thirty minutes, the government invoked a national emergency and declared martial law, grounding all flights across the nation. National Guard troops were instantly federalized again and placed under the direct control of Homeland Security. The Civilian Defense Force was also mobilized and assigned to help man checkpoints throughout the country.

Within an hour, the President of the United States was on television pleading for calm, saying that it appeared the bombing was an isolated terrorist incident and Homeland Security had already begun an investigation. Initial reports were indicating that the attack was an act of domestic terrorism. No matter who the perpetrators were, the President promised swift action against all those who opposed the government of the United States, including those who sympathized with the terrorists. He stressed that there was no room in this crises for any delayed reaction. The response would be immediate and justice would be served upon the heads of those responsible.

CHAPTER 30

RACHEL

The trip was an enjoyable one and uneventful. Brother and Sister Kirtland, who were both gray haired and in their sixties, were interesting and friendly company and so very knowledgeable about Family History, which had been Rachel's calling in her ward before the callout. Brother Desforges, who was driving the sedan, was a little younger, Rachel guessed he was in his fifties though it was hard to really tell. He had a very dry sense of humor and when the conversation lagged, he would tell one of his funny stories which kept all of them laughing. For the entire twelve hour trip they never turned on the radio, preferring to enjoy the lively conversation of their companions.

Brother and Sister Kirtland had been called back to Salt Lake to receive a new assignment. Brother Kirtland had been in the construction business all of his life and Rachel was surprised to find out that this older couple had been one of two hundred couples called by the Church two years earlier to construct several of the camps.

By 9 p.m., it was getting dark, and the travelers were tired. They had been driving for twelve hours straight, stopping only for lunch and dinner and bathroom breaks. Rachel had brought along a substantial amount of New Dollars, given to her by Jared, and had insisted that she buy them all lunch and dinner since they would not let her pay for gas. They had only been stopped once, at the border checkpoint at the bridge outside of Page, Arizona. The border guards had asked them to roll down their windows, and then inquired as to where they were headed. They asked for Bro. Desforges' I.D. and then motioned them through. It had gone very smoothly which gave Rachel a great deal of relief.

Brother and Sister Kirtland had suggested, or rather insisted, that Rachel and Brother Desforges, stop at their house in Spanish Fork. The Church offices were closed, they explained, and they wouldn't be able to get in until the next morning anyway. The Kirtland's said they had two guest rooms sitting vacant, needing someone to occupy them, all in all making it a very hard offer to refuse. The thought of a soft bed, sheets, and a warm shower appealed to all of them.

The house was a large, two story, split level, nestled at the foot of the hills of Spanish Fork in the back of a large cull-de-sac. Brother Kirtland explained that he had built almost all of the fifty-two houses in the subdivision. As he turned on the electricity to the house he told everyone that there would be lots of hot water by the morning. The plan was to get up, shower, and head to Salt Lake by 8 a.m.

Rachel fell asleep instantly as soon as her head hit

the pillow. For the first time in four days she didn't have any dreams. When she woke up early at 5:30 the next morning, it took her a minute to get oriented and remember where she was. For a brief moment, as she lay in bed, enjoying the clean sheets and softer bed in the darkened room, everything seemed like a dream. She had to remind herself that it wasn't a dream, however, and that those events, good and bad, really had happened.

She felt wide awake now, and not wanting to disturb anyone else in the house, determined to do something that she hadn't done in a very long time. Rachel knew there was a jogging and hiking trail up along the mountains above the Kirtland's house. After her mission, she had stayed with an old college roommate in Spanish Fork for a couple of weeks. Her old roommate was an avid jogger and they had gone jogging almost every day along the trail. It was somewhat isolated with rarely another person in sight and the view of Utah valley was spectacular, as she remembered. It seemed like a wonderful idea, and it would give her time to think.

Within ten minutes she was dressed and left the house just as there was light enough to see. She took her water bottle and a light jacket over her sweat pants and tee-shirt. She had thought for a minute about what if anything, to put into her jogging pouch along with her water bottle, and finally decided that since she didn't have her wallet she would take the cash.

In ten minutes she had climbed up to the trail, and

started her stretching routine before her jog. Her plan was to be back before breakfast and take that promised hot shower before leaving for Salt Lake, so she decided to only jog about twenty minutes one way, turn around and come back. She knew that she could run north along the trail and if she wanted to she could take it all the way to where it ended above the Provo Temple. It had been a while since she had gone jogging, but she felt enough confidence in her ankle now to do so, though she decided, just to be safe, she wrapped an ace bandage around it for support.

She planned that as she jogged in the early morning she would think about what she should do next. At this point, she wasn't sure what she was going to do, and really had no plan, but she knew that at least she was headed in the right direction and that much closer to Jared. Granny had said when she got to Salt Lake someone would be able to help her there.

After stretching for a few minutes Rachel stopped to enjoy the beautiful view of the valley as it started to wake up. Most of the valley was still under a light blanket of shadow with their twinkling lights. She could see the houses below, the freeway, farmlands and the lake in the distance at the foot of the brown Oquirrh Mountains. There was even a touch of orange on the distant clouds. It was hard, at this moment, watching this peaceful scene, to imagine that anything was wrong in this world, or that there were problems that could not be fixed.

Just as she turned to start jogging, Rachel glanced

toward the freeway and noticed a long line of green army trucks. *"Another convoy,"* she thought. They had seen a couple of army convoys the day before on the freeway. There hadn't been much traffic on the roads as they had traveled and now there weren't any cars, or vehicles on the road, making the convoy of trucks stand out all the more. She watched them as they drove along and then noticed that there were four trucks just like them driving up the street where the Kirtland's lived.

Rather than starting her jog, something told her to stop and watch them, which she did, intently. *"What would army trucks be doing in a residential area?"* She wondered. She watched as all four trucks came to a stop. After the trucks stopped, soldiers emerged from the one in the lead and the one in back. To Rachel's surprise and horror she saw that they were all carrying weapons. The soldiers divided up with half of them approaching a house on one side of the street and the others advancing toward a house across from it.

Another two trucks arrived on the street, passed the first four and drove a little farther up the road. The light was getting brighter now and Rachel could see more clearly what was happening down below. The soldiers wore what looked like a plain gray uniform; she guessed it was a new one that she hadn't seen before.

After knocking on the door of the house, Rachel watched as a couple of soldiers went in, and within about fifteen minutes out of the house came what must have been the family... a mother, father and three children, two boys and a girl. They were all carrying suitcases and one of the little boys was carrying what looked like a teddy bear. The soldiers helped them into the back of the second truck.

Rachel's attention was then drawn to the house across the street as something came flying through the front window, shattering it. Immediately, three more soldiers entered the house at a run. Shortly, thereafter, the soldiers came out, two of them dragging a man between them. She could tell from his movements that he was fighting and screaming at them, but they were just ignoring him. They were followed by a soldier holding a woman by the arm as she walked beside him. Rachel noticed that this family was not carrying suitcases, or bags as the other family had.

The two soldiers carrying the man threw him on the ground and held him there as the third one tried to put what looked like handcuffs on him. Rachel could see that the man wasn't cooperating and was still struggling against them. One of the other soldiers, who had been watching from a little distance, walked over, and with the, butt of his rifle, hit the struggling man on the head. Instantly, he was still. The other soldier finished handcuffing him and the four of them picked the man up and literally threw him into the back of the same truck that the first family had gotten into.

Rachel noticed one of the other trucks that had come with this group, turning down a side street and driving in an area that was blocked from her view. The soldiers in the street below got back into the lead truck and then drove it up the street towards her. Rachel's heart began to beat louder as she watched the truck turn a corner and come to a stop in front of the Kirtland's house. It was lighter now and the truck and its occupants were closer so she was able to see more of the details. The soldiers once again got out of the truck, and approached the house. One of them went to the back; one went to one side and another one to the opposite side of the house. There were also two near the front door. They had surrounded the house.

Rachel was also able to notice, from this distance, that they didn't look like American soldiers, or uniforms. The uniforms were different somehow, and then she noticed the blue arm patch. *"Those are U.N. soldiers,"* she thought. She decided to sit down on the trail behind some of the scrub brush while she watch what was going on, but to remain hidden. She was frightened at what she was witnessing and felt entirely helpless to assist her friends. In a few minutes, the soldiers emerged from the house with the Kirtland's and Brother Desforges in custody. They were carrying the bags that they had brought from the camp and they were put into the back of the truck. Then the soldiers got in and they pulled away, going back down the street. She watched as the six trucks left the neighborhood together and drove down the road. Although in a state of shock, Rachel now noticed a few other trucks in various locations within her sight and she could see the soldiers with them.

Rachel was stunned. She sat there with her mouth open in disbelief watching the trucks and soldiers moving through the neighborhoods below. Within forty minutes the trucks had all gone and nothing stirred in the streets and houses below, but in the distance Rachel could see more of the green army trucks on the freeway.

The sun's rays were now illuminating the tops of the Oquirrh Mountains with a golden hew. Everything had been so peaceful and wonderful this morning when she had gotten up. And yet, within just a few minutes she had been jerked back into a harsh and ugly reality. Things were not good. There were evil forces in the world and they were at work early today.

Rachel wondered why the people were being taken and to where they were being taken. *"Why not everyone? Why just these people? Why the Kirtland's? How did anyone know that they were even home, they had been gone for the last eight months?"* The questions swirled in her head until it was about to explode. Rachel was starting to panic and realized that she had to calm herself. It was time to stop and make an inventory as she had been taught in her BYU-Anasazi survival class. She had learned that the single, most important thing they teach in the survival classes is mental attitude. If you think you can...or think you can't, either way, you're right. There was always hope. There was always a way to get things done. She could survive because she had skills and determination.

Rachel started her inventory of the things she

knew. She was alone. She had no friends here, in this area, that she knew of. The so called authorities were evil and they were looking for her. There were people trying to kill her and if the authorities captured her, they would surely turn her over to Bennett. There was absolutely no doubt in her mind that Bennett would kill her, given the chance again. She knew that Jared needed her and she had to find him and help him. Somehow, she needed to get to Spokane. How she was going to achieve that, she did not know.

For some reason, probably through inspiration, Rachel had some money and more importantly water, but no food. In her bag at the Kirtland's house were some more clothes, another pair of shoes, a warm jacket and a pocket knife. However, there was no food in the house. They had planned to go out for breakfast on their way to Salt Lake.

As she thought about what to do next, Rachel felt the need for prayer, a long prayer, but in this location she was too exposed. What she needed to find was a place that was off the trail a little, someplace a little more secluded. She got up and walked up the trail a ways. Rachel quickly found a couple of trees and bushes beside a large rock that was shaded and somewhat hidden. She felt good about the place so she knelt down and started praying. She was determined to pray until an answer came. In her mind she replayed the story of Enos in the wilderness who prayed all day and all night before he got his answer. She was determined to do the same.

Many hours later, the sun had set and it was dark

again. Rachel had prayed off and on all day long, not knowing what else to do and she was exhausted. Throughout the day she would pray and then she would wait for an answer, pray again and once again wait for an answer. Nothing came and she wondered if her prayers were getting anywhere, if she really had any faith at all. Towards evening, the doubts that had started to creep into her mind during the day became even stronger. The same doubts that had always been in the back of her mind, now were taking center stage. *"Were the heavens silent because she was not worthy? Was she wrong? Had she misunderstood?"*

As Rachel sat with her back against the rock looking up into the sky above her, she was confused, tired and hungry. She decided that what she needed was to drink the water she had been hoarding all day, and the reason she couldn't think straight was because she was dehydrated. She drank the water slowly, in small sips as she looked at the stars and wondered what she was doing wrong. Why couldn't she get an answer to her prayers? As she sat there Rachel fell asleep, thinking maybe her answer would come in a dream.

A short while later Rachel awoke. There had been no dream. She didn't even know how long she had been asleep since she hadn't checked her watch before drifting off, but looking at it now she saw that it was after midnight. Trying to figure out what she should do next, Rachel decided to return to the house to retrieve her heavier jacket and bag. It was starting to get a little chilly and a slight breeze had come up. Also, it would give her a chance to refill her bottle with water, which she knew was critical to her survival. The moon was up and its half light provided enough illumination to see the trail.

As Rachel approached the Kirtland's house from the back yard, she saw a little light flarc up by the back door. Instantly she froze and then crouched down behind some bushes. It was someone she didn't know, lighting a cigarette on the back porch and then standing to smoke it. She thought, *"He must be a guard of some kind,"* watching as his face light up every time he took a drag on the cigarette. Eventually, he finished his smoke, stamped out the, butt with the heel of his boot and went back into the house.

Rachel realized that there was no way she would be able to get back into the house. Not knowing where else to go, she returned to the relative safety of her prayer spot. As she was nearing it, she decided to keep going, a little farther up, along the trail. The breeze had picked up and it was starting to get cold. The temperature was dropping quickly now and she realized she had to find some shelter to get out of the wind.

Within a few hours she found herself above the BYU campus, but it was completely dark. There were no lights coming from any of the buildings. Walking a little further, and she came to the end of the trail, just above the Provo Temple. It too was dark, but Rachel thought it would at least provide a safe place to stay because of its fence and security. She quickly walked down the trail, through the dark and deserted streets, climbed over the fence, which was much harder than she had anticipated and approached the entrance to the temple. Of course it was closed and dark, but Rachel felt a sense of safety and peace, just being on the temple grounds. She found a spot next to the entrance, out of the wind, and lay down using her arm as a pillow, and tried to sleep. Though her eyes were closed and she was extremely tired, a restful sleep evaded her. Rachel was hungry and thoughts swirled in her restless mind, keeping her awake.

BENNETT

Bennett was furious and was screaming at six subordinates in his office. "I gave specific orders that they were to be left alone." He ranted. "How did they get picked up in the first place?"

One of the men in the office spoke up, trying to defend the soldiers' actions. "The Kirtland's were on the pickup list to be taken to the Homeland camps, sir." He then began ticking off the reasons for the pickup. "Their neighbors had reported them as homophobic; they had not taken the chip, had not accepted any welfare, and had expressed continued dissatisfaction in the government. We didn't realize the Kirtland's were on the Homeland dissident list until after they were in custody. And, we had no way of knowing that was where they were going to stop for the night. Our information was that they were headed to Salt Lake City."

Gaining courage to speak from his co-worker, another subordinate spoke up. "But, she wasn't there, sir. Homeland didn't get her. We don't know where she is. Apparently, she left sometime during the night. We placed a guard at the house just in case she came back for her things."

Bennett's fury had subsided some, but it was clear that he was far from happy with the situation and this turn of events. "I don't know who was responsible for this blunder, but we better find her. What do the Kirtland's and this guy named Desforges know?"

The first man spoke again. "Not much, sir. All they knew was they were asked to bring her along to Salt Lake. They didn't know why, or where she was headed; and they didn't know she had left the house."

"Okay," Bennett spoke, starting out in a relatively normal tone, to bring this briefing to an end. "Process them as normal and have them taken to the Brigham City camp instead of the Delta camp. I want them close, in case I decide to continue their interrogation." Now his voice grew louder until he resumed his rant to impress upon these subordinates that it would be to their personal detriment to disregard his orders. "The rest of you...FIND OUT WHERE SHE WENT. SHE CAN'T BE FAR. SHE'S ON FOOT. GET SOME SPOTTERS UP THERE. FIND HER, AND FIND HER FAST!"

CHAPTER 31

RACHEL

The noise of car engines startled her out of her drowsiness. She hadn't been asleep; she was far too cold and hungry for that, but she had closed her eyes in an attempt to get some rest. It was still dark, but the light of the moon covered the landscape in a pale glow and provided enough light to see, at least from a short distance. As Rachel sat up she could see two cars, stopped at the bottom of the drive in front of the gate. Someone was out of the cars and opening the previously locked gate at the temple entrance, down the slope, about a hundred yards away. She watched as the gates swung open and the two cars drove up the driveway with their headlights illuminating the front of the temple.

The cars drove slowly up the slope and pulled around, coming to a stop near the entrance. The engines and lights switched off as three men got out of the first car and four out of the second. Rachel could see that they were in dark suits with white shirts and ties. One of the men had a flashlight and left the others, disappearing around the side of the temple. Rachel wasn't sure what to do and so she sat, hunched down, behind some bushes to the side of the entrance, hoping they would miss her.

As the men approached, two more flashlights were turned on, and they looked through the glass doors at the front of the temple. One of the men spoke quietly, "President, if you would like, after we finish here, we would have time to grab a bite of breakfast in American Fork on our way back to Salt Lake. President Miller could meet with you there and have breakfast with us." A tall, large man replied in a kind voice, "That would be just fine. This shouldn't take long, perhaps about twenty minutes, or so. Have President Woods and Elder Bingham meet us there as well, if at all possible." Rachel was startled by the sound of the voice, and thrilled. It was a voice familiar to her, one that she had heard a hundred times. It was, she was sure now, the voice of the living Prophet. Just then, from the side, Rachel saw a light come on in the entryway and the doors of the temple open.

With the lights on, she easily recognized the unmistakable face of God's Prophet. Just as she did so, one of the men turned and saw her sitting there, crouched behind the bushes. "What have we here President?" The Prophet turned, along with all of the others and looked at Rachel. As she stood up, she was embarrassed. She was sure it appeared as though she had been spying on the group, but before she could say a word, the prophet spoke to her directly, "And who might you be young lady?"

"I'm Rachel Sinclair from Virginia, President." Her voiced sounded timid to her as she addressed the Prophet.

"And what brings you to be here at this time of the night?" He asked with curiosity, but not accusation.

Rachel rushed into her explanation now, feeling some relief at the opportunity to share it, and also hopeful that this man, above all other's might know what to do. "I was with Brother and Sister Kirtland and Brother Desforges coming up from the camp at Show Low to go to Church Headquarters. But, yesterday morning, while I was out jogging, some soldiers came and took them away. I had no place else to go and I thought it would be safe here for the night." As she finished, Rachel stood with her head slightly bowed and her arms folded in front of her.

"My dear, you are shivering." The Prophet observed. "Come inside and tell us why you were coming to Salt Lake." Turning to one of the other men he said, "Let's see if we can get her a blanket, or a coat, or something to take care of this night chill."

They entered the temple, the Prophet ushering Rachel in front of them. In a waiting room off to the side Rachel was seated on one of the couches. Within a few minutes a blanket was produced and a glass of water that she had requested. The Prophet pulled up a chair and sat down to talk to her face to face. Rachel told him all that she knew about Brother and Sister Kirtland and Brother Desforges. He then asked why she was coming to Salt Lake. Rachel briefly told him about Jared and the attack at his house. She explained that Jared had left the camp to find out what was going on to try and clear their names, that they hadn't heard from him in almost two months and the feeling they had that he was in trouble of some kind, probably up in Montana, near the Canadian border.

It was a wonderful feeling to unload all of her thoughts and emotions on someone who, although she had never before met in person, she felt a keen connection to and in whom she trusted. Rachel explained her need to get to Spokane and in the end she also spoke to him about her dreams and the reason she was in Utah. All in all, the whole explanation took about twenty minutes.

At the conclusion, the Prophet spoke. "Well Sister Sinclair, you certainly have had an eventful time the last few months. Tell you what. We have some things we need to do here. It will take us about twenty minutes. Then, we will see what we can do to help you." Turning to one of the two men that was standing and listening, he said, "Jim, why don't you remain here with Sister Sinclair and keep her company while we take care of our business." The man nodded his head and answered with respect. "I would be happy to President."

"Thank you." The Prophet continued, "Will you also let President Woods know that we will be a little late for that breakfast, but we are still coming. Also," he paused for a split second and glanced at Rachel. "Please explain to Sister Sinclair, what happened in Los Angeles two days ago. Apparently she doesn't know." Turning back to Rachel who was now, slightly confused, he said, "We won't be long."

While the other's were gone, Jim, who was actually one of the Prophet's bodyguards, told Rachel about the nuclear bomb explosion in Los Angeles and the martial law that was now in effect across the country. He explained that the authorities had taken "precautionary measures" and had "temporarily" rounded up people they termed as dissidents, or their potential support groups, in order to prevent further violence, or further difficulties. These families were taken to secure facilities around the country in order to be "safeguarded."

Within twenty five minutes the Prophet and his group had returned. One of the men carried a bag that contained cans of food and a can opener. Another one carried a heavy dark blue jacket. It was a little large for Rachel, but it was much warmer and a welcome addition to the light one she had been wearing.

The Prophet again sat down across from her and spoke. "I think we might be able to help Brother and Sister Kirtland and your Brother Desforges. We thought they might have been picked up, however until your eyewitness account, we weren't sure. You, on the other hand, present a different problem entirely. You would not be safe with us. With all of the checkpoints that have now sprung up, and the roving street checks, you probably would be arrested in short order.

You see, Elder Pinetree contacted us by radio, several hours after you and the Kirtland's left two days ago. He informed us that this Major Bennett was at the camp looking for you and your friend Jared." At this pronouncement, Rachel's face expressed the mixture of shock and fear that had suddenly come over her. The Prophet went on, "We were expecting you at Church headquarters yesterday, but you never came. We understand that the authorities are looking for you now." He paused just long enough for what he was saying to sink in, and then continued. "I understand that you have some wilderness survival skills, is that correct?"

"Yes," Rachel acknowledged. "I was a trainer one summer for the Anazazi program."

The Prophet smiled. "That's very good." He said. "Do you think that you could possibly make it over the mountains to Heber City? Do you know where that is?"

"Yes, I know where it is." Rachel replied. "It's about thirty miles up Provo Canyon." Rachel remembered making the trip many times years ago and was fairly confident of the location.

"That's correct," the Prophet said, pleased that she was familiar with the area. It would make what she needed to do much easier. "How long might it take you to get there walking over the mountains?" he asked.

Rachel thought for a moment and answered. "A day, maybe a day and a half at the most."

"Very good," he replied. "I would suggest that you make your way to Heber, as quickly as you can and go to the UPS store on Main Street. If you can make it to that location, there may be a way to get you to Spokane."

Rachel was overwhelmed with appreciation and gratitude and couldn't say a thing. Sitting there, tears started to well up in her eyes as she stared into the face of a Prophet of God and felt the Spirit testify to her of his divine calling.

The Prophet reached over and gently took her hand in his. "Is there anything else we can do for you Sister Sinclair?" he asked with concern.

Rachel changed her train of thought quickly to her material and immediate needs. "I sure could use a sharp knife," she confessed. "Also some string, or cord and a roll of toilet paper, or some tissue."

One of the men hastily left and within a few minutes returned with three different sharp knives of various sizes, a roll of nylon twine, and a roll of toilet paper. Rachel chose the two larger of the knives and carefully placed them into the pocket of her parka. In his absence, the Prophet had given Rachel clear instructions to leave the temple about fifteen minutes after their departure, while it was still dark, and to start her journey. With the genuine concern of a loving grandfather he advised her to be careful and cautious. He added, "God bless you in your efforts that they will be successful." He then looked directly into Rachel's eyes which caused a stirring in her soul as he said, "Remember, from small, seemingly inconsequential actions much good can be accomplished and many lives can be saved. Listen to the spirit, it will guide you." With that, the dignified group of men in their dark suits left the temple and drove away.

It took Rachel three days instead of a day and a half to reach the outskirts of Heber City. Part of the problem on the first day was a helicopter that kept flying around the mountains causing her to take cover for most of that day, huddled under some trees. She napped as much as she could while in hiding, so that later, in the evening when the moon was up, she was able to make slow, but steady progress. She didn't see the helicopter the second day and so was able to travel, though still slower than what she had expected, or hoped for.

On the morning of the third day, she arrived in Heber, coming down out of the mountains to the south of the airport. The first place she stopped was a gas station on the highway that she found open. Rachel went in, bought some toiletries, including a hairbrush and then retreated into the bathroom to clean herself up.

After making herself more presentable, she purchased some food to eat later. She also bought a pair of sunglasses and the only cap on the rack that fit her, sporting the image of a wasp in black and gold. These were things she had missed and really needed in the wilderness. Rachel left the store and walked down Main Street wearing her jacket, cap and sunglasses looking for the UPS store. Once she located the store, another problem arose... it was closed and wouldn't re-open until noon. Wondering what she should do, she eventually decided to go back to the large Albertsons grocery store she had passed, and wait there. She was encouraged when she saw that the parking lot had only a few cars in it.

Rachel entered the store and realized there were supplies available here that would be invaluable on her journey, and, as the area was preparing for the end of summer and the return to school, the store had a limited selection of back packs that could hold the items she bought. She purchased some clean socks, a bar of soap, and a little makeup. Deodorant, hairpins, a small mirror and a roll of duct tape were also added to the basket. Next, she selected a small package of large black plastic garbage bags, a roll of aluminum foil, some hefty, strong cloth wipes, a small metal cooking pot, and some plastic utensils, including a bowl, cup, plate and a package of lighters. She then chose the largest, plain black backpack in stock, to carry everything in. Unfortunately, the store did not carry a compass, jeans, or a better fitting jacket. Rachel had decided if she had to spend more time in the wilderness, she wanted to have a few things that would make it easier. Yes, she knew that she really only needed a knife to survive, because she had done so, but these extra things just made it easier.

After making her purchases, Rachel applied a small amount of makeup, making herself a little more presentable, in her own mind at least; she put her hair up under the cap and left the store. At about eleven she was hungry again and walked to the local McDonalds where she had a very satisfying, if not healthy, fast food meal full of more fat and grease than she had eaten in months. As noon rolled around, she steeled her courage and walked back to the UPS store. Behind the counter was an older woman whom Rachel guessed to be about 50 years of age. She looked up with a smile as Rachel came through the door.

"Oh, hi," she said in a friendly voice. "You must be Rachel. You're early. I was told to expect you probably later this afternoon. I really appreciate you volunteering to help us out like this. Joan always likes the help and the company. The truck leaves at 6:00 tonight on the dot and you should arrive in Spokane by 6:00 a.m. tomorrow." Then, as an afterthought without apparently needing, or expecting a word in response she added, "Coffee is in the back if you want some."

Rachel hadn't known what to expect, and while the warm friendly greeting was very welcome, it caught her off guard. She had imagined that she was like a spy, going to a meeting place and wondered what she should say to the people at the store. If there was a password she hadn't been told and she didn't know if she should show up and say 'the prophet sent me', or something else. Instead, Rachel simply said, "Thanks, I have nothing to do until then." Then, not knowing what else to do and with her equally friendly nature she added, "Tell me, is there anything I can do to help around here?"

"Not really, at least not until about five, or so." The woman behind the counter now was all business. "That's when Joan arrives from Vernal and we have to unload the incoming packages and then load all of the packages going with you guys to Spokane. As far as the store goes, things aren't that busy nowadays. To tell you the truth, I'm surprised this store is still open even half a day. I guess there's enough business between here and all of the little towns up to Spokane to keep it open. Oh, before I forget, there is a uniform for you in the back. It arrived for you yesterday... hang on here a minute and let me go get it for you."

Rachel was surprised when the woman returned in a moment with a small package in her hands.

"As you know," the woman was saying as she handed the package to Rachel, "company policy is that everyone wears the uniform when working. There's a bathroom in the back," and she tilted her head towards the door she had used a moment ago, "whenever you want to change for tonight's run."

"Thanks." Rachel said with enthusiasm, looking forward to a change of clothes. "I appreciate it. If you don't mind I might as well stay around here until we leave." Rachel didn't know where else to go and hoped that this would work out with the woman who was obviously in charge at the store.

"That would be nice sweetie." The woman responded appreciatively. "I could use the company. It gets kind of boring in here when there's not a lot of business."

Rachel decided to take advantage of the clean clothes and took the package into the bathroom to change. The brown UPS uniform fit well and looking at herself in the mirror, she wondered how everything had been managed. She recalled the words Granny had told her...that if she would go to Salt Lake, everything would work out from there.

She and Abigail, the friendly UPS clerk, chatted off and on all that afternoon. Business picked up and it actually became surprisingly busy with several people bringing in packages to ship and before Rachel realized it, the hours had passed and they were sharing the dinner Abby had brought, just before Joan was scheduled to arrive. When Joan finally did show up, she was a little late, so they had to hurry to off load and re-load the truck before she and Rachel left on the Spokane run, as it was called, with stops in Pocatello, Idaho Falls, Dillon, butte, Missoula, and Coeur D'Alene.

Joan talked almost non-stop in her heavy southern drawl. Her name was Joan Fontaine, and she laughed when she said her mother had gotten the name from an old time movie star. She was originally from Arkansas, and had been driving truck for the past ten years. She had started, at first, to keep busy while her husband was off in the military. He had been killed in Iraq six years ago so she just kept driving. Joan didn't have any children and she liked to listen to country western music as she drove.

She expressed her opinion about politics, asking first if Rachel was partial to the Democrats, the Republicans, or to the new Independent American Party that everyone was talking about. When Rachel told her that she was very displeased with what was going on in the country and didn't align herself with any of the main political parties, Joan chose to talk instead about the bomb blast in L.A. and how the country was going to hell in a hand basket.

The truck was stopped momentarily at each of three different check points, but when the guards recognized Joan they just waved them through. Joan made this run five times a week so she knew everyone and they knew her. Today, there weren't a lot of packages to be loaded and unloaded since it was a Tuesday run, not like it used to be, as Joan explained. However, she was glad for the job. When the driver finally ran out of things to talk about and decided to just listen to music on the radio, sometime after leaving Missoula, Rachel drifted off to sleep, and Joan had to wake her for the deliveries in Couer D'Alene.

CHAPTER 32

BENNETT

Bennett's aide had just handed Bennett a photograph of a woman from the Heber gas station surveillance camera.

"Yep, that's her." Bennett announced as he looked at the photo. "When was this taken?"

"At 7:03 this morning, sir" the young man answered. "The facial recognition software caught it. We'll have someone there in about five minutes to question the store clerk."

Bennett was not happy about the length of time it had taken for this information to reach his office. "That was almost six hours ago. Damn." He paused, thinking how he could make this situation work. "I want all of the surveillance video from that town examined immediately."

"Already in progress sir." He felt fortunate to have a bit of positive news he could relay to his boss.

"Good." Bennett said, "Let me know if anything turns up, immediately. I want to know how she is traveling and when we can expect her to arrive in Spokane. Remembering some details he asked, "Have we made arrangements with the people in Spokane?"

"Yes, sir." The aide answered. "They're waiting for her just in case she makes it that far."

Bennett thought for a minute, weighing the options, before he made his decision and spoke. "I think I will head to Spokane. I would like to leave as soon as the plane can be made ready. See to it."

"Yes, sir." The young man saluted smartly, then walked away quickly to make the arrangements.

As Bennett sat in his chair thinking about what his next step would be after arriving in Spokane, the secure cell phone that he wore on his belt buzzed. When he flipped it open, he was greeted by a red screen displaying the very clear message, "Call Home". Immediately, Bennett entered the secure code and retrieved the text message waiting for him. It said, "Urgent. Go with driver/car now waiting for you downstairs in parking garage."

Bennett did not hesitate to do as he was instructed. He quickly made his way to the parking area and got into the dark blue Continental waiting for him. He recognized the driver as the same one that had driven him and the Commander to that first meeting, several months earlier. Bennett wondered where the Commander was and if he would be at this meeting.

The car again drove into an underground parking lot of an office building up the canyon. This time, there were no other cars to be seen. After parking, the driver turned to him and said, "Through that door there," as he nodded in the right direction. "Up the stairs to the 3rd floor, first door on your right, they are expecting you, sir."

As Bennett walked into the room, there were only two men waiting for him, the Commander and the spokesman from their earlier meeting. Again, there was the single chair in the middle of the room. As soon as Bennett sat in it, the man began to speak.

"There is no need to report about Davis, or the girl," he said in an impatient tone. "She may, or may not lead you to him. Continue to have your people follow her to Spokane. They are now loose ends that must be taken care of as soon as possible. Do you understand?"

There was absolutely no doubt in anyone's mind that Bennett understood exactly the meaning of the instructions he had just been given. "Yes sir." Bennett acknowledged, but even as Bennett answered, he wondered how they knew about Spokane. Was there someone in his office reporting on him, or were they tapping into his communications? Swiftly, he made the decision to perform a subtle, but thorough search to find out precisely where the leak was and fix it permanently.

"Now, Mr. Bennett, one of the reasons you are working for us is because of your unique skill set. First, you have proven to us through your previous work that you can be trusted. Second, you have intimate knowledge of Captain Davis, and third, because of your background and experience in nuclear and biological weapons. I understand that you have handled live Soviet nuclear weapons. Is this correct? Bennett was curious where this preamble was headed, but decided patience when dealing with this individual was the best course of action.

"Yes." Bennett replied. "I have disarmed three of them."

"Is it also correct that you can take them apart, disarm them, and also put them back together?"

Bennett distinctly heard the emphasis on the word 'also' and understood the implication. "Yes, sir." He responded without hesitation. "I can do all those things when the need is present."

The speaker now turned to the Commander who picked up his part of the briefing, "Almost a year ago," the Commander began, "U.S. Special Forces conducted an operation where they discovered over thirty suitcase nuclear weapons destined for the United States. We were able to intercept all of them. Captain Davis was involved in the operation as an advisor.

"However, we did not know, at the time, that three

of the weapons had been sent previously, as a preliminary test. Three months ago, there was a van that crossed the Canadian border. Hidden within the cargo, were three suitcase bombs. The FBI was able to intercept two of them, with the third one slipping through their net. The weapon made its way to Los Angeles, where, as you now know, it was detonated, five days ago. The two other nuclear weapons have recently been turned over to us for use in taking care of a very specific problem." The Commander glanced at the other man and a look that spoke of shared classified knowledge passed between them for an instant.

Bennett was giving this briefing his full attention. He recognized the significance of what he was being told and intuitively knew there would be more forthcoming.

The Commander went on with the information he had to dispense. "The problem we are now facing is one of a growing domestic terrorist threat that is becoming more organized and more fanatical weekly. It appears they are recruiting most heavily among the ultra radical Christian groups who are very much opposed to the actions of the current government.

"At the heart of this growing rebellion is the Mormon Church. Of all of the radical Christian groups, they are by far the largest and best organized. Though the leadership professes complete support and cooperation with the government, many of the members have become decidedly anti-government of late, and are now openly identified by the media as a hate group. The vast majority of their members have defiantly refused to receive federal identification and many people across the country are rallying to them and viewing them as a focal point for a resistance movement. They have become a major obstacle to the stability and the future of this country."

He continued, "Recently, as you are aware, they have solicited the more fanatical members of their religion to leave society and retreat to mountain camps. We are concerned that they are planning either a 'Jim Jones' group suicide scenario, or a full scale rebellion.

"These people are fanatically loyal to their church leadership; they are well organized, and for a civilian populous, fairly well armed. Though we have them under observation, and we have worked to round up their possible co-conspirators still left in society, we are concerned that they could be of tremendous assistance to the terrorists, forming internal terrorist cells in league with the Muslims. Frankly, we are concerned with all religious fanatics and organizations. Conservative Christians, Muslims and Mormons are at the top of that list.

"We have been given the task of taking care of two problems at the same time: first, to destroy the LDS Church leadership and infrastructure. This will allow us to re-educate and matriculate these fanatics from their camps back into society. The second, and perhaps more important assignment, is to show others who choose to rebel against the New World Order, the fate that awaits them. The Mormon Church is to be made the example, cut off the head...and the body will die."

The Commander paused for a moment, eyeing Bennett with a strange mixture of contempt and respect before he continued. "The mission we have been tasked with, and have chosen you to perform, is the preparation for deployment of the two intercepted suitcase nuclear weapons that we will employ to alleviate this problem. The weapons are waiting for you now in a warehouse located on Hill Air Force Base. Your responsibility is to examine them to determine their effectiveness and prepare them for deployment this Friday. You will also be accountable for getting them to their appointed targets and detonation."

"We have learned that the Mormon hierarchy is having an exclusive meeting in Salt Lake for a majority of their church leadership." He consulted his notes for the next details. "Our resources have informed us that their First Presidency, all of the Quorum of the Twelve and a large portion of their regional leaders they call their Seventies will be present in their Conference Center in downtown Salt Lake City at that time. The other location is the Mormon headquarters that they have set up in Cardston, a small town in south western Alberta, Canada.

"Additionally, the head of Homeland Security will also be present at the Salt Lake City meeting. Lately, he has been helping the Mormon Church leadership, against orders. This cannot be tolerated. His demise will leave you in command of the entire region."

The Commander paused again before continuing. "After the weapons are detonated, you are to take charge from Ogden. Further instructions on how to move against the camps will be delivered to you at that time."

"All of the specific's that we have discussed and any other information you may need to know is located in this briefing packet, along with the detailed schematics for the devices." He extended the file to Bennett while finishing his directions. "You will only have forty eight hours to check them over, prepare them, and deliver them to their destinations. Do you understand?"

"Yes, sir." Bennett said, as he quickly reviewed the information inside the folder.

"Do you have any questions?" The Commander asked with a tone of finality.

Closing the folder and looking up, Bennett replied. "Only one sir. Are there any special instructions on how to dispose of Captain Davis and the girl?" It was peculiar to notice that of all that had been said and asked of him in this meeting, the one thing at the forefront of his mind was the elimination of Jared Davis and Rachel Sinclair.

The two other men looked at each other, and the Commander answered simply, "No."

"Thank you, sir." Bennett's short response was sincere. He was grateful for the latitude to dispatch those two in any way of his choosing.

The meeting adjourned and Bennett immediately returned to Blackbird headquarters where he gave orders to delay his departure to Spokane because of some obscure business he had to attend to at Hill Air Force Base. He and his aide, Lieutenant Marston, quickly drove to the location described in the briefing packet. There were four armed guards securing the warehouse when he arrived. Upon verification of his identity Bennett and Marston were allowed inside the building where a dark blue van was positioned. Inside the van were two lead lined boxes containing the weapons. Just as he opened the first box and began reviewing the circuitry, his cell phone rang.

The voice belonged to one of the staff back in his office. "We have been able to confirm that the girl is on her way to Spokane riding in a UPS truck. We have a list of all the stops it will be making en-route. They are expected to arrive in Spokane about 6:00 a.m. tomorrow morning. How would you like us to precede sir?"

Bennett took less than a second to decide. "Let the truck go through. Make sure that no one stops it, or performs any ID checks on the driver, or the passenger. Make sure that it reaches Spokane. I want someone to follow it from a distance, observing it at all times, but staying just out of sight. They are not to be seen. Is that clear?"

"Yes sir."

"I will be finished here in a few hours." Bennett went on. "Make sure that a plane is ready for me. I want to arrive in Spokane before the truck gets there."

JARED

Jared had been in Montana for over a month. It had been a busy time at first, setting up a vigorous exercise program for himself consisting of hiking and the daily cutting and splitting of firewood, using only a old hand lumber saw and an axe. After careful consideration, he had prepared two contingency caches, each with some emergency supplies, including food rations, a first aid kit, and a sleeping bag. He made one cache about five miles from the cabin and the other just over the border into Canada. These 'caches' were his insurance, places where he could "hole up" for a couple of months if necessary.

Being at the cabin once more brought back a lot of memories, as it always did. He had spent several summers up at the cabin as a young boy, learning basic survival skills from his grandfather, including how to shoot, hunt, and track. It was one of those uncommon pieces of property that had remained private even after the surrounding area had become a national forest. When his grandfather died, Jared was surprised to find that the cabin and several hunting rifles, along with a few other odds and ends, were bequeathed to him in his grandfather's will.

Ever since that time he tried to spend at least a couple of weeks every other summer up at the cabin. He had even snow shoed in a couple of times during the dead of winter, through the eight feet of snow that was often present at that time of year. Jared had made a few improvements to the twenty acre property, but not many. On one occasion, he had brought up a couple of solar panels and installed them on the roof, but they became more decorative than practical when afterwards, he changed his mind and decided to keep things more rustic and basic, very much the way his grandfather had kept it. Jared didn't even have a radio, or any other electronic device up at the cabin.

Instead of listening to the radio, or watching television, he found that he preferred to spend his time reading and coming up with ideas for new inventions. He found doing so was very helpful and relaxing, a way to cleanse and refresh the soul, finding peace that would prepare him for the next time he was called into combat where his soul and mettle would be tested.

After several weeks of hard work, getting things prepared and situated just the way he liked them, Jared again took advantage of the time to read, especially in the quiet of the evenings. However, instead of re-reading any of the many classics he had stored in the little cabin library, Jared started on a book he had brought from Granny's house. He hoped it would help him better understand the beautiful, but strange woman he found himself falling in love with.

RACHEL

When Rachel and Joan arrived at the border checkpoint just outside of Spokane at a quarter to six in the morning, they were courteously asked to step out of the truck and come inside. With her constantly friendly, "Ok honey," Joan led the way into the building, but Rachel immediately felt worry and concern come over her. Her fear was that once inside, the office, she would be detained and arrested, but try as hard as she could, she honestly didn't see any other option open to her, except to follow Joan. Once inside they were simply asked to have a seat while a routine inspection was performed on the inside and underside of the truck. "Just being cautious in this time of martial law." the guard had said. "It should only take fifteen to twenty minutes."

Joan was very casual about the whole thing, as if it happened on every run and asked if she could help herself to the coffee. "Go for it," the guard responded. Rachel chose a seat that faced the door in the middle of the room and sat down. She picked up a folded newspaper from the next seat and pretended to read it as she tried to keep an eye on what was going on outside. Neither Joan nor Rachel were aware of Bennett standing behind the one way mirror, watching their every move.

After only ten minutes, one of the guards came back inside to inform the women that the truck had been checked out and they were now permitted to leave. After climbing back into the truck, Joan drove straight to the UPS depot where she and Rachel made quick work of unloading the freight. With the job done, Joan attempted to show her gratitude by offering to buy breakfast for them at a nearby cafe, but Rachel politely declined. She explained that she was anxious to find her friend and spend as much time with him as possible.

Joan had enjoyed having Rachel on this run and volunteered to drop her off at her friend's place before she went on to breakfast and then head to the apartment she kept in the city, for at least eight hours of well earned sleep; but now, Joan was slowly shaking her head as she read the address Rachel showed her, "That's downtown," Joan said with regret in her voice. "I don't like taking my rig downtown unless I have to, especially places like Spokane where there are a lot of narrow one-way streets." Then Joan added as an afterthought, "but, I can take you to within a couple of blocks of where you want to go. There's a nearby freeway exit that will make it easy for me to get back on, once I've dropped you off. It's also mid-morning on a sunny day, so you shouldn't have any problems." Joan's last comment was in regards to safety. Across the country, large inner cities had become increasingly more dangerous. "Downtown Spokane is still pretty safe during the day, but I wouldn't spend the night here honey," Joan went on with additional warning. "Its not like LA, or anything.

Even so, just make sure you're someplace safe before it gets dark."

Rachel genuinely appreciated Joan's concern, wondering herself how safe she really was in this city. She replied, "Thanks Joan, you've been a sweetheart. I'm just sorry I haven't been of more help to you."

"Oh, you have been just fine," Joan spoke up quickly. "And it was great to have company on this run." She then added with hope, "If you need a ride back down to Utah, I'll be leaving Spokane tonight at six. Just remember, the UPS store is out by the airport, about three miles west of town. You're welcome to come along if you want to, but right now, as soon as I drop you off and get rid of this rig, it's time for me to get some sleep."

They reached the downtown exit in just a few minutes with Joan only stopping at the intersection when the light turned red.

"There you go honey," Joan said, indicating that it was time for Rachel to jump out quickly, before the light changed. "You take care."

"Thanks again, Joan," Rachel said as she opened the door, "You've been great." With that, Rachel climbed down the step and closed the cab door. She watched as the light turned green and the semi-truck slowly pulled away.

Rachel took a minute to look around and get her

bearings. According to what Joan had told her, she needed to go three blocks north and two blocks west to get to the address on the paper. If she hit the river, she had gone too far. Rachel hefted her small backpack and started walking. She was tired, but not as tired as she had expected to bc after the long ride. She had slept most of the way from Missoula to the Washington border where they were stopped at the checkpoint. In the back of her mind there was still a nagging concern about a statement Joan had made. She'd said that it was strange that they had not been asked for their IDs at any of the checkpoints. At the time, Rachel had been glad, because she wasn't carrying any identification, and thought it was just an answer to her prayers. Thinking about it now however, something about it, in the back of her mind, just didn't feel right.

Rachel determined to put the worry out of her mind and decided that it was just her lack of sleep that was making her anxious. She focused instead on trying to find the address where she would meet Jared's friend and hopefully find out how to get in touch with Jared again.

BENNETT

Bennett, accompanied by a local homeland security deputy acting as his aide, sat in their dark blue Ford sedan, two blocks away, watching Rachel walk down the city street. They had tailed the big rig to the off ramp from the border checkpoint, and watched as

Rachel got out of the truck and started walking. She had glanced in their direction once, but never noticed anything to increase her suspicion, so she checked the paper in her hand and started walking north.

Driving the sedan, Bennett passed the stoplight and then doubled back and parked the car on the side of the road a few blocks behind Rachel. He wasn't worried about losing her, since he had the RFD tracking chip put in her backpack at the checkpoint, but he wanted to stay close enough to see who she met with and get some idea of what she was up to. Besides, this was a game that Bennett enjoyed more than most, where he played the hunter, stalking his prey.

When Rachel had gotten far enough ahead to be almost out of sight, Bennett and the deputy pulled through the traffic and parked, maintaining a comfortable vantage point. They watched from a distance as she walked two more blocks and then disappeared down another avenue. The traffic was light and sporadic, making it easier to keep up with her. Bennett eased into traffic, drove the two blocks and once more turned down the street she was walking on. Rachel was walking up ahead, then turned the corner, out of their sight for a moment. Bennett eagerly followed, relishing the thought of her leading him to Jared. He would get them both and satisfy the desire for revenge that nearly consumed him. As he had outwardly been trailing the girl, inwardly Bennett had been plotting what he would do to them, especially to her. She was pretty, and had made a fool out of him more than once. A sinister grin came to his face as he imagined how he would exact his vengeance.

After a few moments, he eased the car back into traffic and turned down the street, pulling over to the side. She was walking slowly in the middle of the block now, carefully checking addresses. He could tell from her behavior that they were getting very close.

"Tell the teams to start converging on this location, but to stay two blocks away." Bennett barked to the aide sitting next to him, "I want them prepared to move in immediately when I give the signal." The deputy quickly pulled up a military style radio and began repeating the orders to the occupants of the three other vehicles in their detail, a few miles away.

Bennett watched as Rachel came to a stop in front of the McDonalds restaurant that sat in the middle of the block. She looked down at the paper in her hand and then at the numbers above the glass door as she started moving towards it.

"Is she going to get some breakfast?" asked the aide with a note of confusion.

"I don't know," Bennett answered with more than a hint of frustration. "Maybe." He watched her enter the restaurant and approach the counter to place an order. Something was off and didn't make sense. One minute, she had been looking for an address that was on a piece of paper in her hand, and the next minute she was walking into McDonalds. Bennett picked up the binoculars next to him, and focused in on Rachel, trying to watch her every move through the large plate glass window.

RACHEL

As Rachel turned the corner and saw the McDonalds restaurant, she recognized the beginning of hunger pangs in her stomach. It was now 9:30 am. *"After I get hold of Jared's friend and contact Jared,"* she thought, *"I'll have to come back here and get some breakfast."*

McDonalds, was one of the few fast food companies that had survived the 2nd great depression, as it was now often called, and still had many of its franchises in operation. Most people agreed that what had saved the company was the low price for the quantity, if not quality, of food. Even though now, with the continued economic challenges, the prices were considered high for most people.

Walking down the block and scanning the addresses, Rachel realized that the McDonalds must be close to where she was headed. As she approached the store, she saw the address, and realized that it wasn't just close, it was the exact location where she was supposed to find Jared's friend. She stood there on the sidewalk, confused for a moment, double checking the address in her hand against the one painted on the glass.

There were three cars in the parking lot, and two more in the drive through. It was a slow morning, with just a few people inside now, eating their breakfast. *"Good,"* she thought with a touch of sarcasm, *"Now what do I do? How am I supposed to find Thomas?"*

Rachel decided to get some breakfast and make her next decision as she ate. She had to admit that the smells of the fast food restaurant were quite tempting. After looking over the menu, she settled on ordering a breakfast burrito and a large orange juice. Just those two items alone cost her seven of the New Dollars she carried in her pack. Rachel picked up the tray and took her order over to a table in the corner, wondering what she was going to do. There was no doubt that this was the address Jared had given to her and she concluded that after she finished eating she would go up to the counter and ask for Jared's friend 'Thomas' by name and see what happened.

Rachel realized how hungry she had been as she devoured the burrito. It wasn't until half of the orange juice was gone that she decided to slow down and savor each remaining sip. She recalled that this was only the second orange juice she had had during the last two months. The food had been delicious and since she didn't know when she would be able to eat again Rachel made the decision to purchase another burrito along with another orange juice. When she went back to the counter and placed her order, she asked the older woman working at the counter, "Does

Thomas Jackson work here?

"Oh yes," came the lady's reply. "He's the owner and manager., but he's not here right now."

"Do you have any idea where I might get in touch with him?" Rachel asked as she paid for the food.

"I'm sorry," the cashier replied, "I'm not allowed to give out his home phone number, or address, but he usually comes to work on the evening shift. That starts at 4:00 this afternoon. You could come back then if you'd like to."

Rachel thought for just a second before she asked, "Do you have a pen I could borrow for a minute?"

"Sure," said the cashier and she disappeared into the back, quickly returning with a pen.

Rachel jotted down a short message on the paper in her hand, folded the note, and wrote 'To Thomas Jackson' on the front, and then handed the paper and pen back to the woman.

"Thanks," Rachel said sweetly, "would you please make sure that he gets this note?"

"Of course," replied the cashier as she read the front of the note, "I'll go put it on his desk right now, where he won't miss it."

Rachel smiled as she picked up her burrito and her

orange juice and walked back to the table in the corner once more. She took her time with the food now, enjoying each bite and not hurrying the experience. In reality she wasn't quite sure what else she should do. She thought about staying in the restaurant the whole day, but decided against it when she considered the attention and suspicion that might raise. She even contemplated finding a motel room where she would be able to take a shower and get some sleep, but motels required identification these days, and that was one thing she didn't have in her pack.

When Rachel finally finished her juice and disposed of her trash, she approached the counter once more. All of the other customers had left the store and the woman at the cash register seemed a little bored. She smiled as Rachel walked up. "Is there a mall, or another store within walking distance that is still in business?" Rachel asked. The economic challenges had been particularly difficult for the large inner city malls with high overhead and most of them had closed.

You bet," came the woman's friendly reply. "There's an indoor mall that is still open about two blocks from here. Just go over to that corner there," she said pointing across and down the street. "Then continue on one block and turn left at the next corner. There are some big double glass doors in the middle of the street. You can't miss it."

"Thanks," Rachel said smiling, as she turned to walk out the door, heading for the corner.

BENNETT

Bennett watched as Rachel left the McDonalds and headed further down the street, away from him. She had spent almost an hour in the restaurant and he had begun to get impatient. He watched as she had walked up to the counter and talked to someone three different times. It seemed like she was asking for directions, but something in his gut told him he needed to know exactly what she had asked.

As Rachel disappeared around the corner, Bennett opened his car door at the same time speaking to the deputy, "Let's check this out. I want to know who she talked to and why she spent so much time in there." As they stepped away from the vehicle, he added, "And let's make this really fast."

RACHEL

Just after Rachel turned the corner and had walked about twenty steps, she felt a sudden, overwhelming sense of dread. It was so strong that it stopped her in her tracks. Something was very wrong, and although she didn't know what it was, the feeling was undeniable. She turned around to look about her and see if she could spot anything amiss when a feeling of panic hit her. She started walking back, retracing her steps, but after only two steps she started to run. She wasn't sure why she was running; she simply knew that she had to. *"Faster,"* a voice within her seemed to say. Within a few seconds she rounded the corner at almost a dead run, in the direction she had previously come and then she froze in her steps. Two figures dressed in black were walking towards the McDonalds she had just left. They spotted her at the same time she saw them and they stood there, down the block, glaring at her. She couldn't believe her eyes; it was Bennett. Rachel's heart leaped into her throat.

Both Bennett and his aide came to a dead stop as Rachel came running around the corner. Rachel and Bennett stared at each other for what felt like an eternity, but in reality only lasted a second. Rachel immediately turned around and started running back in the direction she had just come. Just before she went around the corner she quickly glanced back and saw that Bennett and the other man had started running after her.

Rachel ran faster, now in a true, complete panic. Where could she go? There was no question that she needed to find a place to hide, and she had to get out of sight, right now.

She reached the corner and saw the double doors of the mall across the street, just as the cashier at McDonalds had described them. Without slowing down she ran across the street towards the doors.

From the distance she had seen between them, when she first spotted Bennett and the other man, Rachel figured she had almost a block head start and hoped she could make it through the doors before they rounded the corner. She ran to the entrance, opened one of the glass doors and quickly slipped inside.

After getting inside Rachel turned around and watched the corner, peering out through the big glass window at the side of the entry way from behind a large kiosk. She saw Bennett and the other man come around the corner running, then stop when they didn't see her. They started scanning up and down the street and she watched as Bennett started speaking into a small two way radio he was carrying.

Rachel started to do her own survey of the situation as she took stock of her surroundings. There were stairs leading to an upper level and stairs going down nearby. She decided to go up.

As she ran up the flight of stairs Rachel thought to herself, *"If this was a mall, it was an awfully small mall and strangely laid out. It was more like a department store."* At the top of the stairs, she slowed to a fast walk and went down the large hall. She passed a couple of small stores that were empty and then saw a sign with an arrow that read, 'Mall this way.'

Rachel quickly walked down the hall in the direction the arrow had pointed and found more small boutiques and shops. Most were closed, but when she came to one that was open, she could see the whole store from the front window and knew that this was no place to hide.

The need to hide was pervasive; she had to find an out of the way place where she could disappear for several hours, at least. If she went out to the street she felt sure that her pursuers would find her, but if she could wait until there were more people, perhaps then she might be able to get lost in the crowd and escape.

Rachel considered changing clothes, and thus, her appearance, because she had seen it done so many times in countless movies, but she didn't have any clothes to change into. She had left the uniform at the UPS depot when she had changed. Rachel knew that whatever she did, she needed to do it soon; they could be coming down the hall at any minute.

She stepped through an archway and entered the main part of the complex, finding herself on the second floor of a large mall with many shops that extended in both directions. From where she stood there appeared to be four levels, with a few people mingling about, but not very many. She turned right and hurried down the hall past several stores, most of which were open, unlike the ones near the entrance.

On a whim, Rachel saw the elevator doors closing, squeezed between them quickly and pushed the top, button.

When the doors opened she got out and found herself in what appeared to be a large department store. She didn't see anyone as she walked past the house wares section towards the linens and bedding area.

There were several displays of beds, dressers and tables all made up so as to highlight the items on sale. Rachel walked quickly around a partition into a corner area containing a very large, dark wood four poster bed with matching dressers.

She stopped for only a moment and looked at the bed. The covers hung over the sides of the bed almost touching the floor. As she stood there, a thought popped into her mind. The accent lighting here was not very bright. Rachel glanced around and saw that this area was actually out of the way of the main isles and it was difficult to see very far into the rest of the store.

She walked back to the bed and nonchalantly stuck her foot under the edge, finding no obstruction. Quickly she dropped her backpack and pushed it under the bed with her foot while she looked around for one last time; even checking the ceiling for a security camera.

Feeling secure that she was not being watched electronically, or otherwise, Rachel got down on her knees, and then laid flat on her stomach. There was nothing under the bed now except for her backpack and a lot of room that she planned on occupying.

"Perfect," said a little voice in her head. She speedily crawled and scooted until she was completely out of sight. It was dark here, and the dust ruffle hung down to within an inch of the floor, hiding her completely from anyone that wasn't lying on the floor.

Feeling safe in her present location, Rachel started to relax. As she did so, she realized that her heart was beating fast and loudly. She consciously willed it to slow down, controlling her breathing and waiting for her body to respond.

In about five minutes, her heart beat and breathing had slowed considerably, enough so that she stopped focusing on them and started thinking about her next step.

From her hiding place Rachel heard footsteps on the vinyl floor. Probably sales clerks, she thought as she listened to the slap click of hard shoes on the polished floor. She was trying to determine if they were high heels, or men's shoes when the noises suddenly stopped.

Rachel strained her ears trying to hear anything, when she heard a rustling from the side of the bed behind her head. She lifted and turned her head and saw a pair of black men's shoes standing beside the bed. All she could see were the soles and a small part of the tops. As she watched in horror, she saw a hand reach down, grasp the edge of the bedding and lift it, letting in more light.

A face appeared in the opening, and a too familiar voice said, "Hello Rachel." Her heart nearly froze in her chest... it was Bennett.

His words chilled her to the bone and her body gave out a violent, involuntary shiver. Suddenly, she was exhausted and hope drained from her, along with her strength, as if someone had deflated a balloon. After all she had been through, Bennett had caught her anyway. Deep in her heart she knew he was going to kill her, but right now, she didn't care. Rachel was completely overcome with a feeling of despondency and weariness, it was over, and she had come to the end.

She closed her eyes in surrender and wanted to cry, but with the last shred of defiance, she chose not to give him that satisfaction. If he was going to kill her, she wanted to just get it over with. Death didn't frighten her now, she was ready.

Bennett's voice interrupted her thoughts. "Rachel, be a good girl and come out." He was speaking quietly as if to a little child, but there was still a threatening tone to his words. "Don't make me come in and get you, because, trust me, you won't like it if I do."

Rachel opened her eyes and started to move her legs around, without uttering a sound, but before she emerged she thought better of it, and turned around to crawl out headfirst. As she came out from under the bed she saw that there were three other men with

Bennett, all dressed in black uniforms and all carrying guns. Two of them had the same type of stun guns that she had seen in the house in Arizona, pointed at her. Now she understood what Bennett was talking about.

"Cuff her," Bennett ordered one of his men. A man standing next to her, grabbed her wrist and expertly slapped a hand cuff around it, turning her around as he grabbed her other arm, also bringing it behind her back. The other half of the handcuffs quickly and roughly closed around her other wrist.

Bennett spoke into the two way radio he carried, "This is Bennett...stand down, I repeat stand down. We have the suspect in custody. Search is over." The same evil grin that came so naturally to him, once more came to his lips as he glanced at Rachel with a look of utter victory and contempt. He had known all along that there was only one possible outcome and here it was, he had won.

Rachel and her escorts walked down the stairs and out the very large front doors of the mall. No one in the entourage said anything until they were outside of the building when Bennett finally spoke to one of the men, "Go get the car and I'll meet you back at the station."

Directing his next words to one of the others, he ordered, "You go with him. I'll go in your car with the prisoner." Glaring at Rachel he sneered, "I'm not letting her out of my sight." They approached a black sedan that stood, idling in the street. Bennett opened the back door, put his hand on her head and shoved her gently inside.

On the way to the station, Bennett, who sat in front of her, could not resist the opportunity to gloat and so he turned around to face Rachel and spoke in a condescending tone. "You're probably wondering how we found you so fast." He paused, letting the imagined suspense build. "Actually, we've been tracking you since the Arizona checkpoint, thanks to a little chip we had placed in your bag, and you thought you were safe. You see Rachel, you could run, but you couldn't hide." He turned back in his seat with a barely audible snicker, but continued addressing her. "Oh, by the way...thanks for bringing us to Jared; we should have him in custody within the hour. You have been very helpful."

At the mention of Jared, Rachel turned her head away from Bennett, closed her eyes and couldn't stop the tears rolling slowly down her cheeks, despite the promise she had made to herself not to. She had destroyed everything. She had betrayed Jared and deserved whatever fate they had awaiting her.

They arrived at the local Homeland Security station where Rachel was placed in a holding cell. She guessed that it had been the local police station at one time, but all of the sheriffs, local police and National Guard had been federalized and taken over by Homeland Security during the food riots and martial law of the previous summer. At least they had taken off the handcuffs when they put her in the cell. Rachel sat in the solitary chair and rested her head against her arms on the metal table in front of her. She didn't want anyone, especially Bennett to get any satisfaction from seeing her tears, and she softly began to cry.

CHAPTER 33

Two hours later, a woman in plain clothes, with a badge on her belt, opened the door to the holding cell, and walked in. Rachel looked up, wearily, from where she had been resting with her head on her arms. She was still half drowsy when she heard the woman say, "I'm so sorry, there has been a terrible mistake. You are free to go."

In dazed confusion Rachel asked incredulously, "What? I don't understand."

"It appears," the officer went on, "that there is not an arrest warrant out for you. In fact, there is no action of any kind against you that we can determine, except perhaps for a personal vendetta of one Mr. Bennett. Truthfully, this whole situation has embarrassed the department considerably and I have no doubt Bennett will receive a formal reprimand, or worse, before this is all over."

Rachel stood in stunned silence; she could not believe the words she was hearing. The officer, noticing the bewildered look on Rachel's face, explained, "My boss responded this morning to an emergency alert and assisted in your arrest, all based upon the word of this Major Bennett from the Utah Region. He claimed he was working on special orders from the Intermountain Regional Homeland Security

Office to arrest you. Well, after you were located and brought in, my boss checked with Utah."

The woman paused, sighed, and went on, "Apparently, he was not acting with any authority, or official orders of any kind. Since he is part of the Blackbird group, which acts as a support to Homeland Security in a few areas, but not here, I might add... we took his word at first., but after checking with Utah, and then questioning him, we have discovered that this is nothing, but his personal grudge against you, and a couple of others, for reasons that escape us."

"What does this mean?" Rachel asked weakly.

"What it means," the officer went on, "is that he is in a lot of trouble. Abusing one's position of authority is a very serious offense. He has been placed under arrest, pending a full investigation." Rachel's shock became more pronounced.

"Again, we apologize for this terrible inconvenience and the trouble we have put you through in the last few hours. I'm sure that you'll want to file a grievance. If you will follow me Ms. Sinclair there is some paperwork I need you to fill out." The woman turned to open the door and stood waiting for Rachel to follow.

Still confused at this turn of events, Rachel silently thanked her Heavenly Father for the miracle that was taking place. She got up and walked out the door, following close behind the officer, half expecting someone to jump out at her at any moment.

"Right this way," she directed, pointing down the hallway and to the right. They walked down the hallway and entered a room full of desks and police officers, with people talking loudly, and phones ringing. As they entered, Rachel noticed on the opposite side of the room an office with a big window and a glass door. Through the window she saw a man in uniform standing behind the desk, and yelling at three people standing on the other side. From Rachel's viewpoint she could only see their backs. There were two men in sheriff's uniforms with someone in a different, black uniform between them who had his hands cuffed behind him. The officer, behind the desk, who appeared to be in charge, was red in the face and seemed to be addressing his heated remarks to the person in handcuffs.

"Please, take a seat here," the female officer told Rachel, indicating a chair and then walking around the desk and sitting down herself.

"This won't take long," she said. "And then we can take you anywhere you would like to go." She pulled open a file drawer in her desk, reached into it and pulled out some papers.

While she was doing this, Rachel looked back to the office window and noticed that the tirade was finished and the three men had turned towards the glass door. Rachel couldn't believe her eyes. The handcuffed person in the middle was Bennett.

She clenched her jaw and stared at him. If looks could kill, Bennett would've been dead on the floor. The officer attending her noticed the expression and turned to look behind her.

"Yea, as I said...he is in a lot of big trouble."

They both watched as the trio turned and walked out of the office and through the large room. By this time everyone had stopped and was staring. Even the phones seemed to stop their incessant ringing.

Bennett had a scowl on his face and looked ahead of him as he was escorted by the two policemen holding his arms between them. He glanced sideways and saw Rachel; their eyes locked. Despite her anger and freedom, Rachel felt a chill go up her spine, there was more than death in his look; it was pure evil coupled with hatred.

When the trio disappeared down the hallway, Rachel felt a sense of relief spread through the entire room. It quickly went back to business as usual, as if nothing had happened.

"You must be exhausted." The officer's voice brought Rachel back to the present.

"Yes, I am tired, and I really would like to use the restroom." Rachel admitted.

"No problem." the officer responded quickly, "In fact, while you are in the bathroom, I will see if I can speed things up so you can get out of here fast. The bathroom is right over there," she said, pointing to another corner, "down the hall and the third door on your left."

Rachel got up and followed the directions the officer had given. She felt a huge sense of relief at her newly found freedom. As she entered the bathroom she looked at herself in the metal mirror. She was a mess, with big bags under her slightly red and puffy eyes. She washed her hands and splashed some water in her face. It felt good and refreshed her a little.

When she returned to the desk, the officer began to speak. "Ok, I have typed a short complaint for you on this form that will get things started. If this meets your approval, then you can sign it and I'll file it for you."

The officer handed her the form and Rachel read it. It basically said that Rachel had been arrested without cause by an officer, and had been imprisoned without cause, and according to section 34, article 3(B), she wished to file an official grievance.

Rachel signed the paper and handed it back to the woman.

"Great, I've also talked to my boss, the commander, and he has authorized me to give you some remuneration monies for your inconvenience, enough for several meals and a stay in a good hotel." She handed Rachel an envelope, "There should be $250 New Dollars there if you would like to count it."

The officer continued, "Again, we are terribly sorry for this. As a further gesture of our apologies, the commander has authorized me to take you anywhere you would like to go and drop you off. Is there any place special you would like me to take you?"

Rachel thought for a minute and said, "Well yes. I am trying to get to Glacier National Park. Is that possible?"

"No problem," the officer responded. "Though that is a little out of our way. Let's see, I believe the closest town is a place called Eureka, isn't it?

"Yes," Rachel answered. "I have a friend near there I would like to see and I could spend some time there, I'm sure."

"Ok. Just sit here a minute while I make the arrangements." With that, the woman stood up and walked out of the room.

Rachel sat there, finding it hard to believe her good fortune. God had certainly answered her prayers.

About ten minutes later, the woman returned. "Everything is arranged," she said. "If you'll just come with me we'll get you on your way."

They walked back down the hall that Rachel had come from just a half an hour earlier and past the door that she recognized as the one leading to the holding cell where she had been kept. They turned the corner and came to an abrupt halt as she nearly bumped into a smiling Bennett.

"Hello, Rachel," he sneered, "Its good to see you again."

"Here she is." The female officer said without emotion.

One of the policemen standing next to Bennett grabbed her and quickly put her back into handcuffs.

Rachel offered no resistance; she just stood there in as much shock as she had had at her counterfeit release.

The female officer turned to Bennett and asked, "Is there anything else you need from me?"

"Yes," Bennett answered, "Wait just a moment."

Turning to Rachel, Bennett asked with mock sincerity, "Did you like our little play? You see Rachel," he went on, "you have once again been a tremendous help to us. We happen to know that Jared's grandfather had a cabin near the town of Eureka, in the Kootenai National Forest, right next to Glacier National Park. We had checked it once and no one was there, but that was some time ago. It's nice to know that he is there now though. Thanks to you, we will be paying him a little visit this evening."

Bennett turned to the officer that had been part of their charade and said. "Put her in solitary lockup until I return after taking her partner into custody.

Then, I'll transport them both back to Utah. By the way," he said as an afterthought. "Excellent work, we got the information we needed from her in less than thirty minutes of interrogation without breaking a sweat."

Bennett, with more than his usual amount of arrogance, turned back to Rachel. Reaching down, he pulled the envelope of cash out of her hand. "You won't need this where you are going."

Bennett watched the two officers and Rachel disappear down the hallway with a smug look of achievement on his face; he checked the time, pulled out his cell phone and quickly walked down the stairwell. Upon reaching the main floor, one flight down, he walked out into the sunshine and dialed his secure number. The voice on the other end responded simply, "Yes?"

"I have one of the loose ends in custody." Bennett reported. "I'll have the other one shortly. The devices have been prepped and are ready to be deployed. Everything is on schedule."

The man listening was obviously pleased with this news, "Excellent!" he said, and the line went dead as the call was terminated.

Bennett closed the phone. It was true; he did have one of the suitcase nukes prepped and ready to go. It was a simple device, not very powerful. The inspection had been easy, checking the wiring, the connections and the timer. It would vaporize a city block outright and destroy everything else within one thousand yards.

However, the second one, though it also was armed and ready to go, had been in bad shape. It was much larger, more than twice the size of the first, but it was also an older model, one that he did not recognize and had not worked on. He wondered, as he had worked on it, if it were one of the original prototypes of the suitcase device. Essentially, it looked like the core of an obsolete nuclear artillery shell, which had been removed and fitted with a timer. Some of the wiring had even been corroded. As he opened it, he couldn't help, but wonder where it had been sitting all these years.

Bennett had replaced most of the wiring, but the timing mechanism was an old modified system that hadn't been used since the fifties. He believed he had the timing system figured out, but wasn't quite sure. The timing mechanisms on both of the devices had a maximum limit of forty eight hours, in five minute increments. That was one thing he knew for sure, at least for the smaller device. He felt fairly confident that it was the case as well on the larger device, but it was that shadow of doubt that had him concerned. He wanted to return and look it over one more time.

Just before he left for Spokane, Bennett had made arrangements for each of the two devices to be loaded into a separate vehicle. He had then placed the vehicles under the watchful care of his most trusted aide, Lieutenant Marston. Bennett decided this was the time to call him.

"Bennett here," he said briskly as the phone was answered. "I have her and we know where he is, up at his grandfather's cabin near the border. I'll take a team in tonight and round him up. I expect to be back there by the morning with both of them."

"Are there any orders?" Marston asked.

"No." Bennett replied. "I'll be back in time to take care of everything. Just monitor things until I return."

"Yes, sir." The Lieutenant answered and hung up.

Bennett's plan was simple. When he got back to Ogden, he was going to have a little fun with the girl. After all, she had caused him a lot of headaches, furthermore, he had decided, he would do it in all in front of Jared. He smiled deviously as he thought about the reaction that would get from him; it would drive him insane. Bennett relished the thought and the satisfaction he knew he would derive from it.

When he had finished exacting his gratification, he would put both of them in the car with the larger nuclear device and have it driven to Salt Lake. "*Boom,*" he thought, as he mouthed the word. No more Jared Davis, no witnesses, and a mission accomplished. Everything would be tied up neatly with one simple explosion. With the Homeland Security Office in Salt Lake destroyed, it would also leave him completely in charge of the entire region. That would probably result in another promotion. He smiled as he thought about the turn of events. Things were going to end up better than he had dared to imagine.

Bennett looked up into the sky impatiently, wishing it would get dark faster, and then went back into the building to make the arrangements for him and his team to fly out and apprehend Jared.

Later that night, Bennett and six members of the local Spokane swat team, landed about dusk at the little airport a mile north of the town called Eureka. As the chopper blades wound down, two Humvees pulled up. When Bennett emerged from the chopper, one of the drivers stepped out and saluted him. Bennett smiled in anticipation and returned the salute.

Within ten minutes, the men and their gear were loaded up and on their way. They returned the two local drivers to the police station and took off for the cabin. It was a ninety minute drive, but with the GPS guiding them, it was an easy trip through the heavy forest and steep terrain. They would never have found it otherwise. About three miles from the cabin, Bennett and his team stopped to get ready. It was now very dark, especially in the thick woods. They loaded their weapons, painted their faces for additional camouflage and put on their night vision.

Bennett told them they would drive without lights for another mile, then stop. The team would then travel on foot the rest of the way in stealth mode. He estimated that it would take them about ten minutes to reach the cabin and he gave strict instructions that they were to capture the fugitive alive, if at all possible. Bennett made it clear if they were fired upon, however, they were free to respond likewise and they should consider the suspect armed and extremely dangerous.

The team returned to their vehicles, drove the distance and then parked the two Humvees off to the side of the road. Bennett reminded them one more time that he wanted this person taken alive and unharmed, if at all possible. "We have the element of surprise," Bennett said, encouraging the men, "but, by no means should anyone underestimate this man." The four man team then took off, leaving Bennett and the two drivers behind.

SPOKANE, WASHINGTON

Tom and the crew were cleaning up as part of the closing routine at the McDonalds. He often enjoyed this part of his job as it gave him the chance to talk with his employees about the events of the day. A good portion of the discussion had been spent speculating about the woman who had eaten breakfast at the store, then was then chased by two Homeland Security agents out of the parking lot.

They had heard later in the day about the ruckus at the mall two blocks over and of the woman who had been led away in handcuffs. From all reports, it sounded like the same person that had been in the store, and it appeared that the chase that had started at McDonalds had ended for her at the mall just a short time later.

They all had seen this kind of stuff before, especially in the last couple of years. Tom thought back to the times when Homeland Security had even come into the store and taken two of his employees away. One had returned the very next day, detailing the questions asked him about his brother who lived in nearby Coer D'Alene. Six months later, another employee, a former stock broker, before things fell apart, was taken out of the store, never to be seen, or heard from again. It was too bad, Tom thought. He really had liked the stock broker; they'd had some interesting conversations.

After things were well in hand for the closing, Tom sat down at his small desk in the back of the store. He hadn't had time to sit down since he arrived at the store in the late afternoon. The number of employees at the store was always less than needed for optimum operation, not like in the old days, and so with fewer people they all worked harder to get the job done. Tom clearly understood his stroke of luck, purchasing the McDonalds franchise with an inheritance three years before the collapse.

When his parents died in a plane crash, he and his sister had split almost two million dollars in various stock shares and insurance monies. He immediately retired from the service, sold the stocks and bought the franchise, settling down with his family here in Spokane. He had been in the military twenty four years and desperately wanted to put down roots and raise his family without having to worry about the next deployment. He figured at forty six years of age, it was just about time for him to do what he wanted.

The McDonald's franchise turned out to be a godsend. His sister had left her share of the stocks in the market and watched them rise, just as Dad had done, but when the crash came, she lost just about everything. At the very last, she had taken his advice over that of the professionals, and purchased some gold and silver. It had saved her from absolute poverty and having to go on government welfare like so many other people had been forced to do.

At first, he was just the owner and didn't actually work much at the store. With the profits from the restaurant and his military retirement income, he was doing quite well. After the crash, circumstances changed however and finances got tight. That was when he took over direct management of the store. McDonalds was one of the few national franchises that had done alright during the collapse. Only about one third of the stores went belly up. The thing that saved him and his store in particular was that he hadn't borrowed any money to purchase the franchise in the first place. He owned it lock, stock, and barrel, paid for completely with his inheritance. Most of the other local stores had closed, leaving him one of only three stores in the entire city still open.

Lately, if things continued to improve, he had considered opening up another store next year in the north part of town that was starting to come back. Though Spokane had missed out on the riots, the population had been cut in half. Most had lost their jobs and homes and had moved south to warmer climates and many had gone into the tent cities that were prevalent in the warmer parts of the country.

As he relaxed and leaned back in his chair to take a breather, Tom noticed the note taped to the monitor of his computer. However, he didn't recognize the handwriting as that of his Assistant manager, Gerald who had worked the morning shift today. Gerald often left him notes in this way. Tom opened the note and what he read made him sit up straight in his chair. In a woman's flowing script it said, "I am trying to get hold of Jared Davis at the cabin. It is very urgent. He is in danger. There are people coming after him." The note was signed, "Rachel."

Jared and Tom had served together for almost ten years in the military, and had forged a strong friendship. It was Jared that had convinced him to get out and do the franchise thing when he had received the inheritance.

Jared had been in the store just four weeks ago, indicating that he was in some trouble with the authorities. As Tom recalled, he had said they were looking for him to complete an assignment that he didn't want to take part in. He confessed to Tom that he had taken the chip out of his shoulder. That alone would make the authorities very unhappy. They thought of Jared as national property and would have considered such an action a national security issue.

Before Jared left he had given Tom a satellite phone number and stated cryptically that he would be nearby. If there was a problem, or if someone came looking for him, he would like to know. Tom wondered who this 'Rachel' was and just what her relationship was to Jared. After thinking for a few minutes, he flipped open his phone and gave Gerald a call.

"Yea, what's the problem?" Gerald asked, after his boss identified himself. He knew from past experience that Tom only called him this late at night if there was a problem.

"I found a note taped to my monitor." Tom said casually.

"Yeah?" the sleepy employee responded.

Now Tom got more to the point and asked, "Who gave it to you?"

Gerald took a moment to chase the sleep from his brain as he remembered the events of the day. "Some woman came in the store and handed it to Jackie for you." he said. "In fact, about fifteen minutes later, she was chased by a couple of Homeland guys out of our parking lot. The word was that she may have been caught a little while after that over at the mall. Why," Gerald finally asked, "is anything the matter?"

After hearing Gerald's explanation, Tom decided to keep his suspicions to himself and not get his good hearted manager involved in whatever was going on. "No, no problem, I just wanted to know. Thanks Gerald, you can go back to sleep now."

"Will do boss." Gerald said "Goodnight," and hung up the phone.

Tom sat in his chair for a minute pondering what he had just been told. He tried to piece it together and his gut told him that something about this situation was not good. In fact, the more he thought about it the more uncomfortable he felt about what he knew. He didn't like the way the math was adding up. Jared was running from the authorities. The girl knew where Jared was. The authorities now had the girl. Too many people at Homeland were sadistic buggers. He looked at his watch; that had all taken place over twelve hours ago.

He opened the drawer of his desk and pulled out a business card. On the back he had written the phone number for Jared. Tom made the call and kept it short in case someone was trying to triangulate a fix on Jared's location. It was a concept left over from the old military days, but he decided that now it was still good practice. He purposely lowered his voice into a deep southern drawl. "They're comin'." he said. "Get out NOW."

CHAPTER 34

KOOTENAI NATIONAL FOREST,
MONTANA....11:20PM

Anger surged through Bennett when he got the call from the team leader who had arrived at the cabin. "There's no one here sir. It looks like we just missed him."

"Fan out; look for any signs of him...I'm on my way." Bennett could not, would not believe that this had happened; Jared would not elude him again.

Bennett arrived at the cabin in the Humvee five minutes later. He got out of the vehicle and stomped into the cabin. There was still a small fire in the wood stove and the pot of water setting on top was still warm.

"How did he know?" Bennett asked himself and he cursed under his breath, furious at this outcome. For a minute he weighed the option of sending the men after him, but then thought better of it. There was no way these amateurs would be able to track him in these woods at night. Besides, Bennett thought, Jared could pick them off, one by one, at his leisure if he wanted to. In fact, Jared was probably out there right now...watching them from a distance. Bennett's fury generated a low growl. *"No,"* he thought, *"Jared was gone, again."* And Bennett had been burned, badly...again.

He had to think fast and shouted, "He's gone, everyone back into the Humvee. Let's get out of here."

After they picked up the other Humvee and had gone about five more miles down the road with the lights on, the four men silently, on signal, jumped from the vehicles as they slowed down while rounding a bend. Silently, they made their way back to the area surrounding the cabin.

Bennett's plan was simple. First, just in case Jared did come back to the cabin, he would have his people there waiting and watching. He was tired of playing these games though, so this time the instructions were to shoot on sight.

In the morning, if Jared hadn't shown up, he would be back with the Humvees and take all of the food from the cabin. It wouldn't stop Jared, he knew, but it would slow him down. It might even force Jared to expose himself while trying to obtain replacement food. It was obvious Jared had planned to hole up in the cabin for a long time. There was enough food in the metal storage lockers in the cabin to last all winter.

Secondly, Bennett would have the roads out of the area watched discreetly along with other cabins in the area and nearby houses. Most of the area was deserted and the houses had already been stripped of anything of value, including food. There were only a few die hard Montanans left in the area. *"Those too stupid to leave for warmer climates."* he thought. They would be watched.

It was 2:00 a.m. before Bennett got back to Eureka and started looking for a place to sleep...he had expected to be on his way back to Spokane by now. The situation with the devices would have to be addressed in the morning.

JARED

After hiking for ten minutes towards his closest cache, Jared stopped and pulled the satellite phone out of his bag. Turning it on, he punched in the number for Tom. He knew that he needed to make a quick call to learn what was going on so he could finalize his decisions. It was now after midnight. He swung the D bag back over his shoulder and started walking as the call was going through.

"Hello?" Jared recognized the now undisguised voice of his old friend.

"Tom," he said in a hushed tone, "its JD, can we talk?"

"Yes." Tom replied quickly, feeling some reassurance at the sound of Jared's voice.

"Thanks." Jared said, "I assume it was you that saved my, butt big time. I owe you buddy, how did you know?"

"A woman left a message for you at the store this morning." Tom explained. "I got it late tonight., but you should know my friend, that after she delivered the note, she was chased down and picked up by HS. She signed the note Rachel."

In his heart he had known that something had happened, but hearing Tom say her name made his heart sink. "That's bad." Jared responded.

"I didn't think it was good." Tom replied.

Jared asked his friend, "Anything else?"

"You should also be aware," Tom went on. "in case you're not listening to the radio... that a nuclear device went off in LA ten days ago. It was small, but the whole country has been put on lockdown again. There are checkpoints everywhere. Just be careful." he warned. "Beyond that I don't know anything."

"I appreciate it." JD admitted sincerely. "I'm in your debt."

"That's a nice switch for a change." Tom said with a laugh. "Come by sometime and we can chat some more."

"Will do. Off" Jared used the military jargon to

indicate the call was over.

After taking out the battery and stashing the phone back into his bag, Jared quickened his pace a little. His worst fears were confirmed. Bennett had Rachel. That led him to wonder why she had tried to find him. What had caused her to leave the safety of the Mormon tent encampment? The questions swirled in his head, but the answers escaped him. Within a few minutes he had decided his next course of action.

As he hiked down the trail, he passed the path that led to his 'near hole' and kept right on going. His goal was to reach the 'far hole' across the Canadian border by morning, which meant that he had to book it as fast as possible.

He was thankful for the light of the moon. It was a clear, relatively warm night for the mountains and luckily the trails he had to take were not difficult.

Jared figured that Bennett was still looking for him around the cabin and Eureka. *"He might even bring in the dogs."* Jared thought. The plan he had settled on after his call to Tom, was to use the "back door" he had prepared for just such a situation. *"To do,'* he thought, *'the most unexpected and unlikely of actions."* He would hike across the Canadian border to his 'far hole,' a small cache of emergency supplies he had put there two weeks earlier. After reaching that, he could continue north, west, or east. The least likely direction would be east, over the rugged mountain peaks of Glacier National Park. Once clearing the mountain peaks, he could cross back over the US-Canadian border and head south through the middle of Montana. It was an area sparsely populated, and with luck, he would be able to steal some form of transportation and make good time towards Utah.

Jared figured that Bennett would take Rachel back to his home base in Ogden, so that was where he would head. He wasn't exactly sure what he would do when he got there, but by the time he arrived he would have a plan formulated.

If he made his 'far hole' by morning, Jared figured, he would remain there for most of the day just in case Bennett and his men were looking for him. The distance over the mountains was only about twenty two miles and he felt confident that he could do that in one night if the good weather continued to hold. It was late summer, and most of the snow that was going to melt, would be gone, leaving the trails through the passes open. If they weren't, then the trip would take him considerably longer.

BENNETT

Bennett woke up in the morning with a headache. It was 6:00 a.m. and he hadn't gotten much sleep. He was also in a rotten mood. No one had called him during the night, which meant that the four on stakeout had come up empty. He turned down the hall of the local motel and knocked on the doors of the two drivers he had brought with him from Spokane.

"Let's get moving.... NOW," he yelled.

Bennett walked out the front door of the motel and into the front door of the police station, which was conveniently next door. The sheriff was already in, sitting behind a desk with his feet propped up.

"Morning," the Sheriff greeted him warmly. "Coffee's hot if you want some."

"Thanks," Bennett responded. "Anything stirring?"

"Nope, it's usually pretty quiet around here." The Sheriff really didn't really care for the big city types, like Bennett, especially when they came to interfere within his jurisdiction. "The most we do is watch for people trying to sneak across the border into Canada."

The two drivers opened the door of the office and walked in. Bennett motioned to them. "Coffee's there." He said, "We'll leave in about 10 minutes."

"There's a restaurant up the street that should be open about now if you're needing some breakfast." The Sherriff offered, "It ain't much, but it's all we have this early."

"Thanks," Bennett responded, trying to sound sincere. ", but we need to get back on the road. We should be back in time for lunch."

"For lunch and dinner you have a total of three places to choose from." The Sherriff said with a grin.

Bennett detested small towns and their simpleton law enforcement as much as this Sheriff detested him. "Wonderful." he said sarcastically.

After taking another sip of coffee, Bennett decided he had to at least try to play the game. "Sheriff," he said, trying to make it look like they were on the same team. "We didn't pick up the suspect we were looking for last night, though we confirmed that he was there earlier in the day. We need to setup some surveillance in the area. He's on the run, and will need to find food and a place to stay for the winter."

"We could handle that." The Sheriff responded. "I can start making out a plan this morning. Might have it by the time you get back for lunch."

"Good." Bennett said, then pulled out his cell phone and dialed the Homeland Security office in Spokane. "Gil, this is Bennett."

Gil, the former Chief of Police and now Homeland Security Commander in Spokane, responded with curiosity, "Did you get your guy?"

"No," Bennett answered sourly, "We missed him. He was there earlier in the day, but left before we arrived."

"That's too bad." Gil answered.

"Yeah," Bennett went on, "we think he's still here in the area. I'll be coming back later today with the team you loaned me."

"No problem." Gil added, "My orders are to help you in any way that I can."

"You've helped a great deal already. My guess is that we should be back around ten p.m. tonight." Bennett was all business as he ended the call.

A short while later, Bennett and the drivers picked up the team from the woods. They had seen nothing of Jared during the night. Bennett had them clean the cabin out of all the food, just in case, and hauled it all back to Eureka.

Later that day, about 6:00 p.m., just as Bennett and his people were preparing to board the helicopter and take off for Spokane, the Sheriff came to a screeching halt at the local airport. He had just received a report from his deputy in the southern part of town about a suspicious character lurking around a vacant house. Two of the deputies had already gone to investigate and they believed they had the individual cornered in the house. The Sheriff thought it just might be the man Bennett was looking for.

Immediately, Bennett put the chopper on hold as he and his team followed the Sheriff out to the area. In just a few minutes they had arrived and were talking to one of the deputies who already had a map out on the hood of his jeep. He quickly explained that one of the citizens, the wife of a border agent, saw a man lurking in the area he was pointing to on the map. When the deputies arrived, she said she had watched him go into the old Erickson house. While the deputy stood watch with her, they had seen a lone figure through one of the windows. That had been about twenty minutes ago.

The Sheriff explained, "There are only about twenty houses in this area, and they are spread pretty far apart. Most of them are vacant." Pointing behind him, he continued, "I had one of my deputies come up from the south and keep watch to make sure he didn't get out that way. But, beyond that, we haven't done anything. I don't think he knows that he's been seen."

Turning to the deputy standing beside him, the Sheriff directed, "Go ahead and setup surveillance on the west side now... and make sure that he can't get past you without being seen. And whatever you do," he told the deputy seriously, "don't let him see you."

Turning to Bennett, the Sheriff asked, "It's your manhunt, so you're in charge...how do you want to proceed?" Even if the Sheriff didn't care for him, he knew the protocol. After all, technically Bennett was his Homeland Security superior, which now ran pretty much everything.

"Show me the house," Bennett said, taking charge. "And let's set up additional surveillance on it." Pointing to a member of his own team he added, "You, go with that deputy leaving now." Then, to another HS officer, "You get with the deputy to the south and stay in contact." He turned to the Sheriff then and asked, "Is there a building that overlooks the house he was last seen in, one that we can get to without him knowing what's going on?"

"Sure." The Sheriff responded, pointing in another direction. "Over there about five houses down is the Dustin house. It's vacant too, but it's the closest house...about one hundred yards, or so. You can approach it from the back without anyone knowing."

Bennett, nodding to the two other team members while still looking at the map, said, "Ok, you two come with me. Let's go take a look." Speaking to the two drivers he ordered, "Stay here for now and wait for instructions. Let me survey the situation and then I'll tell you what to do. Get your gear ready though, lock and load."

They went to the red brick, ranch style house, with a wooden shake roof that the Sheriff had called the Dustin house. Approaching the back of the house with guns at the ready, the sheriff leaned his considerable bulk against the door, and it easily gave way.

Bennett and the team looked into the living room and saw that the curtains were closed. Bennett carefully peeked out between the curtains and saw the small tan house with white trim. It looked fairly new, but he could see that the grass needed mowing, and there were large weeds growing in the yard.

He spoke into the radio, addressing his team. "This is Bennett. We are weapons free. If you have a clear shot at the suspect, take it. I repeat, if you have a clear shot, take it. Those are our orders." Bennett confirmed that everyone was in place, had clear views, and understood the orders. No one reported seeing any movement.

The problem that Bennett faced now was logistics; Jared had a clear view of the area surrounding the house he was holed up in. It was over one hundred yards to the house that Bennett was in, and any other house was two hundred to two hundred fifty yards away. Bennett knew that he didn't have enough people to rush the house, so he decided to wait until they had a visual confirmation.

They didn't have to wait long. Within about 15 minutes, Bennett saw a figure pass in front of a window. The team on the south saw it as well, but the figure wasn't in view long enough to get a shot off. There was someone definitely in the house, someone who didn't belong there.

Bennett asked the Sheriff if there was any more help he could secure. "You bet," replied the Sheriff happily. "I could have another six officers here in about an hour and a half."

"Get them." Bennett said, determination sounding in his voice. "We're going to need them."

It ended up taking three hours before all of the backup's arrived and were deployed into position. Bennett's plan was to have three vehicles rush the house at the same time, with the supporting people providing cover fire if necessary. The vehicles were to stop, and the officers were to use them as cover to then assault the house and gain entry.

The plan went perfectly except for one thing, there was no one there. The house was completely deserted. In fact, the front and back doors to the house were still locked from the inside. Bennett and his men spent another half an hour in thc dwindling light looking around for footprints, or marks of any kind leading to, or away from the house. None were ever found.

Bennett was beside himself with rage, but knew he had to control it. The thing that bothered him the most was that he, along with three other officers, had seen someone moving in the house, past the window. He had lost almost five hours of time with this fiasco. It was three, or four hours to Ogden, maybe four and half directly from Eureka in the Black Hawk helicopter. Unhappily, he realized that his time was short, and he wouldn't be able to pick up the girl in Spokane and fly to Ogden in time, because he wanted to oversee the weapons send off, personally.

Bennett called Spokane, informing them that he was forced to leave directly from Eureka, flying straight to Ogden. He would then send the chopper back with the team he had borrowed. While on the phone he also made arrangements for Rachel to be transported by vehicle to his office in Ogden.

He consoled himself with the thought, that eventually he would take care of Jared, but he would have plenty of time to take care of Rachel.

After finalizing arrangements with the Sheriff about

continuing the search for Jared, Bennett and his team stepped into the helicopter and it lifted off.

RACHEL

Rachel was still awake when the guards came in, handcuffed her, and told her she was being transported to Utah. She was loaded into a specially prepared Humvee, literally handcuffed to a large metal ring welded behind the drivers' seat. Both the driver and the guard wore blackbird uniforms. The entire trip would take them about thirteen hours, and they expected to arrive between 11:00 a.m. and noon the next day.

CHAPTER 35

JARED

While he was hiking through the Canadian side of Glacier Park, Jared once again pondered his decision to travel in an easterly direction and then turn south. He had studied his topographical map to the point that he had it pretty much memorized and had chosen the general area where he intended to pass over the border back into the United States. He had also made great time through the mountain pass, hiking at night by the light of the moon, arriving before sun up on the eastern side over looking the rolling plains of southern Alberta.

Jared stopped to watch the sunrise in the east while eating his simple meal of Ama-Ama patties. He had found that the Ama-Ama survival food was the very best and had even taken it on several special ops while in the military. This morning he had the raspberry crunch. After breakfast, he started hiking the final three miles down to the valley floor. His plan was to find a safe place to spend the day, and then, at nightfall head south, while still in the trees, and cross the border back into the US.

As he was slowing down and starting to look for a

good place to spend the day in the thick cover of pines...a voice spoke out from behind him.

"Don't move. You have three guns trained at you right now, and if you don't do exactly as you're told, I'm afraid you will have three holes in that nice jacket of yours."

Jared froze and slowly raised his arms above his head.

"Good. Now slowly drop your bag to the ground. Slowly now," the voice instructed.

Jared did just as he was told.

"And now, unbuckle the gun belt...and throw it away from you, very slowly, and with your left hand, if you don't mind."

Jared reached down with his left hand while keeping the other hand in the air. He unbuckled the webbed gun belt carefully and tossed it to the side.

"Very good, now take three big steps forward and lay down on your stomach with your hands clasped behind your head, again, very slowly."

Jared continued to obey, not seeing any other option open to him at the moment.

"Okay, search him."

From his left and a little behind him, Jared caught

the glimpse of a man coming out from behind some bushes with a gun pointed straight at him. The voice giving the orders had come from directly behind him, so he knew there were at least two of them. Jared hadn't automatically believed everything he was told. Experience had taught him that people often lied in situations like these.

He looked at the gun the second man was holding. It looked like a standard issue AR-15 with some burlap wrapped around it. The man was wearing camouflage, with branches, grass, and leaves sticking out here and there, and camouflage face paint, similar to the stuff Jared had wiped off his own face, just the day before. Jared recognized it as a very good job of camouflage. Obviously, this was someone with some real experience. He watched as the man leaned his gun against a tree and carefully approached him. Jared admired his camouflage and behavior as a professional. Whoever these guys were, they knew what they were doing.

Jared decided to take a chance and see what he could find out. "Who are you?" he asked.

"I think we should be asking the questions, don't you?" The apparent leader of the group spoke up from behind him. "Who are you, and where did you come from?"

Now the man who had been speaking to him came up from behind and kicked his legs farther apart as the one on the left started patting him down.

"I'm an American, and my name is Jared." He used his real name, hoping these people were not part of the people he knew that were searching for him back in the states. And if they were, it would do him no good to lie anyway. "I'm on a camping vacation and I just hiked over the mountains this morning." He was trying hard to keep it casual.

Just at that moment, the one searching him discovered his ankle holster and pulled up his pant leg, exposing the weapon.

"Uh-huh," came a new voice from his right, surprising him. "Just another American tourist, carrying a gun in an ankle holster."

Jared turned his head, and saw the man speaking to him now in matching camo to the first, standing only five feet away. *"Wow, these guys are good,"* Jared thought. *"I didn't even hear him coming."*

By this time, the man who was performing the search had taken the gun from the holster, and tossed it behind him, before he spoke. The question surprised Jared. "Nice little gun," he admired, "A Berretta. How many rounds does it hold?"

"Six in the magazine and one in the chamber," Jared answered, a little confused.

"Nine millimeter, or a thirty two?"he asked.

"Thirty two" Jared said. This conversation had him more than a little puzzled, and he was wondering how long it would be before his captors would let him in on what was going on.

"Nice." The man searching him spoke again. "OK, Mr. American Tourist, we can do this the hard way, or the easy way... any more weapons that you would like to declare? I believe that you have at least one, if not two more, somewhere on your person."

Jared made a quick decision and answered, "Just one more. It's a knife on my inside left forearm."

The man behind him said, in a tone dripping with sarcasm, "Yep, just your average American tourist out for a stroll, eh." The man who was searching him unbuttoned Jared's sleeve and withdrew the knife. It too got tossed behind him with the other weapons.

The man standing to his right asked the leader, "You think he's the one we were sent to find?"

Jared heard the voice from behind. "Yeah, he's probably the one, but let's bind him just, to play it safe."

The one who had searched him, and removed the weapons, said in a somewhat kindly, joking manner, "Ok, I'm sorry to have to do this Mr. Tourist, but if you are the one we were waiting for, I'll apologize later." He quickly put Jared's hands in the standard military type hand bind. "But, in case you're not, well, better to be safe than sorry, eh?"

The words, even this whole interaction, confused

Jared more than a little. It didn't make any sense. He supposed that Bennett had outguessed him, that Bennett had covered all of his bases, and had called ahead to have people waiting for him here in Canada, just in case.

Jared spoke up; asking a question that he hoped would shed some light on the situation. "What do you mean, you were waiting for me?" he asked.

The man searching him replied for the group, "Well, we had a tip that someone like you would be coming over the pass this morning, so we've been waiting for you."

While Jared was trying to digest the answer to his question, he heard the zipper on his D bag, and knew they were finishing their very thorough search. The man behind him commented on the contents of the bag. "My, my, all of the gear every American tourist carries with him when taking a stroll through the woods."

There was the rustle of things being moved around in the bag. "Let's see," it was the voice of the one exploring the contents and giving a running inventory of what he found. "A Saiga SKS... six 30 round magazines, all loaded, and an H&K tactical 45 with one... two... three... four magazines. I don't suppose that you have a silencer for it do you?"

Before Jared could answer, he heard the man answer his own question, "Ah, yes, here we are, very impressive."

Jared listened to the sound of magazines being dropped from each of the guns, and the actions opened as the chambered bullets were ejected. Then, he heard the sound of zipping again.

There was a grunt behind him and he imagined his bag, with its hefty contents, being picked up. Then finally the voice from the rear spoke, "Ok, I got it. Help him up and have him walk about ten feet in front of us."

The man behind him who had been searching his bag said with surprise, "This thing probably weighs at least 80 lbs" And then, directing his question to Jared, "You carried this over the pass at night? Remind me not to underestimate you."

The man who had searched him was now back on Jared's left, and his command was void of the levity present just seconds earlier, "Ok, on your feet." And with a guard on each side of him, providing some assistance, he stood up. "No funny stuff now," he was told.

Jared had resigned himself to cooperate with these men, at least for now. Despite their lighthearted candor, it was evident that they were true professionals. So far, he hadn't seen them make one mistake.

When he stood up, he turned around, and finally looked at the man behind him, trying to put a face with the voice. He was a big man, probably about six foot four, and weighing somewhere between 250 and 270 pounds. He was also dressed in camouflage similar to the other two. He had Jared's "D" bag over his shoulders, but on him it looked more like a regular backpack.

"Wait a minute," the leader said, as he took off his camouflaged helmet, made an adjustment and then placed it back on his head. With the helmet off Jared was able to notice the short cropped black hair, dark eyes, and brown skin that wasn't covered by camouflage face paint.

Quickly checking the other two, he noticed the same features. These men were Indians. It had been hard to see at first, under the face paint, but there it was.

The apparent leader spoke to the others, "Let's go." and he motioned the direction with his rifle. "Let's just continue on down this trail to our truck."

"Where are you taking me?" Jared asked.

"There are people waiting for you in town," the big man replied.

"Which town?" Jared asked, feeling this line of questioning was just a little silly, in spite of everything that had happened to him recently.

"Cardston" was the reply.

BENNETT

Bennett had landed at the airport in Butte, Montana, at about 3:20 a.m. because the Black Hawk helicopter didn't have enough fuel left to fly non-stop to Ogden. Originally, there was no hurry, and Bennett was trying to relax while the pilot tried to find someone to refuel the helicopter.

Within thirty minutes, the pilot returned, having discovered that the Butte airport had been vandalized the night before, and what limited fuel had been available, was now gone, stolen by the vandals. The little fuel that had not been stolen had been contaminated with something, they were not sure what. It was estimated that it would take at least three hours to acquire the amount of fuel they needed, and have it brought in from Missoula. And they would need Bennett's authority to get it since, the Missoula airport officials were reluctant to let any of their precious fuel go.

At first, Bennett had fumed over yet another delay, but at last, he calmed down, and started to make the arrangements. It took him twenty minutes to get things moving in Missoula. Then he called his aide, Marston, in Ogden, to have the two men Bennett had hand picked, to start their trip for Cardston. He remembered the conversation he had with the men after arming the weapon, and just before he had flown to Spokane.

After working on the bombs, Bennett had Marston drive one car, while he had personally driven the other car, to the Blackbird underground garage from the Hill Air base hanger. After arriving at the empty garage, Bennett sent Marston upstairs, then had opened the trunks of the cars, and activated the timers on each of the bombs. The first one was set for 1:00 p.m. on Friday, or 1300 military time, as per his instructions, and the second for an hour later.

He then closed the trunks, and also went upstairs, meeting with the two men he had chosen to drive the vehicle to Cardston. "I understand that both of you have been to Cardston before." Standing at attention they both gave the correct response, "Yes, sir."

"Good." Bennett replied. "There is a critical package that needs to be delivered precisely on time in Cardston, Canada, at 12:45 on Friday. Upon final confirmation of orders from me, you will receive the package, and the keys to the car, then you will proceed directly to Cardston. When you arrive, you will park on the south side of the Mormon Temple and wait. Someone will approach you between 12:45 and 13:15 to pickup the package. You must ask them for the password, which is 'Christmas.' After they have given you the correct password, you will give them the package and return here. Is that understood?"

Both of the soldiers nodded briskly.

"I will see you back here on Saturday morning to

report. Are there any questions?"

"No sir," they once again answered in unison. The young men saluted and then left.

Bennett thought, *"One down...and one to go."* He had no concern for the thousands of lives this bomb would take, and did not feel any remorse for these two unsuspecting soldiers. Immediately, he turned his attention to the subsequent chore of arming the second device, and meeting with the next two drivers.

When Bennett had opened the second bomb, it had presented a real mess. He essentially was forced to replace most of the wiring, and jury rigged a timing device, that he had improvised, with a new power supply. He was pretty sure it would work just fine, even though it was still connected to the Russian capacitors and relays. They were old, but they looked in good enough shape to perform their function, and he didn't have the time to hunt down replacements at this late date, so they were left in place. He was in a hurry to get to Spokane.

He finished briefing the second set of drivers with almost exactly the same words as the first. Only they were directed to wait for someone to meet them on the north east corner of Temple Square, in Salt Lake City, across from the Mormon Conference Center, at 1400 hours.

Bennett had wondered how long it would take for word of the explosion in Cardston to be reported. He reminded himself that when he did receive word, he was supposed to act shocked and surprised.

But, this unexpected delay in Butte had upset his timetable, that, plus the idiotic chase of a ghost in that stupid little town of Eureka. He had called Marston, and told him about the delay in Butte, and then instructed him to send the two soldiers on their assignment to Cardston, within the hour. The dummy package was sitting on Bennett's desk along with the keys to the car.

By the time the fuel had arrived, taking even longer than expected, and they were ready to go...Bennett was cursing everyone, and everything in sight. He still had two and a half hours to Ogden, which meant that he wasn't going to be there in time to do anything, except put the girl in the car, and have her driven off to Salt Lake City. It would give him little satisfaction, compared to what he had planned, and he was inflicting the wrath of his disappointment upon everyone he saw. Soon the refueled chopper lifted off and they were finally on their way.

RACHEL

Rachel had been awake all night long, mostly traveling in the Humvee with the two Blackbird guards in the front seat. Her hands were chaffed after being held in front of her for so long, cuffed, with the chain running through the large metal loop welded to the front seat. She sat directly behind the driver, tightly strapped in, with two seatbelts crisscrossing her chest, and one more at her waist. There were two thick Plexiglas plates separating the front and back seats. Obviously, this vehicle had been used to transport prisoners before.

Rachel had tried to sleep, but failed. Everything that had happened to her kept swirling around in her mind. Everything she had done, or tried to do, had turned out wrong. As she replayed the events in her mind over, and over again... she kept asking herself, *"How had things gone so wrong?"*

The thing that tortured her the most was the point where she had felt that she had had a spiritual experience, a dream... actually two different dreams, that, at the time, had felt so right, and yet had turned out so wrong. Rachel even had received confirmation about her dreams by people she trusted, Granny Shumway, and the Stake President.

"How could I have been so wrong?" she thought. *"How could everyone be so wrong? What have I done to deserve this? I must have done something terribly wrong and offended God,"* but, try as she might, asking herself these questions, she could not figure out the reason she was being punished, or had incurred God's wrath.

As the turmoil kept churning in her mind, and in her heart, she looked out the window, and noticed that they had just passed, Butte. The sun was up in the east, bathing the tops of the surrounding mountains in a golden glow. The sky was an incredible dark blue, with just a few clouds here and there dotting the sky. But, the beauty of her surroundings went unnoticed. *'I'm going to die,'* she thought with resignation. *"It's just as well. I don't deserve to live after what I have done to everyone...after what I've done to Jared."*

CHAPTER 36

JARED

On the way into town, they rode in an old brown Chevy pickup truck. Jared was lying in the very back of the truck bed, against the tailgate, with the two smaller Indian guards watching him from their positions up against the back of the cab, with Jared's bag between them. The big Indian, the apparent leader, was driving.

With the rushing wind, it was impossible to carry on a conversation. On the twenty minute walk down to where the truck was parked, no one had said another word to him, or answered any of his questions. The opportunity to make a move never presented itself.

They arrived in town, and all Jared could see above the side of the truck was the top half of some buildings. He had never been to Cardston, and from what he could see from his current perspective, it looked like a typical, very small, Midwestern town. Before he was ready, they made one turn, and then another, and came to a stop in the street.

The two camouflaged guards stood up as the driver got out of the truck. One of them handed his carbine to the big man, and jumped out of the truck, retrieving his gun once he was on the ground. The big Indian went to the other side, and the action was repeated, only with his bag being handed down after the gun. Always, there was someone with a gun watching him no matter what else was going on.

After they had all gotten out of the truck, they went to the back of the pickup, and dropped the tailgate. The leader spoke to Jared, "OK," he said, "Rides over; it's time to go see what they want with you." The two smaller guards helped him down from the truck and onto his feet. He noticed that neither one of them had their guns in their hands while they did this, but the big man did, and he had him covered.

After Jared was standing on the sidewalk, the two men who had helped him down, picked up their guns from where they had placed them, leaning against the front wheels of the pickup, and they escorted him into the building.

Jared read the lettering on the front of the building as he was marched up the steps to the entrance. It said, "Cardston City Offices."

Just after stepping through the doorway the leader told his men, "Wait here." He opened a door and disappeared down a hallway. In a moment, he reappeared with two white haired gentlemen behind him. Jared guessed that one was about seventy five and the other a little younger, perhaps only in his late sixties. They came right up to the group and then turned to the leader. The older one said in a kindly voice, "We didn't say to bring him in handcuffed... would you release him, please?" As he moved to comply, the older man said, "Thank you," to him.

The younger of the two aged men, then turned to Jared and spoke kindly, "We are sorry if this has inconvenienced you." Jared was now thoroughly confused. He had not expected this kind of reception, but, before he had time to comment on his treatment, the older man spoke again, "Tell me...do you by any chance know how to diffuse a nuclear bomb?" The question took him completely by surprise, and the shocked expression on his face proved it.

Jared was so taken aback by the question, he hesitated before replying, but finally, realizing that they were waiting for a reply he answered, "Yes, I do." The younger of the two, grabbed his hand and started squeezing it and said with sincerity and emotion, "Thank you for coming. You are the man we were told would come. We need your help so very much, and I don't think we have much time."

Jared noticed that his Indian guards relaxed noticeably when they heard his answer. The two smaller men looked at each other, and wide grins came to their faces. Everyone lowered their weapons.

The senior white-haired gentleman began to explain the situation to Jared; "You see, we have a nuclear bomb here, and we believe that it is going to go off within the next hour, or so."

The two younger guards looked at each other and immediately tensed back up.

"We were told you were coming," the old man

continued, "and, that you would be able to help us. Will you?"

Before Jared had time to think about it, he found himself answering, "Yes, of course," though he had a puzzled look on his face, which was a perfect reflection of his confused state of his mind.

"Good," the older man continued. "Please follow us."

Quickly, the two men moved towards the front door that Jared had been brought through in handcuffs, a few minutes before. Jared followed the two older men, with the Indian guards bringing up the rear.

As they stepped outside the building, Jared noticed that there were no other cars, or people, on the street, a detail he had missed when brought in. The area was completely deserted, except for the brown truck he had arrived in and a silver gray Ford sedan parked next to it.

When they reached the truck with the vehicle next to it, the older white haired man turned, and said to the big guard. "I suggest that you leave town immediately with everyone else. Get at least five miles away, and take shelter." He shook the man's hand and finished, "Again, thank you for your help."

Without a word the three Indians that had brought Jared into town, got back into the truck, and drove away.

The older man spoke to Jared again as calmly as if the discussion were regarding the weather, "We didn't know if it was a good idea to move it, or not, so we decided to leave it alone. It's about a block from here, just around the corner, and up the street."

The younger of the old men got into the driver's side of the vehicle, slipping behind the wheel, while the older man opened the back door for Jared.

They drove quickly up the street and turned a corner. It was then that Jared saw a couple of local police officers, with two men in handcuffs standing between them. Both of the handcuffed men wore black Blackbird uniforms.

As Jared and his new friends arrived, they pulled up next to one of the vehicles, sitting in front of the deputies and their prisoners. The older man said, "We believe the nuclear bomb is in the trunk of this blue car."

Jared opened the car door and got out. He had felt like he was in a strange, confused play, until now. He glanced at the deputies and the two prisoners standing about twenty feet away, and suddenly everything was very real. He asked, "Who are these two?" To Jared, they looked scared to death.

The older man replied, "These are the men who were assigned to deliver the bomb here today. They really have been most cooperative. It seems that they were told to drive here to Cardston, park, and wait. They arrived early. They were not aware that they had a nuclear bomb in the trunk of their car." He added with a twinkle in his eyes, "Luckily, we did."

Jared and the two men walked the ten steps to the back of the parked blue sedan. The trunk of the car was open slightly. Jared reached over and opened it all of the way.

There was a large rectangular, army green, metal box, with closed latches, that just about filled the entire trunk. On both of the latches there were large brass locks. While still looking at the metal trunk, Jared said to no one in particular, "I need a hacksaw." Then he turned to ask all of the people within the sound of his voice. "By any chance, do you have a power hack saw with a metal blade?"

One of the Sheriffs deputies, standing nearby answered quickly, "Yes." He said, "We have a power drill and a power hacksaw." He walked over to the back of the Cardston squad car and opened the trunk.

The younger, old man told Jared, "We have taken the liberty to have a large variety of tools brought just in case you needed them. We should have most anything that you will need."

Jared walked over to the back of the patrol car and looked in. It was full of every type of tool imaginable, flashlights, pliers, pipe wrenches, screwdrivers, and more.

The deputy opened the back door of the car and pulled out a bright orange Black & Decker power saw, slapped in the 18 volt battery pack and showed Jared a handful of blades.

Jared chose a short, tungsten carbide metal blade and put it into the end of the saw. He then turned back to the officer, and said, "Help me cut the locks off this trunk."

They walked back over to the blue sedan. "Hold the lock out so I can cut it off," Jared said, as he pulled the trigger on the saw, and the blade started vibrating. In a minute they had both locks off. Jared unfastened both latches and slowly raised the lid.

The adrenaline rush he always got at times like this, hit him hard, and he took a minute to regain control before continuing to slowly raise the lid, and look inside.

It was a Russian SDAM 107-D, commonly called a suitcase nuke. They were manufactured in Russia during the 1970's, at the height of the cold war. Jared guessed that this one had a yield of about 1/3 of a kiloton, enough power to destroy a city block outright, and almost everything within a half mile radius. This type was relatively simple in design, having been the upgrade from the initial version of the late sixties. It was essentially the same type as the ones he had observed being defused several months earlier, in Iraq, with the coke machines.

He had personally worked on at least two others just like it prior to the pop machine operation. They posed no unusual problems, except that one had been extremely old, and had not been stored very well, so the wires had corroded. The key to success here was simple, in these bombs the timer was everything. Jared noticed that this one appeared to be in pretty good condition.

He was glad it wasn't an older version that the Soviets had come up with in the late fifties. *"Those were real bears,"* he thought, *"no pun intended."* Basically, they were warheads from old nuclear artillery shells, put together with a patchwork detonation system. He had worked on one of those once. It had not been armed, but he had been given the opportunity to take it apart. It had been a mess; the wires were an aluminum and copper mix that had started to corrode, which made the situation very bad.

The electric timer in those had been designed prior to computer chips, and so the soviet scientists had come up with a wire system that relied on different settings, so that you had a choice of different capacitors and relays. It was difficult to set, and was considered unstable and unreliable, mostly because some of the Russian capacitors had a nasty habit of releasing their electricity early, often shortening the timing settings considerably...to the detriment of those who were carrying them to their destination. Luckily, there were few of them still in existence. Most had been destroyed because they were considered obsolete.

Jared looked in just to be certain, and sure enough, the bomb was armed, and active. He couldn't tell how much time he had, because these bombs had been developed before the days of digital readouts. He figured, when you didn't know the amount of time you had till detonation, it was always best to hurry.

The first thing he needed to do was to shut down the timer, and its connection to the arming mechanism that connected to the nuclear core. Jared looked for the four main wires and quickly found them. Then, he checked to make sure there weren't any hidden wires, anti-tamper devices, or collapsible circuits attached. When he was satisfied that there were none, he also confirmed the power source. The power source in this case, was a new battery. Someone who knew what they were doing had worked on this bomb.

With the wire cutters he had chosen from the trunk of the squad car, Jared made four, slow snips in just the correct order, and defused the bomb. It had taken him a total of four minutes from the time he had opened the box and looked inside.

"Ok." Jared announced to the crowd. "It's defused."

He continued to speak to no one in particular. "At this point, I would normally take the core out, but I don't have a lead container to put it in." Then he had an idea and looked more closely at the small trunk the bomb was sitting in. It was lined with lead.

"Never mind," he said, "the box is lead lined. I'll just leave it in the trunk as the containment repository. I just need to remove the arming device."

He turned to the deputy standing about three feet away from him, "Get me a flat screwdriver please." The officer moved quickly to the squad car and retrieved several flat bladed screwdrivers. Returning, he held them out in his hands for Jared to choose.

Jared picked one and went back to his task. He carefully disconnected the wires to the arming device completely, and then removed the power source. He handed the battery to the officer. "Here, hold this," He said.

Again, he reached into the trunk. He slowly backed the arming device out of the throat of the nuclear core, disconnecting all of the wires, and main link to the core. Jared lifted it out of the trunk, and carried it over to the police car, setting it down in the back seat. With that done, he went back and closed the lid on the trunk, refastening the latches. "All done," he announced.

As he turned around, there were huge grins on the faces of the two older men, and the sheriff's deputies.

The older white haired man stepped forward towards Jared, with his hand outstretched, "We owe you a debt of gratitude young man. Thank you so much."

As Jared took the proffered hand he was looking over at the men in handcuffs. "Do you mind if I ask these guys a couple of questions?" he asked.

"Please, go right ahead." The older man replied. "As

I told you, they have been most cooperative. It seems that they were intended victims as much as we were. We kept them here so that if you needed to ask them something, they would be available."

Jared looked at the two young men in uniform, and saw a mixture of sorrow, relief, and confusion.

"Where are you guys from?" Jared asked, in a friendly tone.

The taller of the two said, "We are with the Intermountain Regional Homeland Security support group out of Ogden."

"Blackbird?" Jared asked.

"Yes, sir," the young man replied.

A thought came to Jared. "Who is the commander of your group?" He asked them. Jared knew the answer already, he just wanted confirmation of his suspicions.

"A Major Bennett, sir."

"So, let me get this straight," He continued. "You said that you had been given an assignment to drive this car up here, park, and wait. Is that correct?"

"Yes, sir," They both said while nodding their heads. The taller one continued on, "We were told to deliver a package, the one sitting in the back seat there, to someone here in Cardston. We were to arrive, and park at this place, and someone was supposed to meet us here at 1300 hours. We were to verify code words, and hand over the package, and then return to home base." The man speaking finished. "I swear, that's all we know, sir."

The other one was nodding his head in agreement.

"What's in the package in the back seat?" Jared queried further.

"We don't know. We were told not to open it, just to just deliver it."

Jared turned, walked to the back of the squad car and grabbed a razor knife that he had seen there while looking at the tools earlier.

"Well, I think we better take a look at what's in the box." He walked over to the sedan and opened the back door. Sitting in the middle of the back seat was a brown box about 18 inches by 12 inches by about 24 inches. It looked like something he would ship via UPS, wrapped in brown paper, and clear, reinforced tape.

He looked it over carefully and it appeared to be the same all over. He gently lifted the box on one end, and discovered that it wasn't very heavy. He opened the razor knife and just as he was about to cut open the top, he changed his mind, and backed out of the car.

"I don't think I want to do that just now." Jared said strangely.

He turned around and walked back over to the small group who had been watching him with much interest.

Jared explained to the people gathered around. "My guess is that it's probably empty, or maybe there's just some trash, or something inside, but I would hate to find out differently."

Addressing the other Blackbird soldier who had remained silent for the most part, Jared asked, "Do you know anything more than what your partner here has said?"

"No sir." The second young man responded. "There were two cars, and two packages. We were to take this one to Cardston, just as he said."

Jared looked at the man with renewed interest. "You said there were two cars and two packages?"

"Yes sir." He repeated. "There was another car just like this one. One of my buddies told me that he had received an assignment to drive a car and deliver a package, and would be gone for the day. We were in the locker room changing clothes and we got to talking. We usually have a poker game on Friday nights, and I didn't know if I would be back in time for it, and so I mentioned that I was going to Cardston to deliver a package and probably wouldn't be back for the game. He said he had also been assigned to drive a car and deliver a package too. He was leaving later today as soon as a female prisoner from Spokane arrived. He was to transport the prisoner and deliver the package."

Jared's heart leapt up to his throat as he listened to the words coming out of the young soldier's mouth. "What do you know about the female prisoner?" he asked intensely.

"Nothing much, except that there had been talk of the Major chasing some fugitive woman from Arizona, and the word was he had finally caught her up in Spokane. He had a lot of the people in the division looking for her. Just before he left to go to Spokane we got the assignment to deliver the package."

Now the other soldier chimed in. "I was one of those working on locating the woman. About two months ago, the Major came back from Arizona madder than all hell. It seems that he had flown down there to apprehend someone and they had escaped. He had us all looking for her and then we spotted her in Utah. He missed her there, but when she was spotted in Spokane, the major flew up to get her."

"Do you know what happened in Spokane?" Jared asked, almost holding his breath.

"Well, apparently she was there, and they caught her after a short chase." He had no apparent fear at divulging this information, after discovering that they had been sent on a death mission. "The major tricked her into telling him where her partner was. There were actually two people they were after, a man and a woman. The major then flew to Montana to look for the guy, but he escaped. The major was madder than hell. I was pulled off the search at that time, and started on our trip here to deliver the package."

Jared's mind was working furiously. He was starting to get more panicked by the minute as the words stumbled out of their mouths. They had no idea of the importance of this information, or what it meant, especially to him.

Jared asked them, trying to keep his voice under control. "Do you know what the woman looked like, or her name?"

"Yes, sir." The shorter soldier replied. "She originally had red hair, but later dyed it black. She was 5 ft 7, weighed about 145, blue eyes, and very pretty. She lives in Virginia sir, and her name is... Rachel Sinclair." Jared said her name in unison with him, and the young man's eyes grew wide in confusion.

Jared's heart now dropped like a rock. His worst fears were confirmed as the pieces fell into place. Bennett had gotten her in Spokane, and had tricked her into revealing where Jared was in Montana. He already suspected that Homeland had her, but now he knew that scumbag Bennett had her, and there was no telling what he would do to her.

Jared had learned in his research that Bennett was known as a sadistic monster, who was not afraid of applying various torture techniques on his chosen victims in order to get whatever information he wanted. In the course of that research, word had come through the grapevine for him to watch out for this guy...he had become a real bad dude.

Jared's blood began to boil as he considered the possibilities. If Bennett had hurt her, in any way, he would pay dearly. There was no place that Bennett would be able to hide, no where in the world. Jared would track him down, find him, and kill him if he even harmed a hair on her head. Then a new fear suddenly jumped into his mind...and he quickly asked.

"Tell me, do either of you know where the other car was headed with the package and this woman?"

The taller soldier spoke up, "Yes sir. The second car was heading for Salt Lake City."

CHAPTER 37

RACHEL

They had just passed Pocatello and were heading south on I-15. Rachel thought about the hair pin she had in her pants pocket. She had meant to take it out and put it into her hair, but with her hands cuffed and shackled, and the restraints across her body, that was now out of the question. By sliding the chain through the ring she could get one hand to touch her knee, but not close to her pocket. To make matters worse, she could see the tip of the hairpin sticking out of the top of her pocket.

To keep her mind focused on something other than depression over her situation, Rachel rethought the steps to unlocking handcuffs, using the hair pin that Jared had taught her while in the tent city in Arizona. She had cornered him one day when she saw someone at the encampment with a pair of handcuffs. The brother had been a police officer on the "outside" and was still wearing his belt with the leather cuff holder in the back. After finding out that he still had the handcuffs, Rachel borrowed them from him for a few days. She found Jared and had him show her the trick he had used to escape from Bennett the first time. "Bend it like a little h," he had told her, "using the holes in the cuffs. And then insert it into the lock

-452-

like so, and then turn it. It even works when it is double locked."

After a dozen tries, Rachel finally got it down to about a minute. It wasn't really that hard, if you knew what you were doing. Jared, of course, could do it in about ten seconds, twenty if his hands were behind his back where he couldn't see what he was doing.

"It was a nice trick," she thought with frustration, *"but it only worked if you could get the hair pin into your hands."* She looked again at the top of the pin sticking out of her pocket and then back at her cuffed hands. Just then, she looked out the window, and noticed a sign that said *"Lava Hot Springs 1 mile."*

JARED

Jared was having a panic attack. It had become obvious to him, after listening to the unsuspecting drivers, that Bennett's plan was to put Rachel in the car with the nuclear weapon, and have them driven to Salt Lake City, where it would be detonated.

Quickly turning to the older white haired man beside him, Jared said, "I need to get to Salt Lake immediately."

Without waiting for an answer, he turned back to the Blackbird soldiers, and asked hastily, "Do you have any idea what time your friend was supposed to be in Salt Lake?"

"Yes sir." The shorter soldier replied, "We discussed it because he wanted to get back to Ogden for the game. He said he had to drop off the package at 1400 hours, and then he would return immediately to Ogden."

Jared looked at his watch...it was noon... he had two hours before the bomb would explode.

He turned back to the white haired man. "It appears that there is a second bomb that is going to be delivered to Salt Lake and set off...probably in about two hours, or later. Is there some kind of plane that can get me there so that I can defuse it?" Jared was grasping at straws. Before he finished his question, he already knew the answer that was coming.

"No," the Old man responded with genuine concern, "I think there might be a couple of private planes out at the airport...but, it would take at least four hours to fly from here to Salt Lake, maybe even five."

Jared was frantically trying to find a solution to this unsolvable problem. "We need to get on the radio, or the phone, or something and let Salt Lake know about this bomb." He grabbed the old man by the arm, stressing the gravity of this situation and searching his eyes for some kind of hope.

The two white haired men looked at each other for a moment and then the older one voiced their thoughts as they turned back to Jared. "They might already know about it. You see, it was Salt Lake that called us yesterday to tell us about this bomb, and that you were coming over the mountain to help us. In fact," he exchanged a look with his companion before continuing, "They told us exactly where we could find you this morning."

Jared physically rocked back on his heels, this answer floored him. How did they know? How could anyone possibly have known about him coming over the mountain? There was no one who knew about his movements, or whereabouts. Bennett might have guessed, but even he wouldn't have known about where, or when, he would appear.

Jared turned to them, and asked the question he had been in the back of his mind from the moment he had met these two. "Who are you?"

"Oh, I am sorry," said the older white haired man. I'm Elder Draper of the Quorum of the Twelve Apostles of the Church of Jesus Christ of Latter Day Saints, and this is Elder Mathews of the Seventy."

Somehow, Jared had known the answer just before he asked the question. They had that look about them, just like Elder Pinetree. He had heard Granny talk about her beloved Prophet and Apostles several times, but he had never imagined that he would meet one of them in person, especially not in a place like Cardston, Canada.

For a moment Jared stood there in silence,

recognizing the importance of these two men, but not knowing what to say.

It was then that the older man, Elder Draper spoke up. "Young man, we are truly in your debt. You have saved our lives, and probably the lives of several thousand people of this community, perhaps even more. If there is anything that we can do to help you, you have simply to name it and we will use whatever powers and means we have at our disposal, to assist you."

The offer for help brought Jared out of his silent shock. "I need to talk to someone in Salt Lake City and tell them how to defuse the bomb that is probably on its way there right now. If it goes off, it will kill tens of thousands, including possibly your Prophet, and other Church leaders who are in the city. According to the information we've received, it looks like it will probably go off in about two hours. There really is no time to waste."

Elder Draper reassured him, "I don't think you need to worry about that. You see, when they called us yesterday and canceled our meetings in Salt Lake today, they mentioned that there were some difficulties that had arisen, but they had everything under control, and we were not to worry about them. We were to just take care of things here by finding you, and having you defuse this bomb. Though they didn't say so, I would imagine that since they knew about the bomb here...they also know about the bomb that you think is headed their way. They have probably already taken steps to overcome the situation."

Elder Mathews added, "They also mentioned that they would probably be out of communication for a period of time, but to go ahead, and continue with our assignments up here in Cardston."

Jared stared at the pair, unable to believe what he was hearing. He had never heard, or experienced, anything before in his life that could compare to this.

The Apostle turned to the Sheriff, "Ed, could we get on the phone and call Salt Lake, just to confirm that they know what Mr. Davis believes is coming their way?"

"Sure," the Sheriff agreed, "let's head back to the city offices and use the phone there. You go ahead and we'll be right behind you with these two."

BENNETT

At their present air speed, Bennett would land in Ogden about half an hour before the girl and the bomb left for Salt Lake. In his mind, he started making mental plans of what he could do with her in so short a time, and then, what he would do, as soon as the bomb went off.

If Bennett hadn't been in such a hurry to run up to Spokane, but had instead stayed where he was supposed to be, he would have had the time to search out and replace the Russian capacitors, and relays in the second weapon. But the decision he had made was typical of Bennett, and the very reason why Jared blamed him for the loss of two team members so long ago. Bennett did not have the patience to perform the tedious and boring tasks, the kind of details that in the business of disarming nuclear weapons, were critical to staying alive.

As it was, when the electricity started filling up the first of the fifteen Russian capacitors, it failed completely, and just passed the electricity along like a bare wire. The next capacitor failed in the same manner, as did the next. The fourth capacitor held however, and worked the way it was supposed to, as did all of the remaining capacitors in the sequence.

Each capacitor had a different length of time that it was designed to hold before releasing its electricity. One capacitor held for twenty four hours, another for twelve hours, and another four capacitors were designed to hold for two hours each. The seventh, eighth, and ninth, capacitors were set for one hour each; the tenth for thirty minutes, the eleventh for fifteen minutes, and the twelfth thru fifteenth, for just five minutes each. By choosing which of the various capacitors were joined together in whatever final sequence was desired, the person arming the weapon could choose any amount of time between forty-eight hours, and five minutes, in increments of five minutes. It was simple, and effective....at least by design.

In reality, Bennett should have replaced the whole thing and started over from scratch. But, as it turned out, he was in too big a hurry to finally catch the woman that had eluded him for so long, and in doing so, he neglected some of the more delicate points of setting the device. He had been preoccupied with his vile imaginings of the depraved things he wanted to do to Rachel, as payback for her disrespect, and he anxiously looked forward to the prospect of getting her under his control, at last. He was going to make her pay for his trouble, and pay dearly. He would take pleasure from her screams and her pleading.

Bennett had set the Russian timer for what he thought was thirty-two hours and fifty-five minutes. However, with the failure of the first three capacitors that he had wired together in the sequence, the time had changed from thirty-two hours to thirty hours and twenty-five minutes.

The explosion was much larger than the experts would have thought from such a small device. In the end, the bomb destroyed four square blocks in an instant, instead of just the two they had expected. The Blackbird Ogden headquarters, and everything around it, was consumed by a huge fireball that disintegrated everything in its path, and turned it into a radioactive mass and mixture of molten dirt, steel, cement, and flesh, that quickly rose into the sky in the familiar shape of a mushroom cloud. It was small by nuclear standards, but, it was definitely in the classic mushroom shape indicating a powerful explosion.

The flash and pressure wave that was generated by the explosion, burned and melted everything within approximately a one mile radius, and then outside of that, for another mile, smashing it all to smithereens, pushing whatever remaining pieces there were further outward.

Those who had the misfortune of looking in the direction of the blast at the moment of detonation, and who survived the hurricane of debris that followed, were instantly blinded by the flash. Those who were close, but who weren't looking in that direction, had their flesh severely burned. Three miles out, the people heard the explosion, and felt the pressure wave push them, knocking some of them to the ground. Windows were blown out, and fragments were blown about as the one hundred fifty mile an hour wind suddenly struck them.

Unfortunately, the car carrying the device had been parked in the underground garage of the Blackbird complex, two stories down, which was directly above the Weber section of the 800 mile long Wasatch fault line, running just to the south of Hill Air Force base. Over the last one hundred years, and especially during the last twenty years, the pressure on the fault running up and down the Wasatch Front had been increasing steadily. Recently, there had been a couple of strong quakes, but instead of releasing the pressure, as people supposed, they actually had done the opposite, resulting in an increase.

The main Wasatch fault was long overdue for a quake that would unleash the pressure. Local geologists, and seismic scientists, had come to agreement on this one point at least, over the last fifteen years. All it took was the little 'love tap' of the underground nuclear explosion, on one of the most critical areas of convergence, to finally convince it to let go, and let go it did. All 800 miles of it.

CHAPTER 38

RACHEL

Rachel was rudely awakened from her reverie, by the swerving of the Humvee across the road and the accompanying curses of the driver. She assumed he had swerved to miss something in the road and was trying to regain control of the Humvee. However, as she became more fully aware, Rachel realized that wasn't the case at all. The Blackbird soldier riding shotgun exclaimed loudly, "What the hell?" She looked out the front window, and saw the reason for his shock and horror. Rachel watched as the road in front of them rose up in a wave about a foot high and rolled toward them. Behind it, she saw another wave, and then, yet another. As she watched in amazement, she realized it wasn't just the road, but the wave extended outwards on both sides of the highway, as far as she could see.

Rachel saw that the next wave was approaching quickly, and she estimated that it would hit the car about the same time that the car was going to pass under the Lava Hot Springs overpass. As it was, it hit the car just as it shot out the other side.

The soldier riding shotgun turned around and said, "Look the $(&#(*& at that," sparing no expletives to described what he had just witnessed. Rachel saw the driver look into the rear view mirror and she could see his eyes open wide in amazement. She tried to turn her head to look, but was prevented from doing so by the seatbelts. She quickly shifted her gaze to look out the window at the side mirror and saw in its reflection the overpass behind them, start to crumble. The supporting column in the middle began to break apart and the span directly over the road they were on shook once and fell to pieces on the road below, in, what felt like to Rachel, slow motion. Huge chunks of concrete were falling down now on the road where they had just been seconds before.

Another rolling wave hit the Humvee and the vehicle bucked like a wild stallion. Because of the restraints, Rachel didn't move, but both soldiers hit their heads on the steel roof of the Humvee since neither of them were wearing their seatbelts. The driver barely held on to the steering wheel during the impact, but regained control over the vehicle with only a minimum of swaying back and forth across the road. Instead of slowing down however, the vehicle hurtled forward since the driver had earlier engaged the throttle lock and was now using it as a makeshift cruise control, which was strictly against regulations.

After regaining control over the vehicle for a second time, the driver reached for the throttle lock handle so as to disengage it. Nevertheless, as he looked down to locate the handle, and with the distraction of the rocking vehicle, he failed to notice that the hidden bridge ahead had collapsed completely and that now, there was empty space for about thirty feet where the bridge had been. The Blackbird soldier in the passenger seat, who might have been of help had he been watching, didn't notice the missing bridge either, since he was still twisted around in his seat, staring at the collapsing bridge behind them and Rachel, who could not have been any help at all in her position as prisoner, did not notice the missing bridge because her attention was still riveted to the side mirror and the reflection of destruction unfolding behind them.

The distracted driver looked up just at the moment the Humvee left the ground and started slowly flying through the air in a short downward arc. Rachel saw the empty space beyond the side mirror and only had time to close her eyes. The soldier riding shotgun had only a fraction of a second start turning around to see out of the corner of his eye the large pieces of jagged concrete fill the view of the windshield from side to side before the vehicle made impact.

The Humvee hit the road and debris below with a resounding thud and chunking sounds. The force of the concussion threw Rachel against the restraining seatbelts, which actually, in the end, saved her life. The front of the Humvee, though tremendously strong, was shoved into the front of the passenger compartment, crushing the two soldiers and pushing the driver's seat back at least a foot. The men didn't feel the crushing blow of the actual impact however, because they had both been killed instantly when their heads hit the windshield simultaneously.

Rachel woke up to find herself hanging upside down with a splitting headache. She shook her head, trying to clear it of the confusion, and recognized that she hurt everywhere, and that the action of shaking her head only made things worse. She was also having a difficult time breathing, and every breath sent a sharp pain throughout her chest. The thought occurred to her that she must have cracked a rib.

With her eyes open, and her head hanging down, she almost touched the back of the dislodged front seat. As it was, her hair was laying in a tangled mess on top of the clear, but cracked Plexiglas. Through the pain, she slowly turned her head, and saw, between strands of hair, that both of the soldiers were obviously dead. She closed her eyes tightly again, attempting to block the image of the tangled mess of flesh and blood, steel and glass.

It was at that moment Rachel felt the rumble of the earth begin and everything around her started to tremble violently. It seemed to shake the Humvee much the same way her family dog shook his favorite chew toy when clenched tightly between his teeth. The shaking increased and the roar grew louder, seeming to emanate from everywhere at once, and then, slowly, it grew softer. She involuntary flinched as she heard a large chunk of concrete hit the underside of the overturned Humvee, just above her feet.

Rachel realized that she needed to get out of her upside down prison, or she was likely to be buried here alive. She opened her eyes with a new resolve to escape and then quickly closed them again as she began to pray.

When she opened her eyes, she saw that, with the seat pushed so close to her, her hands could now reach the seat belts. She first undid the lap belt and her knees dropped onto the seat. She was kneeling now, as she held herself up with one hand, and undid the two seatbelts that crisscrossed her chest. After releasing the second chest strap, she was able to breathe easier, and she took big gulps of air. With each deep breath, the pain shot through her chest from the front, to the back.

"Well, at least I'm alive," she thought, as she involuntarily winced with each breath.

Now, she could concentrate on getting her hands free. As Rachel reached for the hair pin in her front pocket there was another rumble, but this one was different. It didn't shake as violently as the previous one and the sound had changed. She paused, trying to figure out what this was and why it felt so different. Then one, terrifying word filled her mind... **VOLCANO**, followed quickly by a second word, adding to her terror...**ERUPTION**.

As the thoughts attached to these two words flooded her mind, they brought with them a string of ideas. First, was the thought that she was near Lava Hot Springs, a commonly known volcanic area. The next thought was really an impression. Rachel knew in that moment that the surrounding area was entirely volcanic and she needed to get out quickly.

Then, another thought filled her mind, but this was more than a thought; it was almost a vision. In her mind's eye she could see a tremendous earthquake, and then one, and then another volcano erupting with large, dark plumes of smoke and lava shooting up from the middle and flowing down their sides. Next, in her vision, Rachel saw the ground open up with huge columns of water shooting up from the openings, quickly flooding the valleys. She remembered the dreams and visions she had read of this event, and as she did so, a voice seemed to penetrate her mind. *"Hurry,"* it said. *"Get to higher ground...hurry."* And the strongest urgency filled her whole soul from top to bottom.

It was at that very moment, that Rachel underwent a spiritual experience unlike any she had ever had before. Her whole being seemed to fill with light for just a moment, and she felt a peace fill her heart to overflowing. Everything around her seemed to stop in suspended animation, and she felt that she was being wrapped in a cocoon of warmth, and comfort, and love. It lasted for only a few seconds, but it thrilled Rachel to her very core, and she knew that she would remember this feeling for the rest of her life. She sensed that someone was next to her, caressing her head with tenderness. Rachel closed her eyes in an effort to hold onto the sensation, and try to feel the actual touch of the hand she was so sure was near, but the urgency filled her heart again, and she realized that she needed to free herself, and get to higher ground quickly, before the water arrived.

She opened her eyes, and with purpose and determination, she pulled the hairpin out of her pocket. She was careful to hold it securely so that she wouldn't drop it and lose it to a spot she couldn't reach. As Rachel went about the process of bending the pin this way and that into the proper shape, and inserting it into the handcuffs, she felt as if a hand was helping her, guiding her trembling fingers.

The handcuffs fell away, and she started to leave them where they lay, but again, Rachel received a strong impression to take them with her. She thought to herself in almost a prayer, *"What do I do next?"* Immediately, she could see in her mind's eye what she needed to do.

Quickly, she turned around on the back of the Plexiglas, and slowly turned over on her good side, so that her feet were facing the side window opposite her, and she started kicking. The unbroken window quickly shattered on her second kick and fell away. Rachel turned over and crawled towards the now open window, past the back of the front passenger seat, and popped her head out to look around.

"Hurry," the voice in her heart and mind was saying, *"The water is coming."*

With that, she pulled herself out of the wreckage and stood on top of a large piece of concrete roadway that the crumpled Humvee was leaning against. Rachel climbed down the side of the concrete and stood on the road. It was littered with various sized chunks of concrete with pieces of rebar sticking out from them at all sorts of twisted angles.

Rachel looked around her at the two disconnected

sides of roadway that, at one time, had formed the overpass. She looked behind her, away from the Humvee, and took a step in that direction. It was clear of debris and went down towards the valley. She stopped, and this time purposefully asked in her mind..."*Which way do I go?*" Immediately, her efforts were rewarded, and she had the distinct impression to go back towards, and past, the Humvee, the piles of concrete, and the large metal girders. "*Go up not down,*" the voice seemed to say.

Rachel's obedience to the prompting was immediate as she turned around, and started climbing over, and around. The obstacles in her path. As she was almost past the debris, another rumble began. It seemed stronger, and somehow closer than the earlier one. This time, the ground shook more and the feeling of urgency filled her heart again.

As she climbed over the last of the debris, Rachel had an uncontrollable urge to run, so she started jogging. This side of the cross road was angling back towards the Lava Hot Spring turnoff, and was slowly going up the eastern side of the valley. Rachel guessed it was the farmers' access road. Suddenly, there was a huge rumble, and the ground shook hard enough that it caused her to stumble, almost knocking her completely off her feet. She stopped where she was, and tried to remain standing, as the ground shook violently. There was a huge roar, and what sounded like a tremendous explosion that filled the air. Rachel looked up into the sky, directly to the east in front of her, and saw a huge black column of smoke shoot straight up into the sky. It was very close. Quickly, the sky became dark as the black cloud began to spread out before her very eyes.

Rachel was shocked and confused when snow started to fall from the sky, and then she realized that it wasn't snow... it was ash that was falling. The rumbling and shaking slowed, and Rachel started running again, this time in earnest. Her side was also hurting now, she hadn't noticed it since the climb out of the car, but now, she was suffering ...with sharp, shooting pains accompanying every breath.

"Please Heavenly Father, help me have the strength to keep on running. Help me, help me, please," Rachel prayed out loud now in her renewed fear. The pain didn't stop, but she was able to keep running. In fact, she was able to pick up her pace even faster.

The ash was falling more heavily now, and the wind picked it up and blew it sideways a little. Rachel saw what she thought was the remains of a gas station, with some other buildings, up ahead, and she decided to make a run for them to try and find some shelter. With this thought in mind, she again picked up her speed as the road leveled out and she ran on flat ground.

Rachel reached the shelter of the buildings quickly, and was happily surprised to find that she wasn't completely exhausted. Her side still hurt every time she took a breath, but it was bearable. The buildings she found were in pretty bad shape, and Rachel began to look for a place where she could take shelter from the falling ash. Again, a strong impression let her know that it was not a good idea; she needed to get to higher ground. Looking around the corner of a partial wall, Rachel saw the black cloud towering over her that had come from where Lava Hot Springs used to be. It was so very close and seemed to go straight up into the black clouds filling the sky. Turning to the south, she looked in the direction of the highway and saw another column of smoke rising in the distance. *"A second volcano,"* she thought... *"This is definitely not a good development."*

The rumbling had dropped off a little so that it was only a dull roar now, instead of an overpowering reverberation. The ground also wasn't shaking hard like it had, but the ash was still falling. The wind had picked up and was blowing harder now, but luckily for Rachel it was blowing the ash away from her. She felt the need to repeat the question she had already asked, but instead of thinking it, this time she said it out loud, as if she were talking to someone standing near her, and asking for directions..."Where do I go now?" Her voice was soft and quiet against the noises all around her and, once again, she received her answer.

Rachel looked up and immediately spotted some trees growing on a low hill top in what she guessed was a northerly direction. The hill was across the road from where she was and up along the bluff past a few broken houses. She knew that was where she needed to head. But, just as she was ready to start running again, she heard a different noise and stopped.

This sound was a whooshing noise mixed in with the sound of the volcanic roar. It was coming from down in the valley and Rachel turned towards it. What she saw was unbelievable. Rachel watched as a wall of water twenty feet high rushed down the valley floor towards the south and then joined another body of water swirling in the distance. Where there had previously been a large open valley, there was now a rapidly rising lake of brown water. It was simply incredible! Rachel stood frozen in awe as she watched the water rapidly climb back up towards her from the newly formed lake and begin to fill the valley. When the water had risen to about twenty feet from the roadway where she was standing, she woke up from her trance, turned around, and started to run up the hill. She prayed that she would make it, the water was coming fast and she realized that in about a minute it might reach her.

Rachel tried to run faster as she headed straight towards the hill. The roar of the volcano filled the air and more ash was falling, making the air feel thicker as she ran. The whooshing sound was gone now, and curious as to what was happening, Rachel chanced a quick look back. The scene that lay before her froze in her mind and frightened her beyond anything she had seen today, up to this point. The water had already started to swirl around the base of the buildings she had just left, and part of the parking lot was now covered with water. Beyond that, in the distance where there had been a valley and a road...lay a swirling lake of brown water filled with trees, branches, and debris. Rachel gasped, as she glanced the remains of a barn, and a house, floating in the dirty water as well, slowly moving southward. The newly formed lake stretched from side to side in the valley, and as far as Rachel could see, to the south and to the north.

Catching her breath became increasingly more difficult as the hill became steeper. Her side was really hurting, and with every step now the pain shot through her entire body, no longer limited to just her chest. Rachel's pace slowed, but she kept going, determined to reach the top of the hill before the water below reached her. She ran at a slow jog now, focusing on just putting one foot in front of the other.

Rachel glanced up to see how far away the crest of hill was, and found to her delight that it was directly in front of her, perhaps only five hundred feet more. But, when she returned her gaze to the ground beneath her she heard a gurgling sound behind her. Rachel glanced back quickly as she kept moving forward, and saw that the water was only ten feet behind her. She realized that it was going to catch her before she reached the top.

Rachel willed herself to run faster, regardless of her pain, or weariness. *"Step, step, one more step, take another step, step,"* it was all that she could think about now. She looked down at the ground near her feet out of the corner of her eye, and saw that the brown water was only a few feet behind her, and rising fast. In another minute she would be running in the water. With what seemed like a superhuman effort, Rachel tried as hard as she could to increase her speed, but the ground was quite steep now, and she just could not go any faster, in fact, she was slowing down.

Just as Rachel raised her head to gauge her distance to the top of the hill, a cold wetness sloshed around her left shoe. No sooner had she pulled her left foot out of the water than her right foot was suddenly covered with a cold wetness, as well. Now both of Rachel's feet were in water, and she sloshed with every step, slowing her down even more.

She was close to the top, perhaps only one hundred feet more, but Rachel realized that before she reached the top of the hill, she would be swimming. She recognized that with each step she took the water reached higher up her legs. She guessed that in about twenty more steps she would have to swim for it. She started wondering what kind of current this water had and if she had the strength to fight it. Rachel couldn't dismiss the big question in her mind right now, how long could she last, swimming in this water?

Rachel was slowing down with each step she took through the water and she was already completely exhausted. She hurt everywhere, especially her side. She quickly realized that she wouldn't last ten minutes in the cold water.

As these thoughts plagued her, still she slowly moved forward and upward, until suddenly, she realized that the splash and pull of the water wasn't higher up her leg. She took a few more sloshy steps, and made a conscience note that the water was not getting deeper. As she took yet a few more steps, climbing higher up the hill, the water level began to drop. Rachel, weary from exhaustion, then realized that the water wasn't dropping, it was staying level, but she was climbing out of it. With three more steps her feet touched dry ground. She kept going, though slower now, and the incline started to round off, no longer so steep. It was then Rachel saw she was standing at the summit of the hill, near a small cluster of trees.

She stood there, her energy completely spent and her legs weak from the exertion. The ash was swirling around her face like snowflakes in a snowstorm, but she didn't care. She didn't even have enough energy to lift her head to see the clouds above her. Standing on the hill, Rachel heard the roar of the volcano and the ground trembled, so once again, she willed herself to lift her feet, one at a time. Moving slowly, she looked up and saw a tree, heavy with green leaves and a thick covering of gray ash. However, under it, the ground was clear of the gray substance that covered the rest of the area.

Rachel trudged slowly, dragging her feet through the ash, one after the other. When she reached the tree she ducked her head under the branches and literally collapsed on the ground. As she did so, the pain from her side shot through her body, but she was too tired to do anything about it. Rachel lifted her arm to pull her sleeve over her mouth and nose, closed her eyes, and with her last thought of *"Thank you Heavenly Father for saving my life,"* she fell asleep on the spot. The trembling of the earth, and the deep rumbling noise that filled the air, seemed to lull her into a deep sleep of complete exhaustion. She then dreamed a most marvelous and wonderful experience.

CHAPTER 39

"Upon My house"

"Behold, vengeance cometh speedily upon the inhabitants of the earth, a day of wrath, a day of burning, a day of desolation, of weeping, of mourning, and of lamentation; and as a whirlwind it shall come upon all the face of the earth, saith the Lord.

"And upon my house shall it begin, and from my house shall it go forth, saith the Lord;"

The devastation throughout Utah and Idaho from the earthquake that followed the explosion, was tremendous. The large faults went first, creating a shaking both vertically, and horizontally. It lasted for a full thirteen minutes, but it seemed like an eternity for those who were in it. Later, it was decided by the seismic scientists that it was 8.5 on the Richter scale, though there were some who wanted to place the measurement closer to 8.7 because of its duration.

One of the main points of the argument was that the frequency of the shaking set up a resonation among the sandy floor and benches of the Utah valleys. When the resonation reached a certain oscillation point, the water saturated ground, acting first like jello, vibrating like crazy, and then the sand

and clay underwent "liquefaction," making it flow like water. The debated question was this: Was this part of the calculation of the original strength of the earthquake, or was it just to be listed as part of the resulting damage? To the people who had survived, it really didn't matter.

There were two major after shocks, continuing the damage that occurred shortly after the main quake, the first was 7.1 on the scale and the second at 6.6. And so, in the end, the Wasatch Front had suffered three catastrophic earthquakes in a period of forty-eight hours. The two aftershocks really didn't matter much though, almost everything had been destroyed by the first quake, with the liquefaction of the underlying strata, and so there really wasn't much left to be shaken down by the time the so called aftershocks came around. Except for the most recently built, or modified, heavily reinforced buildings, everything else was simply reduced to a twisted pile of rubble three to four feet high.

Then the fires started, almost everywhere at once. With broken gas lines, ruptured gasoline tanks at thousands of fuel stations, propane tanks, and downed "hot" electrical lines in every neighborhood, it was inevitable. Within minutes of the initial earthquake, there were explosions everywhere. As the shaking continued, the explosions increased. When the shaking finally stopped, over a thousand columns of smoke drifted skyward, and the number grew larger by the minute.

With just about every overpass completely

destroyed, and the streets buckled...making most of the roads impassable, the local police and fire departments couldn't get to any of the fires if they wanted to. Of course, if they had, the water that the fire trucks carried wouldn't have lasted more than thirty minutes, at most, and then, because of the broken water lines, their water supply would have been depleted. Besides that, a much larger problem was that most of the police, fire and emergency services had been completely destroyed; their vehicles were buried under tons of rubble. They would never go anywhere.

Estimates of the initial death toll from the first earthquake were set at 300,000 to 400,000 throughout Utah. Most of the estimated casualties had died as a result of the thousands of collapsed high rise buildings and apartment houses. The majority of those who survived, dwelt in private residences, and were not in the downtown sections of the cities when the quakes occurred. The survivors crawled out from under their crumbled wooden structures to face a whole new set of problems.

What made a horrendous situation even worse were the flood waters from broken dams throughout the Intermountain region.

For those dams along the Wasatch Front, such as those at Jordanelle, Pineview, Rockport, East Canyon, and Echo reservoirs, most sustained catastrophic damage and failed almost immediately, sending their massive waters down their respective canyons. Dams further out, sustained cracks allowing their contents to empty out slowly, resulting in fewer casualties and less damage comparatively.

When the Jordanelle dam gave way, the wall of water that resulted was estimated by survivors watching from above, to be from seventy five to ninety five feet tall. A huge section of the dam just gave way, releasing over one hundred billion gallons, to the valley below, all at once. It only took three minutes before the water hit the little community of Heber, and, two minutes after that, most of the town simply ceased to exist.

The lower Deer Creek dam had already broken, with a huge crack in the recently reinforced barrier and the reservoir was slowly draining. When the water from the Jordanelle came screaming down the narrow canyon, and then hit the Deer Creek Reservoir, the pressure was too much and the entire dam just gave way all at once, not just a piece, or two at a time. With the water from the two reservoirs filling the very narrow Provo Canyon, two things happened. First, the water climbed up to almost one hundred feet as it hit the narrow parts of the canyon that had collapsed during the earthquake, making the canyon even narrower. Second, the water increased tremendously in speed as it raced down the canyon.

The mouth of the canyon that was the most narrow to begin with, and because of the earthquake, had become even more so. When the water reached it, the water's speed, along with its depth, increased to an even greater degree. As the wall of water burst forth from the mouth of the canyon, it was a boiling mass of mud, boulders, trees and cars, not to mention the remnants of Heber City buildings. It was 125 feet tall and traveling at over 100 miles an hour, taking out anything that stood in its way like a gigantic, high pressure sprayer.

The water had already scoured the Provo canyon, pushing everything along in front of it, so that when the water hit the cities of Provo and Orem it just picked up the rubble from the earth quake and swept it away as well. Those who had survived the devastating earthquake had just begun to crawl out from under the rubble minutes before hearing the roaring sound; most had only 10 seconds to watch the wall of water before it came down upon them.

This scene was repeated up and down the Intermountain West to one degree, or another. The result was an estimated 360,000 additional deaths from of all the dams, and the resulting flooding, mostly in the Weber and Utah counties.

Up in Southeastern Idaho, the dams broke, but the resulting floods were not as spectacular, or as murderous. Essentially, after the earthquake which did do severe damage, but not catastrophic, the region saw a repeat, on a larger scale, of the Teton dam disaster of 1976, only this time there was more water.

Almost as one, as soon as things stopped shaking and people crawled out from the destroyed buildings, entire communities realized the immediate danger of the dams bursting and subsequent flooding. They had learned their lesson well almost four decades earlier.

Even though the electricity was out, within minutes their fears were confirmed by an extensive emergency short wave radio network, set up over the last several years. The many emergency plans devised for just such an occasion as this were immediately activated.

Even with the tremendous death toll from the earthquake, fires and floods, the majority of the population of Utah and Southeastern Idaho survived, though the destruction was almost complete. That turned out to be the least of their problems.

Fourteen thousand years ago, Lake Bonneville was, at its largest, about 325 miles long, 135 miles wide, and had a maximum depth of over 1,000 feet. It covered most of the present state of Utah and Southern Idaho. It was just one of several large bodies of water that filled the ancient Great Basin, which extended from Oregon and Washington, down to Arizona and the California Baja, so long ago.

Then, massive earthquakes caused the land to raise up, and emptied most of the lake to the west and north. Evidence then indicates that the land raised a second time and the lake grew smaller, becoming the current Great Salt Lake, also creating what some call, the underground Bonneville River, which now flows below Utah, Arizona, and Nevada, finally emptying south into the Baja. For some, this is the only explanation of the fresh water flowing into the Baja sea of Mexico, making it an unusual estuary, full of partly salty, and partly fresh water, teeming with unusual sea life.

The evidence of the lake, and the massive topography changes that occurred anciently, are numerous. The various levels of the lake Bonneville shoreline could be seen up and down the mountains of the Wasatch Front, often as high as nearly 1000 ft above the then level of the Great Salt Lake. From Idaho, through Utah, and down into Arizona, the huge 800 mile long Wasatch fault line was often easily seen, with as much as 200 feet of relief in some places.

No one was exactly sure about what happened, but it was theorized that the massive earthquakes caused the Wasatch fault to shift back again, somewhat closer to its original position, and the whole region dropped a average of 200 feet in most places, and up to 500 feet in several others.

The Oquirrh Mountains essentially ceased to exist, and flattened out, becoming rolling hills, with a few small peaks still showing here and there all the way out past the Nevada border. The towering Mount Timpanogos was shaken to the point that it seemed to disappear, flowing down into the American Fork canyon. The same thing happened to other canyons, long famous for their ski resorts and fabulous powder snow, became buried under millions of tons of rock. The Wellsville Mountains, between Brigham City and Logan, were among the other ranges that also essentially disappeared.

One of the end results of this commotion was that with the drastic changes in the topography and the lowering of the entire region, suddenly the ancient

Bonneville Lake, and river, were forced up to the surface in a huge hurry. Great cracks in the earth opened and geysers were seen to shoot up as high as 100 ft, with huge towers of water. Many of these geysers were seen in the Great Salt Lake, with a few others here and there along the Wasatch fault line.

Further north, there seemed to be a large group of these geysers that occurred just south of Pocatello, where two new volcanoes suddenly appeared. These new volcanoes were actually part of the huge volcanic edge of the great Yellowstone caldera, which underlies the entire area. Their sudden emergence helped alleviate the pressure of the largest volcanic formation in the world. Without the pressure release they provided...the whole caldera would probably have exploded in a massive display of power, equivalent to a potential 1000 very large nuclear weapons going off at the same time, flooding the upper atmosphere with dust and debris that would have brought a cooling to the entire planet, ushering in a sudden, global ice age.

In the south, the release of the Wasatch Front fault was felt all the way down to Arizona. In Southern Utah, the earthquake was felt as a 7.0, from Delta to St. George, collapsing houses and buildings, and causing extensive, but not catastrophic damage, similar to Southeastern Idaho. However, many of the long dormant volcanoes in the area, part of the southern extension of the Yellowstone Volcanic system, became active, especially Pine Valley Mountain, which exploded into activity, spewing smoke, fumes, toxic vapor, ash, and lava, as it once did anciently. Lava bombs started fires everywhere over a 20 mile area of dense forests. Streams of lava flowed down new channels.

As it was, along the main part of the Wasatch Front, in some places the great walls of water from the broken dams were followed by a huge flood of water from below. A wall of water fifty feet high swept over the lower part of the Salt Lake Valley, from the direction of the Great Salt Lake, like a huge, inland tsunami. By the time it hit the higher portions of the valley, its force was greatly diminished, eventually coming up about twenty five feet on the outside wall of the great Salt Lake temple.

It was interesting to note, over a year earlier, because of the mounting protests and riots in downtown Salt Lake City against the Church, the four barred gates in the ten foot wall surrounding temple square had been replaced by solid steel plates with all of them being reinforced by sand bags. Like so many other church properties, temple square had been closed completely. Ten foot high fences had been erected surrounding all Church properties in Salt Lake, including the great Conference Center, and behind those fences was a wall of sand bags, erected to the same height, since so many vandals had started shooting through the fences at the various buildings.

This kind of vandalism had occurred at many other temples, including all of the LDS temples and church buildings in California, and on the East Coast. Even though they had been closed and the lights turned off, there were those that still sought their destruction. Along with the closures, and the potential for vandalism, most of the temples had had their furniture, paintings, chandeliers, and other items, removed and stored for safety. The beautiful art glass windows were boarded up to protect them from the random shootings that happened frequently. The ensuing result was that the temples, and a few of the other Church owned buildings in Utah and Idaho received some damage from the earthquakes, but remained standing, and were generally sound structurally. The main Church office building, had been damaged and condemned by the previous 5.3 and 6.0 earthquakes that had occurred months earlier, and was already in the process of being torn down. The massive Wasatch earthquake finished the job.

After the waters of ancient Lake Bonneville returned to what used to be its level at the 5000 foot mark along the region's vallies the destruction and death toll reached truly catastrophic proportions. As much as 90% of the population simply ceased to exist, snuffed out in a matter of hours.

CHAPTER 40

EPILOGUE

JARED

They called Salt Lake, and Elder Draper had just been connected to the office of the First Presidency when the phone line went dead.

As they stood around staring at each other, wondering what had just happened; the Sheriff's radio started squawking. Everyone turned towards the radio to listen. "This is Canadian Border Security to all points. Please be advised..." It was easy to hear the level of tension in the voice as he relayed the news. "We have picked up a report from the United States that a massive explosion has just taken place in Northern Utah, at the United States Hill Air Force Base located near Ogden, Utah. It is possibly another nuclear attack, and America has been put on high alert, and full lockdown. Again, we have received an official report from the United States Homeland Security that a possible nuclear detonation has just taken place at the US Air Force base near Ogden, Utah and they are initiating a full, high security lockdown of the entire country. All planes in US air space are to land immediately at the nearest suitable airport, and all US citizens are ordered to return to their homes immediately as the danger is assessed."

Jared looked at his watch and spoke out loud. "That's almost two hours earlier than we expected. Also, it was in Ogden instead of Salt Lake." Jared was trying desperately to figure out what this meant.

Elder Draper looked at him solemnly, and asked, "What do you think might have happened?"

Jared thought for a moment, and then replied, "These devices are old, and if you don't know what you are doing, they can go off prematurely."

"Do you think that is what happened?" Elder Draper asked.

"Maybe," Jared answered. "At least it is a possibility."

Just then a deputy who was monitoring a local radio station interrupted.

"Another report breaking in," he said. "This is confusing. Now, someone is saying that there has been a massive earthquake in Utah, probable epicenter 2 miles north of Salt Lake City, Utah. Possible massive casualties. No word coming from Utah. Communications and power are all out in the area."

In an attempt to get more details the Sheriff turned on a small television he kept in the office, catching a news report already in progress.

"Scientists from the USGS Southern California Earthquake Center at Caltech are saying that a massive earthquake, possibly 8.5 has hit the Salt Lake area. No direct word from Utah as of yet. All communication is down throughout the area. Electricity is out in the region and has affected the power supply in other western states. Cascade power failures in the grid are taking place throughout the entire northwest. There are also conflicting reports of a massive explosion that occurred just prior to the earthquake in the same general area. Authorities are trying to clarify the details. We will report them as they are received."

Jared sat down on a nearby chair, and put his head in his hands. *"Is she dead?"* He asked himself. *"What has happened?"* Even Jared, with all of his experience, was having some trouble putting the pieces of this puzzle together, and his worry and concern for Rachel weren't making it any easier for him to think clearly.

Elder Draper approached him quietly, "You're worried about your friend, aren't you, son?" The kindness in his voice calmed Jared momentarily, allowing him to feel a tiny bit of hope, if only for a moment.

"Yes, I am." Jared responded

"Do you have family in the area?" The Apostle asked.

"No, I don't." Jared answered, now hanging his

head as he leaned forward in the seat. *"Family,"* he thought to himself, and images of Granny and Rachel came into his mind.

"I feel impressed to tell you that the person you seek is still alive, though all is not well." Elder Draper's words brought Jared out of his thoughts. Even though he did not understand what kind of power would give the gentle old man this kind of insight, he found himself trusting and believing his words.

"Do you have any idea where she might be?" Jared asked, in almost a pleading tone.

"No, I am so sorry," Elder Draper replied sincerely, "I do not."

Jared's mind started to work with what he knew. Elder Draper said that Rachel was alive, but something was still wrong. If she needed him, he had to figure out a way to help her. Jared started working out some of the math. If she was supposed to be in Salt Lake by 1400, and the bomb went off two hours early, where might she have been when it went off?" He knew with a little concentration he would be able to come up with the solution.

After a few minutes of calculation and looking at a nearby map hanging on the wall, Jared had his answer. *"She is probably somewhere between northern Utah and Idaho Falls."*

"I need to get some transportation." Jared said out

loud now to everyone in the room.

"Well," said Elder Draper, "we just happen to have a car, or two, that you can use."

Jared turned to the two Blackbird soldiers, standing handcuffed in the room, listening to all that was going on. "You want to help?" He asked getting their attention. "I sure could use you."

The taller, but younger looking recruit asked, "What do you have in mind?"

Jared paused for a moment trying to gather his thoughts. A plan was starting to formulate in his mind.

He approached the soldier. "Sergeant, what's your name?"

"Blake Richards, sir."

"Where did you serve before Blackbird?" Jared asked next.

The man straightened up, and with pride answered, "Eight years with the 101st Airborne, Sir."

Jared replied with satisfaction, "The 'Screaming Eagles.' What was your MOS?"

"I was a medic and communications specialist, Sir"

Jared thought, *"A medic could be very good to have*

along in this situation." Jared continued his questioning, "How long have you been with Blackbird?"

"Only about six months, Sir. They came through and made offers to a lot of us that we really couldn't refuse."

Turning to the other Blackbird soldier, Jared asked, "And what about you?"

"Frank Alvarez. I served six years with the Marine 1st Expeditionary force." The man answered proudly. "When I left, I was a 2nd Lieutenant in Civil Affairs."

"Have you seen combat Frank?" Jared asked somberly.

"Yes sir. I had two tours in Afghanistan, and Blake here had one." He followed up, "I haven't always been civil affairs. Prior to that, I lead a forward observation team."

Jared was pleased with the information he was receiving from these two and saw just how he might use this to his advantage. "How long have you been with Blackbird?" he asked.

"About four months, Sir."

Jared paused for a moment before asking his next question, "Frank, Blake...Why would Blackbird, or Bennett, want to kill you two?"

This was something they had both been trying to figure out in their own minds. "I have no idea" The ex-marine, told Jared...looking him directly in the eye. There was an anger smoldering behind those eyes, and Jared knew these men had no allegiance left to the man, or the organization that had betrayed them.

"Why...would Blackbird want to kill thousands of innocent men, women, and children?" Jared's words challenged the men.

The Lieutenant Alvarez was the one who answered again, "Honestly, I have no idea. Blackbird has been a pretty good outfit to work for since I've been in. Bennett has been a pain in the ass, and there have been some rumors about him, but up until now everything has been on the up and up."

"Uh-huh." Jared's reply was absent minded as he was now deep in thought.

"Family?" He asked them.

"Both of us are currently single," The Lieutenant answered. "Though I've been dating a local girl pretty regularly. It's starting to get serious," He added.

"Would you like to go and find her and see if she is alright?" Jared's question was sincere, sensing the feelings this young man had for his girlfriend.

"Yes, Sir." He answered eagerly

"How about you?" Jared asked turning to Sergeant

Richards. "Would you like to go back and see if you can help?"

"Absolutely," The man replied with more than a little anger in his voice. "I'd also like to find Major Bennett and ask him a few pointed questions, if you catch my meaning."

Jared had carefully considered his options and this seemed like the only one with any chance at success. He crossed his arms in front of his chest and looked the men in their eyes again, trying to gauge their response as he asked them, "Would you mind taking orders from me as we go back down there and see if we can help?" Jared paused. "As you are probably aware, someone very dear to me is also down there in that mess, and I need to find her. And, I would dearly love to ask Bennett those same questions."

"Before you answer let me tell you a little about myself. I'm retired Special Forces, Captain, with 22 years and so many combat ops I've lost count. I'm not sure who we can trust yet... so we need to trust each other; otherwise we'll all end up dead. As it is, we would effectively be on a special ops undercover mission into what could be a hostile war zone. There are people who apparently want each of us dead... but, on the other hand, we could help save a lot of lives and perhaps make a difference. Are you in?"

The Sergeant spoke without hesitation, "I became a medic to help save lives, Sir. I would very much like to go with you to see if I can be of assistance."

The Lieutenant took his turn to answer. "It would be an honor to serve with you, Sir." His sincerity was evident. "I would very much like to find Jennie and her family and make sure that they are alright."

Turning now to Elder Draper, Jared asked, "What do you think?" In the short time he had known him; Jared had already begun to respect, and appreciate, the special insight this man had. He had a feeling that the Elder would have something to say about his plan.

"It feels right," Elder Draper responded.

Jared, addressed the Sheriff..."Would you please release them?" Pointing to the handcuffs as he spoke, "Into my custody, of course."

The Sheriff looked at Elder Draper, who nodded his assent, then walked over and unlocked the handcuffs.

"Good." Jared said as he shook the hands of the two recruits who had just joined his team. "I'd like to leave in an hour, or as soon as we can get things ready. There is one other thing we need to do." He said matter-of-factly, "We need to secure the weapon."

Three hours later, after the individual parts of the nuclear weapon had been well hidden in separate locations; Jared was standing talking to Elder Draper and Elder Mathews.

"Before we leave," Jared addressed them. "I would like to ask you one last question."

"Anything," Elder Draper replied with a smile, and a look it his eyes, that made Jared feel that the man could see directly into his heart and mind, knowing what he was going to ask before he formed the words.

"Something has been bothering me a great deal," Jared went on. "How did you know exactly where I was this morning? I mean, how did 'Salt Lake' know about me coming over the mountain? They apparently called you, and told you I was coming and where I was going to be, before I was even sure what my plans were, or knew if I was traveling in this direction." He had been thinking about this since the details of their foreknowledge were revealed.

Elder Draper searched Jared's eyes for a minute before responding. In that brief minute, Jared felt as if his soul was being laid bare, and examined piece by piece.

After a moment Elder Draper said, "I will tell you, but, you will probably not understand." He paused, and Jared was concerned he might not continue. After a moment's hesitation, the Apostle spoke again; "You see, the Urim and Thumim has been returned to the prophet."

"You mean the two special stones, or whatever they were, that Joseph Smith used to translate the book of Mormon?" His comment surprised and pleased the two General Authorities, and they smiled as he went on. "You see, I have been reading your Book of Mormon the last little while. And I wondered a lot about what that thing was."

-495-

"Yes...the very same." Elder Draper responded. "You see, not only can the Urim and Thumim be used to translate ancient languages.... a Prophet can use it to see anything, when the Lord directs him to "ask and look." The Prophet Joseph Smith was directed by the Lord to use it many times for warnings, and information when mobs were coming to search for the plates, so that Joseph could move them. But, with the Urim and Thumim, a person can see not only things in current time, he can see into the past, as well as into the future, and in whatever detail the Lord chooses"

"You mean like some kind of a super computer that can see into space and time?" Jared knew his words were inadequate for what he was trying to ask, but even with his experience and learning, this was a totally new concept.

"Something like that." Elder Draper encouraged, and then continued his explanation. "My guess is that the prophet was directed to use it, to see what was coming...and then was able to tell us when and where we could find you, and also about the bomb in the car."

Jared's responded, "Well, I guess that explains it," not really comprehending what he had just been told at all. The ramifications boggled his mind. It was something that he was going to have to think about for a very long time. However, he shelved it in his mind for another day, and, as he shook Elder Drapers hand he spoke from his heart. "Thanks for everything."

Elder Draper, realizing that Jared did not fully understand what he had just been told, reminded him as he climbed into the silver gray sedan, "Remember, if there is any way we can assist you, please do not hesitate to contact us, and do not hesitate to ask for help from those places of refuge I gave you directions to. If they have any questions, have them radio me up here. Also, we have resources in many places and can help in ways that you may not think possible." Jared recognized his last words as a huge understatement, but just nodded his head.

"And finally," Elder Draper concluded, "I leave upon you, and your companions, an Apostolic blessing, that you will be successful in your efforts, and that you will be protected, and watched over. Though things may seem grim at times, don't give up, have faith in God, and it will all work out right."

As Elder Draper and Elder Mathews watched Jared, and the two former Blackbird soldiers drive off, Elder Draper spoke to his companion, "The Lord definitely has His hand upon that young man."

Elder Mathews responded, "I was thinking of something like a modern day Captain Moroni."

Elder Draper smiled, "Interestingly, so was I." After a pause he added, "We will need a lot of men like him for what is coming..."

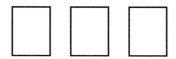

NOTES:

1. Many of the events described in the story are found in numerous dreams and visions, most of which are found in the revised Dreams and Visions of the Last days book. Some liberty has been taken to fit them into the story line.

2. The trick with the hairpin and the handcuffs actually works. It is actually not a trick, but an escape technique taught in SERE school. There is a video online that shows the technique. Also, on how to get out of the new "strap" cuffs that

3. In 2006 the Provo paper published a preparedness

section giving worse case scenario if the Deer Creek and Jordanelle dams failed. Some of the things mentioned that aren't pretty:

*Flooding down Provo River 21-50 ft. The Utah Valley Regional trauma center flooded to the 4th floor.

* Most of Provo under 7-20 ft. of water

* Much of Orem (which is kind of on a bench) 2-6 ft. of water.

* If an earthquake is involved, then liquefaction (quicksand effect) would occur all around Utah Lake, mostly on the East side where everyone lives. And in what is called the Riverbottoms.

4. For a map of the ancient lake Bonneville go to ...
http://geology.utah.gov/online/m/m-73.pdf

Other good resources about the ancient great Bonneville and other ancient lakes and their release floods:
http://imnh.isu.edu/digitalatlas/hydr/lkbflood/lbf.htm

A good article about the ancient lake that covered almost all of Nevada:
http://en.wikipedia.org/wiki/Lake_Lahontan

5. The great earthquake, and particularly the flood of Utah/Nevada/Idaho are mentioned in several dreams. There is also evidence in the scriptures about them. In Revelation Chapter 12:14-17...the dragon/devil persecutes the woman/Church. The Church escapes the persecution by fleeing into the

"wilderness" for 3 ½ years and is free from the persecution during that time. If you think of the Salt Lake wilderness as the wilderness mentioned here, (possibly confirmed by D&C 86:3) then persecution arrives after 3/12 years (Utah is made a territory and the antagonistic "gentile" Federal judges are appointed and arrive, bringing with them the persecution...and the next big thing John describes is to destroy the Church with a flood. However, the earth opens its mouth and swallows the flood...which matches closely many of the dreams about the event.

The better reference, however, is contained in Isaiah Chapter 4:

After describing the cleansing and destruction of Jerusalem and Zion(America) in chapter 3...in chapter 4 Isaiah then describes that those who have survived the cleansing are holy and blessed. Interestingly, inverse four the "daughters of zion" are cleansed by water..."washed away the filth of the daughters of Zion" a reference to water being used to cleanse. Whereas, in Jerusalem the survivors there were cleansed by judgment and burning.

6. For maps about the liquefaction in various Utah areas:
http://geology.utah.gov/utahgeo/hazards/liquefy.htm#liquemaps

7. There is some evidence that a pandemic of some kind happens before the callout. However, the

great deadly plagues happen soon after the callout. I have decided to address this in the next book in the series.